B' ?C 'Gl C

CW01395186

Summer's Last Retreat

CHAPTER ONE

Olwen pushed the almost empty cart up the steep hill, past the row of small cottages that stood at right angles to the seashore and grunted as the wheels stuck against a large pebble. She slithered in her soft leather shoes as she manoeuvred the cart's wheels until she could continue, her groans an accompaniment to the squeaking of the cart.

She was small and very thin, her knees looking swollen against the stick-like legs that were revealed as she bent about her task, but there was no look of sickness to account for her waif-like thinness. Her blue eyes, large and with a hint of violet in the whites, were clear and constantly smiling. Wrinkled laughter lines already showed on the freckled and suntanned skin. She looked like a leggy seven-year-old, but was in fact approaching her fifteenth birthday.

There were fewer than a dozen small fish left to sell and she looked hopefully up at the door as she knocked on its painted surface. The door opened and before she could shout out the list of fish she had to offer, the woman shook her head and waved her away.

Olwen's heart fell. If Mrs Baker had bought from her she would have been able to go home and wash herself free of the fishy smell that followed her like an aura and attracted the wider aura of small flies.

'No fish tomorrow, mind,' she shouted, 'it's Saturday and Dadda takes all we catch to Swansea market, remember!' She waited hopefully for a moment but the door did not reopen and she continued slowly up the hill.

Mumbles village where Olwen and her family lived was little more than a gathering of cottages where the inhabitants made their living from the sea. The beach which she had just left at the foot of the hill formed one end of a six-mile crescent with dunes and flat ground along its length. At the

1

other end of the crescent of sand and shingle, to the east, was the town of Swansea.

To the west of the village were steep cliffs, falling almost vertically down to jagged outcrops of rock, and small walled fields made a higgledy-piggledly pattern interspersed with narrow green lanes. In some, crops waved in the summer sun, and in others, sheep grazed contentedly on the rich grass.

Below the cliffs, narrow gullies gave the fishermen the opportunity to gather lobster and crab to add to the fish caught from the boats that went out daily from the small harbour. On days when there was no market, women and children cooked or cured what they needed for themselves and, as Olwen was doing now, tried to sell any surplus.

Olwen looked up at the sun. It was already mid-morning on a fine July day, and if she did not sell the fish soon it would be fit only for feeding to the pigs. There was always William and Dorothy Ddole of course. The wealthy Ddole House, the largest in the village, had dozens of servants and workers, and Florrie the cook usually accepted anything she had to offer. But it was such a long walk and the weather was becoming so hot.

A thin stream of water ran down the side of the lane and she gathered some in her small hands and poured it over the fish to make them look less dry and glassy-eyed, then continued upwards, calling,

'Fresh fish, last few to sell cheap. Fish to sell cheap,' until at last a door opened and a woman emerged, taking her purse from the pouch at her waist. She beckoned to Olwen with a scolding look on her face.

'There's a disgrace, your mother sending you out on such a hot day to sell fish for her! What's she doing that she has to make you push that heavy cart? It's work for a grown woman and there's you hardly more than a baby!'

'Going on fifteen I am,' Olwen said, stretching herself up to look taller. 'And Mam didn't make me. It's just that she can't come herself, she's going to have our new baby soon and the fish would have gone to waste. A-w-ful wicked that would be, the vicar was saying that only last Sunday in his sermon. Now, will you buy the lot for a penny, Mrs Powell?'

'A ha'penny. I saw you trying to hide their staleness with water, my girl.'

'All right then, a ha'penny, but Mam won't be very pleased with me.'

'And an extra farthing for your cheek,' Mrs Powell laughed as she counted out the coins into the grubby hand. Olwen pocketed the money and with the cart rolling ahead of her, she ran back down the lane shouting back her thanks.

She took the cart to the beach intending to wash it in the tide before pushing it home, but instead, leaving it behind a clump of wild spinach, she went to where a crowd was gathered around Kenneth-the-Post who was sitting discussing all he had learnt on his journey around Gower. He was the Letter Carrier for Mumbles and Gower and on Fridays, his day off, he habitually sat on the bank outside his house, smoked a clay pipe, which others filled for him, and allowed neighbours to ask about distant friends and exchange local gossip.

Olwen approached the group but she had eyes only for Barrass. She watched his eyes, waiting for him to see her and smile. He was standing near the cottage, already at eighteen a tall young man but odd-looking with his ill-fitting linen shirt, baggy, half rolled trousers, and bare feet. His appearance was further impaired by his shaved head and the patches of angry spots around his head and neck and on the exposed part of his legs. He was strongly built, with the gleam of intelligence in his dark brown eyes, but although many people spoke to him in a friendly way, he stood alone.

Olwen called to him and clambered across the springy turf to stand beside him. She was rewarded with a smile.

'What have you been doing – as if I can't guess,' he smiled. 'Smell the fish before you come into sight I can.'

The other young people, standing apart from him but near enough to hear, all wrinkled their noses in exaggerated dismay and she butted a few of them with her fair head before Barrass held her still, which was what she had hoped for. There was a wonderfully safe and contented feeling when Barrass held her, even if her mother did constantly warn her about standing too close to him. The fact that she defied the warnings gave her a certain notoriety and importance within the group of friends. She smiled around at the circle of faces and hugged Barrass even tighter.

She dreamed of him being her special friend, although, as she was three years younger and looked half her age that was unlikely. Still, he didn't tease her too much and he rarely ignored her, and for the moment that was enough. His strange appearance troubled her not at all. She looked into his eyes and saw the person, the outside trappings becoming unimportant, invisible, the reason for them forgotten – until she was harshly reminded of them.

Kenneth-the-Post sat puffing on the long white pipe, looking important in spite of his lack of height. He wore the red waistcoat and tall black hat that was the unofficial uniform of the King's Letter Carriers, even on this day when he had no official duties apart from entering in his books any letters that were handed in for forwarding to Swansea sorting office. The horn which he blew to announce his arrival at the places where he stopped was at his side, a badge of his calling and a boost to his ego. The Letter Carrier was an important man in the small village where he lived and he never missed an opportunity to display his position.

'An ale if you please, Ceinwen,' he said to his wife, sharing a look of superiority among his admirers like an actor on a stage, 'then I will rest ready for my early start in the morning.'

Ceinwen, his plump, dull-looking wife who had been leaning out of the window of the white cottage listening to the chatter, disappeared inside to reappear in the doorway with a foaming pewter mug in her hand, a bored look in her brown eyes.

'Can I come with you tomorrow?' Barrass asked him. The young man stepped towards Kenneth as he asked the question and the crowd leaned away from him, some run-

4

ning with exaggerated fear and giggling at each other in shared amusement.

Barrass appeared not to notice and he looked at Kenneth, his eyes liquid and pleading as he willed the older man to agree. 'I have no work to do for Pitcher at the alehouse until the evening. I'll carry your bag for you.'

'You know I can't do that, boy!' Kenneth looked pompously outraged at the idea. 'I alone have responsibility for that bag and its contents, you know that! But, all right, you can come. I'll be glad of your company for part of the way. I have two letters for the Reverend Benjamin Hill, Rector of Rhosili, and it's a long way. But keep your distance, mind!'

When Kenneth stood and bade goodbye to his audience, Barrass rejoined Olwen.

'Where have you left the cart?' he asked. 'Would you like me to push it up the cliff path for you?'

'No, I'll leave it by Dadda's boat, it'll be safe enough there, but you can help me scrub it,' she said, and taking hold of his strong arm near the frayed end of his too short sleeve, she pulled him towards the beach while he mockingly laughed at her puny strength.

Together they washed the wooden cart, scrubbing it with bunches of the reeds that grew around the earthen path, then she filled her arms with the rich green sea spinach for the family's evening meal and set off home, parting from the tall, peculiar-looking boy with undisguised regret.

The cottage where she lived with her parents, Peter – known to all as Spider – and Mary, and her brother Dan, was high on the cliffs above the beach and the village that huddled around it. Built of hardened, firmly pressed earth, it had been whitewashed at the beginning of every summer for many years and was a dazzling sight in the afternoon sun as she approached it. Spider was in the yard and she called as she ran towards him, chattering almost as soon as she was within hearing.

'All the fish is sold,' she shouted, 'and I've brought spinach for Mam to cook for tonight. Can I have a farthing for a bit of ribbon for my hair?'

5

Her father stood up, tall and unbelievably thin, and shaded his eyes.

'Damn me, girl. I don't know where you get the strength from that little body of yours to make such a row! Hush for the sake of the people within the five miles that can hear you!'

'Food will shut me up, Dadda. Will we cook the spinach for supper? Has the baby come yet?'

Spider held out his long arms and lifted her up to hold her high against his chest.

'Come you and see.' He bent his head and lowered her carefully as they entered the small, dark room which was insulated from the sun by walls two feet thick and tiny windows covered with curtains of sacking tied back with cheerful ribbons.

'Mam?' Olwen whispered fearfully, the mysteries of child-birth making her tremble and cling more tightly to her father. He carried her up the ladder set on a bank of earth against the back wall that took them up to the two small bedrooms, one of which was divided with a curtain and shared by Olwen and Dan.

Her mother lay on the bed on the floor near the small window. Her face, half hidden by shadows, looked tired and old, and Olwen felt fear tighten in her stomach. Then her mother's eyes lit up and her face widened into a smile, and Olwen slid down from her father's arms as the bed covers were lowered and the head of her new brother was revealed.

She stared down, marvelling at the perfection of the tiny being.

'What will we call him, Mam?'

'How d'you know it's a boy?' Peter laughed.

'Granny Hughes told Mam it would be a brother for me.'

'She was right, and we thought to call him Dic.'

Olwen savoured the name for a moment, frowning in concentration.

'Yes, baby Dic. That will do fine. Where will he sleep? Will he come in with me or share with Dan?' Olwen asked. 'It's a bit of a squash for us isn't it?'

'Always room for another cariad,' her mother replied.

'Then if there's always room for another, couldn't we ask Barrass to live with us until he finds a place?' Olwen poured the words out, knowing it was the wrong time but unable to wait. 'He's been thrown out by Mrs Baker after only two weeks. Sleeping under a pile of old wood he is.'

'You know we can't, Olwen,' her father said patiently. 'He's never free of fleas and your mother wouldn't like the house overrun, now would she?'

'I'll scrub him myself, Mam, honest. I'll go over every inch of him I will. I promise.'

'No, Olwen. Until Barrass manages to stay free of those things he won't find a place with any decent family, nice as the boy is,' he added as Olwen began to pout. 'Fond of him we are, and sorry indeed for his predicament, but we can't give him a home.'

Olwen couldn't sleep that night – partly because of the heat close under the thatched roof, and also because of the tiny baby, mewing occasionally, in her mother's bed. It was an exciting thought, having a new brother to look after, and she gave up all attempts to sleep. Dressing quickly she went stealthily down the ladder and out of the house. She would sit on the cliffs and look down at the sea and think about Dic – and Barrass.

The sea was so smooth she imagined she could walk across its dark blue surface all the way to the distant coastline of Devon, seen so often and looking so temptingly near. The fishing boats went across there often, she knew that, and had listened with envy to tales told by her father and Dan, and all the other men who earned their living from the sea. One day she too would leave the village and travel to new places. For a while she daydreamed about setting off with Barrass carrying their possessions on his broad back to seek what adventures they could. Oh, if only her body would grow, so that such dreams were not so ridiculous.

There was a quarter moon and its strange light did little to display the scene. Gradually her eyes grew accustomed to the darkness and she could make out the rocks around her and the shape of the cottage behind her, only the thin edge of the thatch caught by the moon's glow, a black silhouette huddled against black trees and bushes in contrast to the lighter sky.

She lay back on the cool grass and thought about baby Dic and wondered if he too would be small like the rest of the family. He might be very tall, like her father and Dan, but without flesh on his bones to fill him out. Her brother Gareth, who had died while serving as a soldier, had also been thin, but not very tall. What chance had she of ever becoming rounded and shapely? She took in a deep breath and blew it out noisily in a sigh.

How she longed to grow tall and womanly like Blodwen, the daughter of Ivor-the-Builder, who she frequently caught Barrass staring at with an adoring light in his eyes. Blodwen had always looked grown up and womanly, while she, Olwen-the-Fish still remained a child. Skinny legs that refused to show any curves, a body so thin she was often mistaken for a boy. Even the fringe of her hair was scrappy and uneven where she had tried to fashion it into curls and burnt it off with an over-hot poker. The rest of her fair hair was long and straight, but that did not seem to make any difference to her boyish appearance. She thought: Small, thin and looking so young, how am I ever going to make Barrass notice me?

A chill breeze disturbed the grasses around her and she was about to return to the house and her warm bed when she heard feet scuffling through the long grass behind her. She tensed, wanting to move but held by fear. Perhaps she would not be noticed if she kept very still – her frightened mind spared time to think that there was some consolation in being so small. The footsteps came closer and stopped, not far from where she sat trying to sink into the grasses and wild flowers. She held her breath, then a voice she knew said,

'Olwen. What are you doing out so late?'

'Early more like, Barrass,' she said, her voice trembling

with relief. 'There's glad I am it's you. I thought it might be robbers.'

'And what would you have to steal?' He slithered down beside her and stared out across the glassy sea. There were still no white wave-edges to be seen in the milky darkness, the waves, even with the rising morning breeze, hardly making a sound as they touched and then left the rocks below them, the tide gently reaching fullness.

She remembered her news and hugged his arm. 'Barrass, I have a new baby brother and his name is Dic! What d'you think of that, then?'

'Good news. Will you give your mother my best wishes? When it's light I'll gather some flowers for her.'

'Pity it's not a sister, mind,' Olwen sighed. 'It would be nice to boss a sister around. A brother will ignore me after a while and – '

'Hush!' He put a hand on her mouth to stop her chatter and they both sat straining their ears until the sound of a small boat, oars lightly touching the surface of the calm sea, reached them. Olwen nodded to tell him she understood and he removed his hand. They sat looking into the pearly light of the incipient dawn until their eyes gradually made out a small fleet of boats, shipping their oars as they reached the rocky cove below them.

'Can we move closer to see?' she whispered close to his ear.

'No! It's far too dangerous! Foolish girl!'

'Please, Barrass. I can be so quiet I make a fish sound like a fairground, honest.'

He rose to a crouch and held out a hand for her to go with him. She kissed his fingers in silent thanks and he stifled a laugh. What a funny little thing she was.

They walked cautiously, stepping on tilted, pointed toes through the swathes of tall grasses, hardly disturbing them and making very little sound. Gradually they moved lower, avoiding the clearly defined paths and instead, pushing gently past bushes, along narrow animal tracks until they could look down on the cove that was a beach only for the lowest hour of the tide.

'Not a sound, not a movement now, or we're dead,' he whispered in her ear.

She pulled his hairless head close to her and whispered back, 'And cover your head then, or we'll be spotted for sure. There'll be too many moons in the sky!'

Again he stifled a laugh. But he took a battered old hat from his pocket and pulled it over his shining head.

They watched the scene below them and marvelled at the efficiency of the men involved. Small boats were emptied and rowed silently away, while others were dragged to the side of the rocky plateau and held securely by ropes wound round a rock by brawny arms. Already there was a procession of men and donkeys making their way across the cliffs and heading inland with heavy loads. One of the men walking to and from the boats was exceptionally tall. Both knew it was Spider, but neither mentioned the fact. Olwen knew that, unlike the rest of the villagers, Barrass did not believe that those who could avoid paying revenue to the king should do so. It was the only thing about which they disagreed.

An hour passed and they lost count of the number of journeys made from the now faintly discernible ship outside the bay. They could only guess at the cargoes being illegally landed, and did not move until birdsong was the only sound disturbing the dawn.

'A lot of them were strangers to me,' Olwen remarked. 'Do you think one of them might be your father, Barrass?'

'Who knows? But I doubt it. He wouldn't be involved in anything that broke the king's law.'

'Oh Barrass, bringing in a few packets of tea and some tobacco isn't serious. We all buy things from the smugglers that we couldn't otherwise afford. Mam and Dadda aren't "lawbreakers".'

'I don't know very much about my father, only the little my mother told me before she died, but I do know he carried the King's Mail. Imagine that, Olwen, being responsible for carrying letters for King George III! Whoever he was, my father wouldn't have done anything to risk losing that trusted and honourable role. I want to follow him one

10

day, so I too have to avoid anything less than legal. Tall, broad of the shoulders and very strong he was, and so noble and honest. Head and shoulders above other men, and people looked up to him because of his admirable example as well as his exceptional height.'

Olwen knew his fine eyes would be glowing, as they always did when he spoke of the father he had never known. He had moved closer to her as the need for quiet was still imperative, with watchers on the cliffs likely to stay until the processions of men and donkeys had gone from the area. She snuggled against him, wishing the moment could go on for ever, not wanting to talk, content for once to listen, knowing that talking about the mysterious man who had fathered him would keep him with her longer than anything else.

When he left her, she did not go back to the house. The events of the night and the thrill of sharing them with Barrass had sent all possibility of sleep from her. She sat with her arms around her knees, continuing to watch the sea changing colour as the sun rose and the day began. Then gradually she became aware that her fingers were busy in her hair and on her back, and that something was tickling her in unexpected places, and she sighed.

Once again she regretted her defiance of the unwritten rule not to stand too close to Barrass. Without a doubt she had caught some of Barrass's army of fleas. That meant a scrub – and a clout from Mam. Still, it had been worth it. Glowing with happiness, remembering the feel of his body curled close to hers, she stretched, yawned and prepared to leave the area of flattened grass where they had sat and talked like the friends they were.

One day, she promised herself, they would be much, much more. The few hours she had spent with Barrass were hers to be savoured over and over again, long after the sting of the clouting had been forgotten. Sighing again, this time with the accompaniment of a smile, she stood and wandered back home for a few hours' sleep.

It was a Saturday and Spider needed Olwen to help him take the fish to market and sell his catch. She had hardly

11

reached her bed, it seemed, when he shook her and told her it was time to rise. The morning was warm and she could see from the sun that he had allowed her to sleep well past her usual time.

Spider had put down nightlines and with the falling tide, he had walked along the shore with Dan, gathering in the lines and the fish they had caught, and now had the catch loaded ready for the walk into Swansea Market. When Olwen stepped out into the sun she saw her brother staggering back with a basket filled with mackerel caught from the boat just outside the bay. The silver and black fish gleamed in the early morning sun, their beauty not yet fading.

Loading their fish on the pannier baskets of a borrowed pony, along with one of the blankets Mary had made on her tall loom, they all set off across the sands, heading for St Helens where they would leave the sands and walk the further mile into the town's market, at Island House in Wind Street. They had to hurry, both because of the tide already on the turn and because the first to arrive made the best sales; they were already late due to the time of the tide and the recovery of the nightlines.

The market was on three sides of Island House, whose overhanging roof, supported by wooden pillars, formed a veranda that gave shelter to the butchers already stripping the carcasses hung on hooks above their wooden chopping tables. Local farmers shouted against each other, all insisting that their eggs were still warm from the hens, their cheeses and butter the most tasty in the whole kingdom, and that their root vegetables were still crying their earth tears at being pulled from their beds.

Olwen loved the market with the hordes of people all either looking for a bargain or trying to convince others that they offered one. Performers fooled around the shoppers, depending on the good humour of the day to persuade a few coins from limited pockets, and music vied with the shouts of the vendors to the same aim. The smells were a symphony of such variety that Olwen gave up trying to recognize any individually, accepting the whole as The Smell of the Market.

She begged a penny from her father and bought herself a drink of lemonade from a stall, smiling at the notice displayed by the man selling pure and health-giving mineral water, warning customers who sent servants for their supplies to demand a receipt, 'for they might be tempted to fill up your containers elsewhere and pocket your money and bring you an inferior product'.

In spite of their late arrival, the fish was quickly sold and they prepared to walk back, this time overland, the road turning inland at St Helens to pass through Sketty and, crossing the Clyne stream at Rhyd-y-Defaid, Sheep's Crossing. They were all a little reluctant to go; there was still plenty to see and the crowds were in a good humour, some dancing accompanied by an old gypsy with a fiddle who had been playing for most of the day without any sign of tiring.

Olwen turned and saw that Spider and Dan were already moving off. Clicking to the pony, she hurried after them.

On the following day she found herself in Swansea again. Emma Palmer, whose husband Pitcher owned and ran the alehouse close to the shore, wanted a message taken to their twin daughters' school, and Olwen offered to go. There was little to do and the prospect of a trip into the town was too tempting to refuse. She looked for Barrass, then Arthur, Pitcher's fourteen-year-old pot-boy, to go with her but could find neither, so she went alone.

The message delivered and the reply pushed safely into her deep pocket, she wandered around the houses, absorbing the sights, so different from the usual market-day hubbub. It was after six when she saw the post-boy, his horn raised ready to blow and announce his arrival with the 'Swanzey Bag'. Olwen stared at him, as Barrass and his quest for his post-carrying father made the man of more than usual interest.

The man was quite old, grey hairs falling about his shoulders from under his hat like a collar of dirty lace. She stared at the dust-covered features, wondering if this was the man for whom Barrass was searching, whether this

13

long-nosed, wild-eyed and drab individual was the father Barrass dreamed of finding. He looked so unlike the sturdy, dark-eyed Barrass that she doubted it.

Then she squeezed her eyes tightly shut and tried to see her father as the boy he had once been, comparing his face with Dan's. Spider and Dan both had brown hair and a serious expression that belied their sense of fun. But would she recognize Spider as the father of Dan if she had never seen him before? She shrugged and gave up the puzzle. How could anyone see in a complete stranger something to tell them he was their long-lost father?

'There goes Ben Gammon,' Olwen heard someone say. 'Been travelling the same route for almost thirty years and hardly missed a day.'

Ben Gammon heard the remark and called out, 'Thirty-six year no less and, I says to myself – why, I hopes to go on for a few more yet.' He grinned as he slowed his horse to walk through the crowded street, blowing a kiss or giving a nod to faces he recognized, like a royal procession, aware of his importance. Olwen, intending to tell Barrass about him, stared at the man, determined to take in every detail.

Ben Gammon's eyes were bright in the dust-rimed face but they were blue, not the deep brown she would expect Barrass's father to have. The skin on his face was loose and flabby and he slouched as he rode past to the sorting office. He was dusty and brown as the end of a hot, dry summer, and the only thing that shone was the horn tucked in his belt. From Barrass's description she doubted if this was the man, but she would tell him anyway; best to humour him, she thought, copying a constantly repeated remark of her mother's.

She turned her face towards the sun and headed for home, her thoughts dwelling on the news she had for Barrass. She was very tired, having walked twelve miles two days in succession, but as soon as she had helped to prepare the evening meal, she went to find him.

Barrass was sitting near a small fire over which he was baking a couple of fish. Wrapped in mud and green leaves they were beginning to send out a delicious smell. Behind

14

him, set against a tree jutting out of a steep bank, was a precarious-looking lean-to. Made mostly of timbers gathered from the beach below, it seemed likely to collapse at the first strong breeze. She sat beside him, chattering non-stop as usual.

She told him at once of the arrival of Ben Gammon, and described him.

'Dirty you wouldn't believe! Hardly an inch of him clean enough to see if he was a man or one of those monkeys we saw at last year's fair!'

'And you think a man like a monkey could be my father?' In mock anger he rolled her over and over on the dry summer grass until she warned him that his fish would burn, to be free of his tickling.

'What do you remember about your father, Barrass?' she asked. '*Really* remember.'

'Nothing, I suppose, although the stories my mother told and which were repeated by others to entertain me when I was small are so real I know I'll recognize him when we meet. He was taller than most men, and broader. Upright in behaviour too,' he assured her with utmost faith and conviction. 'He had large, brown, soulful eyes. Too much red hair, not bright red mind, more with a hint of red, like some fine polished wood. That much my mother told me.'

'That man I saw today, his hair was grey so there's no telling what it might have been once. Oh, Barrass, how can you hope to ever find him after such a long time? Sixteen years, longer than I've been alive.'

'I just know that I'll find him.' He spoke quietly and Olwen did not argue. Everyone was entitled to their dream.

'Shall we go down to the beach to cool our feet after this?' she asked as he carefully unwrapped the food and began to share it between them.

'No, I have someone to see,' he said, and no matter how she pleaded, he refused to tell her where he was going.

'I don't care. *And* that fish was not as good as if *I'd* cooked it!' She glared at him and ran off.

She didn't go home but waited until he had washed his hands, face and prickling bald head under a small stream sprouting from the rocks close by and set off for the village, then she followed him.

Barrass had something to be proud of. For several weeks he had been building himself a home. A derelict stone barn, used occasionally by sheep sheltering from a storm, had become, after several weeks of work, a rainproof dwelling. A piece of tarpaulin given to him by a sailor had become the roof, and the walls, shored up with baulks of timber dragged up from the beach, were whitewashed and clean. Local people, while refusing to invite him into their clean homes because of his fleas, were willing to help in any other way they could, and he had been given oddments of unwanted furniture. He already had a table, a straw-filled cushion on which to sit, a jug and plates and a cup from which to drink. He had made a hearth for his fire and a wooden platform for his most precious possession, his fea-ther-filled mattress.

Before she had become too ill to work, his mother, whom he only vaguely remembered, had worked on farms, doing seasonal work throughout the year, travelling great distances to find fresh employment as one season's work finished.

At the last place where she had been able to earn a few shillings to keep them in food, she had been given a few pieces of ticking, which she had patiently sewn together. With Barrass helping her, she had filled it with feathers and down gathered from the farmyard ducks, geese and hens. It was this, his only possession, that Barrass had managed to drag from one home to another as he was passed around the village by people willing, then unwilling, to feed and clothe him.

The cause of his constant moves had always been his fleas. No one at any time associated the problem with his mattress. Or if they had, they were unwilling to take from him the one thing he had to remind him of a mother who had died before he was two years old.

He had been shaved of his hair at an early age, the dark curls dropping around him as he sat, frightened and unable to complain, utterly dependent on the perpetrators. His clothes had been burnt on more occasions than he could count in attempts to solve the problem, and he had been given an odd assortment of both boys' and girls' clothes to cover himself.

All through the summer, when he had been living with a family on the estate of William and Dorothy Ddole, he had worn nothing but a girl's dress that was short and hid very little of what showed the incongruity of the pretty pink, lace-trimmed garment. This had led to the nickname Bare Arse, which had gradually become Barrass, the name by which everyone knew him. His real name had been forgotten years ago and Barrass he remained. The fleas remained also.

On the day Olwen followed him, he went to the house of Ivor Baker the builder and his wife Winifred, and asked to see their daughter Blodwen. She came out and leaned against the door post, looking at him with utter disdain.

'What do you want?' she asked.

'I have something to show you. Will you come and see?'

Without answering him, she closed the door and watched from a window to see how patiently he would wait for her. Then, when she thought she had tormented him enough, she wrapped a black shawl around her shoulders and stepped out to join him.

'Keep your distance, mind,' she warned. 'Fleas I can do without.'

He walked ahead of her, smiling his delight that she had agreed to come, leading her up to the top of the cliffs by a path through the steep woodland where a stream filtered through rocky ground and wild flowers abounded, fed by water, nurtured by the rich leafy soil and the sun that found its way through the parasol of leaves. Birds sang all around them, quieter now that summer was well under way, but rich still with the melodious blackbirds and thrushes who nested within the rarely visited wood.

'Lovely isn't it, Blodwen?' Barrass called back, but she only complained,

'What d'you think I am, a goat? Fancy making me walk through this steep wilderness. I'm almost persuaded to turn

17

and walk back down!' She stopped for a rest and looked back at the slope behind her. But curiosity urged her on.

'Not much further,' Barrass promised, and he offered his hand to help her up the last few yards.

'Move away,' she said rudely. 'I can manage without you touching me.' She flinched slightly at the look of embarrassment that crossed his face. But it's best he keeps his place, she thought. She didn't want anyone to think she was a friend of the homeless, flea-ridden orphan! Why she had come was a mystery to her. She usually avoided him and, apart from an opportunity for rudeness and a giggle with her friends, ignored him completely. What could he have that would interest her?

Barrass took her through a field that had been cut for hay, and on to where the barn stood, near the edge of the cliffs looking down on the one- and two-masted boats that lay at anchor along the shore.

'I have a home of my own now,' he said proudly. 'Still an orphan of course – until I find my father. But no longer homeless and dependent on others for shelter.' He stood well back for her to look inside.

'Call this a home?' Blodwen laughed. 'My dadda's pigs are better housed.'

'You don't understand,' he said, his fine eyes clouded with disappointment. 'It's a place of my own, I don't have to ask for someone to give me a place to sleep any more. When winter comes and the storms begin, I'll have my own place.' He hesitated at the doorway, which she had not entered. The door was a frame on which pieces of tarpaulin had been nailed. He pushed it to one side.

'Look and see what I've done inside,' he pleaded.

Gesturing for him to stand well back, she went in.

It was surprisingly light, with three windows on the landward side open to the summer air. He had framed the windows with wood but they lacked glass. The whitewashed walls gave it a certain orderliness and she saw that wood was piled ready to burn near the roughly hewn stones of the hearth.

'You aren't going to live here, are you?' she said, hiding her surprise at its neatness and cleanliness.

She continued to look around, intending to share a laugh with her friends over the boy's attempts to make a proper place for himself. She nodded towards the bed on its platform near the fireplace.

'Your filthy old bed and a few sticks of furniture in a hovel like this and you bring me to see it? I'd be too ashamed to show anyone if I lived in a place like this.' She leaned away as she passed him and ran out of the door, her laughter coming back as she hurried down the steep wooded cliff.

Olwen heard the last of the conversation and the derisive laughter, but seeing the hurt expression on Barrass's face, decided it best not to show him she was there. She went slowly home to bed and lay wondering when he would tell her about his home, and why she had not been told of it before. Was he hoping to marry Blodwen? She sat upright in bed with the shock of the idea. In spite of her tiredness, the thought kept her awake for almost an hour. If only he would be patient and wait for her to grow up!

Arthur worked as a pot-boy at the alehouse for Pitcher and Emma Palmer, and whenever he was free he would look for Olwen. If there was no possibility of her being with Barrass, she would go with him and wander along the narrow and sometimes precarious paths on the cliffs above the village. They would talk, sharing confidences and just enjoying each other's company. Arthur had a dog, which, as Pitcher would not allow it inside, slept in a barrel laid on its side in the yard behind the alehouse.

One morning, when there was no work for her, Olwen went to the alehouse and, seeing the dog dozing in the barrel, guessed that Arthur would not be very far away. She stepped inside, where Blodwen's mother, Winifred Baker, was scrubbing the slate-slabbed floor, and called him.

'Give me a hand with the last of these jugs and I'll be able to go out for a while,' Arthur answered in his high, girlish voice that had not yet broken. 'There'll be some wild raspberries on the cliffs.'

19

Stepping carefully over the wet surface, she went into the large, cool kitchen and began washing and drying the big jugs with which Pitcher served his ale and porter.

'Barrass has built himself a house and he thinks I don't know,' she began. 'Not a word, mind. I'll take you there if you like.'

By the time the pots were all clean and put back in their correct places in the barroom, rain had begun. Taking a grain sack from the pile in a corner, they covered themselves against the wet and ran out. They ran through the scattered houses, climbed through the steep woodland and reached the top breathless but hardly damp.

They went slowly as they approached the building, looking to see if there was anyone inside by peering through the open window-spaces. Everything looked the same as when she had been there before. They opened the makeshift door and stepped inside.

'There's clever he is to make this from a few old walls,' Arthur gasped. 'Who'd have thought to whiten the walls an' all. Looks fit for someone like William Ddole it does, not Barrass. He hardly looks the part, does he, with no hair and pimples and God knows what else besides.'

'Where *is* Barrass, I wonder,' Olwen asked. 'Best not to let him catch us here, not until he tells us about it himself.'

'Gone with Kenneth-the-Post. I saw them go this morning. Soaked he'll be in all this rain with all the miles he'll be walking just to keep little Kenneth company.'

Olwen looked at the wood ready for burning near the roughly built hearth.

We could give him a surprise and light his fire for him. What if we lit it now, then come up later to add some fuel? That would please him.'

'But first we'll pick him some raspberries,' Arthur said. 'The rain won't harm us, and it would all be such a surprise.'

They gathered some of the luscious fruit into a wooden bowl they found on a windowsill and left it on the table. A flint and rag had been placed ready on the hearth and Arthur managed to strike a light and start the wood burning.

For a while they sat beside the comforting glow and talked, then, as time drew near to the moment when Pitcher would begin shouting for his pot-boy, they added more fuel and left, well pleased with the surprise they had prepared.

Some of the wood was well dried but the piece they had added from the pile Barrass had begun outside was still damp from the sea and it hissed a protest as flames began to lick around its edges. the fire burned unevenly, the dry logs on one side being reduced to ashes quickly while those on the other smouldered and resisted the heat.

When Olwen walked up later to see if the fire needed more fuel, her eyes glowing with thoughts of Barrass's appreciation of the welcome when he arrived cold and wet and tired from his long walk, she saw smoke filtering through the trees, held low by the damp air. There was a great deal, and it was coming from the barn.

The truth hit her like a hammer blow. Somehow, she and Arthur had burnt down Barrass's new home. What she did not know was that she had also relieved him of the source of his fleas by burning his most treasured possession, his mother's feather mattress.

CHAPTER TWO

The rain was heavy as Dan strode across the cliffs towards the house where Markus lived. He did not relish meeting with the surly blind man who was rarely seen but who, as an organizer of the smuggling that went on in the area, was feared by all. The lonely house on the edge of the cliff path was avoided by the locals, especially after dark, but today Dan sang as he walked, a pleasant, powerful tenor voice that seemed at odds with his thin frame. He sang songs of the battle against the sea that was always a part of his life, and some of his favourite hymns, apparently indifferent to the pouring rain, his long legs stretched at each step and his head held high.

He wore a linen smock over trousers and a thick fisherman's jumper. Gaiters on his lower legs protected him from the wet grasses and a large, wide-brimmed hat given to him by a French fisherman covered his head. The clothes were generously cut and hung loosely on him.

He sang because he would meet Enyd, daughter of Kenneth-the-Post, that evening. Although they rarely met without some disagreement rising between them, he knew that eventually she would consent to be his wife. The thought quickened his already fast pace and he was glowing with exertion when he reached Markus's.

'Markus is from the house,' the watchman said as Dan prepared to knock at the large, rambling farmhouse. 'Gone this long time and no knowing when he'll be back.'

'Oh, then I must leave this message with you,' Dan said hesitantly. 'Mistress Dorothy Ddole asked me to deliver this invitation. Kenneth will not be back this way for a day or so and she wished him to have it at once.'

He handed the folded and sealed paper to the watchman, protecting it from the rain until the last moment by using his hat.

22

'There's a package here for your mother, young Dan,' the old man said, and searching in the shelves in the porch-way, he gave Dan a small box. Dan thanked him, made him promise to deliver Mistress Ddole's letter as soon as his master returned, then headed back home, still singing, clutching the box under his smock to protect it from wet. He guessed what it contained; tea, legal or otherwise, would not benefit from a soaking!

He could barely see the sea as he walked back along the path, although the hiss of it and the slap of waves touching the rocks accompanied his singing. In the stretch below his home there was a tunnel in the half-submerged rocks; at high tide the waves thundered through it and burst out with a roar. Childlike, he stood and listened to it. The ill-tempered sound amused him and could be heard even when the tide was an amiable one like today when it was beaten down by the heavy rain.

Still singing, he climbed the steep grassy slope, slithering on the wet grass, to call a greeting to his mother.

'A gift, Mam, as we expected,' he said as he stood at the open doorway. 'Tea and something else which I will leave you to unpack.'

'Wait while I see,' she said, smiling as she took the package from his wet hands. She handed him a mug of hot cawl from the cauldron hanging by the fire and when he did not enter, said, 'Going straight to see Kenneth, are you?'

'So wet I am, it hardly seems worth warming myself. Besides I'd fill the house with steam and Dadda would find you disappeared.'

Mary laughed. 'I don't think that makes sense, but I know what you mean!'

She opened the carefully wrapped parcel to reveal a pound of tea and a small square of richly coloured silk, enough to make a shawl. She handed it to Dan.

'Take it for Enyd,' she said, 'it's too grand for me. She will enjoy wearing it for sure.'

'Thank you, Mam! Enyd will love you for it.' His eyes gleamed with the prospect of pleasing Enyd as he watched

23

Mary fold the silk and pack it neatly back into its paper. 'Is there anything for me to do before I go and call on her?'

'Go you, and be sure to be back in time to get a change of clothes before you stiffen with the cold. July it is and there's us chilled like it was winter.' She bustled around the small, overfilled room and put the treasured tea in its place in a cupboard, smelling it in anticipation of the first brewing.

The tea was part of his father's reward for helping with the unloading of a few nights before. The rest of the payment, a small amount of brandy, would come at night, left in the hay-barn. Tea was easily scattered on the windy cliffs if there was any sign of the excise men, but brandy gave out an unmistakable smell, impossible to disguise. Extra precautions were made when that was shared out.

As Dan walked down to the village, his hands found the statue he had made for Enyd. The wooden cross, with the body of Christ intricately carved, had taken him several days, between other work, to complete. He wanted to look at it before handing it to her, to make sure he could not improve it further, but the rain prevented him. He did not want it to be wet with rain as if he had been careless. It was not a casual gift from a boy to a girl, it was an act of love to have carved it and an act of his love for Enyd that he should give it to her.

She opened the door to his knock but before she could greet him, he heard her mother's voice call shrilly,

'Hello Dan, go straight round to the chickens, will you? No sense treading through the house all that mud and rain for me to clear up.'

Dan remembered with a smile that Ceinwen had recently bought an old carpet from Emma Parker at the alehouse and the care of it made her over-fussy about feet. He smiled ruefully at Enyd and walked around to the back yard.

Enyd was a serious-looking girl, with a slight haughtiness about her that discouraged most of the young men who were at an age for courting. But Dan seemed to ignore the occasional rebuffs and continued to see her at every opportunity, unafraid to show how he loved her, determined

24

to wear down resistance by perseverance. He loved the way her soft brown hair fell from the combs and ribbons with which she attempted to control it, and how it glinted with touches of gold in the sun, and her small neat figure that already hinted at the plumpness to come. He loved the occasional smile he managed to produce around her tightly closed lips, and dreamed of softening their harshness with his kisses. He knew that without her parents' insistence that she found someone more worthy, she would have consented to be his wife months ago.

Kenneth kept chickens – or at least he bought the eggs and set them beneath a broody hen, then left all the care and management to Ceinwen, insisting he had no time for such things. They had some young cockerels to be killed and this was the reason for Dan's visit. Dorothy Ddole had a fancy to hold a small party for their friends, and needed a dozen roasting fowl and two dozen large plaice. Dan and Spider were supplying the fish, and Dan had been asked by Ceinwen to slaughter the fowl and take them to Ddole House.

When the task was done he called for Enyd at the back door. She had been waiting in the outer kitchen, where a multitude of household jobs were done – everything from cleaning and polishing Kenneth's bag and boots, to the care of sickly young animals and the preparation of food. He bent to kiss her but as usual, she turned her face away, allowing him only a touch of her baby-fine hair. She was always unwilling to kiss him when there was the possibility of her mother appearing. Away from her home she was different, although she was still held back by something she would not explain.

'I have a present for you, Enyd,' he whispered. 'Two in fact, one I made and one from Mam. Now which will I give you first?'

'Yours please,' she said, and gave him just the hint of a smile.

He handed her the statue and looked at her face, hoping anxiously that she was pleased with it. When she glanced up at him, her eyes were dark with emotion.

'Dan, it's beautiful, did you really make it? Oh thank you! It shall stand beside my bible and hear my prayers every night, and I'll say one for you to keep you safe from the dangers of the sea. Oh, Dan, thank you.' She touched his cheek lightly with her lips, pulling him down to reach, then released him and stepped back as if embarrassed by her show of feelings.

'Glad you like it,' he whispered. 'I didn't show anyone I was making it. I wanted it to be completely yours and mine.' He laughed nervously to hide his pleasure at the way his gift had been received, and said, 'Want to see the other present now?'

'Yes, please, but it can't be as wonderful as this.' She continued to stare at the small statue, whose face was perfectly sculpted to show the expression of joy that transcended pain and grief, then glanced at the tall figure beside her as if unable to believe that those huge, knobbly hands had carved a thing of such delicate perfection.

She marvelled at the silk for the shawl and promised to make it ready to wear on the following Sunday. But her eyes drifted back to the statue, and she finally said,

'Dan, if you can carve wood like this, couldn't you make a living from carpentry instead of bringing in fish? I fear for you and would be far happier knowing you were safe on land.'

Dan sighed. The moment of happiness was spoilt. Every chance she had, she brought up the subject of his leaving the sea. He looked at her face, seeing now only the spoilt expression, the slight pout that showed how much she wanted her own way. Nothing had been said about marriage, but he knew that she was telling him as plainly as she could, that unless he found some different way of earning money to keep her, then the answer to the as yet unspoken question was no.

He walked back up the cliff path slowly, still ignoring the rain, but the joyful singing had ceased, and his steps no longer bounced with happiness. What sort of a wife would she be if she expected him to become someone different from the man he was? Couldn't she understand that he had

26

not known any life but that of a fisherman, and wanted no other?

He wished briefly that he had not given her the statue. Henry Harris, secretary to William Ddole, who collected works of art, had surprised him by buying a previous carving from him, and had paid generously. It had been of one of the oyster boats that worked in the bay, complete with all the fittings: the sails, the dredge and winch and tiny members of the crew. Harris had asked to see any other models he made. He would surely have paid well for the cross.

But no, he was acting like the spoilt child he was accusing Enyd of being. The statue had been made for Enyd and her being afraid of the sea was not sufficient reason to begrudge it. But he was silent and far from content when he reached the cottage on the cliff top.

As Olwen ran down from the burning barn to tell Arthur what had happened to the magnificent surprise they had planned for Barrass, she saw Enyd walking across to the alehouse, shrouded in a cloak and hood and lifting her skirts high to avoid the mud. Olwen was fighting back tears and she did not want to talk to Enyd, but as they were both heading in the same direction she could not avoid waving and shouting a greeting. They met at the porch and as Olwen pushed at the door, Enyd stopped her. Aware of the girl's distress, but not interested in the cause, she showed her the beautiful carving and said,

'Dan gave it to me. Such a clever one, your brother. In some other, more enlightened home, his talents would be encouraged. He wasn't intended to waste his time gathering fish, a job anyone could do. Such a pity he didn't have parents who could see that, don't you agree? Not a word to Mary and Spider, mind, but you understand what I mean, don't you?'

'Oh yes, I understand!' Olwen forgot her manners in her distress at burning down Barrass's new home and poured out her anger at the prim-sounding girl. 'I understand that being a fisherman is not good enough for the likes of you. What is your father anyway?'

'He's a carrier of the King's Mail! Meeting important people every day.'

'He's a messenger! Passing messages between his betters! That's no great improvement over a family who brings food into the village whatever the cost. Fancy talk and fancy ideas you've got, Enyd, and far below what my brother deserves for a wife!'

Tears flowed and Olwen ran to the back room where she knew she would find Arthur. Enyd stared after her, surprised at the outburst, wondering about the cause. It was not herself, she guessed that much. The girl had been white with shock before they had spoken.

The sound of running feet and squeals of laughter made her look along the dismal street and when she saw the twin daughters of the alehouse keeper, she stepped out into the rain to greet them.

'Pansy! Daisy! How fortunate. I might have missed you. I've called to show you what Dan has made for me.'

'Enyd, how beautiful,' Pansy said, shaking her head free of the hood that had protected her between the carriage which brought them home and the porch. 'Come in, won't you? Mamma would like to see it, I'm sure.'

'I cannot,' Enyd said. 'I must go and talk to Dan. I'm afraid, even after his wonderful gift I was less than kind. The boy needs a pleasant word or he'll be downcast.'

The three girls, the twins eighteen and Enyd almost two years younger, giggled together like conspirators as Enyd exaggerated Dan's lovesick advances and her own coolness, and in return heard the twins' latest adventures.

Above them a window opened and the twins' mother Emma leaned out, holding a book over her head to protect her wig from the rain. She called down with the full force of her far from genteel voice, 'Pansy, Daisy, come in at once! How can you behave like the lower classes, shouting in that unladylike way and causing uproar? Get in this very moment. Why have we been paying good money for fine schools to teach you the way to behave? For you to carry on like this? Oh my goodness, what *will* people think?' The window slammed shut and, stifling their giggles behind gloved hands, the twins nodded farewell to Enyd and went into the alehouse.

Emma stood at the head of the stairs, arms on ample hips, demanding an explanation of the rowdy display. 'Mr Palmer?' she called in a voice loud enough to loosen the rocks in the quarry behind the house, 'I think you should come and talk to your girls.'

'Leave them, Mother,' said Violet, her eldest girl. 'It was only harmless fun.'

'That, Violet,' Emma stormed, 'is up to me and your father. *Pitcher*?' she shouted again.

Below her, Pitcher grumbled and left the barrel he was rolling for Arthur to deal with, and hurried to berate his daughters for whatever they had done to displease their mother.

Afterwards while Olwen waited for him, Arthur handed Pansy a small cardboard box. Daisy went upstairs and Pansy lifted the lid to see a few choice wild raspberries resting on a bed of white crinkled paper.

'I picked them for you this very afternoon, in the rain,' Arthur said in his high voice, feeling redness suffusing his cheeks as Pansy smiled her thanks.

'I'll hide them from Daisy and eat them all myself,' she whispered, ' – in bed.' She replaced the lid and tucked the box under her wet cloak. Giving him another dazzling smile, she tripped up the stairs after her sister.

Arthur stared after her for a moment, his adam's apple dancing puppet-like on the string of joyous rapture. Then he turned to where Olwen was waiting, her shoulders hunched with sobs. For a moment he hesitated, not rushing as he normally would to comfort his friend. After an encounter with Pansy he needed to be alone, to think about the few words they had exchanged and commit them to memory, to relive time and again the excitement of their brief communication. Olwen was his dear friend, the closest he had ever been to having a sister, someone to call his family: but Pansy was his love.

Olwen was inconsolable and the words she uttered made

29

no sense to him so he was relieved when he saw Barrass entering the alehouse.

'She's upset, but she can't tell me why,' he said as Barrass came at once to place an arm around the sobbing girl. 'Perhaps she'll talk to you, Barrass, I certainly won't do today.' Thankfully Arthur escaped to dream about Pansy Palmer.

'Olwen, what is it? Has someone harmed you? Tell me and I'll go and make them sorry.' The sound of Barrass's soothing voice sent Olwen into even louder crying. How could she tell him why she was upset? Once he knew she had ruined the home he had just finished building he would never speak to her again. She should tell him at once, but she could not. How could she when it would mean he would push her away from him? The very thought made her sobs increase in volume.

Barrass led her to a bench seat near the fire and sat beside her, rocking her as if she were a baby. She breathed in the scent of him, relishing with a sort of desperation the wonderful sensation of having his arms around her, holding her close. His attention and concern were balm even though she guessed it would be for the last time. Slowly her sobs eased, but whenever he tried to move her away from him she began again. She was cheating, allowing him to comfort her when she knew he would never forgive her for what she had done, but the need for his love was intense. For the last time, she pressed herself closer, savouring his near-ness to remember when she was no longer his friend.

She opened his coat and dug herself as deeply as she could so she was pressed against his beating heart, and in a muffled voice said, 'Barrass, will you always remember I'm your dearest friend?'

'And I am yours, Olwen. You were my friend when I had no one else. I'll never forget that. Whatever it is, you can tell me.'

'Perhaps later,' she whispered, 'perhaps later.' This moment was too precious to spoil. Unseen by her, Barrass smiled. She really was a funny little thing. How he would miss her if she weren't there. But his thoughts didn't go any further, they drifted to Blodwen.

Enyd was older than Olwen by two years and although the gap between herself and the twins did not seem to matter, between herself and the small, innocent Olwen the differences were enormous. Enyd had broken out of childhood some time before while Olwen still loved to play games with the younger children, snowballs and wild tobogganing in the winter. Hide and seek in the summer, racing about on the fields and in the sea, shouting and screaming wildly with the rest. The girls were separated by thoughts, knowledge and attitudes.

They were divided too by the rather exalted position Enyd believed she held in the community, compared with Olwen's status as the daughter of a fishermen. Their differences were further exaggerated by Enyd's envy of the affection in which Olwen was held by the villagers. Her own aloofness, created by the friendship with Emma's twins, and the insistence of her mother that she had more in common with the wealthy family at the alehouse, was to blame. The illusion of importance was nurtured by both her parents. They created a position of superiority and encouraged her to be contained by it.

She walked back home, wishing she had not said those foolish and hurtful things to Olwen about her family. She stood at the bottom of the bank below her home, looking up at the neatly curtained windows, remembering the poor but friendly comfort of Dan's home and wanting both. She wanted enough money to live in moderate comfort, and wanted Dan to share it with her. But not, she reminded herself, with Dan the fisherman. That she could never live with. Her thin lips tightened even further as she climbed the bank and pushed open the door.

She could not settle. She sat looking at the little statue and gave it to her mother to admire, then sat again, thinking of the loving hands that had carved it for her, knowing that thoughts of herself as well as the figure suffering on the cross had filled the carver's mind. His love for her was so

31

plain to see, so why wouldn't he leave the sea for her and find a more respectable job? She sighed, put her cloak back on and prepared to go out into the pouring rain once again.

When she arrived at Spider's house, Dan was drying his clothes around the fire on which Mary was preparing their food. A fish baking in the oven with some small potatoes was sending out delicious and mouthwatering smells and Enyd tried to ignore it, telling herself that her own meal of lamb, bought from the Swansea market, was far superior. But her stomach told her different.

'There's plenty for an extra one?' Mary invited.

'Thank you, but Mam is cooking roast lamb for today.'

'I'll walk you back,' Dan offered when Enyd had shown the statue to his mother. But they walked away from the village, along the path above the sea.

He took her hand and they walked close together when the path allowed, separating as briefly as they could when it became too narrow. They could not see the water but heard its monotonous coming and going, without the punctuation of the seabirds that usually glided over the incoming tide to scavenge what it brought. They did not speak, each wanting to say what was in their mind but afraid, knowing that the result would be an argument and a walk home in a different sort of silence.

'You don't like the sea so you are afraid for me,' Dan ventured. 'I know it and respect it, but I am not afraid or I would never be able to earn a good living from it.'

Enyd swallowed the impulse to beg him again to forget fishing and find himself better work. This was not the moment, in pelting rain with him squelching beside her in wet clothes and a chilling body.

They were taking the path down to the village when a rider appeared at the side of them and called for Dan to stop.

'Dan. May I please ask what you have been doing up here in such weather? Something very important to keep you from a warm fire and a comfortable chair?' Daniels, Keeper-of-the-Peace, pushed his way between Dan and Enyd and demanded an answer.

32

'Mr Daniels, we have been walking, nothing more.' Dan smiled disarmingly. 'What else could we be doing in rain such as this?'

'Who is your companion?' He leaned down to peer at Enyd and was at once apologetic as he recognized her.

'Miss Enyd? I am sorry to delay you, but can you explain why you are out at such a time? There can be no pleasure, surely, in a stroll and a discussion with rain falling down your neck and soaking your clothes.'

'That, sir,' Dan replied, 'would depend on your companion. I have been most content, and the state of my clothes will soon be rectified. I wish to see Miss Enyd safe home, then I will go and enjoy my mother's ministrations like any spoilt son.'

Daniels nodded and allowed them to pass. He had no liking for staying out in the rain and could see no purpose in asking any further questions. Seeing the young couple were wrapped in the foolishness of love was explanation enough. He smiled a little, then turned his horse and headed for home.

He had travelled miles that day to attend a meeting to discuss the need to bear down hard on the smuggling that was almost blatant in the area of his jurisdiction, and he had been told quite firmly to deal with it. He shrugged in his wet clothes even as he thought of it. How could you deal with something that involved the whole village? Especially when that village considered the extra income and luxuries their right?

He was tired and the discomforts of the day's riding in the unpleasant weather became more apparent. He frowned as he glanced down at his expensive leather boots which had been cleaned with such care the previous evening, and the cloak made of fine wool which he had been too vain to protect with a waterproof that smelt of mildew. The brim of his hat was falling in waves about his head. Why did his masters insist he waste a day just to be told what he already knew, that smuggling was a pest and costly nuisance?

When Enyd had closed her door, Dan decided to go and

see Ivor-the-Builder. He had long intended to make a truckle bed for when baby Dic was old enough to need one. Ivor would have some small pieces of wood to sell cheap and a few nails too. The bed he planned would slide out of sight under a cupboard during the day and be trundled out at night.

He wondered if he *could* learn to live without the sea, if perhaps he could spend his days making things from wood to sell at the markets. It would entail a lot of travelling, to other markets in other towns and villages, and fairs. He would have to spend long hours alone in a barn with only the rasping and banging of the tools to listen to. The companionship he shared with his father would be sorely missed. And what of his father? He couldn't manage the boat and nets alone. Perhaps Olwen would go with him? She was small but strong, and would probably relish the adventure.

He stopped to relieve himself against a tree but was startled to see a blaze of red, and made out the shape of a soldier hiding in the leafy green. The desire to urinate left him. First Daniels asking questions and now soldiery. He walked on without speaking to the boy and thought he had better warn his father and the rest to be extra careful for a few days, until the soldiers' enthusiasm was lost to boredom.

He found Ivor at home, the rain making his work of building a new barn for William Ddole impossible. Invited inside, Dan explained his reasons for the call, and when he and Ivor went to the barn to choose the wood, he said in a half-whisper,

'It's getting that you can't pee in the hedges without sprinkling a soldier!'

'I saw two of them half hidden by the big chestnut tree,' Ivor laughed. 'They try to hide, hoping to find out something that will lead them to so-called criminals, yet insist on wearing their bright red coats. Do they think us blind?'

'Still, even though we laugh at them, we must warn people to be extra cautious for a while,' Dan said. 'The deliveries of gifts must wait a while, I think.'

34

'Leave it for today, few will be out in this. I'll send messages tomorrow.'

Dan gathered up the strips of wood Ivor had supplied, then asked, in a moment of impulse, 'What chance of my working as a carpenter, Ivor? Would I be good enough?'

'If you spent the time with me, eventually you would pass muster, but I can't see you leaving the sea for the monotony and frustration of learning a fresh trade, boy.'

Dan laughingly agreed. Now, although he had been light-hearted in his question, he could tell Enyd that he had at least tried and been turned down!

He adjusted his load and set off home, thinking of the food and warmth and dry clothes, bending in his haste to be there now there was nothing more to keep him away. At the top of the cliff he smelt smoke. Low and creeping about like a lost fog, its acrid smell puzzled him. Who would be stupid enough to try and burn out of doors in weather like today?

CHAPTER THREE

When Barrass reached his new home that evening he stared in disbelief at the smouldering building. It was still raining, steady, relentless rain that filled the air with warm dampness, no fierce storm but surely enough to hold back a fire?

He stumbled towards the already blackened walls and tried to look inside. The smoke billowing out forced him back, but he knew without having to see that all his possessions were gone. He felt the walls, warm and damp. It would be hours before he could sleep in the meagre shelter they offered. Where could he go? His old lean-to at the beach had disintegrated days ago.

The temptation to walk and keep walking until he collapsed with exhaustion welled up in him. Why should he stay here, where someone could do this to him? Then a devastating thought came into his head. Who could have come here to this isolated place and deliberately burned his home? The only one who knew of it was Blodwen, the girl he had allowed to share his secret. He sat down on the wet grass and fought to hold back sobs of dismay.

He moved towards the building again, wet, cold, hungry and miserable. It will smoulder until there's nothing left, he thought, and the only thing to do is walk away. He dragged his feet reluctantly down to the village and there, in a corbelled pig-house, mercifully empty, where he had found shelter before, he slept.

The first person he saw the following morning was Kenneth, who was setting out on the horse he regularly hired for the journey to Swansea to pick up the post. He used a horse to collect the mail, yet was too mean to hire again for the longer trip around Gower delivering it, when he would walk and spend a night at the furthest point of his route before returning for home.

'What's the matter, boy?' Kenneth asked as he saw the

drooping figure standing halfway up the bank. 'Want some breakfast, do you?'

'I made myself a home,' Barrass told him, 'and yesterday, someone burnt it down.'

'Never! Well there's a thing! Sure you weren't careless with the fire yourself?'

'I hadn't lit one.' He took the piece of bread and chunk of cheese offered by Kenneth and went on his way. 'Tell Blodwen Baker, will you?' he called back.

All day he wandered aimlessly around the village, waiting for the opportunity to confront Blodwen and ask her why she had done it. Then, when he was building up the courage to go boldly to the door of her house, she came past where he was sitting on the wall in front of the alehouse talking to Arthur.

'My house was burnt down last night,' he said, his face reddening as it frequently did when talking to Blodwen. 'Someone went up there and deliberately ruined it.'

Blodwen, who was with her mother, just shrugged and the two women passed him without a word. Although it was not unusual for Blodwen to ignore him, for Barrass that day it seemed an act of guilt.

Arthur reddened too. He had been waiting all morning for the opportunity to tell Barrass what he had done. If Barrass had been less distressed he might have noticed the boy's nervousness, his anxiety to please him and the way he agreed, almost before he had finished speaking, with everything Barrass said. Barrass could not know that the boy was waiting for the accusations to begin, brought almost to the point of tears when none came.

When Olwen came to sell fish to Pitcher, Arthur exchanged a look with her of anxiety and remorse.

'I've been making a home for myself,' Barrass told her, 'and spent ages getting it finished and dry for the winter, and last night someone burnt it down.'

Olwen hesitated. It would be so easy to lie – Barrass had no idea that she had found out about the place. Then she knew with childlike conviction that she had to be honest

37

with him, he was her special friend and no untruth must spoil that.

'I – I planned a surprise for you, Barrass,' she began. 'I wanted you to have a fire to welcome you home after walking all those miles in the rain and I lit a fire in the hearth. I did it proper, mind. Built it just as Mam does. But I suppose it must have fallen from the hearth and caught the straw on the floor alight. Barrass, I'm sorry.' She began to sob as he stood over her, his brown eyes frowning. She flinched ready for the blow that must surely come. 'I'm sorry, I really wasn't careless. I wanted to surprise you.' She blinked her eyes open, expecting to see his arm raised to hit her, but to her amazement he was calm and almost smiling.

'So it wasn't Blodwen,' he said softly. 'Now there's a relief.'

Olwen glanced at Arthur and back at Barrass, her normal ebullient nature quickly restored.

'You aren't mad at me then?'

'Glad I am, glad that it wasn't Blodwen as I thought. She wouldn't really be that cruel, would she?'

Arthur, wanting to own up and take his share of the punishment that Barrass was certain to give, was confused. Barrass looked pleased! He swallowed nervously. 'We didn't mean it to happen,' he mumbled at last.

Barrass turned to him so swiftly that Arthur fell off the wall in his haste to avoid the swipe that must now certainly come. He wriggled away as he was offered a hand to help him rise.

'So you were in on it too? What is it about me that no one wants me to have a home of my own?' Barrass asked, but there was no rise to his anger.

Once it was clear that Barrass was not going to lose his temper and hit them, Olwen felt suddenly sick. 'You were so glad that Blodwen hadn't done it – you don't really care about losing your home, do you?' she said, bending forward at the waist and trying to look threatening. 'Barrass, you aren't going to *marry* her, are you?' The dismay on her small face and the scolding in her voice was comic and Barrass burst out laughing.

'I want to be someone important when I'm a man,' he said when his laughter subsided. 'And for that I'll need a wife who wants the same.'

'I'm important,' Olwen said stoutly. 'I'm the daughter of the finest fisherman in the whole of Wales!'

Barrass tousled her hair, making the damaged fringe stand up comically, and laughed again.

'Come on, let's see if there's anything to save.' How could he explain about choosing a wife to a girl who was still a child? And how could he tell her that the place he had worked on, and of which he had been so proud, meant less than a temporary shelter, a shack made of driftwood or a borrowed pigsty, after the curt dismissal of his efforts by Blodwen on the previous day?

The three of them set off, Barrass taller and larger and making the guilty pair look smaller than usual by comparison. Arthur and Olwen were dressed with reasonable neatness but Barrass was a sight that made even those used to seeing him stop and stare.

His face was a mass of angry sores where fleas had bitten, and his clothes were made for someone other than he, so they were like a second skin in parts and drooped over his body in others. The trousers were torn and shortened by the fringing of age, and showed ankles as badly bitten as his face, bald head and neck. Children jeered at him as they passed, jumping away from him and calling him names. He seemed unaware of it, he had suffered it all his life and thought it unlikely to change.

Olwen and Arthur walked a few steps behind him until Olwen realized that this might be taken for fear of catching his fleas, and she moved up to walk as defiantly close to Barrass as she could without actually tripping him. She was his only real friend and he must be regularly reminded.

They had walked only a few yards before Arthur was halted by the shouting of Pitcher warning him that the cleaning of the yard was waiting to be finished. Reluctantly, Arthur returned to his work and Olwen skipped happily along beside Barrass.

It was clear there was nothing to be done to save any of

the contents of the old stone barn. The tarpaulin had fallen early victim to the flames and once that had gone, there was nothing to stop the rain spoiling anything the fire did not destroy. Barrass shrugged and walked away.

'There's plenty of time for me to find somewhere before the winter sets in,' he said. The realization that Blodwen had not ruined his home made the loss easy to bear.

Olwen believed that it was her cheerfulness that had helped him over the shock and disappointment, and she joked and laughed and was excited and happy when he joined in her merriment. 'Please God, keep him away from pretty girls while I grow up,' she muttered to herself, an often repeated prayer.

In the alehouse Arthur worked in the cold cellar below the barroom, but even there he could hear the shouting between Pitcher and Emma on the first floor. He crept up the stone steps and, pushing his head up above the trap door, listened with a grin on his thin, almost skeletal face. It was not the first time he had heard them quarrelling and the subject was not new.

'But Mr Palmer,' Emma said, her voice rising in a parody of the well-spoken woman, 'Mr Palmer, we must do all we can to help our daughters. How can they attract the attention of suitable young men if all we have is this small room, and it overlooking the yard with all its muddle of barrels?'

Emma was short and well rounded, small features taking up only the centre of her plump face giving her a doll-like appearance. The cap she wore wobbled as she scolded him, a frilly frame for her puffed cheeks and the double layers of her chin. Her well-shaped hands fluttering around her middle made the chains on her brass chatelaine jingle their disapproval.

'It's how we earn the money to buy all the fancy clothes you insist they need! Stop pretending we're something we ain't, Mrs Palmer. You shame me from myself. Make me feel like apologizing for being Pitcher Palmer, alehouse keeper, and I once had a pride in being just that. Shame me from myself, that's what you do, Mrs Palmer!' His voice was raised with anger, although Emma sensed his defeat as he looked away from her and lowered his head.

Emma sobbed, not softly but with all the breath she could find within her large bosom. She breathed deeply and let it out in wails of dismay until Pitcher lowered his head even further and gave in.

'All right, we'll make you a drawing room if that's what you really want, although I can't see what the hell we need such a place for. Got enough rooms as it is, seems to me.'

'Thank you, dear Pitcher.' Emma's voice had lowered to the refined tone she normally used. Only on occasions of anger – or when she was quarrelling with Pitcher – did the careful and controlled voice slip.

Pitcher went downstairs from the room which Emma called the parlour and towards the door leading to the yard. He passed the cellar entrance and could hear Arthur busily moving things about and whistling while he worked, but was unconvinced that he had not stopped to enjoy the row.

'If you missed any of that, let me know and I'll fill in the gaps for you!' he growled as he passed the trap door.

Adjoining the alehouse was a building that had been empty for several years and was in a bad state of repair. He stared up at it, working out how best he could incorporate the two buildings into one, allowing for a room large enough for Emma to call a drawing room and use when the suitors she dreamed of were invited to call.

It did not take Barrass long to realize that, for whatever reason, he no longer carried fleas. The confidence that brought gave him the courage to refuse when Pitcher offered to re-shave his head. He knew that at last the hair could be allowed to grow.

By the time Pitcher was ready to start on the rebuilding work, Barrass was transformed into a handsome youth who attracted the admiring gaze of most of the local girls – and their mothers.

'If you want work permanent,' Pitcher told him one day, 'you can come-along-a-me. I want a strong lad to help shift some rubble and get everything ready for the new walls.'

'Any chance of a place to sleep?' Barrass asked.

'Not if you got fleas, boy. Mrs Palmer won't stand for you to bring fleas into her house.'

Barrass pulled off the worn and too large shirt he wore, showing the almost healed spots on his powerfully built body. 'Not a bite to be seen.'

Pitcher nodded. 'All right, boy, you come-along-a-me and we'll find you a corner somewhere.'

'He could share the cellar with me, Pitcher,' Arthur offered.

So Barrass found himself a home of sorts and work to keep him fed and, eventually, clothed with garments that fitted him.

The cellars beneath the alehouse were extensive, leading back further than the house itself and reaching to the storage barns and the malt-house beyond the yard. In the first of these was stored the ale and small beer which Pitcher and, when she could be persuaded away from her social calls, Emma made. Beyond that room were several others, one of which held the brandy, gin, and wines bought legally and with proper receipts from the suppliers in Swansea, but which he had no licence to sell.

Another room, half hidden by a collection of rarely used barrels and boxes, held the results of other transactions: Wines and ankers and half-ankers of brandy that had arrived at night without the need for receipts, just a quick exchange of cash and the constables and customs none the wiser, although members of both organizations frequently applauded Pitcher on the quality of his liquor.

He studied the layout of his building carefully and began to draw an idea of what he envisaged, to discuss with Emma. Using the upstairs rooms for a drawing room was not what he wanted. He had a long-held dream of several properly furnished bedrooms to rent out to travellers.

The room where he sold his ale and food was not large and he did not want to extend it, but furnish a second one so he did not have to turn away the occasional visitors who asked for a room where they could eat in private. With some of the upstairs rooms decorated and furnished, he could accommodate visitors. Travellers came for the sea air, and if he had a comfortable house, they would stay and spend their money with him instead of at the inns, taverns and alehouses six miles away in Swansea.

He imagined the house full of beautifully dressed and wealthy gentlemen – sometimes with their ladies – all sitting at well-filled tables beside his fire, and all having well-filled pockets. But first, as Emma constantly told him, his daughters had to be settled. Once they were off his hands, he could then turn to increasing his trade.

In the large, rambling, once beautiful old house about two miles inland from the seaside village, Dorothy Amelia Ddole sat examining the house accounts. A strikingly handsome woman in her late forties, she wore her iron-grey hair pulled back in an untidy bun at the nape of her neck. Her eyes were deep-set and alert, as if waiting and watching for someone to make a move of which she did not approve.

She was very thin, almost gaunt, and her height of almost six feet emphasized her lack of roundness. There was a hardness about her, an expression that made people a little afraid, yet there was humour too in the eyes and the set of her mouth. With her at the round table near the mullioned window was Henry Harris, the secretary whom her husband still employed although the need for him was no longer valid.

Henry Harris was an old man, and when William Ddole gave up the two small mines and the shipping rights he had inherited from his father, he kept the old man on, unwilling to allow his servant to face the workhouse. So Harris lived frugally but with sufficient comfort in a house near one of the farms.

Dorothy pointed an imperious finger at an item in old-man's spidery writing and demanded that he read it out to her.

'Really, Henry, your words almost leave the page as soon as they're written! Haven't you the strength to press a little harder on the quill? I swear I will open this book one day and find all the pages as clean as when the book was delivered!'

43

'Sorry, Mistress Ddole, but I find it difficult to form the letters some days. Most days I manage well enough,' he added swiftly, 'most days I manage very well.'

'Will you try to work faster on those days and rest when things are not well with you?' She spoke loudly and harshly, but there was no anger in her for the old man. She used the same tone whether she was speaking to a friend, her children, her husband or a recalcitrant puppy.

'I will try, Mistress.'

To Henry Harris she sounded more cross than usual and he gathered his papers together, anxious to be gone before her patience finally gave out and she told him she no longer needed him. Without the few shillings she and her husband paid him he would be hard put to pay for food and the services of Bessie Rees who came in daily to attend his wants.

He hurried out of the house, the books and papers under his arm, a small, anxious man, thin and bent with age, white hair flying around his head and shoulders. Before he had gone more than a few yards he was called back. Dozy Bethan, called so because of her dreaminess, who worked in the dairy and the stillroom, invited him to stay for a drink of buttermilk, which she knew he loved.

They went around the house and re-entered at the door of the kitchen, where Florrie the cook and Carrie, the daughter of Bessie Rees, his cleaning lady, were preparing vegetables for the evening meal.

Henry was right about Dorothy Ddole being more than usually irritable, but the reason was not himself. She had suffered periods of intense pain in her stomach. She at first put these down to too many sour apples, which she loved, then, as the pains grew more frequent and intense, to indigestion following her long rides straight after a heavy meal.

Doctor Percy had at first given her some powdered oyster shells, which he had dried in the sun and ground in a mortar before sieving it into a fine alkali powder. It had eased her discomfort for a while. She had tried eating less, and in fact that was not a hardship as her appetite was no longer as healthy as it had once been. Now she had decided to call in Doctor Percy again to ask for more of the soothing medicine he gave her.

The doctor arrived as Henry Harris sat sipping the delicious cool buttermilk which, Henry did not fail to notice, had been taken from the pail ready to feed the piglets. The thought did not spoil his enjoyment. Dozy Bethan might be irritatingly slow in all she did, but he knew she was meticulous in cleaning her utensils.

When he was leaving he passed the door of the study where he had been looking through the books with Mistress Ddole, but stopped when the door began to open. A rather shy man, he could not face explaining about his invitation to sup buttermilk in the kitchen with Dozy Bethan and Cook, so he darted back into the nearby doorway of the drawing room. What he overheard startled him.

'A temporary affliction, Mistress Ddole, of that I am sure,' Doctor Percy said. Then after a few whispered words from Mistress Ddole which Henry did not catch, the voice went on, 'I'm sure we can relax and not worry unduly, nothing more serious than a temporary affliction, Mistress Ddole. The pain we can do something about. We must not worry, it will be as transient as a summer storm.'

Mistress Ddole came further out of the room and Henry heard her say urgently – and for her, quietly – 'And you will say nothing of this to Mr Ddole if you please, Doctor Percy.'

'Not a word, not a word. No purpose served in worrying William unnecessarily, Mistress Ddole. We'll see how things progress, shall we, and make up our minds at a later date? Now, shall we meet again next week? But, please send a servant for more of the medicine or for me to call if you are further worried. I am at your service, Mistress Ddole, at your service.'

Mistress Ddole spoke again, too softly for Henry to hear, and the doctor replied,

'Of course I will be silent of the matter. I am not a scaremonger, as you must surely know. Not,' he added hastily, 'that we have anything to fear.'

Henry gasped, his hand over his mouth to hush the

45

sound. So this time the rumours were true! Doctor Percy's bumbling reassurances were proof enough. She really *was* ill. He hurried off as soon as the doctor had mounted his horse and ridden away to his next call. Bending further forward in anxiety to begin his arrangements, Henry hastened home.

He had work to do. He needed to arrange things so that William Ddole understood how indispensable he was. He would make sure no one but he could manage the accounts of Ddole House and its farms. Once Mistress Ddole was gone, he felt sure that William would want to retire him and take on a younger, fitter man and that he *must* avoid – whatever he had to do to the neat and carefully kept books.

A few moments later Dorothy Ddole went to the stables and demanded that her horse be saddled, then, after taking a spoonful of the medicine the doctor had left her, rode out at great speed, scuffing dust and hay out of the stable in a cloud. She galloped past Henry and on across the muddy fields as if trying to escape from the devil. All day she rode, the horse lathered and distressed as she urged him on to chase anything that moved – including a child caught climbing down from a tree with some cherries, who had to jump first through a bush and then into a stream to escape. Back home, she bathed and dressed, and when her husband came home she was calm, and apparently without a care.

In Pitcher's alehouse it was Emma who dealt with the accounts. She hated anything to do with the way they earned their money, but knew that if she left it to Pitcher, many accounts would not be served and many more forgotten. At the end of every month she sent Arthur, or one of the boys who hung around looking to earn a penny, to the various houses where goods had been delivered or food and drink taken at the alehouse and for which the money was still unpaid.

She tutted disapprovingly as she looked at the money owed by William Ddole. He made his own ale and had need to buy very little, having his own supplies of wine and spirits brought in from France, yet the account for drinks supplied when he brought people to the alehouse to discuss business deals had mounted up, and for the past several months had not been paid. She went to the top of the stairs and called her husband.

'Don't upset yourself, Emma, they're like that, the wealthy, often leave things for months but they always pay in the end. It isn't the likes of William Ddole we have to worry over, you just try getting that miserly old Kenneth to pay what he owes, that'll keep you busy till Christmas!'

'No, husband, this will not do. I want you to send someone with the account and a note saying to "pay it at once if you please". Then they'll be shamed into settling it.'

'And maybe go somewhere else in future! This isn't the only alehouse in the place as well you know! No, just send the account at the usual time and we'll see what happens.'

Emma did not reply. She did not lie to him, she simply did not do as he asked!

'Barrass,' she called out of the first-storey window, 'I want you to come here without showing Pitcher. I have a job for you.'

Barrass dropped the length of timber he had been carrying up to where the alterations were under way, and ran up the stairs.

'I want you to take this bill and this letter and hand it to either Mistress Ddole or her husband. No one else, mind.'

Barrass promised and set off to walk to Ddole House.

Olwen was walking back down the steep hill, pushing her empty cart. The morning was dull, the rain had eased to a fine drizzle, filling the air and making visibility poor. She could not see the line of fishing boats along the shore until she was almost upon them, and when she did, the figure jumping suddenly out at her with a roar made her scream with shock.

'Barrass! You nearly made made my heart stop!'

'Where are you off to? Still selling your fish?' He peered into the empty cart and added, 'Oh, I see you are finished. Best to get home then out of this rain.'

'I went to Ddole House and they bought all I had. It seems they have a lot of guests this evening and intended to send the boy into the market. I arrived just in time to sell them mine. Wasn't that lucky?' Her sun-freckled arms stuck out from the sleeves of her cloak like pea-sticks, so tiny compared with his, and she bent back to look up at him as she spoke. He smiled and touched her fair hair affectionately.

'That's where I'm going, to Ddole House,' he told her. 'Special delivery of a letter from Mistress Palmer.'

'So, you are a post-boy after all,' she teased. 'Where's your leather bag then?'

'When Kenneth retires, perhaps I'll be old enough to take his job.'

'And marry Ivor-the-Builder's spoilt daughter too?' she jeered. 'Fine life she'll give you, that one!'

He darted at her as if to pull her hair and she stepped away and rumbled on with her empty cart.

She stopped and turned to watch him walking away. His hair was thick and as black as the coal that colliers dug from the earth, and with the dampness of the day, tightly curled. When he had been an object of ridicule, his face had been like a faded picture – dull, spotty and unworthy of anyone's time – but with a frame of dark hair, the dark brown eyes had been given a setting that increased their luminosity, and that same face had a sense of importance. Now there was interest shown by all who looked at him. No one jeered any more and no one ignored him.

She sighed dejectedly. He was catching everyone's eye now. Oh why couldn't he have kept his old fleas for a few more years? What chance do I have now, of him waiting for me to grow up? Even Blodwen looks at him with a sparkle in her eyes. Why was I born so late? Why haven't I grown faster?

As she walked along, her hair and clothes soaked through from rain, the hem of her skirt dragging on the wet roadway, she suddenly gasped out loud as she remembered Penelope. William Ddole's daughter had spoken to her about Barrass when she had called to sell her fish. Of how she had heard

48

that his appearance had dramatically changed from oddity to appealing young man. And Barrass was going to see her!

Oh, fancy lady or not, she was another one to save Barrass from. Olwen sighed, and leaving her cart turned over near her father's boat, ran to follow Barrass and hopefully prevent him finding favour with Penelope, however unlikely that might seem. She had no idea what she would do, but at least there was a chance of preventing him from captivating Penelope and making her cow eyed about him like the rest!

With the rain on the ground she had felt no discomfort as she walked around selling her fish. But now with the sun, watery at first, showing itself in a brightness that surprised her, she became conscious of soreness in her bare feet. She dawdled and wandered away from the direct route to Ddole House, forgetting temporarily her need to watch Barrass. When she found herself wandering in the wrong direction, following a stream, marvelling at its clearness and the fish visible in its depths, she hurriedly left the coolness of the water and the shade of its willows and ran across the fields to the big house.

To her relief, when she went to the kitchen door and asked for Barrass, Dozy Bethan said he had seen the mistress and was already on his way back. She was glad she had come, for now she would not spend the early hours of the night imagining them together.

Olwen did not go home. The sun, once a soothing comfort, was blazing in complete disregard of the time of day and she felt the need to cool herself off near the sea. Cutting across the field where the ruins of Barrass's barn stood, she slid down through the steep wood and on to the beach. Her eyelids were heavy with the need to sleep and seemed determined to droop. She picked her way slowly across the warm pebbles, working her way towards the beach below her home and, with words her mother would have been surprised that she knew, cursing Barrass for being so handsome.

Darkness fell suddenly as if the sun was ashamed of its unreasonable behaviour, a shy performer unexpectedly aware of an audience, and sank hurriedly from sight beyond the dark blue, calm sea in embarrassment. Mary and Spider looked anxiously at the path from the village, wondering where Olwen could have got to.

As the evening became silent and still, Spider went to look for her. Within an hour, Barrass, Arthur, Pitcher, Kenneth and several of their neighbours were out on the roads and paths, calling her name. The moon rose, spreading its eerie light across the water, and they were still searching.

It was Arthur who saw her. He leaned over the sheer edge of the cliff and looking down, saw her spreadeagled far below.

'She's fallen! Quick, over by here! Fallen over the edge, she has.' His high-pitched voice carried to where Barrass and Spider were searching among the thick hedges bordering the small fields on the cliff top. They ran with a wail of anguish, to where Arthur stood, dancing up and down in distress, crying and pointing downwards.

'By there she is, down by there,' he kept repeating.

Barrass and Spider ran to the edge, where normally they would never have attempted to climb down, and lowered themselves over the side. With hardly a pause to feel for safe holds, they worked their way down to the still figure, slipping occasionally but never stopping to consider their danger. Believing in their grief and disbelief that they could, by their very speed, alter what they would not accept.

They reached her together, and as they called her name, despair in both their voices, she stirred and said sleepily, 'My feet, Dadda, they're a-w-ful sore.'

Barrass and Spider turned their heads in unison to where her feet rested in a cool, weed-fringed pool. It was Barrass who carried her home.

CHAPTER FOUR

At first, Olwen could not understand her newfound popularity. Girls who had rarely even noticed her – let alone stopped and spoken to her – were suddenly calling her, asking her to share their activities, and treating her like a young woman instead of a child. She stared hopefully in a mirror whenever the opportunity arose, hoping for a change in her appearance, but so far as she could see, there was none. She was still small, skinny and very much a child. She swelled with importance when Blodwen invited her to come along on an errand for her father.

Then realization hit her like a wild gust of autumn, with a fierce humiliating violence that threatened to dislodge her heart from her flat chest. They were friendly with her because of Barrass! They followed her with the assurance that eventually she would meet him and ease the first moments for them.

She almost hated him then. Barrass, whom she had befriended when no one would even stand close to him! When he looked funny with his bald head and spotty skin. Now he was pursued by everyone, and *she* was being used. Very soon, she saw with mature clarity, she would be left out.

She was standing at the bottom of the bank on which Blodwen's house was built when the realization happened. She and Blodwen were intending to go to the alehouse with a message for Emma. Olwen was wondering how best to deal with the situation when Blodwen's appearance on the step decided her.

Blodwen was dressed for visiting in a full-length coat and skirt of fur-trimmed blue that fitted around her waist in a way that made her look taller and, Olwen's jealous heart told her, elegant. Blodwen even had a hat riding on her piled-up hair, feathers waving in the breeze. Worst of all, she had colour on her face: touches on her cheeks and something brightening the already red lips.

'Wait till your mam sees you in that lot!' Olwen shouted. 'If you think you're walking with me looking like that, you're wrong!' She flounced off – leaving Blodwen to hurry after her in shoes that were probably her mother's Sunday pair – and then ran ahead to tell Barrass to be prepared for a laugh.

Barrass did not laugh. He looked in amazement at the beautiful girl who stood before him, a letter for Emma Palmer in her gloved hand.

'Called on Enyd I did, and her mother asked me to bring this for Mistress Palmer.'

She held out the letter, not a chink in her confidence to show how she had had to plead with Ceinwen to be allowed to bring the letter. He stuttered shyly and offered to show her up to where Emma was sitting sewing a new flannel shirt for her husband.

Olwen watched his behaviour with growing dismay and when Blodwen had slipped into the room above and closed the door, she picked up the nearest object, a copper jug, and threw it in Barrass's direction.

'You aren't fun any more,' she condemned.

'I have to be polite to her,' Barrass reasoned, picking up the dented jug. 'It's her father I want to impress. I won't stand a chance of him putting in a good word for me with the King's Mail when I apply for work if I tell his daughter she looks daft, now will I?'

'And you think she looks daft?' Olwen asked hopefully.

'Nearly as daft as you when you try to look angry with me,' he said.

But something in his voice told her that he was not being truthful, that Blodwen's appearance with her newfound adulthood had disturbed him. She tried to convince herself that the dishonesty was the greatest hurt.

Emma sat looking out of the window after Blodwen had gone, reading the outside of the letter the girl had brought. It was from Ddole House and for a moment she had savoured the excitement, not opening the seal, just staring at it, trying to imagine what it might contain. An invitation? An opportunity for her daughters to meet marriageable sons of the Ddoles' wealthy friends? Her fingers fiddled with the seal until it finally broke and the letter was unfolded. Then her plump, beringed hands trembled as she read and reread the brief note.

Mr and Mrs William Ddole
request the pleasure of the company of
Mr and Mistress Palmer and
the Misses Pansy, Daisy and Violet Palmer
at a party
given in the garden of
Ddole House
on Tuesday at four o'clock.

It was signed in the large, curlicued hand of Dorothy Ddole. Emma stared at it, tears of joy brimming in her eyes. Then she clutched her heart in an exaggeration of alarm.

'Pitcher?' she called in her loud voice. 'Pitcher, come here at once, there is some urgency.'

Pitcher came running up the stairs, still carrying the pewter mug he had been idly polishing with a duster.

'What's happened, wife?'

'This!' she said dramatically. 'An invitation to Ddole House for our daughters and after you sent that rude note to Mistress Ddole demanding money. Money! Oh, Mr Palmer I'm so shamed.'

'*I* sent it? Mrs Palmer, it was you who insisted!' He went on reminding her of how the firm demand for payment had come about, but Emma was not listening to him.

'Dresses! They will have to have new dresses. And a cloak in case the weather is inclement. New gloves. What they have are quite unsuitable. Oh dear, where do I start!'

Pitcher left her, still clutching the precious invitation and clucking like a broody hen, and went back downstairs. He was pleased. All the expense of the School for Ladies and the never-ending demands for new clothes might after all be worth while if even one of his daughters made a good marriage.

At eighteen the twins were already showing their mother's inclination to plumpness. Violet, the older by four years, was a constant worry to Emma with her lack of interest in the young men her mother introduced.

Emma gathered her daughters around her and produced the long-hoped-for invitation with a flourish. The twins began to discuss with great excitement the new clothes and accessories they would buy. Violet tried to sound enthusiastic, but the thought of an evening feeling like an unwanted piglet on the last day of the fair did not move her to joyous imaginings.

There was very little time for all the arrangements and Emma sent at once for the dressmaker. Mistress Gronow had some difficulty in convincing her that it was impossible to make three new dresses by Tuesday, and Emma, with tears of disappointment, had to agree to having their newest dresses freshened up.

'I'm quite happy with mine,' Violet told her, 'so let Mistress Gronow concentrate on Pansy and Daisy.'

Her mother applauded her generosity, not knowing how the ordeal of the pinching and pulling and standing for an age while pins were poked into the hem irritated her eldest daughter, and how glad she was to avoid it.

Barrass was sent with the acceptance to the party, and was invited into the kitchen to wait for Mistress Ddole's response. It was Dorothy's fifteen-year-old daughter, Penelope, who came back telling him there was no reply but to thank Mistress Palmer for her promptness.

Penelope, who did not remember ever having seen him before, asked him, 'You are new in the village?'

'No, Miss. Born here I was, in the house of Ivor Baker on Village Hill.' He showed no nervousness as he met her gaze steadily, the ale that Bethan had handed him still in his hand.

'I don't remember seeing you before,' Penelope said, as she looked into the deep brown eyes in the tanned and handsome face. 'Do not let me interrupt your refreshment,' she added as he was about to put the pewter mug down on the scrubbed wooden table.

'Pardon me, Miss, but you have seen me before. I had no hair then, and I suppose it makes a difference to how you remember me. Barrass they call me although I doubt it's my real name.'

'Barrass? But – ' She stared at him, trying to see in this curly-haired, personable and confident youth the ill-kempt beggar boy that everyone said bred fleas as if cursed. There was no sign of the sores and spots that had once encrusted his face and neck.

'And what do you do, Barrass?' she asked. 'Work for Palmer as a potman?'

'More as a general handyman.' He leaned casually on the high-backed rocking chair that stood close to the cooking range, wondering why Penelope, who had never given him more than an occasional word, should be staring at him with such intensity. He was relieved when she finally nodded and left the room.

'You've made a triumph there, boy,' Cook chuckled. When Barrass asked what she meant, she went on, 'Miss Penelope sees the man and not the errandboy, you might say. There, what do you think of that, then?'

'I think I could drink another mug of ale,' Barrass replied.

Dorothy Ddole knew she was seriously ill. She also knew that, no matter how encouragingly he spoke, Doctor Percy could do nothing. For the time left to her while she was able, she decided to concentrate on getting a husband for Penelope. Her son, Leon, was a major in the army and could manage well enough with his father's help, but a girl needed a mother to guide her in such an important matter. To this end, she decided to arrange several parties.

It had not been her intention to invite the boring Palmer girls, but having been let down at the last moment by the four daughters of a friend, who had suddenly been afflicted with summer colds, she had thought it the best way out of her difficulty. The woman had hinted often enough after

55

all, and surely wouldn't mind being told so near the date. My desperation helped her in hers, she reasoned.

She took a spoonful of the medicine Doctor Percy had sent over and went on compiling lists of food, guests and seating arrangements for the entertainments. At least she would go out with the house ringing with laughter and music, and perhaps see her much-loved daughter happily betrothed.

Pitcher was pleased with the way Barrass was working. The boy learned fast and was already beginning to form letters and read some of the simpler words sufficiently well to check that the deliveries were correct and there was no shortfall. Gradually, in the few weeks he had been there full time, he had become almost indispensable, especially now when Emma called her husband every other minute with a new problem over this fast-approaching party. So it was with a shock that he was called upstairs to be greeted with the words,

'Barrass must go!'

'Mrs Palmer. What you do up here in your domain is yours to decide upon and rightly so, but down there, where I earn the money that allows you to deal with your domain, that's *my* domain and will continue to be so.'

Immediately, they stood glaring at each other like fighting cocks, walking around each other as if preparing to go for the jugular. With the words 'He's paying attention to your daughters, Mr Palmer!' Emma touched it.

Since the brief encounter with Penelope Ddole, Barrass had gradually become aware of his attraction for women. She had opened his eyes to something that everyone else had seen for some time. His reaction was not the expected one. His own sensuality had not become a strongly felt need so it was with amusement that he reacted to his newfound power.

He watched the unease in the eyes of women he met, and quickly learnt ways of pleasing them – or adding to their discomfort. The first girls on whom he practised, simply because of their propinquity, were Pitcher's daughters.

Violet succumbed first and would wait about in the passages for a word or a glance. The twins were too wrapped up in their party arrangements to notice him for a while, but one day he managed to remind all three of the change in him.

Pitcher was in the malt-house supervising the last stages of the latest brew and Emma was sewing new trim onto the bonnet that Pansy would wear at the garden party. The girls were at their books with the teacher who called to help them with their French lessons, when there was a resounding crash from the part of the house where the rebuilding was under way.

Barrass ran from the cellar with Arthur at his heels to find that a partly demolished wall had sunk into a dusty pile, taking with it the new window frames that Ivor had just finished making. The glass panes standing ready to be installed had all shattered.

While Arthur began to straighten out the mess and the French teacher dealt with Emma by waving smelling salts to and fro under her nose, Barrass found himself comforting the girls after their fright.

In his new role as an acceptable young man, he observed – coolly at first, and with amusement – the way they gently pushed each other out of the way to be nearest to him. Eventually he was hugging the three of them, with the twins wrapping themselves into his body in a way that aroused feelings he had only just begun to recognize. Violet had stood back a little at first, but eventually even she found a way to be within the reach of his powerful arms.

The cameo was still intact when Emma, fully recovered and curious to understand the simpering and crying from her usually sensible daughters, came into the room. To her credit she said nothing to Barrass, who gave the girls a final comforting hug and then departed, or to the girls who stared after him with such a look of longing in their eyes that she wanted to scream. She simply opened her formidable mouth and shouted for Mr Palmer.

When she explained why Barrass should leave, Pitcher looked serious.

'But he's only a boy,' he began, having recovered somewhat from the shock.

'Yesterday he was a boy, today he is not!'

'I'll think about what you say,' Pitcher promised, wondering how he could keep the boy and appease his wife.

'I want him out of the house, Mr Palmer, I wouldn't ever sleep easy in my bed knowing he might be prowling.'

'I need him here if the work you want is ever to be finished,' he warned. 'There's never been a boy who works as well or as fast. The choice is yours, Mrs Palmer.'

They eventually agreed that he would stay, but only until the work on the new drawing room was completed. That couldn't wait, not with the party, where they were sure to meet new and exciting friends, so near. A drawing room was essential if Emma's dream of a social life were to become a reality. But, she warned Pitcher, Barrass must not come further than the bottom of the stairs!

Hearing this, Barrass was more amused than ever. He went about his work pretending not to notice the girls hanging over the banisters and stifling giggles as he plodded to and fro with planks and bricks for the new room. Amusing they might be, but there were other girls to fill his few spare hours, whose mothers were not so anxious.

Olwen sat on the newly turned earth and planted small, straggly cabbage plants in the well-watered holes she had prepared. She worked at a steady pace, unhurried and apparently content in her boring task. She hummed softly as she pressed the plants firmly into the ground.

The smiling young face did not reveal her disappointment, her eyes were as blue as the sheepbit that had until recently peered out from the grasses, and they were wide and sparkling with no sign of a frown. Her mouth, with pink lips parted slightly, was soft and generous and her forehead was fuller than of late, making her face round, open and with an honesty and an offer of friendliness that gained her affection wherever she went. But today the happiness that showed was a half truth.

Not a moment before, she had heard voices, low and confidential, passing close to where she worked. Raising herself to her knees and peering through the grasses, she had seen the tall, broad figure of Barrass pass by, in neat new cream and blue striped shirt and trousers of brown velvet, clasped tight below the knees with knitted socks. The person he was talking to in such a conspiratorial whisper was Blodwen.

She stood up and for a while their voices were brought back to her by the wind – too faint to be understood, but the tone sufficient to explain the meaning.

'Blodwen of all people!' she muttered in disgust, threw the remaining plants into the last hole and kicked the earth impatiently around them. Running at first, softly on bare feet, she followed the strolling, chattering couple, the water-filled leather bucket in her hand. She felt hot, as if her disappointment had fired something inside her, and she pulled apart the braids holding her hair and let it fall. The clean wind from the sea took it and lifted it like a newly opening golden flower.

They were walking with the slow stroll of those with loving on their minds, the slowness a disguise for the impatient intent. Blodwen's feet almost left the ground as Barrass's arm tightened occasionally around her. His hand was under her arm, and Olwen knew just where his fingers were wandering.

The pair slithered down a steep sheep track to the beach, where the rocky coastline gave a hundred small and secret coves. Olwen waited on the cliff top some twenty feet above the place the couple had chosen, and waited as Barrass kissed Blodwen and lowered her onto the hard surface of the sun-warmed plateau.

With infinite care, not wanting to land in their laps, she approached the edge, and slowly tilted the bucket, pouring the muddy contents over them. Before they realized what had happened she had followed the water with a shower of small stones which she kicked over the edge with her tender toes.

She scuttled back along the path and was bending over her plants, humming softly to herself, when the bedraggled pair passed by. She increased the volume of her singing, the words appropriate as she reached the chorus:

> Sing me soft water a lullaby low,
> Sooth me soft water as gently you flow.
> Anger assuage as my body's caressed,
> Cleanse me soft water as by you I'm blessed.

It was a song asking the spirit of the spring to calm them with softly flowing water; a wife before her wedding asking to be a patient and loving wife and mother; or an ill-tempered child to be soothed; or someone grieving and unable to find peace of mind.

'What do you know of water this evening?' an angry voice called, and pushing aside the tall seed-filled grasses, Barrass stood glaring down at her, his eyes flashing with outrage. His clothes showed dark patches where the water had caught him, and mud streaked his shoulder.

Olwen looked up guilelessly and nodded towards her empty bucket. 'Only that I am out of water to start these poor plants growing. You can fill it at the spring if you've a mind to?'

'Don't pretend to have been sitting there in innocence!'

'Sitting here? Sitting here? These plants won't dig themselves into the soil, more's the pity. Working hard I've been and my back's a-w-ful stiff.' She rose to her feet and smiled at Blodwen, who was hanging back, half hidden by the broad shoulders of Barrass.

'Hello, Blodwen, been for a walk, have you? It seems I must walk also, if Barrass is unkind enough to refuse my request.' She pushed past them on the narrow path that led from the cliff edge garden to her cottage, swinging her thin hips and singing softly, but Barrass called to her to stop.

'Here, give it to me, I might as well fill your bucket, little slip of a thing that you are. I doubt if you *could* carry it more than half full.' There was doubt in his eyes though as he looked at her and added, 'But a half-filled bucket might have been enough.'

'Enjoy your walk?' Olwen asked Blodwen as Barrass set off with the empty bucket.

'Someone threw water over us, and what Mam will say I daren't think.'

Olwen was gratified to see that Blodwen's head had taken most of her share of the muddy water and her once neatly tied hair was falling across her face. She was wearing a most unsuitable dress of pale mauve material, with flowers sewn all around the hem. Olwen looked at it with only a brief flash of guilt.

'Serves you right for wearing such a daft dress for walking on the cliffs! And,' she went on, lowering her voice as Barrass returned, 'lucky you were that it wasn't nearer the village or it might not have been just honest muddy water that was thrown!'

William Ddole stood at his study window watching the carts arriving. Seven so far, varying from the simple flat-backed farm carts locally called gambos, which were pulled by small ponies, to the grander, two-horse affairs – velvet lined, beautifully polished and driven by liveried coachmen who unloaded great boxes of clothes and jewellery for the occupants to array themselves with. Most of the conveyances were small multi-purpose waggons which their owners had decorated for the occasion. The cart containing the Palmers with their three daughters was one of the latter.

Emma had bought some curtains discarded from the living room of a wealthy family. These she and Violet had carefully draped around the edges of the cart to give it an air of grandeur and respectability, Emma dreaming of one day owning a proper carriage in which she and Pitcher would ride with their daughters and, she begged of the Lord above, their daughters' husbands.

William smiled as he watched the plump and overdressed Emma being helped down by her husband. She brushed herself down as if emerging from some terrible ordeal, then

61

set about fussing over the three girls, straightening their long, full dresses, adjusting their knitted shawls and touching their hair to make sure they looked their best.

Of the four women, William thought Violet benefited most from her mother's efforts; the young woman had a natural elegance, a way of walking and standing tall, so she gave the impression, even at this distance, of looking the world in the eye and expecting life to treat her as a woman of some importance. He was curious to meet her at this semi-formal occasion.

He waited as other carts, riders and walkers arrived and were bustled inside by the heads of their parties, and saw the efficient way his stable boys dealt with the horses. Then, as the rush of arrivals trickled to a few, he sighed and prepared to meet his guests.

He was not a tall man, and a little overweight, but there was about him a confidence and authority that made him stand out in any company. For the evening party he had not dressed very splendidly, even though his wife had complained that seeing the fine clothes of their host and hostess as well as those of the other guests was an important part of the evening for many. But his apparently casual clothes had been chosen with care. He had intended to be noticeable.

His coat was a dark green cloth with a high, stand-up collar trimmed with green of a lighter shade. He wore breeches which ended in leather riding boots, well polished and very new. His cravat was yellow, the only splash of bright colour on his person apart from the thin band, also yellow, that held his long hair back in a twist. He knew from experience that as darkness fell it would be easily seen.

His face was ruddy, his hands and nails marked with work and he looked what he was, a successful farmer on a small estate, whose wealth was not sufficient to exclude him from an occasional day's work. The house had been built by his grandfather, but having given up the business interests he had inherited to buy an army commission for his son, William no longer had the means to live in the way his grandfather and father had. But he had found a contented balance between the richness of their lives and the poor conditions of his tenants.

He walked through the house which contained some beautiful furniture as well as simple, locally made pieces, touching some and stroking their smooth, polished surfaces, using his admiration of them as an excuse to delay the inevitable boredom of making himself pleasant to people who were too shy of him to be the natural selves they were when he met them on their own home ground. He wondered idly why Dorothy had insisted on the party; it was an ordeal for everyone, this mixing of the moderately rich and the poor.

There was a nervousness about him that suggested more than the prospect of meeting a few local people. He straightened up and prepared himself for the smiles he would show his guests, and stepped out into the slightly overcast afternoon.

The invitation was for four o'clock, when the well-to-do would have finished their main meal and before the working classes were ready for theirs. As he walked across the grass to find his wife, William could hear the anxious scolding of Florrie the cook, making sure all her efforts were presented properly and at the correct time. His smile was a natural one when he went to stand by Dorothy's side.

'Where have you been, William?' she demanded in a disapproving whisper. 'I've been making excuses for you for an hour!'

'Watching them all arrive,' he whispered back. 'A lovely sight, all in their best, all so pleased that you invited them. Tell me, why did you invite so many? Half of these I hardly know.'

'I felt the house needed a cheerful few hours. I needed a few cheerful hours.'

'There is nothing wrong, is there?' he asked and she shook her head and smiled, looking down at him in a fond way before turning to greet a late arrival.

He watched her go – then his heart gave a crazy leap as a shadow passed over and on her face he saw the clear image of a skull. He turned away, reeling in his agony. It had happened again, the thing he dreaded. Twice before he had received that same vision, on his baby daughter who had not survived to her third birthday, which they had at that moment been planning to celebrate, and on his mother, just a month before she died.

He tried to force the fear away from him, turning and hurrying back to the house, afraid that his wife would see his fear and wonder at it. The vicar had told him it was simply a symptom of his own anxiety and not a sign from God that he must prepare to lose a loved one. He sustained himself with a brandy from his cupboard.

It was only his imagining, he *must* believe that. But it was impossible for him to put aside the dread and fear. He had guessed, in spite of her constant denials, that she was ill, but the face of death he had seen on her was something he was not ready to look at. How *could* he? Dorothy had been his love since they were children, his life would have no meaning without her. He took several deep breaths then set his face in a smile before rejoining her.

He and Dorothy spent the next hour trying to persuade everyone to mix with others, to make new acquaintances. But although they managed sometimes to split the closely huddled groups of family or friends long enough for strangers to exchange a few pleasantries, they quickly lost confidence and scuttled back to their own like disturbed field mice at harvest time, pressing together and looking out on the world from the safety and assurance of their own kin.

They talked nervously and stared uncomfortably at others doing the same. William hid his irritation and his desire that they were all gone back to their homes, and chatted with everyone, apparently concerned only with his duties as host. He often stood alongside Dorothy, but he refused to look at her for fear of seeing again the terrible sign of death on her beloved features.

Violet was one they tried to encourage to leave her mother's side and seek fresh conversations. They talked to her briefly, then, having introduced her to Edwin Prince, a local farmer, left her, to walk with their daughter Penelope.

'This, my dear Penelope, is hard work,' William sighed.

'Why won't these people move and make new acquaintances when the opportunity is offered? I can't think what your mother was doing, trying to make a social evening with such people. Kind as they are, they will go from here without having learnt a thing and leave your mother and me exhausted.'

'Wait till the dancing,' Penelope laughed. 'That will break a few inhibitions. I think Mother feels it her duty to make a contribution to the local people, Father, and would like to encourage a greater friendliness. She says they all work so hard and for such long hours, their lives are spent without having done anything but work and worry. She feels it her duty to do something to alleviate their short and difficult lives when she can.'

Her words were ominous. Did Dorothy dwell on death? Was she aware that death walked beside her? He looked around for something to help take his morbid thoughts away.

'There is someone you should meet, my dear,' William said, and Penelope glanced across the crowded garden to see a well-dressed young man just entering through the side gate.

'John,' William called. 'So pleased you could come. May I introduce you. Penelope dear, this is John Maddern, a partner in some new business ventures of mine who is just arrived from London. John, my daughter, Penelope.'

He left the young couple talking to Dorothy and wandered slowly towards the house. It was hardly six o'clock yet the day was darkening. He called to Dorothy,

'My dear, shouldn't we start on the food? If it rains we'd be hard put to find room for all these people inside.'

Trestle tables had already been set up under the trees and spread with white linen cloths. He watched as Florrie and her assistants began scurrying to and fro with dishes and platters of food. Cooked meats and vegetables arrived at the same time that boys were bringing the last of the chairs. As people stood to approach the table, the seats in which they had been sitting were taken by the young boys hired for the evening to help serve, and placed with the rest

65

at the tables. William sat beside his wife and started a conversation with the people around him, but he frequently glanced at his watch, dropping it back into his pocket and hoping that no one, noticing his obsession with time, would interpret it as boredom.

The meal lasted for two hours, then a dozen musicians trooped into the garden and settled themselves to play. Dorothy, having failed to find William, began the dancing with John Maddern, then they separated and John sought Penelope while Dorothy, unable yet again to find William, chose Carter Phillips, one of the local farmers who earned extra money by delivering and carrying for local people.

William slipped into the house and ran up to his room, hoping no one had noticed his disappearance. He pulled off the brightly coloured cravat and braid and changed from his shining new boots into an ancient, well-worn pair which he had hidden at the back of a cupboard. When he left the house, with darkness shadowing the scene, the lanterns in the dancing area emphasized the blackness where the light did not reach. He moved cautiously until he was no more than another shadow.

At the tables where drinks were being offered to the thirsty dancers, John Maddern came to ask for a glass of ale for William on two occasions during the following two hours.

Edwin discussed his enjoyment of the evening and added, 'I was just this minute talking to your husband, Mistress Ddole, see him over there in the far corner, his bright scarf like a beacon? He says he hasn't enjoyed an evening more.' He pointed back into the shadows under the trees. 'Over there he is, talking to young Thomas about his record litter of seventeen pigs.'

A yellow scarf was just visible – too far away for anyone to see that it was not William Ddole who wore it.

'Made us all laugh he did,' added another man, who called himself Oak-tree after a tree that grew beside his house and around which a wall of his stables was built. 'There's a one he is for good stories.'

Although absent for more than three hours, no one at

the party would believe William had not been there all evening. He reappeared when the dancing was still in full swing, with a glass in his hand and a group of friends all sharing with him a joke or two and, draining the glass, he invited his wife into a gavotte.

Many of the young people who had not been invited to join the party had crept through the fields to watch. Along the hedge dividing the garden from the fields they crouched in silent groups and looked through the leaves at the colourful and merry crowd in fascination.

Olwen, who had climbed out of her window to join her brother as he slipped from the house, stood between him and Enyd's brother Tom, who at seventeen was only a few weeks younger than Dan and was on leave from the army.

Tom was not in uniform, having been given instructions not to remind his neighbours that he was a soldier in the hope that he might pick up some information about smuggling. Olwen felt conscious of his eyes on her several times and glanced at him curiously, surprised to realize that instead of the small, rather weedy boy who went away, Tom had grown and filled out.

She caught his eye as she looked at his rather thin face, and was disconcerted slightly when his eyes softened with admiration and interest. She turned away and smiled to herself. It had been a trick of the poor light. No one looked at her like that – the way Barrass had of showing his admiration of a girl with scarcely a movement of his brows or more than a slight relaxing of his face, a softening of his mouth. She changed her position so they were separated by several of the uninvited watchers.

After watching for a while and laughing at some of the more portly women's attempts to trip lightly through the dances, and wonder at the enormous amounts of food still being piled onto the tables, she moved along in search of Barrass. But he was not there.

Barrass had been relieved of his duties that evening, and at four thirty by Pitcher's clock had set off to walk to Swansea. Since Olwen had mentioned the post-boy she'd seen there, he had been considering how he could meet the man and find out if he knew anything that would lead him to his long-lost father.

The tide would be high at around ten o'clock so there was time to walk across the bay. He took off the shoes he wore for work and, barefoot, struck out across the ridges of wet sand.

As usual there was a small crowd waiting for the arrival of the Swanzey Bag. Besides the officials waiting to sort the contents and give the post-boy the letters to take back with him, others hovered in the hope of learning some news.

News-sheets from London were delivered to those wealthy enough to pay for them and even, occasionally, a newspaper abandoned at an inn and brought, tattered with many readings, with the letters. There was usually someone in the crowd able and willing, for a few 'generosities', to read aloud the news-sheets and the letters received by those slow at their reading, and on occasions draft out in neat hand their reply. Barrass waited with the rest for the post-boy's horn announcing his imminent arrival.

Ben Gammon, the post-boy, was as Olwen had described him, grey, straggling hair, long nose and a face barely to be seen under its coating of dust. His leather bag, strapped across his back was also covered in thick deposits, and in the creases of the red waistcoat the colour was lost under layers of it, built up over weeks of dry weather and streaked from the days of rain.

The crowd moved back to allow the horse to reach the doorway of the sorting room and Ben dismounted with a sigh of relief. A boy ran out and took the horse to feed and water him, and the crowd surged forward again. Those expecting a letter went into the sorting room and waited for the bag to be opened.

Inside, Barrass could see a table, and an official sitting there with an opened ledger into which he wrote names as the man with the bag called them out. Beside the man at the table was a box into which he put the monies paid to him for receipt of the letters as they were claimed. A man came out holding a letter and looking anxiously around him.

Guessing the reason, Barrass offered to read it for him, having learnt from Pitcher the rudiments of his letters, but an angry man pushed him out of the way, hissing at him,

'Keep away, you! Trying to steal my generosities'll get you more than you bargained for!' He held out his hand to the holder of the letter, who offered a coin in payment, then the pair went to sit on a convenient wall to read the letter by the light of a hand-held lantern.

Barrass waited for Ben Gammon to re-emerge, and spoke to him.

'Sir, I believe my father was a post-boy like yourself. I have lost touch with him this many a year and wondered if, by looking at me, you can remember seeing my like among those you work with?'

Ben looked at him, curiosity in the dust-fringed eyes. Then he laughed, opening wide a pink mouth almost devoid of teeth apart from a few unsightly stumps.

'Damn me, boy, I bet there are a thousand who beg to know their fathers, and a goodly number of them from those such as I, wandering here and there with no one to keep a suspicious eye on us! Aye and there'll be many a lad wanting to claim *me* as their father!'

'I did not think that you – that I – '

'Handsome enough you are boy, not to say striking, and many might be proud to claim you. But I know of no one you resemble so much as for me to exclaim with amazement and wonderment, "Damn me, boy you must be the son of — " anyone that I've ever seen.'

From the nearby inn a boy came out with a foaming mug of ale, which Ben sank without pausing for breath. Then, following the boy, he went to the inn. Already men were reading aloud from the papers he had brought, and receiving coins to continue, and ale to sustain them when their audience thought them about to falter.

Barrass lingered for a while, watching the old man eat his meal at the inn doorway and the crowds discussing the news, and exclaiming and laughing at the gossip he also brought with him. He saw a fresh horse brought out and the bag handed back and fastened onto another post-boy's shoulders. This one was young and Barrass thought it useless to inquire of him about a father who had disappeared so many years before. He waved and shouted with the rest as the boy set off on his journey to hand the letters to the next relay carrier on the way to Monmouth and London.

The crowds remained for a long time after the departure of the post. Ben was busy with his cronies, exchanging gossip and world news, giving out the latest London opinions confidently, reporting who said what and why with great authority, although he had never travelled further along the route to London than Monmouth.

Ben Gammon would spend the evening at the inn and sleep there, ready to return with a fresh post-bag on his part of the relay the following morning. By the amount of ale that found its way down his throat, Barrass wondered if he would ever be able to wake sufficiently to mount his horse. He remembered how the man boasted of never missing a day in thirty-six years and supposed the ale could not harm him overmuch, and he ordered one for himself.

Although disappointed not to have discovered a hint to his father's whereabouts, Barrass was not unhappy with his visit. There was something exciting about being in a crowd, especially a good-natured one such as this, and he spent an hour talking to strangers and felt thrilled to be among the first in the town to have the latest news of the world beyond the village. He turned for home, more than five miles through lonely paths, excited, and imagining how he would share what he had seen and heard with Arthur when they were in their beds below the alehouse.

When he reached the village, he walked up onto the cliffs intending to sit for a while and think about the evening and about his father. He brought Ben Gammon's face to mind, trying to imagine a man in similar clothes but who had his own face. If he could picture him, even if it were mostly invention, it would bring him closer and restore Barrass's failing belief that one day they would meet.

If he had someone of his own he would not feel so lacking in love. He would have more confidence in himself too. No one, apart from Arthur who seemed not to care, was so completely alone in the world. He longed for a family, even if they were the most unpleasant people on God's earth, to give him roots in the place where he lived. He had always felt tolerated rather than loved. That, more than any of the other deprivations he suffered, hurt him most, not having someone to whom he truly belonged. He smiled then, thinking of Olwen: someone as near to a loving sister as he would ever have.

He walked slowly and with great caution, heading for the edge of the cliffs from where he could look down on the wide bay. It was cold and he covered his head in his coat to keep his ears from stinging in the wind. He went past Olwen's house, all in darkness, and smiled at the thought of the excitable young girl lying peacefully still and silent on her bed. Then without warning, he was seized from behind and a hand covered his mouth before he could cry out.

His mouth was covered with a band of rough cloth and his hands tied behind him. Then he was manhandled across the turf unable to see his attackers, losing all sense of direction and expecting at any moment to be thrown over the cliff to his death. He railed silently against the unfairness of not knowing why.

To his surprise he was forced to bend forward until the top of his head waᶜ stuck fast in a hole. He was to suffer the indignity of having his head pushed into a rabbit hole, and a stake pushed between his legs and into the ground, making it impossible for him to move. He tried to mumble his protests but no one wanted to hear, then he was left alone, uncomfortable and wanting to scream with rage.

It was more than an hour that he stayed there, stiff, uncomfortable, and, now the fear of death had left him, angry at the humiliation. All around him the night's silence was broken by soft footsteps, the creaking of leather and the unmistakable smell of horses passing close by. Then all was silent again apart from the moaning of the wind through the distorted trees nearby.

When he thought his neck must surely break, the stick was withdrawn and the tie around his mouth cut away.

The knife touched his neck, pausing momentarily in silent warning. Then he was alone, picking himself up and easing the painful stiffness from his neck and back. He waited a moment, a defiance making him refrain at first from running like a scared rabbit. Then, moving faster and faster as the darkness pressing on his shoulders seemed to threaten him with unimaginable phantoms, he headed back to the village, not looking up until he reached the open door of the alehouse.

CHAPTER FIVE

Barrass felt the anger of the unfairly treated, the fury of a young man made to feel foolish. The morning following his encounter on the cliffs, he went up to see Spider to talk out his grievances, filling the cottage with his resentment.

He paced to and fro across the small, over-filled room, his long legs stepping over the piled logs near the hearth, the baby's cradle, the low stool on which Olwen sat most evenings, and knocking over the pile of nets and lobster pots which Spider had been sorting for mending.

'I want to go to the Keeper-of-the-Peace,' he said, and as Spider shook his head, added, 'But it was an attack! I did nothing to warrant it! A man pushed me into a rabbit hole and kept me a prisoner for such a time that I thought my back and neck would never be straight again.'

'Calm yourself, boy,' Spider said. 'You're talking like an old woman.'

He knew that Barrass would have more sense than to make a complaint about the men on the cliff once he had talked out his anger, but it was important to stop him raising his voice in accusation within the hearing of anyone but his closest friends. Although there had never been any trouble with those involved in the night activities, Spider knew that, when necessary, those concerned would not hesitate to use force to protect themselves.

There were violent men involved in the local smuggling, however unworldly they might seem if met in their everyday lives. The penalties were severe if they were caught: transportation, flogging, imprisonment and even death if any of the revenue men were harmed. The revenue had too few men and often had to stand and watch as dozens of the locals brought their spoils up from the boats, knowing that with the sentences facing them, they would kill if necessary to evade capture.

'You don't understand,' Barrass went on, refusing the offer of a chair near the fire, which Spider had vacated for him. 'I want to be a part of the King's Mail. I don't want anything to suggest that I am anything less than completely honest.'

'Why should having your head stuck in a hole make anyone thing you're dishonest?' Spider laughed, trying to jolly the boy out of his rage.

'Because if anyone saw me coming down from the hill last night and knew that a transaction had taken place, well they would surely not believe I was staring at the stars! Now would they? I *have* to tell what happened, so I'm clear of suspicion if anyone talks.'

'No one'll talk, boy. Why should they? Everyone in the village save one or two suspect characters has benefited. Including me and Mary. I doubt you'll say no to a cup of fine tea, now would you?' He nodded to Mary, who sat, with baby Dic held 'Welsh Fashion' in a thick blanket which went around a shoulder and under her arm, wrapping the baby firmly against her. 'A small drink of tea for the boy? It'll calm him, my dear.'

'I can't!' Barrass was horrified at the idea and stepped away as Mary pushed the kettle nearer to the heat of the fire.

'Now you're being daft, boy. Many's the saucer of tea you've enjoyed here.'

'I can't risk being accused. I have to keep an honest record. I don't want to lose my chances of working for the Post.'

Spider and Mary shared a glance of wry amusement.

'Honesty isn't the word I'd use for some of the King's Messengers, Barrass,' Mary said softly. 'The news-sheets are always reporting on the dishonesty of the men who collect money for the King's Mail.'

'She's right. There's two in Swansea prison right now.'

'That's why I don't want to take any chances. Lock me up for sure they would if anyone saw me coming down from the hill last night.'

74

'And what would you have been be doing up on the hill last night?' a voice asked.

Barrass turned in alarm to find Olwen, hands on hips, glaring at him from the doorway. From one hand hung a couple of silver fish. Her hair was blown untidily across her face in a cobweb of gold, half hiding eyes that flashed with suspicion. 'Which girl did you take up to cuddle in the darkness last night, Barrass? Getting talked about you are.'

'Talked about? Who has been talking?'

'Blodwen for one. She says you no longer like her. And Enyd has been spreading stories about the girls you take into dark corners for a cuddle. Is that true? And them in the alehouse, the fancy Misses Pansy and Daisy. They talk about you all the time and drive their poor mother to distraction. That's right, isn't it, Mam?'

He smiled at her, relieved that the talk was only about girls.

'Truth is, Olwen,' he teased, 'you're the only girl for me. Waiting until you're twenty I am, then I'll give up all the rest.'

His words were so near her dream that she gave a scolding growl and threw the fish at him. They caught him across the shoulder and, being far from fresh, spread a slimy wetness on one side of his face. Shrieking with laughter, she ran from the house followed by Barrass.

'He'll soon forget his anger,' Mary laughed. 'So young he is, that he can be filled with a man's anger one moment and be a silly young boy the next.'

'I'll have another word with him though,' Spider said thoughtfully. 'We don't want him complaining loud enough for the night-owls to get alarmed, do we? Best he keeps his mouth well closed.'

Later that day, when Spider's warnings had made Barrass's complaints subside, Barrass was asked by Pitcher to deliver a package to Ddole House. The alehouse keeper explained that there being no post on that day, the delivery was a favour for William and Dorothy Ddole. It was not until he was at the kitchen door of Ddole House that a shower of sweat burst out on his skin, giving him the sensation of being drenched in hot water.

Florrie the cook opened the door and smiled at him. 'Ah, at last! We were down to the last makings and the mistress *do* like her – ' She did not finish the sentence, but Barrass could have finished it for her. The package, he knew with certainty, was illegally imported tea, presumably part of William Ddole's reward for his assistance on the previous night. Barrass had always lived apart from the village, but he knew its ways. He thought again of being forced to stay in that ignominious position on the cliffs while the smugglers walked past him with their illegal goods – he remembered every moment with clarity.

The touch of the jacket worn by his assailant came back to him, and the smell of a certain fine tobacco rising from it on the clean night air. It had been William Ddole who had imprisoned him in that humiliating manner! He thrust the package at Florrie, muttering,

'Thieves involving the innocent is a crime worse than the theft from the king's purse! They should be punished and stopped! Making the innocent take their risks for them is wicked!' and ran back to the alehouse.

Daniels, Keeper-of-the-Peace, was in his thirties, a widower with five children whose ages ranged between six and fifteen, and a serious-faced man who rarely smiled. He was smartly dressed – over-fussy, many thought, about his appearance – and never stepped out of his door without first making sure there was not a speck of dust on his shoulders or a touch of mud on his boots. It seemed to those who knew him that he led a comfortable life, with the older children caring for the youngest and all of them finding work either in the fields or doing chores in some of the richer houses. Yet the expression on his countenance showed nothing but gloom.

He had accepted the post some eight years before, with a sanguine attitude, knowing that if he were to live long enough to enjoy the standing in the community it gave him, he had to suffer both periodical deafness and occasional poor sight. Over the years he had frequently been called to deal with evidence of smuggling, and each time he found, after apparently diligent effort, that there was nothing to lead him to those responsible.

On the occasion when Barrass had inadvertently become involved, Daniels was pushed to greater effort. He had been warned by his superiors yet again that the night activities must cease. In trepidation, he set off to start questioning people about where they had been during the Tuesday night. He began with Betson-the-Flowers, knowing what she would say and knowing it would not be the truth.

Betson lived in what remained of a house, far above the steep cliffs and beyond the barn which Barrass had tried to make into a home. Her room was always filled with flowers, gathered from the fields and hedges, and brought back to be lovingly arranged in whatever pots and bowls she could find. It being autumn, she obviously found it difficult to fill her room with flowers but, not to be outdone, she had gathered branches of leaves tinted by the coming of winter into a thousand beautiful colours. The displays included huge clouds of traveller's joy and sprays of late blackberries, the fruit adding a texture and a brightness which reflected in the polished surface of the tables she had acquired and patiently cared for, and the shining windows. People soon forgot to notice the cracked walls and the almost non-existent ceiling in the glory of the magnificent exhibition.

She had a regular stream of visitors, all men and all willing to pay her with a variety of goods for a few moments or several hours of her company. Many came just to talk, to be fussed over and made to feel wanted and important for an hour or two, but others needed more. There was only one room, so when she did not want to be disturbed, she draped a piece of frilly curtain over the window and no one called until it was removed.

Daniels made his way along the rutted path to her door and glanced at the window to make sure it was clear. Betson had seen him coming and opened the door wide in welcome, her long red hair hanging down over the black dress she habitually wore.

77

'He was here with me. No names, mind, but *here* he was.'

'Betson, I haven't even asked a question yet!' Daniels said with a groan.

'No matter. If he says he was here, then it's *here* he was!' Betson insisted.

'Only one?' He quirked an eyebrow quizzically.

'Course not only one! Whoever you wants, if they say they was here – '

' – then it's *here* they were,' Daniels finished. 'Thank you, Betson, I don't know what I'd do without your cooperation!'

Daniels rode around the village, a notebook in his hand, making what he could of the vague and apparently helpful information he was given. His questions were answered with great enthusiasm, men and women wearing an innocent expression, with eyes popping in their willingness to help, but no one saw or heard a thing.

Only when he questioned Barrass did he have a suspicion that the boy had seen something that troubled him, but try as he might, he could not get more than 'I do not agree with the boats,' from that young man.

From his wearisome questioning throughout several days, all he had learnt was that apart from Barrass, who had been in the town, everyone had been either with Betson-the-Flowers or at the Ddole House party. He braced himself for an interview with Dorothy Amelia Ddole.

Leaving his pony with a stable boy, he knocked on the kitchen door and waited, notebook in hand, while Florrie brushed the flour from her hands and the kitchen maid took off her sacking apron and cleared away the bucket and brush with which she had been scrubbing the floor.

'Mind you don't slip, and please to stand on the dry bits,' Cook demanded as the tall imposing officer of the law finally entered.

He sometimes thought that Florrie was more terrifying than Mistress Ddole. Yet he had begun to discover a softer side to the woman, a hint that perhaps she looked kindly on him. He smiled at her, the unusual expression lighting up his hazel eyes and surprising Florrie with the interest they showed. Somewhat flustered, she pushed Dozy Bethan

78

aside, led him into the house herself and knocked on the door of the drawing room to tell her mistress he was arrived.

He found Dorothy Ddole lying on a couch in front of a blazing fire. Beside her was a basket of sheep wool, gathered from the hedges where the sheep had dragged past, and washed until it was soft and clean and free from dead leaves and other debris. She was carefully sewing a layer of it between pieces of cloth to make a quilt, patterning the stitches into scrolls and flowers. She looked unwell and he paused, wondering whether to make his excuses and leave the questions for another day. Her answers, like those of Bethan-the-Flowers, were a foregone conclusion anyway – she had seen nothing and heard even less! But when she looked up, she smiled and the tenseness he had seen left her.

'Daniels. *Do* come in. How can we help you?' Before he could answer, she called, 'Bethan! An ale and a bite for Mr Daniels if you please.'

'Cook says *she's* bringing it, Mistress,' Bethan replied with a bobbing curtsey as she entered the room.

Daniels knew that the bonhomie was a farce and this would be as hopeless as all his other attempts to discover what had happened on Tuesday, but at least the ale was good – freshly brewed and in a glass as delicate as any he had seen. He carefully straightened his trousers, adjusted his coat to prevent creasing and settled down to enjoy it.

'I am told that you want to question everyone about where they were on Tuesday evening, Daniels?' Dorothy eased herself to a more comfortable position and smiled at him. 'You could have saved yourself a lot of riding if you'd come here first. Everyone who is anyone was here.'

'A party I understand, Mistress Ddole.'

'Well, it seemed to me that so many of the villagers have nothing but drudgery in their lives. I thought to give a little excitement. It's so little to do, a bit of extra food, some ale, a few bottles of spirits – ' she stared boldly at him, her deep-set eyes brightening with humour ' – bought from Pitcher as I'm sure you will have checked.'

'Of course, Mistress Ddole.'

'Apart from those things – which we can easily afford – then all it took was a few hours of our time, mine and my husband's.'

'And he was here all evening.'

'As host, where else could he be?'

'Were there any who refused your kind invitation, Mistress Ddole? Any who made an excuse that they could not attend?'

'Really! Who would dare?' She laughed again and this time, the sparkle in her eyes faded as she held her stomach and swallowed painfully.

'Is anything wrong? Is there anything I can do?'

'Ring for Bethan if you please. I need some more of Doctor Percy's medicine for this indigestion. She will have to go and fetch it.'

'They say brandy is soothing for upsets of the digestive system, Mistress Ddole,' he said dryly.

'Yes, so I have heard. Perhaps I will instruct Pitcher to send some for me,' she replied with equal drollery.

Emma's excitement showed no sign of decreasing. Since the Ddole party, when Edwin Prince a local farmer and a friend of the Ddoles, had shown such an interest in Violet, Emma had been in a state of euphoria. It seemed far more exciting to the mother than the daughter, although, as Emma assured Pitcher,

'Our eldest daughter *is* looking different since that night, Pitcher, sort of woken up, and brighter than a new taper.'

Emma was sitting in the parlour fixing some fresh braid on a winter dress belonging to Violet, and Pitcher had come for a brief rest. The men sitting at the tables outside the alehouse in a benign, watery sun were settled into a game of draughts with a full quart mug at each elbow. They wouldn't be needing him for a while.

'Our Violet is walking about in a state near to dreaming – surely you have noticed, Pitcher?'

'Well, now you mention it, I did have to call her three times to warn her that the flooring was up in the back room, and at the time I felt certain that she was about to step out into nothing and disappear down the hole. Yes, Violet has something on her mind now you mention it. I suppose he's all right, this Edwin? Seems a mite strange for him to be thirty and never married. Not nothing unpleasant about him, is there, doesn't beat his servants or anything I suppose?'

'Of course not, Mr Palmer! Give me credit for having some sense! I have made diligent inquiries of a confidential nature and there's nothing to fear.'

'Where is she now?'

'She said she wanted to walk by the water and think about things. I do think I'll go and find her, perhaps it will help her to have her mother to talk to. At such times, a young lady needs the ear of someone who understands.'

'You understand, do you?' Pitcher grinned, leaning closer to his plump wife. 'You being experienced in love and all that yourself?'

Emma laughed coquettishly and gave him a gentle slap. 'Now, husband, don't start making me blush.'

A few minutes later she stepped out of the front door, nodding politely but with the right amount of coolness to the men sitting at their game, and walked along the road to find her daughter. She was in a pleasant mood, but the smile that moulded her small features into a smudge of wrinkles rapidly faded when she found her eldest daughter. Violet was not dreaming about Edwin Prince, she was almost arm in arm with Barrass.

Violet moved away from Barrass as she saw her mother bearing down and hurried to greet her, patting her brown hair nervously.

'Mother, I'm so pleased to see you, now we can walk together.'

Emma glared at Barrass, who stood hesitantly, wondering whether to stay or leave. Wordlessly, she caught hold of Violet's arm and led her away, tripping over the uneven ground in her haste.

An hour later, Barrass was again homeless and without work.

Violet's room was at the back of the house, overlooking the

81

confusion of the building work. She sat at her window that evening, listening to the gentle breathing of her sisters, unable to sleep. Her thoughts were not about Edwin, on whom her mother had built such hopes, but about Barrass.

The yard lay in darkness, the archway leading to the malt-house an empty black tunnel. She was tempted to give up all attempts to sleep and light a candle; perhaps she would go downstairs for a drink of water, that sometimes calmed her into sleep. She sat perfectly still for a while longer, too awake to sleep yet too lethargic to move. Then she became aware of a movement in the tunnel of blackness near the malt-house.

She instinctively moved back from the window, as if even at this range needing to seek the safety of further distance. Then curiosity overcame the temporary fright and she peered carefully out again. It was Barrass. Without even seeing him she knew suddenly and clearly that it was Barrass. Picking up a candle and flint, she glided softly down the stairs, through the dangers of the half-built room and out into the yard.

She paused for a moment waiting until her eyes had readjusted to the different light of the open air and then a movement caught her eye and a voice whispered,

'Miss Violet! What are you doing out here at such a time?'

'Barrass, I knew it would be you. I've come to say I'm very sorry to have been responsible for you losing your home and your work.'

'It wasn't your fault, you didn't do anything wrong. It was me. I had no right to talk you so boldly. Don't you worry, Miss Violet, I got what I deserved. And,' he added slowly, 'it was worth it.'

'I'll try to talk to my father tomorrow,' Violet whispered back, then she shivered and drew her thin shawl closer around her shoulders.

'Look, you're getting cold. Go in now before I have your illness to bear as well as the scolding I caused you.'

His voice was soft, caressing as a warm breeze, and

instead of moving towards the door and safety, Violet stepped closer to the shadowy figure near the archway.

'I don't want you harmed, Miss Violet.'

'I know,' she whispered, her voice uneven, tormented by a constriction in her throat.

'Can't bear the thought of you being cold.'

'The night is kindly. I don't feel cold.' How could she tell him that just knowing he was near was warming her blood in a magical way?

'Would you like to put my coat over your shoulders, Miss Violet?'

Even the way he spoke her name was different from how it had sounded before. She stepped nearer to the archway and felt his arms touch her as he placed his jacket around her, sparking off a desire that made her gasp. Then they were pressed against each other, his strong body moulding hers against him, a perfect completeness. His lips soft and welcoming, his male smell, the roughness of his clothes all added to the flawless moment.

He released her gently, and pushed her towards the doorway. 'You must go, we shouldn't meet again. I – can't trust myself,' he muttered, stumbling away from her into the darkness of the archway.

She followed him, then handing back his jacket, returned to the house. Not see him again? Compared with the dull, over-polite young men her mother had insisted she meet, how could she ignore Barrass, who had woken her up to womanhood?

She was still awake, sitting at her window, watching the dawn rise over the sea, when the servant girl came in with water for her to wash. She soaped her body slowly, aware of its promise of new delights, dressing with greater care than usual, in a brown taffeta dress with a flowing wide skirt that she knew showed her figure well, and a bonnet of darker brown to match the chiffon sash.

The twins watched her go downstairs then giggled.

'This Edwin must be something quite out of the ordinary to make our dear sister so much changed!' Pansy whispered.

'Yet he seemed a dullard, and with such an ungentlemanly way of dressing! A farmer whose hands are marked by the soil. Oh, the thought of being touched by such hands!' Daisy replied. Both girls shuddered delicately at the thought.

'But it must be nice to meet someone who makes every moment a dream. Our dear sister can perhaps see something in Edwin that we cannot,' Pansy said. The more kindly of the twins, she was less happy than Daisy to criticize others, less inclined to remind those she met of the differences in their education and style.

Daisy lowered her voice even more and said, 'But Pansy, my dear, what can Edwin see to admire in our dear sister Violet? Dull brown hair, mud-coloured eyes, never a smile to lighten anyone's day. A brown streak of solemn indifference!'

Both girls continued giggling as they completed their preparations for the day, then, calling for the servant to carry down their shawls in case they needed them, they tripped happily down the stairs to greet their parents at breakfast.

Barrass did not go to see Spider and Mary to tell them of his loss of a home. People were showing him an increasing lack of friendship and although he had no idea of the reason, he was so used to being an outsider that he accepted it stoically, and waited for things to change. Because of several rebuffs, he didn't want to talk to anyone, even the kindly fisher family to whom he always looked for comfort and friendship. Besides, what was on his mind was not his homelessness – after all, that was hardly something new.

Since those few moments in the archway with Violet, his mind was filled only with her, memories of her slim and sensuous body causing an agony of desire. Even when the night approached and he had made no effort to find himself a new home he did not concern himself with the practicalities of shelter and sleep. He would wait behind Pitcher's alehouse and perhaps be rewarded with a glimpse of Violet. That would be comfort enough.

The night was cold but the wind was almost nonexistent,

the sea a low murmur with the regular sound of clinking, clattering pebbles as they were dropped by the slow out-going waves. He had brought two sacks he had begged from Ivor Baker and filled with dried seaweed for a pillow of sorts to protect his back from the worst of the night chills. He settled himself as comfortably as he could, leaning up on one elbow, watching the doorway for the appearance of Violet.

She came when all the lights in the house had been snuffed out, wearing a billowing nightgown of embroidered cotton, a nightcap which matched it, soft slippers and, shrouding it all, a thick blanket worn as a shawl. She made no pretence at being surprised to find him there, but walked towards him and tilted her face for his kisses.

His hands were warm as they moved slowly over her skin, touching her slender neck and moving down to the ribbons that held the top of her gown laced in a frill of crocheted flowers. He pulled them and the restraining material fell away from her breasts, which swelled under his touch.

They both groaned softly under the spell of discovery, their movements soon as rhythmical as the waves touching the shore, with the falling of the pebbles a hypnotic accompaniment. Then they lay still, clinging to each other as if afraid to admit that, for a time, the magic was past. They risked staying together, hardly speaking, relishing the closeness, the sense of belonging, until a cockerel crowed from a nearby fence and warned them it was time for people to start their day. Reluctantly, Violet left the archway and went across the littered yard and back to her lonely bed.

It was the twins who woke first that morning and they had to shake Violet out of her dreams. If they were curious about the look of wonderment on their sister's face, neither mentioned it.

Emma saw that her daughter was different. But as she became aware of it only after Kenneth had brought them a letter containing an invitation to visit Edwin for afternoon tea, she presumed the farmer was the cause. She re-read the short note aloud and smiled at her daughter, whose bright eyes smiled back at her across the table.

'Thank goodness you had the good sense to send that Barrass packing, Pitcher,' Emma sighed later as she sat looking again at the invitation. 'Once Edwin proposes to Violet, there might be a chance of his friends meeting Pansy and Daisy. Just think of what you risked by having such a one as Barrass on the premises near your beautiful daughters.'

'Aye, but I miss the boy, there's none so willing and so skilled who will take so little money, Emma my dear. Your drawing room will cost me more than I'd had a mind to pay.'

'Mr Palmer!' Emma exploded. 'Surely you can't put money above the welfare of your daughters?'

'No, my dear, but if you'll come-along-a-me and look at my accounting, you'll agree I'm sure that things is less than fine with us. And,' he added in a low voice, 'with the Keeper-of-the-Peace wandering around asking questions and poking his nose where it shouldn't be poked, it doesn't do for us to be seen to spend money we can't explain the earning of. Daniels is being more persistent of late and we don't want no trouble, not if we wants to impress people like Edwin. Best if we let him come back, wife, or the work'll never be done before Pansy and Daisy are well and truly settled in the chimney corner.'

'Don't even think such a thing!' Emma waved her fat little hands at him, the rings catching light from the fire. 'Perhaps if he worked in the yard but found somewhere a long way off for to sleep – '

News that Barrass no longer had anywhere to sleep reached Olwen via Arthur. He had arrived at her door with his dog as she returned with her father and brother, having helped them gut their catch. In the distance the gulls could be heard screaming and clacking as they argued over the offal she had discarded.

'If you've finished for the day, shall we walk on the cliffs?' Arthur suggested and, as she began to refuse, he went on, 'No use looking for Barrass. He set off before dawn to go into Swansea.'

'What for?' Olwen asked, at once wondering about a pretty young woman. 'Who does he know in Swansea, then?'

'He's borrowed a horse from the stables and hopes to ride with the post-boy. He wants to talk to others on the route and show himself and ask, "Have you seen my dad?" Daft if you asks me.'

'But how will he get back in time to help Pitcher? He won't allow him a day off for sure, until that drawing room is finished.'

'He isn't working for Pitcher any more.' Arthur's face closed up, warning Olwen that he would not tell her the reason. He knew only too well Olwen's reaction to the thought of Barrass with a girl.

She pestered and pestered, until he admitted, 'It's something to do with Violet, and that's all you're getting from me. Right?'

'But surely Barrass isn't fancying that Violet now? She's a-w-ful old and has long straight hair and a long straight body and is as pretty as a yard of mucky pump water!'

'I'm not saying he has a liking for her, but that's the reason he's been booted out into the cold.'

'Out of his mind he is for sure. Is there a full moon? Granny Hughes would say he was afflicted by moon madness.'

'Full moon or not, he's without a home again. And him with not a flea on him. Pity for him,' Arthur piped, as shrill as the seabirds wheeling above them.

'I'll ask Mam again, she always says there's room for another, but perhaps that means when she is going to bring me another brother,' she frowned.

'We could go and have a look at the old barn, see if we can make it weatherproof again?'

They walked across the fields and were surprised to see a small group of soldiers half hidden in the trees. One of them was Enyd's brother Tom, called in for some exercise or other about which the youngsters did not bother their heads. Olwen carefully avoided him as they passed the bushes in which the small groups were quietly waiting. They also saw Enyd and Dan, who were too busy arguing to heed them. The couple parted then, Enyd walking back to the village and Dan striding off along the cliffs at speed, anger apparent in their attitude and haste.

'They must love quarrelling, them two,' Arthur said with a shake of his head, 'it's all they ever seem to do.' They discussed the stupidity of adults as they walked towards the scorched barn.

The day grew warmer, autumn's last fling before retreating, the air was moist and sweet after an earlier refreshing shower and as the temperature soared, late insects swarmed and birds sang.

While Olwen and Arthur, accompanied by his dog, searched amid the blackened walls of the barn in a hopeless attempt at planning repairs, Barrass was talking to Ben Gammon. He noticed, as he rode beside the post-boy along the tracks, that the man's hair gave a hint of former redness. Could this elderly man be the father he had dreamed about? He forced his memory to give a picture of his own face and compared that image with the man riding beside him. There was nothing to hint at a relationship. Everything about the man was wrong, and, he decided finally, Ben Gammon was far too old.

The thought of his young mother with a man who must have been approaching fifty made his lip curl in disapproval. Then his thoughts flitted back to Violet, who was hardly out of his mind for more than a moment. She was older than him, and that was not always a good thing. Childbearing became more difficult as a woman grew older, and while a man could always give a child to a woman, at least according to what he had learnt in conversations with Spider and Pitcher, a woman's body grew too old to receive it.

It was something to be considered when a man chose a wife, he understood that, but Violet had chosen him and he wasn't planning to tell her she was wrong. His knees trembled as he thought about the previous night and imagined how it would be on all the nights to come. Four years wasn't an impossible difference, was it? He wondered who he could ask. Somehow it didn't seem right to question Pitcher!

They reached the point at which Ben Gammon handed over his bag to the next man on the route and Barrass went forward with interest to meet him. The sorting office was at an inn, and the horse stood ready to depart, the rider leaning against the horse's flank puffing on a clay pipe.

Barrass could see at a glance that the man was not a candidate for the role of his father. He was tall and broad, but barely twenty-five years old. Barrass asked the usual questions and the young man smiled and repeated much of what Ben had said: a request to find a father among the travelling post-boys was not an unusual occurrence.

'I'll bear your likeness in mind, boy,' he promised. 'And should I ever come across a man who looks so like you I'll say, "Well I'm damned if that isn't like young Barrass", and I'll send a message to you as fast as this here horse can gallop.'

'He even talks like you,' Barrass said with a smile.

'So he should, my boy, for he *is* my son and proud of him I am, so much I wished I'd married his mother!' With a laugh, Ben trotted off to where his wife and family waited for him.

Barrass rode back to the village, allowing the horse to set its own pace, his disappointment overriding his haste to be back where he might catch a glimpse of Violet Palmer.

When he reached the village, the road took him along the edge of the tide and before he came in sight of the alehouse, he heard voices raised in anger. He touched the flanks of his mount and hurried to see what was the cause of the riot and rumpus.

On the beach a fire had been built and around it, crowds of people had gathered. Driftwood had been brought and in unusual extravagance, was being thrown into the blaze. Olwen and Arthur were two of the first people he recognized and he demanded to know what was happening.

'My dadda has been arrested,' Olwen sobbed. 'Along with Dan and Pitcher and a dozen others.'

Before he could hear more, stones began to be lobbed

in their direction and Barrass quickly shielded the girl from the danger.

'What has happened to them?' he demanded angrily. 'Why are they throwing stones at you?'

'It's you they're meant for, flea breeder!' a young boy shouted, and Barrass asked again what was the reason for their anger against him. No one spoke; they just muttered among themselves.

It was Olwen who told him that they were blaming him for giving information to the customs men. Arthur reluctantly admitted that it was so, and they had been warned not to talk to him. They walked with him, moving fast to escape another volley of stones, as he took the weary horse back to the stables. Then they sat to tell him the full story.

'Somebody said too much and there were raids on three houses in the village and two beyond,' Arthur said in his squeaky voice. 'That Daniels must have tricked them into giving the names of others and a group of revenue men were sent over from ports as far away as Cardiff and Fish-guard. They all swarmed in and took prisoners. Treated them rough too, so they say, pushed the women out of the way with the butts of their firearms.' Outrage made his voice so high-pitched, it seemed he was about to burst into song.

'What will you do, Barrass?' Olwen looked at him with such trust, so confident that he would be able to free her father and the others that he felt a stab of sickness.

'What *can* I do? If no one trusts me, there is nothing I can suggest that will even be be considered!' His dark eyes showed dismay and hurt, and Olwen hugged him, reassuring him that as always he could rely on her support when other faces turned away.

He looked at the sky, it must be after eight o'clock and he knew that in a few hours Violet would be waiting for him. What did it matter that everyone else accused him of disloyalty?

'There's nothing we can do tonight. Go to bed, both of you, and I'll think of something tomorrow. I promise.' He crossed his fingers as he said the words, having not a single thought that would lead him to an idea. All he could think of was Violet, offering her long slim body to him in the darkness of the archway behind the alehouse.

'Will you walk home with me, Barrass? I'm a bit frightened now that Dadda and Dan aren't there.'

He nodded. 'Come on, Arthur, we'll walk Olwen safe home then go and see if Mrs Palmer will have me back, for a while at least. She'll need someone to help with the casks with Pitcher away, won't she? I needn't sleep in the house, the archway at the back will do,' he added, half to himself.

Emma reluctantly agreed that Barrass should help out during the day, but insisted he found somewhere else to sleep.

'Although I don't know whether I should have you on the premises,' Emma sobbed, her face a red, shiny mask of distress. 'Seen talking to Daniels you were, and not a day later, the men were taken from their homes.'

'Mistress Palmer,' Barrass sighed in exasperation, 'Daniels was talking to *me*. The same as he talked to everyone else in the village. He was talking to Mistress Ddole. Do you suspect her of talking of things best not mentioned?'

'Stay until Pitcher comes back, then he can decide on the rights and wrongs of it all,' Emma said, knowing that she needed him if the alehouse was not to close.

Violet joined him an hour after the house had fallen into silent darkness and Barrass thought he had never been so happy in all his life. The misunderstanding about the men would soon be cleared up, once they were out of prison, and surely that was simply a matter of time? There would be no evidence of their guilt and of a certainty, no one to speak against them. He put it all out of his mind and luxuriated in the pleasures of exploring Violet's willing body.

The next morning, while he was cleaning barrels and bringing fresh supplies from the brewery beyond the archway, Olwen arrived breathless and smelling of fish.

'Mam and I took baby Dic out in the boat and we caught enough fish to sell from the cart,' she explained hurriedly.

'I can't help you,' Barrass began, 'I've got too much – '

'Oh yes you can! I've had an idea!' Her young face was lit up with excitement as she absentmindedly wiped her hands down her dress to clean off the fish scales that lingered.

'To sell the fish?'

'To help my father!' she announced, pulling him to leave his work and listen. 'I know where the boats have left a crop of barrels which they intended to gather later. Out in the bay, not far, and I can row there easily if you won't come with me. I thought if they were gathered while Dadda and Pitcher are in prison, and the revenue found out, they'll have to let them all go. They can't be guilty if the crop is harvested while they're in prison, now can they, Barrass? You will help, won't you? Yes, I knew you would!'

Olwen was referring to the method of weighting a barrel down out at sea, and tying others to it so they floated. Touched with white paint to be invisible in the foam-tipped waves, the floating crop could remain there until the revenue had given up their searches, then harvested at leisure.

'Olwen, I think you should leave alone things that don't concern you. You might end up in prison yourself. How will that help? And those men don't play children's games, as you well know. If they thought you were taking what's theirs, you might not live to tell the tale.'

'But you will help us, won't you Barrass? If we leave evidence of our activities, and a trail leading the customs to the place where we hide the barrels, they'll believe it was men from another village using our beach and not Dadda and the others, and they'll have to let them go.'

'Olwen, we can't! The risks are too great, both from the revenue men and the others. If they get wind that you're stealing those tubs, it will mean death. Young as you are you know what that means!'

'Stop going on as if I'm a child! Young as I am I know a lot of things, Barrass!' She placed her hands on her hips and glared at him. 'More than you think. And if you don't help us, I'll tell on you.'

'Tell what? I haven't been involved with smuggling,' he whispered.

'I saw you making cow-eyes with that Penelope Ddole. I'll tell her father and he'll have you whipped.'

Relief made him smile. 'I'll think about what you suggest and, if I do agree to help, it's without you being there. You must stay close to your mother and baby Dic, and invite others to stay with you for evidence so no one can say you're involved. Right?'

Olwen did not agree, she lowered her head as if in submission but her mouth was tight and her forehead wore a stubborn frown. Barrass went about his work content that he had discouraged her, and sure that, eventually, Spider, Pitcher Palmer, Ivor Baker and the rest would be freed for lack of evidence. His confidence was unfounded.

A week passed and there was news of a trial. Olwen came to him again and this time he could not refuse. Although he had been treated with ridicule and indifference, and now distrust by the villagers, these were his friends, and what Olwen suggested did have a faint chance of success. And surely the revenue men would not be on the cliffs looking for suspects if they believed they had them all in prison?

He felt momentary guilt at the thought that in helping Olwen with her plan he might miss Violet's nightly visit. He would have to explain to her that it was to help free her father, although the actual facts of what he was going to do would be held back from her as from everyone else.

To free the men of the village would surely improve his standing in the community, help people to forget his past and treat him as he deserved? Pitcher and Emma would perhaps be grateful enough to consider him as a son-in-law when the time came for him to take a wife. Violet was too old for there to be other suitors. She would surely wait until he was ready.

The other aspect of his decision-making was the look on Olwen's face. Silent for once, pleading with her lovely blue eyes, knowing he *could not* let her down. It was more than he could resist. Olwen, who had been his friend even when no one else would have him near. He nodded.

'All right, on the understanding that you stay clear away and make sure that you and Mary have visitors to vouch for your being indoors all evening. Arthur and I will do what you suggest. You can go to the Keeper-of-the-Peace at a signal from us, and tell them there's sounds of activity on the beach and remind them that it must be men from other villages.'

He studied the tides and the state of the moon, made his plans with Arthur, sitting on the planks which lay ready to be made into flooring for the new room, then sent Arthur off for a few hours' sleep and waited for Violet. He had been excited to see that the tide made it possible to see her and share an hour of her loving before he need wake Arthur and set off on their adventure.

CHAPTER SIX

There was no moon and the night was dark and still as Barrass and Arthur made their way down to the water. It had an oily blackness, with only the thinnest of white lines showing at the edge of the tide. If he could find his way, following Olwen's directions, to the place where the smugglers had hidden their cache, the task would be easy. He found Spider's boat without any trouble – Olwen had hung a piece of white cloth on the beam end to help them – and they began to push it off the gravelly shore into the water. Arthur jumped in and, after a few more steps, with the water rising up his legs, Barrass joined him.

They took an oar each and gently touched the water, trying not to make a sound. To Barrass, who was not used to boats, the tide running so gently was surprisingly strong, and soon the boat was once again touching the pebbled beach, the grating deceptively loud in their anxiety to be unheard.

They pulled on the oars, but the water was too shallow for them to make any headway and the only result was the slap of water against the boat's side ending in the warning sound of the pebbles under it.

'I'll have to push it further out,' Barrass whispered. 'Fine start this is.'

'It looks so easy,' Arthur said. 'If that skinny little Olwen can manage this boat, we ought to be able to make it fly.'

A second attempt brought them no nearer to floating the heavy craft and it was not until Olwen appeared out of the darkness, stiffling giggles, that they eventually made away from the shore.

'I thought I told you to stay in the house!' Barrass whispered, his voice hissing like the sea in his anger. He was more upset at her seeing him failing to move the boat, than for disobeying him.

'Mam will be believed when she says I was home and in bed,' Olwen said, 'and if I don't help you shift this boat you'll be sitting here for everyone to see when dawn breaks!'

This time, with Barrass giving a push, Olwen managed to float the boat and get her under way. She refrained from teasing Barrass, guessing that with his nerves taut with the prospect of the night's work, he would be in no mood for raillery. Instead, she worked the rudder and with confident ease, directed the boat towards the place where she had seen the captive tubs floating amid the foam further along the coast.

They put up the smallest sail and tacked across the curving sweep of the bay and out, past the headland where the gibbet stood – a frightening sentinel and a warning to those intent on breaking the law. They had to go out some distance from the shore to avoid the Mixen sandbanks and the hidden arms of rocks which were known to Olwen from her regular, lifelong trips with her father and Dan.

They rarely spoke, only when Olwen pointed out some landmark, like the large white cross that was visible even in the blackest night, which fishermen had painted on the cliffs as a guide to navigation. Or the odd shapes of some of the the rocks and her private names for them, which, as a child, had helped her to remember their sequence and know where she was.

No lights showed. If there was anyone else abroad they gave no sign. Olwen shivered slightly, realizing as if for the first time just what risks she had persuaded Barrass and Arthur to take.

She knew that Barrass was still angry, both at being persuaded into undertaking this adventure and for being unable to launch the boat. He had been made to feel humiliation, and in front of a girl who could do better. Although his face was hidden by the darkness, she guessed that it would show foolish resentment. There seemed nothing she could say to ease his embarrassment. Best she forgot it for the moment, once they were busy with the tubs he would likely forget it too.

As they drew near to the place she had memorized she

glanced up at the rocks surrounding the small bay, trying to find the shapes she needed to enable her to find the exact spot. She screwed up her eyes, searching for the formations she called rabbit's ears, two narrow peaks close together. Then a sloping series of folds like the feathers on a duck's back. Lining them up as she had done before, with a projection at the western end which showed between the 'ears' and a small rock jutting out of the sea towards the east, she found the tub with little delay. With Arthur's help she heaved the anchor overboard.

Silently, their plans discussed thoroughly before they had set out, Arthur and Barrass went over the side, each with a knife in his belt. Barrass swam down strongly, his hand touching the cord which held the floating tub. Down in the frightening blackness until his hand touched a second tub.

Down again, his lungs beginning to pain him, then he abandoned the dive and returned to the surface, where Arthur was treading water beside the boat. He nodded to Olwen, filled his lungs and disappeared once again under the silky black water.

This time he went down to the bottom, not more than nine feet, where the anchoring tub lay half buried in sand. He cut the rope and five tubs were brought to the surface, where they were held by Arthur and Olwen until Barrass was back in the boat.

He lay panting for a moment, then he and Olwen hauled the tubs aboard. Arthur clambered over the side to join them and lifted the anchor.

'Best we don't waste too much time,' Arthur warned, his voice echoing over the silent water. 'The alarm will be given at a certain time, and we've no idea how long we'll take.'

Markus Grand lived in a large house five miles along the coast from the place where the small boat was making a landing. He knew the cliffs intimately so that his blindness was no drawback, and he habitually walked at night. On this occasion, hearing Arthur's voice coming to him across the water, he halted in his tracks, one foot remaining in the air, the other on the grassy path leading, at a long slow angle, to the top of the cliff. His ears were keen and he stood immovable as he detected other sounds that enabled him to understand what was going on. He knew that a small boat had been out near the crop of tubs and was coming into the small beach below him,

Moving stealthily, he returned down the path he had been climbing and reached a level track between the steepness of the grass-covered cliff and the drop onto the rocks. A bank of earth rose to four feet on the landward side, brought down from the sloping land by countless winters. On the other, a few bushes gave scant protection from the barely perceptible breezes coming across the water.

The tide was slack, hardly more than thirty-five feet, and there was no violent splashing, only a lapping and an occasional rush as gulleys were filled by the tide. Markus headed swiftly for the beach, his feet making little sound, bent forward to make himself invisible behind the stunted bushes that struggled for sustenance on the rocky ground, his walking stick only occasionally touching the path.

Where the track widened above the beach, he stood and listened again. He heard the complaining of the rowlocks as oars moved within them, heard the shaking and squeaking of the sail as it was lowered down the mast on metal rings. How little time he had. They were almost onto the beach. In moments they would be off with his tubs.

The steep climb was the quickest, but would he be in time to catch them? He could do nothing alone, that much was certain, so there was no choice, he had to make the climb, and make it fast! He turned and jumped up the bank of earth and began scrambling up the grassy hill to the top of the cliffs. He ignored the sharp scratches as he pushed his way through brambles, and the bruises when he tripped over low scrub and loose boulders.

Breathing painfully, he forced himself on to where a group of cottages stood, all built one against the others as if, like a house of cards, they would all fall if one moved by an inch. He knocked on the door and told what he had heard. Within minutes of his arrival, seven men, armed with sticks and knives, were on their way to the bay with others sent for to follow.

Markus's keen ears heard them go, although they moved as quietly as possible. He walked to the edge of the grassy cliff, below which was the narrow path, a thin hedge and then the rocky shore. He sat to listen and follow the scene to be enacted below him, cursing his blindness.

In Spider's cottage, Mary sat watching the time slowly passing on the watch belonging to Pitcher. Emma sat with her, and when the hands eventually reached a quarter after midnight, another guest, Bessie Rees, who worked for Henry Harris, stood to leave.

'Best I go and tell Daniels,' she said, 'me having no man to plead for, they'll believe me to be public-spirited and not trying to protect my own.'

The others agreed and Bessie wrapped her shawl tightly around her head and shoulders, and set off to find the Keeper-of-the-Peace.

They had waited impatiently for the time to report the activities on the beach, the minutes crawling past as they sat, each imagining the dangers the three young people faced. Now the time had come, Bessie ran as if *her* life were in danger along with theirs. Through the dark streets, dreading to meet a stranger or be accosted by a madman on the prowl, she lifted her skirts and made her fat legs twinkle, white in the darkness, like wood-shavings blown by a wild wind.

Her appearance, when she finally woke Daniels, was startling. Her hair had fallen from the shawl and hung in an untidy cage across her face. The skirts of her grey dress were still held high and on her face there was a look of such fear that in the spluttering light of his candle, Daniels thought he had answered the knock of a revived corpse.

'I was just coming from Mary's, comforting her I've been, on the wicked miscarriage of justice that has robbed her of her men, when I heard some strange sounds coming from the bay below the house. Men, it was, and dragging something. Certain to be them smugglers that got our men accused, imprisoned and facing trial I thought, and as fast as my old legs could run, I came to get you. Come on,' she added as he did not move. 'Catch them for sure we will if only you'll hurry yourself!'

Daniels dressed himself quickly, wondering who he could ask to accompany him. There wasn't much chance of catching anyone with only old Bessie Rees for support. Collecting a gun, a lantern and a heavy stick, he left the house with his wild-looking visitor. He paused only to knock on the doors of three men from the village, sending messages for the rest, and urged Bessie to go and rouse Edwin and tell him to bring men. Then, with some trepidation, began to run towards the beach below Spider's cottage. He had not gone far before there were eight men running with him, each having armed himself as well as he could, with a stick, axe or knife.

The boat reached the small beach and Barrass and Arthur jumped out to haul it up. Olwen jumped out beside them and ran to the rocks leading up to the plateau of flat ground above. It was a steep and difficult climb, the handholds painfully sharp on the barnacle-encrusted rocks, the pools unseen in the darkness, a slippery hazard.

She could see nothing and climbed blindly, her shins scraping excruciatingly on the uneven surface. Apart from the small sounds of the two below her on the pebbles, the night was still and apparently innocent of watchers, though the stillness was menacing, closing in around her like an enveloping black cloak. Fear tightened her muscles, clenching her small jaw until her teeth ached.

When she reached the top she waved an arm as a signal for them to unload the tubs, hoping that against the almost indistinguishable skyline they might see the movement and know she was safely off the beach.

The first tub was taken out and Barrass and Arthur carried it between them to where they planned to hide it. As they bent to place it in the hollow in the rocks, a voice said softly,

'Thank you, these are ours I do believe.'

100

'Run!' Barrass shouted, and Olwen bent and scuttled away, up and inland, not daring to look back, dreading to see Barrass knocked and beaten senseless by the men who had been waiting for them.

At a deep bush-filled corrie she fell to the ground and, trying to control her rasping breath, waited to see if she had been chased. No one came, there was no sound. She crawled across the dew-wet grass back towards the beach.

The sound of footsteps stopped her and, heart thumping against the hard earth, she curled herself up, hoping to avoid being seen. Then she realized that the footsteps were approaching from inland, and saw about eight men marching, with little attempt at concealment, towards the beach. She sprang up and hailed Daniels, the Keeper-of-the-Peace, who was leading them.

'Oh, Mr Daniels, I was trying to get to you. Quick, the men are beating Barrass and Arthur to a mash.'

'What on earth are you doing here?'

'Don't stop to ask questions now, please, Mr Daniels, come and save Barrass and Arthur.'

Breathless and frightened as she was, Olwen ran with the men, who, although well known to her, looked fearsome, larger than life and alien in the darkness. Their outlines with the sticks held threateningly made them look like a race of wild invaders, and Olwen had to fight a fear of them as well as what awaited her on the beach.

She sobbed as she ran behind them, determined to keep up. There had never been a night so dark or one that so surrounded her with the threat of unimagined horrors.

She could see in her mind the battered body of Barrass draped over that of Arthur whom he had fought to save. Why had she persuaded him to do this? She was the cause of his death, and how would she live without him?

Barrass backed away from the group of men come to claim the tubs, trying to reach the rocks and a chance of escape. He hoped he would not catch his foot against a rock and fall. Once he was down, there was no chance of escaping the weapons they held, barely seen but clearly imagined.

The thought of an axe splitting his skull made the pain of it as real as the actual blow. He heard whispered voices, and shadows moved to get behind him. He knew that his time had come, and wished briefly that he could have found his father before the end. A momentary fear for the safety of Olwen, a mild curiosity about the rocks and stones that fell around them, then he stiffened himself for the vicious blow.

The man stood in front of him, both hands holding an axe raised back behind his head, a soft sound of pent-up breath as he prepared to strike. A smell of sweat and tobacco and stale seawater filled his nostrils, and he realized that the sound of air filling lungs came from himself.

Then other voices coming from the top of the rocks began to shout in warning, and the man who held the axe high, relishing the chance of a clear blow to his head, suddenly fell backwards, hands around his throat. Men were swarming over each other, some trying to escape, others determined they would not. Barrass felt his knees give way and he sank to the ground, praying that he would not be hit by either side in the madness going on around him. Stones still flew through the air, voices growled, groaned and panted as he slithered on hands, feet and bottom to where a rock would give some shelter.

The battle on the beach was almost over when Olwen and the tail end of Daniels' group reached the steep rocky approach. She slithered down, uncaring of scratches and cuts. Arthur climbed down from the top of a steep pinnacle of rock where he had been sitting throwing stones down on the men trying to reach him.

The rest of the party were carrying the tubs up the difficult route to the top of the rocks and the attackers were held with much enthusiasm by the last of Daniels' men.

Barrass was hurt, but not as badly as Olwen had feared. Arthur's stone-throwing had deterred much of the treatment the men had tried to hand out. She washed his face, which had received a few minor cuts, and then, hands on hips, threatened that he must see Doctor Percy as soon as possible to have the bruises and swelling lumps dealt with. Daniels agreed and thought that the expenses might be met by the revenue men when they heard about his bravery.

Up on the cliffs, Markus listened, tried to make sense of it, and again cursed his blindness.

When all the men had been captured and tied and the tubs safely confiscated by Daniels, Olwen began her explanations, willing Barrass to let her finish before adding anything that might jeopardize their story being believed.

'Barrass and Arthur overheard something at the alehouse that made us believe the tubs were being collected tonight, so we set out in Dadda's boat to catch them.'

'That's right,' piped up Arthur, 'in the alehouse it was, wasn't it Barrass?'

With as little embroidery as possible, Olwen described their intention to discover who the men were and show the revenue men that it was not Spider and Pitcher and the rest who were guilty of smuggling.

They never did find out how the men knew they were coming, although, as the cliffs were rarely empty of people watching, it seemed likely that someone had heard the boat and sent a warning.

Each of the five tubs contained four gallons of brandy and would have been bought in France for sixteen shillings. With the duty at eight shillings per gallon, it had been worth a fight to try to recapture them.

When Olwen was told that it would be at least a few days before the men were released, she decided to take the boat out and catch some fish. The sea was calm, and she had proved on the night of the tub-gathering that she could both handle the heavy boat and navigate sufficiently well to reach the fishing grounds out in the channel.

Waking in the early dark, even before the thin wail of Dic warned her that morning was near and he was hungry for food, she dressed warmly and set off for the beach. She met no one as she made her way to the line of boats along the shore. The night fishermen were not yet back and the men intent on finding a few codling and perhaps a late-season bass not yet prepared to depart.

Pushing the boat out was harder than she expected. With Dadda and Dan it seemed like a toy to push; on her own, it strained her shoulders and pulled at her back muscles so she almost gave up the idea completely. When it did move, it was with a sudden surge of a larger wave so that it went onto the water in a rush and she landed with her face on the wet shingle.

Jumping into the now lightly floating craft, she began to ease it away from the shore until another large wave lifted it and sent it soaring over the surface of the sea in joyful movement. She stepped up the mast and the sail was soon filling with a rising wind. Taking the rudder, Olwen sat back to enjoy the excitement of the morning's wakening, throwing back her head in pleasure as an occasional gusty wind blew her hair streaming out behind her in a silken banner.

Setting her lines with paternosters baited with brightly dyed feathers which were clearly visible in the calm, quiet waters of the bay, she sailed in a circle continuously casting and hauling in, bringing a harvest of writhing, silver fish on board to gasp and struggle as she began to pull for the shore.

When she returned to the beach, there were a dozen hands willing to help her bring the heavily laden boat ashore, and among them was Barrass. She could see at once that he was not pleased.

'Showing off again are you, Olwen, showing me what a strong girl you are compared with me?'

'Oh, Barrass, there's daft you are. I was wide awake and it was such a temptation that I just went off and didn't tell a soul. I'd have called for you to come if I thought I could have woken you. Shall I? Next time?'

'I'd have to sit there with you telling me what to do.'

'So what's the matter with that? I had to for years before Dadda would let me even touch the rudder. Tell you what, we'll go fishing off the next bay and you can learn without anyone knowing, then you can sail her in right under the admiring noses of the fishermen as if you've been doing it all your life.'

'All right, just don't go off out there on your own again, it isn't safe for someone as young and small as you.'

Olwen knew he was only pretending to be afraid for her to cover up his own lack of skill, but she smiled and nodded.

'I won't go without calling for you to come with me, I promise,' she said contritely and with ambiguity, fully aware that she had deliberately avoided a promise not to go out without him, agreeing only to call for him first. If he did not answer her call then she could go off with a conscience only slightly clouded.

On the day when Emma took her three daughters to tea with Edwin, she was filled with anxiety. It was clear that dutiful as Violet undoubtedly was, she did not want to go.

'But, daughter, when will you get such another chance as this? Edwin is a fine and wealthy young man. You'll have a life of social standing such as many a girl would envy. New clothes for every special occasion, and, from what I have learnt, daughter, there will be plenty more of those.'

'But Mother, I find him so distressingly boring. His attempts at humour so predictable.'

Emma hid her expression as she thought with irritation that 'boring' was the word most frequently used about Violet!

'Violet, dear, won't you try to find something to start a conversation? Think of a few subjects that he would be sure to know a thing or two about, and start him talking. There's nothing a man likes better than being allowed to talk on his favourite subjects and to be thought clever. Now what about pigs?'

'Pigs, Mother?' Violet raised a thin eyebrow and looked at her mother with mild amusement. 'What on earth should I know about pigs?'

'Edwin is fond of them, so they say, and successful at bringing them to a fine size for the September Fair at Neath.'

'That should fill at least half a minute.'

'Violet, dear, what do you *wish* to talk about?'

'I dream of talking to a man who has adventure in his heart, someone who will take risks and not be more worried about getting a butter stain off his shirt than about the fate of the men fighting in France against Napoleon.'

'That, dear daughter, is man's talk and shouldn't fill your thoughts for a moment. Soldiering indeed! What have your teachers done to fill your head with such stuff? Is that what we have paid good money for?'

'Not soldiering, Mother, but stirring tales, people who have done exceptional things, left the safety of their homes and gone boldly out into the wild, wide world.'

'The town of Swansea is wild enough for me with sea-farers bringing the troubles of the world to its doors, and as for people leaving their homes, well, you are lucky to have a home such as this, and look around you if you are in doubt. Just poke your well-dressed head out of the window and look at some you see passing.'

'You are right, Mother, and I am ungrateful. I will do my best to be polite to this – farmer who pretends an interest in me, for your sake.'

'And I'm expected to thank you for that? And me trying to cope with all this with your father in prison? Oh you're a cruel girl and that's for sure.'

'It's fortunate that Barrass agreed to come back and help you, isn't it, Mother, after you threw him out into the cold.'

'Enough, daughter, I won't have the boy mentioned. If you think he's the one to tell you stirring tales, then I fear you are out of your head. Fleas, rags and no home, that's his background, and don't you ever forget it!'

'No, Mother. Now, what time do you wish us to be ready?'

'Four of the clock and not a minute later.'

Edwin Prince lived in a traditional Welsh long-house built on a rise of land with a view all around. In the centre of the single-storey building was an archway leading to the yard behind. To the right of the arch were two living rooms and to the left the barns used by cattle. Behind it, some distance from the house, were two small buildings with large enclosed areas around them, which housed his pigs. A new piggery was under construction, built of brick and large enough for several sows.

The house had windows added in the roof and Edwin had built a staircase of stone which led up to a platform jutting out halfway into the living room, on which he had a bed. A railing of carved wood protected him from falling to the ground floor. He used the bed very little.

All day he spent either supervising the work on his farm, or visiting friends to play cards. At night, when most people slept, he went about a different sort of business.

His farmworkers, as with those in the farms around, were paid a pittance for their long hours of hard work. Their homes were theirs only as long as they stayed in the farmer's employ so they were captive, unable to risk the poor wage and the sometimes precarious roof to find a better life. The unseen assistance Edwin gave his workmen and women was the night hours spent collecting and distributing illegal imports.

A packet of tea plus a few shillings for two hours' work was worth the risk of being caught and sent to prison, or, in extreme cases, death or transportation to colonies across the sea. Those who worked for Edwin knew that he would protect them as diligently as he could. The income the trade represented meant the difference to him between barely existing, and a full social life and all the comforts he required.

Edwin had left the fields, where he had been watching the men digging out the last of the root crops and carting them to the storage sheds beyond the piggery, and walked back to the house, shouting for water for bathing.

This fascination with a soak in a tub of water was still a source of amusement to his housekeeper, Martha Baker, sister-in-law to Ivor-the-Builder. Since she had come to work at the house four years before, she had never failed to smile at the idea of her employer, lying full length and wearing nothing more than a nightshirt, in hot, soapy water while he read a few pages of a book. Not once but some-

107

times twice in a week he would shout for water and wait while the bathtub was filled, before locking the door and settling himself to enjoy the odd practice.

She and the two servants, Sally and Megan, had frequently stared with suppressed chuckles through the large keyhole and watched as he lay, blissfully unaware of being watched by eyes wet with tears of laughter.

'Bless my old boots but that steam must be doin' strange things to his skin. I mind when I've spent time a washin' of his clothes how wrinkled my poor fingers do get,' Martha Baker remarked. 'Now I wonder if that's fashionable then, to have fingers all wrinkled?'

'It ain't fingers but the rest of him what'll be wrinkled, Martha. Them hands of his never gets near the water from what I see, always turning the pages of that book.'

Edwin rose from the water, bubbles and creases making the white nightshirt seem like a fanciful gown of lace, in a haze of steam. He reached for the towel placed ready for him on the back of a chair near the fire and, putting it on the floor beside the tub, stepped out.

This was the stage at which the eyes at the keyhole changed rapidly, each person being scrupulously fair at having only the count of five before allowing the next to have a turn. Today it was Martha who saw him pull the nightshirt over his head and she gasped and almost fainted away as he turned to face the door wearing not a stitch, to pick up his book and place it away from the danger of spillage.

'Never saw that much even when me and Mr Baker was married!' she gasped as Sally and Megan helped her to a chair and a small brandy for medicinal purposes.

Unaware of the stir he had caused in his female staff, Edwin dressed in his newest suit of grey woollen cloth ready to greet Violet and the rest of Pitcher's family. He called for Martha and reminded her that there would be cakes needed for tea and some bread thinly cut to be spread with some of her raspberry preserve. He thought she had been crying and vaguely wondered why, not knowing it was tears of laughter she was, with difficulty, keeping in check. He sat watching out of the window for Pitcher's cart to arrive.

Barrass was driving them. In the absence of Pitcher, there was no one else, and although Emma was quite capable of managing the small waggon and the amiable horse, she thought it important to give a good impression and had even found a suit of clothes for Barrass, which, although a bit tight across his shoulders, gave an air of elegance, or so Emma thought.

Barrass felt Emma's eye on him as he helped the three sisters out of the cart, placing the stool on the ground so they would not have to stretch their legs too far. He was unable to resist clasping Violet's waist as he helped her down to the freshly scrubbed steps, and did the same with Pansy and Daisy so she could not complain. When it came to helping Emma herself, he thought it wise not to attempt anything so gallant, and offered his hand with a polite bow.

Edwin stood at the door to greet them and offered his arm to Emma to escort her inside. Tall, dark-skinned and with an intriguing hint of foreignness about him, he smiled back at the three sisters, giving each a personal smile. His eyes paused only momentarily longer on the face of an indifferent Violet, who allowed him to take her hand as if it were a separate thing.

He was amused to see the way Emma's eyes darted about the room, taking stock of the few pieces of good furniture as well as the untidy desk that stood near the window, on which piles of papers tempted gravity.

'My apologies, ladies,' Edwin said, waving a deprecating arm. 'My drawing room is also my study, I'm afraid, and has the look of an office rather than a comfortable place in which to sit and enjoy pleasant company.' He smiled at Violet again, a warming smile with a hint of amusement in the dark eyes. 'Seems I need a good woman to show me how I should live.'

'Is this the only room?' Emma asked, seeing with surprise the precarious room above them and the windows letting in the light on both sides.

'I have plans to rebuild, or at least, to add on at the back of the house, perhaps a double storey to include a couple of bedrooms so I can entertain properly.'

'And when would you be planning to do this?' Emma was clearly unimpressed with the house which she had been led to believe was important and rather grand. What on earth did three servants do to keep themselves occupied, she wondered primly. Why, she and Spider had to do with only two!

Violet handed her cape to the servant who hovered near, and walked to look out of the window at the back of the room. The yard was cobbled and well swept, but the view was of pigsties – in no way the garden of a gentleman. The man was a farmer and, rich or not, would never be anything more. There was a partly finished building at a point furthest from the house and this she guessed was the newest pigsty.

'The pigs are to be housed comfortably before you attend to yourself and your servants, I see,' she said with a glance at her mother. Well, she had done what her mother had asked, hadn't she, and mentioned the man's pigs?

To her consternation, Edwin burst into laughter. It angered her rather than flattered her and she said, sharply,

'Oh, I see it takes but a small wit to amuse you greatly.' At which he laughed even more.

'Before we take tea, would you like to walk around the out-houses?' Edwin asked. 'It's already dark, but we have plenty of lanterns and if you are interested in the pigs' welfare – '

'Thank you,' Emma replied swiftly, 'but I think I have a mind to sit here before your blazing fire and leave the outside viewing for another day.' He sensed in her reply a hint that 'another day' would be a long time in the future if at all. Violet, who had begun to rise, sank down again in relief. At least in here, she couldn't be expected to discuss the merits of the various breeds of pigs!

Pansy and Daisy began to relax when tea was brought by Mrs Baker and two young maids, and the uneasy group sat to enjoy it. Most of the conversation was instigated by

110

Emma or Edwin. The three girls only added a word or two occasionally and at their mother's insistence. Violet was aware of the nearness of laughter in her twin sisters and, guessing that it was due to comparison with other, grander tea parties, began to feel a proprietary protectiveness towards Edwin. However, she did not make an effort to develop a friendly conversation, but sat watching him when she thought he was not aware of it.

When she did speak, Violet smiled secretly at how promptly Edwin gave her his full attention. Always with that fascinating hint of amusement brightening his eyes and upturning his full and sensuous lips.

'My daughters are talented musically and in all the social needs of a wife, Mr Prince,' Emma told him at one stage in the stilted conversation.

'Now what needs would those be, my dear Mistress Palmer? Besides music and the running of a household, what else could there be?'

Edwin looked boldly at Violet as he asked the question, his eyes glancing down to where her softly rising breasts showed in a nest of lace. Violet blushed but Emma seemed unaware of the innuendo in the question and went on airily.

'Manners, Mr Prince, manners and the way to behave in any situation.'

'*Any* situation, Mistress Palmer, how very full their education must have been.' Again his eyes caused Violet to blush and she stood to shake crumbs out of her skirt. She should leave, the man was impossible. But she found herself smiling in spite of his audacity and did not move from where his eyes could find hers.

When it was time for them to leave, Emma was very undecided about the suitability of Edwin as a son-in-law. He was obviously wealthy, but he equally obviously did not spend it. There was nothing worse than a mean husband, and however anxious she was to have her three daughters married, she would not, could not inflict a mean man on any one of them.

Oh, she sighed silently, if only Pitcher were free. He would know more about the man than she, a mere woman, could be expected to discover. She was still not sure whether to be pleased or concerned at the glow of excitement on Violet's face when they reached home and sat down in the oil lamp's gentle light.

Violet was far from dissatisfied by the afternoon's entertainment. Edwin had asked her to play the spinet, which she did, and he had stood close to her, his hand touching her shoulder as he leaned over to turn the pages of music for her, his fingers moving her hair disturbing more than her tresses, unseen by Emma and in no way accidental. He was impressing his personality on her, making her feel in the brief time they were there, that he was attracted, had guessed that she was also not unaware of his interest, and that she would not be discouraged by Emma's lack of enthusiasm. All the time they were there, she found his eyes on her, silently sharing his enjoyment of the occasion, nurturing an understanding unseen by the others, laughing with her at her mother's anxieties, which Emma failed to hide.

Whatever her mother might say now she had visited, Violet wanted to see him again, and soon. There was something more to Mr Edwin Prince than she had suspected. That night she did not go down to join Barrass in his lonely archway behind the house, but slept and dreamed of another pair of brown eyes, wicked brown eyes, smiling at her and flirting with her in the presence of her mother and sisters as if they had not existed.

CHAPTER SEVEN

Between the work at Pitcher's alehouse, Barrass filled his time with either fishing in the bay with Olwen, or helping her and Mary to sell their catch. He had been so wrapped up in thoughts of Violet, he had not really considered how difficult it was for Mary and Olwen to manage with Spider and Dan in prison.

There had been no date set for a trial, and the initial optimistic supposition that Spider and the others would soon be released was not borne out by events. Olwen's concern was that having so many men in custody, no one was looking for evidence that they were innocent, only thankful they at last had someone to blame for the trade that went on between the village and the coasts of France and Holland. William Ddole had made repeated visits to the prison and had employed the services of a lawyer, but so far there had been no hopeful news to report.

Olwen spoke of nothing else as they rowed back from a fishing trip off the headland.

'What will become of us if Dadda and Dan are trans-ported?' she asked time after time. 'I'm a-w-ful scared.'

Barrass knew that her real fear was that her father and brother might receive the death sentence. He tried to reassure her.

'I have no doubt that they will come back to you,' he told her. 'There was no violence against the revenue men, so there is no need to worry about a hanging. Taken from their homes peaceably they were with not even a voice raised, so sure they were that they would not be kept once inquiries proved nothing. No one will come forward and give evidence against them, that's for sure. And the evidence they have can't be strong.'

'Perhaps what you say is true, Barrass, but will they worry about evidence? Twist you all up with words they can. They

113

want to show they've been doing their work proper, and the men they've taken will serve their purpose, innocent or guilty!'

Barrass pulled the boat up onto the shore and helped Olwen to haul out their catch. A poor one that morning, and he knew that unless they were more successful on the mornings to come, Mary's small supply of food would dwindle at an alarming rate. He had to think of something to do to add to their income, and glanced hopefully at the house where the mail was gathered. Perhaps he could find time to assist Kenneth and earn a few more pennies.

Enyd answered his knock later that day, a notebook in her hand, expecting it to be someone with a letter to send.

'What d'you want?' she asked coldly. 'Move off, we don't want scruffs like you littering the place. Important people come here and we can't have them upset by a sight like you.' As she said it she knew she was being unfair. A sight he certainly was, but a sight to make a girl's heart flutter, except her own. She did not want him, but resented the fact that others certainly did. They both stood there, Enyd at the half-opened door and Barrass on the road. Kenneth came out, a small figure in a full-length dressing gown of red, and looked at them curiously.

'Barrass. What are you wanting?' Kenneth asked in his rather pompous voice. 'Don't waste the girl's time if it's only chatter you want.'

'I came to ask if there was a chance of helping you,' Barrass said. 'Truth is, I need to earn some extra, there's someone who needs it see, and I thought, if you needed someone to go and collect the post or – ' He dried up as Kenneth shook his head.

'Nothing so casual will suit the King's Mail. Only I can collect from Swansea, no matter how I feel about the long ride, it's me and only me they'll give the letters to. Unless I make arrangements for you to be an appointed servant of mine. But at the moment I am well able to do the work myself.'

'Perhaps you should put my name forward as your servant

then, in case there's ever a day when you can't go.' Barrass looked up at him, hope in the moist brown eyes.

'I'll think about it, Barrass, I'll think about it.' He ushered his daughter inside and, following her, slammed the door firmly.

Barrass turned away dejectedly and wandered back to the alehouse.

During the evening he helped Arthur carry drinks up from the cellar and rinse out the empty mugs as customers departed, alternately boring and heavy work with large pitchers to carry up and down stairs, remnants of food and drink to clear and barrels to heave about. The weather was cold and a heavy rain was falling as he stepped out into the yard to run for the shelter of the archway. Towards the end of the evening the barroom had become quite chill, the fire having been allowed to die down. And with washing the mugs and the tables in icy water, he was very cold when he went to his bed.

He sat shivering in his temporary shelter in the archway, unable to sleep, his thoughts wavering between the hope that tonight Violet would return to him, and intermittent concern that he should be finding a way to help Olwen's family. He wrapped the sacks tightly around him in an effort to warm his chilled body and tried to bring thoughts of Violet to mind to help make his blood run faster.

He was roused to sudden excitement when he saw a shadow appear in the doorway of the house and he sat up, straining his eyes to see if it was Violet, but the voice was Arthur's.

'Come on, Barrass, sleep in the cellar with me, there's daft it is for you to be sleeping out by here in this weather. *She* won't see you. Up long before she's roused herself we'll be and who else is to know, or care?'

Stiffly, and still shivering, Barrass rose and followed Arthur to the cellar door. Although without heat, the cellar was out of the biting wind and the cold rain that constantly found places through which to seep and wet his clothes. The covers Arthur had collected for him were soft and thickly filled with sheep's wool, the mattress comfortably

115

packed with dried heather, and he felt the comfort of it and was filled with ineffable sadness that such simple luxuries only rarely entered his life. He fought back the tightness in his throat that threatened tears of self-pity.

As he lay, wrapped in a cocoon of slowly enveloping warmth, his thoughts rose to where Violet lay under the same roof. There would be a fire in her bedroom, and warm, clean clothes to wear when she rose, warm water to wash herself, a servant to cook and serve her breakfast. He imagined the soft, sweet-scented bed in which she slept and wondered why life treated some so well and ignored the simplest, most basic needs of others.

It was still raining when he rose and began his day's work. He was outside the alehouse in the rain and the darkness, carrying out some of the unwanted pieces of wood to clear the ground for the next stages of the building work, when he saw Kenneth setting off for Swansea to collect the letters. He called to him, receiving the briefest of nods in response, and watched as the darkness swallowed him up, listening until the lonely sound of the horse's clopping hooves faded away.

Everything of late seemed to emphasize his solitary and worthless state. Everyone walking away from him. Enyd, for whom he felt no desire, but whom he had hoped to cultivate as a friend, was cold and indifferent; and Violet, so loving and then leaving him without a word. Even Kenneth had no time even to wish him a good morning. He forced a brief smile as Olwen's small and lovely features filled his mind. He pictured her standing before him, hands on slim hips, face raised to look into his eyes, perhaps frowning in mock dismay at some slight offence, or laughing him out of some disappointment with her blue eyes twinkling with good humour. She was his friend and never thought anything but the best of him. He threw down the last of the wood and, calling to Arthur to explain his absence, ran up on to the cliff to Olwen's cottage. At least there, with both Spider and Dan away, he would be of some use.

Kenneth worked a regular weekly routine, collecting the

116

three evening deliveries to Swansea on the morning following their arrival. On Sunday, Tuesday and Friday, the post-boy brought letters in to the Swansea sorting office at six p.m. and on the mornings of Monday, Wednesday and Saturday, Kenneth rode in on the hired horse and collected the letters for Gower and took in any that had been left with him, in time for the next outgoing mail at six a.m. He brought the collection back to his house and rested while Ceinwen sorted them into the order of his calls, then he set off again to walk around the peninsula, delivering and collecting. He would stay overnight at either Port Eynon or Rhosili before finishing his round to arrive home in the afternoon or evening of the following day.

On this Wednesday morning Kenneth wished he had asked Barrass to go with him. The rain, although a part of his life and rarely noticed, was cold, and the walk around the isolated farms and houses would be a lonely one with few people out and about with whom he could stop and share a few minutes of pleasant gossip.

He put the letters into his leather bag and after a brief chat over a mulled ale with Ben Gammon, rode home. In the small room which he used as a sorting office there were several letters for him to take between neighbour and neighbour. Ceinwen had listed them with a note of the fees payable. He stopped only long enough for her to put a parcel of food into his bag, and he to take a warming sip of brandy, before setting out on his two-day round.

He would be glad when the morrow came. Thursday was the best day of the week. He would arrive late in the evening to be fussed over by Ceinwen, who always worried about him being out alone and with little means of protection should someone wish to rob him. He would be allowed to relax and sit near the fire in his favourite armchair to savour the prospect of Friday, always a free day, when there was no travelling and only the letters handed in to Ceinwen or Enyd to be dealt with on the following day. Yes, Thursday was a day to savour.

The deliveries were few on that Wednesday and he spent a lot of the day sitting discussing the imprisonment of the local men with the villagers of Port Eynon. The conversation was wary, as the local men were afraid of unfriendly ears overhearing things that could be passed on to the revenue men. But they stated their conviction that before the month was out, the Mumbles men would be freed.

When he rose the following morning there was a package in the pocket of his coat that he had not seen arrive. It was addressed to William Ddole and he pushed it out of sight deep in the leather bag.

'Little hope of a personal delivery for that one,' he muttered grimly as he went down to break his fast. 'I'm not visiting that prison even for William Ddole, and that's where he spends most of his time, talking to those that the law is holding!'

Thursday was the day he called at Morgan's farm. There were never any letters to deliver or to collect as neither the farmer nor his wife was able to read. He stopped there each Thursday to buy eggs for Betson-the-Flowers.

One day when he had met her by accident in the green lane that passed her hovel she had asked him if he would bring her some eggs the next time he passed. She had held out a couple of coins, leaning languorously against the doorway and tilting her hips towards him in a provocative pose so well practised that she did it unconsciously whenever she spoke to a man. He agreed, with some trepidation, half tempted to refuse, knowing that to be seen visiting her would lead to only one conclusion.

That conclusion would have been correct after his second visit and since then he always took her some eggs and an occasional fowl on Thursdays, and never asked for the money.

It was only a little past noon when he came in sight of Betson's semi-derelict cottage and he increased his pace in anticipation of her welcome. She always kept Thursday afternoon and evening free and he knew she would have a meal and a roaring fire ready for him. He counted himself very lucky that in all the months he had been calling on her, he had never once had to change his plans. He had never met anyone and had to turn away in disappointment, or bluff an excuse for being there. The good God approves, he thought irreverently.

The ground was soaked with the day and night of rain and his boots were heavy with mud. In the shelter of an overhanging fir tree he stopped and tried to clean them with a small fallen branch. Walking on, he cut across a field of soaking wet, over-long grass which he hoped would make them even more presentable. He was just pushing his way through the hedge when a voice hailed him. He groaned inwardly. Now he would be unable to visit Betson, and what's more would have to find a way of filling in the time until he could go home. If he were once early on a Thursday, it would be difficult to explain his lateness on others!

'Barrass,' he smiled, tilting his head forward to allow the rain to pour off the brim of his hat. 'And what are you doing out in such weather?'

'I chopped a load of firewood which I've sold to some of the cottagers. It's money for Spider's family, not for myself, mind,' he added quickly as he saw Kenneth's face show disapproval, 'and I didn't charge them much.'

'Would you like to earn another sixpence?' Kenneth asked as an idea formed in his mind. 'For Spider's family if you wish.'

'Well, thank you, yes,' Barrass said, surprised. A sixpence would buy bread for a week.

'I have a package which is addressed to William Ddole. If you would take it for me, I still have a number of letters to deliver and it's getting late.'

Sheltering the package as best they could, it was transferred from Kenneth's pocket to Barrass's, and without looking at it the boy set off back the way he had come. If he wondered where Kenneth was heading, he said nothing and, after waiting a moment for him to disappear among the trees, Kenneth sighed with relief and went through the doorway and into the open arms of Betson.

She laughed as she stripped off his soaked clothes, making roguish fun of the way the cloth clung to his wet skin and refused to free him. Then, with the garments hung on a clothes horse near the fire to steam and dry, she began

119

to rub his body with a soft towelling cloth. Before she had dried his shoulders his desire forced him to forget the need to be dried and he reached out for the buttons that held her skirt in place. In a whoop of laughter Betson slapped his hands in mock propriety then fell to the floor and rolled against him, encouraging his hands that were stiff with the cold to fumble awkwardly at the rest of the fastenings.

He failed and pulled clumsily at her, catching her skin in the folds of the cloth and making her gasp with the shock of it. She stood up and turned away then, as if in disapproval, and for a moment his heart raced with the thought that he had seriously offended her, but before he could think of a way to persuade her back into his arms, she turned to face him and with a slow smile, pulled on a red ribbon and allowed her dress to fall free. She wore under it only a pair of broderie anglaise pantalettes cut to knee length. A slow pull on another ribbon and they were gone.

Barrass clutched the sixpence as he ran towards Ddole House. He wondered how best to spend it. On flour perhaps. If Spider and Dan were to stay in prison through the winter months, it was essential that Mary had food for her family. But perhaps it would be best to hold it and wait until he had more. A sixpence was a lot of money for someone like him, without anyone dependent on him, but to Mary with Olwen and little Dic to care for and a husband to visit and supply with extra comforts, it was little enough. His hands stiff with cold he slipped the coin into a pocket with difficulty, and ran on.

At the field from where he could look over the hedge and see the house, he stopped. In the gloominess of the late afternoon a man was leaving the front door of the house, and Barrass saw that it was the Keeper-of-the-Peace. At once caution bade him stop and consider the message he had come on. Could it be something innocuous? It had to be. It had come from Kenneth's bag. But he knew that the King's Mail did not accept parcels for delivery. Had Kenneth trusted him with a package that the law would like to see? No, he would not!

He half hid in the hedge and using the soaking wet jacket he wore as protection, drew out the package. There was no post mark or an indication of how much there was to pay, and it had no seal to close it, only string. A cold sweat broke out on his forehead, competing with the icy rain.

He thought to run but he had left it too late, Daniels had seen him and hailed him.

'Barrass? You're soaked right through, boy, and living in someone's yard, how will you dry yourself?' He took hold of the boy's shoulder and marched him to the kitchen door of Ddole House.

'Florrie?' he called, ignoring Barrass's protests. 'See this boy, come with a package it seems and so wet he'll flood your floor. But can you do something about his clothes? I swear the lad has no others and will suffer pneumonia if left to his own administrations.'

'Come on in, and stand on the mat while I find you something dry to wear.' Florrie tutted and sighed and shook her white-capped head but ran at once to the cupboard where extra clothes were always in readiness in case one of the servants needed them.

'Try these for size,' she demanded, then she took the package from him and passed it to Daniels. 'Seeing as how this was your idea, Mr Daniels, put that on the fender where it will dry, will you? And put his jacket, poor thing that it is, to dry on the clothes horse.'

Barrass avoided Daniels' eye as the tall man took the package and almost absentmindedly opened it. It contained money.

'And where did you find this, boy?' he asked in a soft voice. 'Not yours for sure.'

'It's addressed to William Ddole,' Barrass said, deciding not to say who had given it to him. Always best to say as little as possible, Spider always told him.

'There's no name that I can see,' Daniels said.

Barrass hid behind a cupboard door, pulled off his clothes and put on the ones Florrie had handed him. How could he explain without mentioning Kenneth?

'Ah, that will be mine, Daniels,' a voice said and Dorothy

Ddole strode into the kitchen, making the two servants stand up and bob a curtsey, which was noted but ignored.

'Yours, Mistress Ddole?' Daniels raised an eyebrow questioningly.

'Payment for a horse,' she said briskly. 'Came adrift, did it? Lucky that money isn't made of sugar or I'd be down a few pounds!'

'May I ask who sent the money?' Daniels asked politely but with an edge to his voice that indicated he would insist on an answer.

'Markus, that man who lives further along the coast. He wanted a sure-footed mount for that sister of his.' She turned to where Barrass was standing in trousers too small and a jacket that held his shoulders back like a vice. 'What's happened to you? You look as if the rain has shrunk you, or rather your clothes.'

'I took the liberty of lending him some, him being soaked bringing your packet,' Florrie told her and Dorothy laughed, smiling at the others to join in.

'I'll try to find you something better fitting, Barrass. Come, Florrie, there's sure to be something that my son has no further need of.' She led Florrie and an uncomfortable Barrass out of the kitchen but stopped at the foot of the curving staircase, her hands pressing against the pain in her stomach. 'Second thoughts,' she said in a low voice. 'I have things to do. My daughter will show you.' Then, as Penelope appeared at the top of the stairs, she went into the drawing room and closed the door.

'All right, Florrie, I will find him something,' Penelope said when the situation had been explained.

So, as Kenneth was lying naked with Betson, on the floor of the old cottage, Barrass was naked behind yet another cupboard door, while Penelope and her giggling maid, Carrie Rees, gave him an assortment of clothes to try on.

They arrived home at the same time, Kenneth with clothes only partly dried, and very uncomfortable, and Barrass warm, dry, fed by Florrie, and with a brown paper parcel holding his discarded clothes, wearing a set of good quality under and outer wear such as he had never seen before. Both were well content with their day, Kenneth glowed with memories of his time with Betson, and Barrass with thoughts of Penelope's kindness.

Daniels rode along the cliff paths in the slippery mud to where Markus lived with his sister and her children. The rain had stopped and the air was pure and fresh. But although the ride was a pleasant one apart from the danger of the horse slipping, he had not wanted to make the journey. He knew he had to talk to Markus and have the explanation of the money confirmed without allowing time for a message to be sent, but it had been hard to leave the warmth of the kitchen where the preparations for supper were sending tempting smells to torment his empty stomach. Florrie had seemed about to invite him to stay and that thought too made the journey a tedious duty.

He was greeted by Markus with irritation and scant hospitality.

'Money, for Mistress Ddole? How would I remember what it was for? A horse probably. Now if you don't mind, I have a book being read to me and it seems a more interesting way to spend a dark evening than talking to you. Good day to you.' Daniels was ushered into the kitchen where he was offered an ale and a bite to eat, which he refused. Sadly, he reflected that he might just as well have stayed with Florrie and her excellent cooking.

Barrass was still worried about the package Kenneth had asked him to deliver, and between jobs at the alehouse, he ran up over the cliff to Olwen's home. The day was cold, the sun fitful, but Olwen and Mary were outside dyeing skeins of sheep's wool and draping it to dry on bushes nearby. Olwen's hands were stained purple with the blackberry dye. Mary smiled a welcome and went into the cottage.

'Barrass.' Olwen ran to greet him, her hands held clear of his new jacket. 'There's smart you are!' She admired his new clothes with a smile hiding a feeling of dread. Now the girls will be chasing after him even more, she thought miserably. 'Will you stay for a bite of fish?' She nodded to the oven where loaves were cooling and fish already prepared for baking. '*I've* made the loaves today *and* prepared the fish. I've stuffed them with herbs and leeks and they'll be very good. You'd be surprised what a good cook I am.'

'Yes, Barrass, stay and eat with us.' Mary came out of the cottage with Dic in her arms. She put the baby down in his wicker cot and sighed. 'Do you know he's already too long for his cradle, Barrass. Another long-legs like his father for sure.'

'Pity help me,' Olwen sighed, 'he'll catch me up in no time. Mam, why was I so small when all the rest are so tall?'

Barrass caught Mary's eye and shared a smile over Olwen's constant lament.

'I'll still look seven when I'm seventeen,' she went on, 'and children will want me to play games and young men will pat my head and call me a good little girl when I'm twenty-seven!'

Barrass laughed out loud and she reached for a skein of wool and began swinging it threateningly.

'Now, Olwen,' Mary warned, 'not with him looking so smart in his new clothes!' and Olwen placed the intended weapon back on the branches of a blackthorn bush to dry.

'Mary, I'm worried about a package Kenneth asked me to deliver to Ddole yesterday,' Barrass explained. 'It contained money and there was nothing to say who sent it. Daniels saw it and if it's stolen or something – '

'Don't worry about it,' Mary smiled. 'We had a bag of coins too, they look after their own to make sure the men don't talk and involve others.'

Barrass was reminded that although he had lived in the village for nearly all of his life, he was still an outsider, uninvolved in the day-to-day lives of those he called his friends. His concern for Mary and his small efforts to help her were superfluous. The villagers all looked after their own.

'Come on, Olwen,' he said then, 'get those fish in the oven and let's go and catch some more.'

'Tide's wrong, silly,' she said, rinsing out some more of

the dark-purple wool. 'Besides, I have to finish this job first or Mam'll shout.'

'Tomorrow then?'

'All right, come back and eat supper with us and we'll make plans to go in the morning, right?'

Barrass wanted to see Penelope again. He knew that there was no possibility of her ever looking at him with more than kindness, but he wanted to thank her properly for the clothes and show her he was not just a homeless beggar, dependent on handouts. He walked tall and strode out confidently. His knock on the kitchen door was loud and authoritative. He did not really know why he felt the need to impress them except that arriving as he had with soaked and ill-fitting clothes he had looked his worst, and recently, events had told him that he was less often dismissed without a second glance. He asked to see Mistress Ddole, thinking that if luck was with him, he would also see Penelope.

He was discomfited when he saw that the Keeper-of-the-Peace was there again, sitting in the large wooden chair near the fire and drinking a mug of ale. He stretched himself up and stared at the man boldly, and hoped that the quaking he felt in his knees did not show. Then he saw that the table was set, that the solemn-faced man was free of his coat and hat and was sitting relaxed and obviously not on duty.

It was Penelope who waited for him when he was shown into the parlour. It was hard then for him to retain the slightly haughty expression he wore, but the new clothes helped. He knew that the transformation they had made was having an effect. Penelope raised her fine eyebrows in surprise.

'Barrass?'

'I've come to thank you most kindly for the clothes, Miss Ddole, and to tell you that I will take great care of them, I value your generosity so much.' He had been practising what he would say all through the walk but the words came out in a less orderly way then he had hoped. But she seemed well pleased.

'Thank you, Barrass. I think they have made quite a difference. If there are any more, I will send them to you.' She looked away and asked, 'Where do you live, Barrass?'

'Nowhere, as yet,' he said. 'I sleep at the alehouse.' He couldn't tell her that he slept on old sacks under an archway. 'I am looking for a suitable place to make comfortable. I did have an old barn,' he added, 'but it was burnt down and all my possessions with it.'

'Thank you for calling. I will bear in mind your need for a home.' Penelope watched as he walked out, then sat for a long time thinking about him.

That night he stayed for a while in the archway, still nursing the vain hope that Violet would come, but when the cold became too much he joined Arthur in the cellar and dreamed about Penelope and Violet, both girls looking at him with that unmistakable speculativeness that tells a man his advances would not be rejected.

On the following morning he woke with his thoughts still on Violet and Penelope and completely forgot his promise to help Olwen take her boat out.

Olwen waited in the darkness with the wind giving occasional gusts to match her own sighs of impatience. Under her warm shawl her hands were on her hips as she stood watching for Barrass's arrival and her spirits sank lower and lower as time passed.

'It's those clothes,' she muttered angrily. 'Thinks he's above helping me with the fish now he's got new clothes. Afraid of getting them messy and the girls complaining of the smell, no doubt!'

Mary called to her softly, her silhouette touched with light from the oil lamp behind her.

'You don't go on your own, mind, not until the light is strong. Dangerous it is for you to be out on your own in the day, but you must not go out in the dark.'

'No, Mam. Oh! I think this is him now.' She hurriedly kissed her mother goodbye, and talking to the empty path, pretended to greet Barrass. She wasn't going to stay here and wait for him a moment longer. Still pretending for her mother's benefit that he had arrived, she ran towards the beach, the wind clutching at her clothes, chilling her thin body and pulling her hair free of its scarf.

It was colder once she was out of the shelter of the bushes and trees around the house, the wind was keen and blowing with sudden force that made her crouch and spread her arms preparing to grab at the grasses at her side if the gusts were strong enough to dislodge her from the path.

She raised her head occasionally hoping to see Barrass approaching. If he arrived after she had left Mam would give her a clout for disobedience. Still, they needed to bring in a good catch and if she waited for Barrass until it was too late for the tide, she would waste a day. Besides, she took pleasure in the anticipation of telling him how she had gone out without him, making him feel guilty for his neglect.

All the way down the path she rehearsed their quarrel. Her pert face wore an expression of offended dignity as she imagined wringing every last drop of his guilt from the situation. How could he just forget? Surely there weren't any girls about at this time of day to distract him?

At the bottom she pulled her shawl closer around her and waited a while, her eyes piercing the darkness, and hearing only the creaking of the boats on pebbles and the slapping of ropes against masts. She was so intent upon watching for Barrass she ignored the signs of an approaching storm.

Several of the boats were already out on the choppy water with their nets being hauled across the bay, their owners hoping to be back within the safety of the headland before the storm hit.

Olwen threw the box of bait into the boat and launched it. It rode the white-tipped waves with ease, the wind behind helping, even though she was not using a sail. She did not intend to go outside the bay, where though the water was shallow there was a chance of a reasonable catch and, waking up suddenly to the impatient pushing of sea and wind, she cautiously shipped the oars and let the boat ride while she threw the anchor overboard.

For a while she concentrated on the nets, but when the

boat began to corkscrew she decided that common sense was best obeyed and she lifted the anchor and tried to pull herself back to the shore. It was then she felt the stirrings of fear. The boat did not respond. As soon as it was free, it jerked towards the open sea and no matter how she tried to persuade it, she was taken on past the headland and out to where the wind was suddenly wild and threatening.

She was no longer in control but small and defenceless, at the mercy of the mighty strength of an angry sea. She had only the sturdy, carvel-built wooden boat between her and death under the swells that tipped the boat first one way and then another. She could not row, and even attempting to lift the sail to ride with the storm would send it over the side in a moment – and her with it for a certainty.

The tide turning saved her. The wind slightly eased its ferocious game, the centre of the storm passed over her and allowed her to master the oars again. Crying in her despair and helplessness, sobbing her remorse at her stupid prideful disobedience, she struggled to pull herself back to the shore with arms weak and aching with fatigue. Her teeth were pressed over her bottom lip in an effort to hold back the tears flowing down her white face.

Where was Barrass? Why had he let her down? In her predicament she blamed him. Blamed the fancy clothes those at Ddole House had given him, blamed his fleas for deserting him and allowing others to see, as she had always seen, how beautiful he was.

The morning did not really break, the storm clouds overhead held back the dawn, and sea and sky were one purply blackness in which she was the only living thing. She had nothing on which to judge her position, the coast was lost in the haze. Her crying increased in volume and was not even heard by a seagull.

The whole sea was empty, there was only her stupid self in the whole world. Her voice wailed her misery as she allowed the boat to take her where it chose, her arms no longer able to pull on the oars, even if she were able to judge which direction she should take.

She sat there, the uneasy motion of the boat making

128

sickness a possibility, the final humiliation. Dejected and afraid, she waited, saving her strength for the moment when she would sight the shore. Whatever piece of coast she saw, she would not try to guess where it was, but would pull herself in and get off the frighteningly undulating water. She began to bale out the water that had settled at her feet, discarding the fish she had caught and wondering if she would ever dare step into a boat alone again.

Thunder rumbled around her, distant but adding to her fear. The clouds moved, but without a sign of breaking – black, ominous and low enough to almost blanket the sea. Then, there was a thin sliver of brightness on the horizon, and she watched, afraid to blink for fear of it disappearing, dreading that it was her imagination playing tricks. But it grew and showed up the scene. First the sea, which changed colours like the palette of an insane artist, then the cliffs – unfamiliar but surprisingly and thankfully close, white foam dashing against them and rising high.

Rowing in was difficult, as she had to watch for rock hidden in the unknown waters, choppy with the threads of the dying storm. Lightning still flashed to startle her as she stared out across the wildness of the white, boiling surf searching for a place to land.

As she came close under the towering cliffs she saw a small sandy beach and cried with relief as she managed to point the bow towards it and allow the waves to push her in. The tumult seemed to stop with a suddenness that made her think her ears had been affected as she reached the shallow water. The boat glided with unbelievable orderliness onto the beach's gentle slope. She climbed out and pulled as hard as her weakened muscles would allow, trying to get the boat well up on the sand. Then she fell onto the shore a few yards above it and cried herself to sleep.

She was woken by the touch of the waves on her feet and she sat up immediately, to see the boat bobbing in the surf far out where she had no hope of reaching it. In front of her the sea, still showing its fury, and behind her steep, jagged rocks rising to the now blue sky. From the marks on the rocks she saw with horror that the tide would cover the small beach. She had to move, but where was there to go? Above the gusting wind, she shouted,

    '*Barrass!*'

CHAPTER EIGHT

The coast near the village was largely mudflats, with shifting dunes partly covered with marram grass, sea poppies, sea spinach and rock roses. The area from which the boats sailed was shingle, with rocks rolled about by the wild tides, an ever-changing situation. From where the moorage ended, and the beach changed from small pebbles to large rocky formations, the surface beyond the beach changed dramatically from low accessible ground to steep cliffs.

It was some miles away that Olwen spent the night huddled at the lip of a cave, which in its dark interior promised shelter but repulsed her by its secretiveness. She did not sleep, but dozed and woke with fright at the thought that she had read the signs wrong and the tide would swoop into the cave, breaking her against the cruel rocks or dragging her into the relentless rock-bound sea.

Far above her, unseen and unheard, men and women searched through the night, calling her name, crying in their despair. As morning broke in shining splendour as if to compensate for the sullenness of the previous day, she rose, shivering, hungry and afraid. In front of her the water was swollen and frightening in its bulging rise and fall, bloated with the storm. Behind her she could see no way up the cliff.

There was only one thing to do and that was wait, in the certain knowledge that everyone would be searching. All she had to do was wait. Waiting, she decided after only an hour, was the most difficult pastime of all. She began to gather winkles, and thought that if no one found her, she could at least eat them raw. Then she put aside the thought of food, it was making her digestive juices run and remind her of the hours that she had passed since she had eaten. A thin trickle of water seeped through the rocks nearby and she slaked her thirst thankfully. After a while she slept.

Barrass had spent the night running across the cliffs from Thistleboon to the sea, his feet making a close pattern of zig-zag lines in the wet grass. All the time, he called her name, his pleas unheard, the roaring wind snatching it from his mouth whistling its laughter at the weakness of his voice. Thunder growled and lightning flashed and it was as if the whole world was against him finding her.

In the morning he met others and demanded to know where they had been, how diligently they had examined every bush and hollow. Then, wailing in anguish, he went on with his search.

Exhaustion made him rest at Mary's house and take a hot drink, not caring for once that the tea she offered him was from the boats.

'There are plenty on the cliffs, more have come since daybreak. I think I'll go down and look along the dunes and where she set off from.' He could not be still even long enough to finish the tea. 'Perhaps the boat only went out a few yards and was beaten back by the winds. She's so small, her little arms could hardly have made much headway. Oh, why did I forget her?' he groaned.

Mary listened to him, her face frozen with anxiety, her gentle eyes wide and staring, as if Olwen would materialize in front of her if she believed it strongly enough.

'Yes, Barrass, try the beach,' she whispered. Dic began to cry and she sat rocking him, not aware of Barrass's leaving.

Barrass ran down the path from Mary's cottage to the village and on to the end of the small beach. The gale had caught some of the boats and they lay drunkenly leaning, half filled with water, many with their boards split. One had an enormous boulder inside it as if dropped casually in by a giant hand in the rage of the storm. It seemed unlikely, he thought vaguely, that it could ever be removed. Boulders too littered the path along the edge of the water, and he thought he saw a figure lying amongst them and ran with a cry, to find only seaweed-draped rock.

The sea was apparently quiet, the surface not breaking,

but it was rising and falling with ominous strength. The threat was there and he knew that further out, the movement of a small boat would be violent. He looked out to sea and with the good visibility that sometimes comes before or after a storm, saw an emptiness that renewed his fear for Olwen's safety.

Then a sound came on the air that puzzled him and he looked around for the source. Surely it was men singing? He climbed onto the highest dune and shaded his eyes, looking first at the sea, then along the path leading down from the inland track which led to Swansea and Gower. The sound became stronger, the voices raised in thanksgiving, the words of the hymn swelling as the singers turned towards him. They had found her!

He slithered down and ran, shouting her name, towards the group of men he could now see approaching the beach. He had to look down to prevent catching his feet on the storm-strewn rocks, eyes filled with anxious tears so when he looked up he did not recognize them, thought them a band of ruffians, ex-soldiers maybe, bent on mischief, and he paused, disappointed and prepared to run back to the shore. Then his heart somersaulted within him as he saw that the group was the village men released from prison, and sadly he knew that the jubilation was not for the rescue of Olwen.

'Keep back, boy,' Spider shouted, barely recognizable in tattered clothes and a scruffy beard, hair unkempt and flying in the wind like a tattered sail, 'It's *we're* the ones with fleas now!'

'Spider, it's Olwen. She's been missing in the storm all night,' Barrass shouted, and the joyous singing stopped as if cut off by the baton of a fine conductor. But it was not his words that stopped them. They had been unheard. He watched in disbelief as the men stripped off their clothes and threw them in a pile on the sand. With wild shouts that sent a flock of gulls into the air with clacking complaint, they ran through the dunes, the mud and the rocks and dived into the water.

They played like children, washing themselves clear of

the stink and infestations of the prison cell where they had been incarcerated for more than two weeks. Barrass ran to where they shouted and called and splashed but he couldn't make anyone listen. A pair of legs appeared as their owner stood on his hands under the waves – long and skinny, they could only be Dan's. He saw Spider like an amputee crab leap on Pitcher's muscled back and allow himself to be carried out further and tossed over humped shoulders into deeper water in gales of excited laughter.

'Get a tinder and burn them clothes, boy, will you?' Spider shouted. 'We're never wearing them again!' Then seeing the consternation on Barrass's face, he stopped, hushed the others and listened as Barrass shouted,

'It's Olwen! Missing in the storm she is, lost since last night.'

The splashing and foolishness stopped as suddenly as the singing as the men strode out of the water and without bothering about their nakedness, discussed this new tragedy. No one gave a spoken instruction but they formed an orderly group, lined up in threes and trotted through the village, each man breaking off when he came to his home. Starting with fifteen, there were still ten naked and unshaven men running towards them when Emma and her three daughters came out of the alehouse to step into their waggon.

She screamed and fell back in a faint – which she thought the most ladylike way of coping with the terrifying sight. Before she fell, she begged her daughters to cover their eyes. She kept hers tightly closed and so did not see Pitcher run towards her, and it was only when he tried to carry her indoors and failed to lift her that she realized who the men were.

'Pitcher! They've driven you mad! My dear husband has been driven insane! Oh dear, what will I do!' She screamed at her girls to turn away and walk into the house, then, using her woollen tartan cloak to cover what she could of her husband's anatomy, she staggered with him into the house, sobbing and crying in her embarrassment and her relief at his safe return.

Violet paused at the door, but after a brief and undisguised stare at the wild-looking men in their nakedness,
she looked at Barrass. He was dressed in good wool-cloth
trousers in brown tweed and a Welsh flannel shirt with
sleeves rolled up his strong arms. There were leather gaiters
around his calves and she could not look away from him.
He stepped towards her, his eyes holding such longing that
a faint cry escaped her lips before she turned and ran to
join her family.

For a moment Barrass forgot Olwen, then he turned from
the door and ran to catch up with Spider, whose long,
skinny legs were causing laughter and jeering among those
honest enough to stand and watch, and more hesitant
amusement for those who only peered from behind curtains
and shutters.

A young man from the quarry ran down with some reed
pipes and began playing a lively tune to which the naked
men started to dance while continuing on their way, their
legs kicking in the air in bawdy abandon. Children appeared
like magic and began to dance after them, jeering and
laughing. Old women covered their faces with their aprons
but peered brazenly over the edges, their faces red with
uncontrollable laughter.

When the rest had dispersed among the scattered houses,
Spider ran beside Barrass up the hill to where Mary was
waiting. Arthur from the alehouse had seen the men and,
witnessing their march around the houses, found time to
go and warn Mary of Spider's homecoming. She ignored
the laughter that Spider's followers could not hide, and
got on with preparing for her skinny husband's enormous
appetite while telling him all she knew about Olwen's disappearance.

She had bread and cheese set out neatly on the small
table, and clothes airing near the fire, but Spider ignored
both and clung to her, whispering her name, telling her of
his love, and Barrass stood there, wondering how they could
even think of each other when their daughter was missing.
Then guilt made him remember how the thought of Violet
returning to him had made his mind wander from its pur-

pose. His disapproval and his guilt showed in his dark eyes when they released each other and Spider began to dress.

'Tell me, where have you searched?' As he ate and dressed, Spider absorbed the facts, then, with another hug for Mary, set off to look for his daughter.

'But where's Dan?' Mary shouted after them.

'Gone to see Enyd, I think,' Spider shouted back. 'Don't worry, he's perfectly all right.'

'Visiting without any clothes on?' Mary screamed. 'What's the matter with the boy?'

'Love, I think.' The words drifted back on the wind as Spider and Barrass disappeared down the path.

Kenneth heard the commotion and, with Ceinwen and Enyd, stood outside his door on the bank high above the path, from where he had a clear view through the village. At first they did not realize that the men they were watching were without clothes, they thought it was some mad game, bathing in the cold month of October. Young men often challenged each other to such crazy dares. But as they watched, each of them slowly saw that the men were naked, only body hair and unshaved beards covering them. Enyd held her breath and said nothing, curious and hoping her father would not realize before she had had a good look. Ceinwen also ignored the truth. She screwed up her eyes, fascinated to have such an unusual and interesting view of her well-known neighbours. But Kenneth gave a roar of anger and pushed them both inside as soon as his slower eyes appraised the situation. He warned them to stay inside and stood waiting to see what the explanation could be. Then a man broke off from the rest and came his way.

'Dan!' Kenneth said, his voice full of disapproval.

'Can I see Enyd?' Dan asked, his young face smiling as he covered as much as he could of his unacceptable parts with his long, slender hands.

'Damn me, boy! No, you can't! Get away from here and make yourself decent!' Kenneth waved the boy away, then turned round in horror as Dan apparently waved at someone

136

looking out of the window. 'Enyd! Get you away from that window! Have you no shame!'

'Lend me a coat or a blanket then, will you,' Dan insisted. 'I'll clap hands if you say no, mind.'

Agitatedly Kenneth turned round and round, wondering who to shout at next, the boy or his women, then he called for a blanket.

'And shut your eyes when you bring it out!' he added with hysteria in his voice.

Dan wrapped the blanket around him and said, 'Now can I see Enyd?'

'Take one step nearer and I'll report all this to the Keep-er-of-the-Peace,' Kenneth warned. 'Causing a public dis-turbance this is for sure.'

Dan shrugged and walked away, with a pretence at waving to someone at the window, which made Kenneth turn around again in rage.

At the bottom of the track leading to Kenneth's house, where there was a seat on which the elders of the village sat and smoked their clay pipes on warm summer after-noons, Caleb, a cottager, waited for him. He sprawled relaxed and unconcerned about his nakedness as if enjoying the sun. That his skin was blue with the cold he seemed not to notice. He stood up as Dan came towards him.

'You got one then,' he said, gesturing towards the blanket.

'Told you he wouldn't refuse,' Dan laughed. 'I'd rather frighten him than my mam! Come on, let's get home and then we can go and find that sister of mine. Sheltered somewhere along the coast she has for sure.' And sharing the blanket between them they walked home.

The search for Olwen continued all through that day and when darkness began to close in and threaten them with another night of anxiety, Barrass discussed the coastline with Dan and Spider.

'It would have been westwards she'd have gone from what I've understood of the freak storm, if she had been outside the bay,' Spider said. 'There's stretches of coast without any beach to speak of and she's probably sheltering against the rocks somewhere.'

'Without shelter and food, she'll be in a sorry state if she isn't found tonight,' Dan whispered. His mother was standing at the door, holding Dic and staring at where the track led up from the village, wanting to see as far as she could for the earliest glimpse of her lost daughter.

'I'll go along the cliff path and call,' Dan said, for his mother to hear. 'Got a loud voice I have, she'll hear me for sure.'

'I'll go across to the next bay and search from there,' Spider said.

But Barrass knew he had already covered that area and he decided to run for as long as the light held, then continue on, working his way along the distant shores where they had not yet searched beyond the bay of Caswell. The wind had been stronger than the men in prison would have realized, although they had seen the boulders and stones brought in by the sea and could guess at its ferocity. Most winds came from the west, this one had been easterly.

With food in their pockets for when they found her, the three men set off.

During the hours of daylight Olwen had entered the cave, just as far as the light travelled, leaving the darkness deep under the cliff unexplored. She found a few rags, and remnants of a fire suggesting that someone had sheltered here before. There were tapers too, and she wished she had some means of lighting them. Light would have been almost as comforting as a fire. There were empty boxes too, some broken, but with nothing to hint at their previous contents. She sat on one of them, wrapped the old tattered clothes about her and waited for the sound of someone calling her name. She did not stay in the cave long, but wandered outside, seeing the sea rising once again towards afternoon, and saw in its dark surface the remnants of her father's boat.

'If I live, he'll kill me,' she sobbed aloud.

With her father in prison and no boat to catch fish, how

would she and her mother and baby Dic manage? Winter was fast approaching and it was frightening how quickly the store vessels of flour and oatmeal and all the other essentials were emptied. The thought that her mother would not even have her, Olwen, to help was a thought that froze her blood.

As darkness fell she sat outside the cave, glancing out to sea in the hope of seeing a boat searching for her. She held the ragged clothes she had found in the cave to wave, should anyone come close enough to see her. All day there had not been a sign of a vessel of any kind.

The wind was wailing slightly around the rocky cliffs, and she began to imagine the sound of a voice in its song. Then, her heart racing, she realised that it was not imagination. It was her name, and the voice calling her was Barrass's. He had found her.

'Barrass! I'm here!'

Using the rope he carried, Barrass lowered himself down to join her and held her close in his arms while she cried in relief. She was such a tiny little thing and he had feared he would never see her again. He was overwhelmed by a powerful feeling of protective love, his arms tightened around her and it was a long time before they moved.

When she began to climb the rocks, using specially good hand and foot holds to rest periodically, Barrass was behind her, determined she would not fall, and when they reached the top, he asked her why she still carried the bundle of rags.

'I don't know,' she said, shivering with the cold night wind. 'I suppose they saved me from being frozen and too stiff to leave the cave. They were to be a flag if I saw one of the boats looking for me.'

'You don't need them any longer, I'm here and from now on I always will be. I let you down yesterday or you'd never have set out in such dangerous weather. But I won't, ever again.' He picked her up and carried her back in the dark along the tracks, her arms around his neck, her head tucked into his neck. Olwen was so happy she cried all over again.

Olwen's family were in trouble – with no boat they had no

139

livelihood. For several days Dan and Spider tried to fish in the river, but eels were their only catch. And fishing from the shore with borrowed lines was no more successful.

In the front garden of Mrs Powell's house at the top of the row of cottages rising up from the beach, there was an old boat. The gunnels were rotted away, there were no oars, several of the planks were splintered, and the outside was badly in need of caulking and repainting, but Barrass knocked on the door one day and asked if he could buy it.

'I haven't much money,' he admitted, as the keen dark eyes of the frail old woman looked from him to the boat, assessing her chances. For years it had only provided shelter to a wild cat, snails and several dozen spiders. She doubted if it were still usable, but if it meant a little money, she was not going to say so.

'How much?' she asked.

'Seven and sixpence,' he said boldly.

'It's worth more than that!' Mrs Powell said, sounding more hopeful than she felt.

Barrass shook his head and stepped a few paces away from her door, his head bowed in disappointment.

'Can't manage more,' he said, 'and even that will have to be sixpence a week.'

As his footsteps removed him further from her door, slowly taking away the chance of a few shillings, she called him back as he hoped she would.

'All right then. Seven and sixpence, and you'll have to buy yourself some oars as I used them for firewood last winter. And the sails will be in a right mess. Eaten by mice for sure.'

Barrass smiled, his face lighting up and making the old woman smile with him.

'Thank you, Mrs Powell, I'll be back with Spider, Dan and Arthur in less than an hour.' He handed her a pile of coins. 'There's the first one shilling and sixpence, my life savings that is.'

'Never better spent,' Mrs Powell assured him, and hurriedly closed the door for fear that someone would see the transaction and plan to rob her.

It took a few days before the boat was ready to put on the water, but when they did float her she at once gave them the feeling of being a reliable craft. She rode the waves easily, with no hint of unevenness in the way she moved. There was a firmness about her that promised many years of safe sailing. With oars borrowed and the seats still without paint, Barrass was taken on a maiden voyage of the boat they called *Olwen*. After a few more days of work, Spider and Dan were taking their place at the market, insisting that theirs was the freshest fish anyone could find.

Spider promised to repay Barrass, but he refused.

'I owe you that for the way I let her down that morning,' he said. 'I'd never have let her set off, and she only did it because she was angry with me for not coming as I promised. No, the fault was mine and I'd be happier if you'll let me pay for it.'

'She's very fond of you, isn't she?' Spider said hesitantly. 'I think too fond, her being so young and you ready to be off with girls and almost a man. Not that I mind, nor do I think you'd ever harm her,' he added, seeing the boy begin to protest. 'But I think it might be an idea if we found her some work, something further away from the beach, then she wouldn't have time to go off on mad fishing trips to repay you for kissing someone else.' He smiled and to his relief saw the smile reflected on the boy's handsome face. 'She's young, and I don't want her hurt, so us sending her away would be a kindness and she wouldn't blame you.'

'I'll miss her,' Barrass surprised himself by saying. 'I think of her like a sister, someone to look out for, and protect.'

'You can still do that, we aren't sending her far, only to work at the Ddoles' house. Dorothy Ddole is ill, although she will not admit it, and her daughter needs extra help.'

Barrass's heart leapt guiltily as he thought at once that he would have an excuse to call and perhaps see Penelope.

'I'll go and see Olwen when I can,' he said, hoping Spider had not seen the sudden emotion that flooded his face. 'As often as I can. You can tell her that.'

'Not too often, boy,' Spider warned. 'Not to feed her

141

idea that she's your protector and give her the wrong impression, like.'

Barrass nodded but felt an inexplicable disappointment.

Barrass was kept busy that evening, as all those who had been freed from the prison gathered in the alehouse to celebrate their good fortune. Caleb, who rarely left his small primitive cottage at the edge of a small woodland, surprised everyone by his joviality. He was a small, dark man; even the greying of his hair and moustaches did not lighten his features, but more emphasized them, so he looked as if he were wearing someone else's hair. He got up several times, and lubricated by the fast flowing drink, sang them songs of ancient battles and saucy loves.

Everyone was in party mood and Pitcher, the host, was generous with his drinks, refusing payment often, and supplying food without a thought to charge. Emma, upstairs reading one of her favourite novels, while her daughters were entertaining Enyd with accounts of their recent partying, was content to allow the extravagance, knowing how easily she could have lost him for ever.

Barrass noted that although Dan was there, enjoying the evening with the rest, Spider had not put in an appearance. He knew, with a trace of envy, that Spider would not want to leave Mary and Dic and Olwen, whom he had expected never to see again after the two near disasters of imprisonment and shipwreck. Barrass wished he too was a part of such a loving circle.

He was puzzled by the men's attitude towards himself. None of them had come and thanked him for the part he had played in their reprieve. The story of how he, Arthur and Olwen had risked death to gather in the tubs and throw suspicion on others was well known, yet none had come to congratulate him on the way they had executed the daring action.

He was observed with uneasy glances as he went in and out of the tables and benches gathering mugs and jugs to be washed and exchanged or refilling them on Pitcher's instructions. Talk, so lively and excited, slowed as he approached, and heads were lowered as if in secrecy. He had proved his loyalty to the villagers even to the point of defying the law, *and* the smugglers who would not have understood his reasons for robbing them.

At ten o'clock Emma came down into the bar, a place she tried to avoid, preferring to ignore the way they earned their bread and pretending some other, more genteel existence.

'Mr Palmer,' she called in her softest voice, 'a word if you please.'

Pitcher ran to her, pushing his way through the merry crowd, knowing she would not be best pleased if he were to keep her waiting there among what she called the carousers. 'What is it, my dear one?' he whispered close to her ear.

'Enyd wishes to leave and I would like Arthur to walk with her if you please, Pitcher, my dearest love,' she whispered back, her eyes glowing as if the words were the sweetest love song.

'I will 'tend to it at once, my precious.'

But it was Dan, seeing what was happening a few minutes later, who walked her home.

They did not go straight to the house on the bank, but, tempted by a surprisingly beautiful moon, walked towards the lonely beach, where the shadows of the boats loomed large and distorted by shadows. They sat for a while, leaning against the bulk of one, holding hands, saying very little, each thankful that the separation was over.

Dan bent to kiss her but she turned away.

'Oh, Enyd, why do you pretend you do not care?'

'It is not that I don't care, you know full well that I do,' she said and although he could not see her clearly, he could well imagine how her lips were already tightening and thinning to that hard line that was often accompanied by a frown.

'Then why do you not say you love me?'

'Because you do not show that you love *me*.'

'How can I show you, when on most days you will not even let me kiss you?'

'I have a desire to kiss you now,' she said softly and turned towards him. His long arms wrapped them together and she opened her lips with a kiss as soft and giving as he had ever experienced.

'Enyd, will you be my wife? I can't be happy without you, say it is the same for you?'

She pulled away from him and stood up, staring out over the sea, where the moon spread a golden path, an invitation to step onto it and journey to imaginary lands. He stood beside her, his arm on her shoulder.

'Why do people talk of a silver light from the moon?' she whispered. 'Here it is pure gold.'

'Like my love for you,' he replied.

'So strong is it?'

'Stronger than the wildest wind.'

'So much so that as soon as you were freed from that awful prison, you ran first to me?'

He chuckled. 'Without first getting dressed!'

'No, Dan, you ran first to your true love, the sea.' She once more pulled away from him. 'You couldn't wait to worship in its waters. The sea is your first and only love, I come a poor second to its witchery.'

Dan dropped his shoulders; she was doing it again. Every time they began to get close, she shied away like a fey horse. Something was preventing her accepting his love and he was more and more certain that it was not the sea.

They stood silently staring out over the hushed sea, the breeze hardly moving Enyd's long hair. The night was perfect with the moon's golden path a magical sight but ignored by the unhappy lovers. Filled with ineffable sadness, the beauty adding to his melancholy, he touched the top of her head gently, and led her home.

Emma was so happy to have Pitcher safely home that she did not argue when he asked her if Barrass could stay.

'He works well and there's no worry about Violet now that she and Edwin are getting on so well, is there?' he said.

'You're right, Pitcher, my dear husband,' Emma said. They were sitting on the big armchair near the fire; the

144

three girls were at a musical evening given by one of Emma's friends on the outskirts of Swansea, and they were enjoying a rare few hours alone. It was Sunday and the alehouse was silent and empty.

Emma's weight on Pitcher's legs was threatening to incapacitate him for hours but he could not ask her to move. Her plumpness was a joy to him, and the occasional discomforts well compensated by her generous loving. At forty she was still like a young girl in the way that she welcomed his attentions and he thanked God every time he went to church for giving him such a blessing.

For Emma, life was perfect. With Pitcher home and unharmed she was in the mood to agree with anything he suggested. Violet had been meeting Edwin frequently, accompanied by her two sisters and her mother of course, but there was a growing affection between them, of that Emma was certain, so what harm was there in allowing Barrass to share their roof? After all, the preacher was always reminding them about the blessing of helping others.

In the cellar below them, Barrass was holding on to Arthur's legs while the boy cleaned the bottom of a cask. When they had done they sat in the light of two tallow candles, and drank the ale and ate the bread and cold meat that Emma had provided for them. When Arthur, tired out and ready for sleep, settled under his covers, Barrass lifted the cellar door and looked out.

The alehouse was in darkness, but lights crossed the windows, showed the heavy dark furniture in the bar in flashes of yellow, as the waggon drew up outside.

'I'll go up and see if they need any help with the horse,' he said, but there was no reply. Arthur was already asleep.

He hesitated as the girls stepped down from the waggon assisted by Pitcher, who had gone to fetch them home. Then as Violet passed him, she touched his hand. So light was the touch he wondered if he had imagined it, or whether it had been accidental.

'Can I help with the horse?' he asked Pitcher as the three girls disappeared into the house.

'Thanks,' Pitcher said, and together they unharnessed

145

the animal and rubbed him down before giving him his meal. Then, with a nod of thanks, Pitcher dismissed him and Barrass walked towards the door. Then he stopped.

'I think I'll have a bit of a walk before I go to sleep,' he said, and the older man nodded again, went in and closed the door.

Barrass stood in the yard, his senses heightened with anticipation. Had Violet meant anything by that touch? Again he could not decide whether it had been intended. She had not spoken to him for weeks – content, apparently, with the attentions of Edwin. Had she changed her mind, and grown to want him again as he wanted her? He knew that once loving was a part of your existence, it was difficult to live without it. Was it the same for a woman?

There were no seaweed-filled sacks to sit on now, he had thrown them away when he had begun to sleep once again in the cellar. But there were always clean sacks around that had contained the barley grain for malting, and he collected several and made a place where he could sit in reasonable comfort.

The moon had waned to a half, shedding a thin, translucent light over the yard and silvering the edges of the buildings, so they appeared as insubstantial as gossamer. It touched her clothes as she stepped silently out of the door and gave the illusion of ethereal beauty as her face was illuminated. There was no place more lovely for them both that night than the yard behind the alehouse. The breeze wafted the scents of the sea towards them and overcame even the strong smell of brewing. The builder's rubbish that was spread around them lost its shape and became as beautiful in the gentle moonglow as banks of flowers in some heady woodland.

She floated towards him as if he were dreaming, and fell into his arms with a sigh.

'I've missed you so much,' he groaned as his hands began exploring her perfectly formed body.

'And I you. I thought I could forget you, but seeing you again is like a constant ache being eased.'

146

'Although I have so little, my life lacks nothing now you are back with me,' he sighed.

Throwing off the blanket that covered her, she allowed him to ease away her nightgown and, shivering deliciously in the cold night air, she snuggled against him, pressing herself close, guilding his hands to her warmth, each aglow with the joy of fulfillment.

Edwin stood at the window of his room, shivering a little as the wind found a way through and touched him with a cold draught. Behind him, his two dogs were lying in front of a log fire, their heads on the fender of brass. The desk was littered with plans of the building he had designed.

The men outside were working on the footings of the extension to the house and soon he would have to move out, temporarily, while they broke through and joined the new to the old. Further off, the piggeries were almost completed – and below them the secret room that he hoped would add a margin of safety to his other activities.

Enlarging the house was part of his preparations for his proposal to Violet Palmer. He had known, even before seeing the surprise and disappointment on Emma Palmer's face, that no woman of any standing would consider allowing her daughter to live in the house as it stood. There was nowhere to entertain, nowhere even to eat with any pretence of comfort. And the bedroom, propped up above one half of the room like a mantelpiece designed by a nincompoop, as he often referred to it, would hardly be a suitable place for a wife to sleep, with servants coming and going between the outbuildings and the house to attend to fires and the like. No, he could not dream of marrying until the sprawling new addition had risen up, tall and grand, behind the old single-storey long-house.

It grew dark early and he waved to the men as they stopped work, gathered their tools and set off home. They had been working since before daylight and apart from a brief rest to consume their food, had worked steadily and well. He promised himself that he would pay them extra should they finish the work ahead of schedule.

CHAPTER NINE

Violet watched Edwin as he sipped the tea her mother had poured for him, and felt the same stirrings of excitement that she always felt on seeing him. It was now late October and he had become a regular visitor. She glanced at her mother, whose enjoyment of the genteel scene was clear to see.

Violet wore a new dress of red wool, its full skirt half hidden by the wrap-around overskirt in the same colour but in softer material, gathered to fullness on her slim hips. Her waist was small and held in even further than was natural by a band of stiffened material. Down the front, where the overskirt divided, there was embroidery of trailing honeysuckle, which Emma had stitched specially for today. Violet knew that, for once, she looked at least as attractive as her sisters. That knowledge, and the interest and admiration in Edwin's brilliant, intelligent eyes made her glow.

She held out a hand, in the lacy gloves her mother had insisted she wore, and as she took his empty cup his fingers enveloped hers for a brief moment. She bent her head shyly, knowing that her responsive elation was plain for him to see.

Her sisters talked about the party they were to attend, and shared with Edwin their enthusiasm. He responded by promising that as soon as he had finished the rebuilding at his house, they would be invited to a party as large as any they had yet imagined. But all the time he was talking, Violet had the conviction that his replies were automatic, formal, polite, and that his thoughts were on her.

Emma, who had powdered her face and added colour to her cheeks in honour of his visit, sat, red and moist with the heat of the room and the feverish exhilaration of seeing this personable young man coming to court her eldest daughter. She seemed unaware of the gentility of the afternoon tea party being encroached upon by the sounds from below. All she could see was the trio of her pretty daughters, talking and enjoying the company of a darkly handsome young man with wit and mannerly behaviour. She was so proud she almost burst into tears on several occasions.

The sounds from below, she gradually realized, were being overwhelmed by a beautiful singing voice. Edwin too heard the voice raised in perfection to a note high above the usual barroom singer's ability. Violet stood and opened the door to allow the sound to swell around them, and while the song lasted, none spoke.

'Who is it?' Emma asked. 'I've never heard such a voice, not in church nor anywhere.'

'I do believe it's Dan, Spider's son, Mamma,' Pansy said. She looked away from her mother's inquiring stare. Really her mother was irritating, you couldn't mention a man without her wanting to know at once if he were a possible husband! 'I've heard him coming in with the boats once or twice.'

Below them, the applause had finished and the voice began a haunting love song. Although they could not hear the words, Emma and her daughters were all affected by its sadness. As applause rang out and jugs and mugs were banged on the tables in approval and voices shouted for more, Pitcher's voice could be heard shouting, 'Order!'

Emma smiled as she wiped away a tear. Trust Pitcher to make sure they ordered between one song and the next. He knew the value of entertainment to bring in extra customers, but did not want the audience to forget the ale that they had come to sup!

'What a find!' Edwin said. 'I will remember him when I plan the house opening party near Christmas time.'

'So soon?' Emma smiled. 'How exciting to have a house enlarged by more than twice and in such a short time. Pitcher is so busy with the alehouse he has less time than he would wish to get on with our new drawing room. But when it *is* done, it will be a place to be proud of. Velvet drapes are ordered, Mr Prince, green velvet drapes! And a set of chairs and a couch of the finest quality and in that same elegant colour.'

'I see I must come to you when I need advice on furnishing with good taste,' Edwin replied.

'Me or my eldest daughter,' Emma replied with a fond look at Violet. 'So clever with colours she is, you'd be amazed at her many skills and abilities.'

Violet guessed that her mother was about to go into a long list of her accomplishments, and to discourage her, she begged them all to listen again to the voice beginning a third song.

A successful afternoon all round, Emma decided, and the evening promised a full room, if Pitcher could persuade young Dan to return for a few more songs. She sighed her satisfaction as Edwin rose to leave. Then he said the words that above all others could make the day a perfect one.

'Mistress Palmer, do you think I might have a word with your husband before I leave? I have something I wish to ask him.' Edwin's eyes were not on Emma, but on the blushing face of her eldest daughter, and Emma had to hold onto the fire screen for fear that she would faint right away.

'Go and ask your master if he can spare a moment or two for Mr Edwin Prince,' she said breathlessly when the servant answered the ringing of the handbell. She ushered the giggling Daisy and Pansy out of the room and, with a look of ecstasy on her plump face, nodded to Edwin and followed the twins, leaving Violet and Edwin alone for a few precious moments. She carefully left the door open and coughed to remind them she would not be far away.

Edwin stepped closer to Violet and offered her a hand to rise. In a moment they were in each other's arms and when their lips touched, Violet was embarrassed to realize that her urgency was hardly met by his. She felt him stiffen in surprise as she softened into the kiss, where he was obviously expecting a light touch, a cautious welcome to his arms, and nothing more than a formality.

She stepped away from him embarrassed and ashamed. She had shown her experience and now perhaps Edwin would reconsider his intention to propose marriage. He would not lack knowledge of other women, of that she felt sure, but a man never expected the same experience in the woman he chose for a wife.

When she looked up at him, he was staring at her in that attractive way that made her feel she was the absolute centre of his attention.

'I have the feeling, Violet, my dear, that I shall enjoy getting to know you when you are my wife.'

She smiled tremulously, wondering if he had truly believed that her forthrightness when he took her in his arms was from an overwhelming love and not from previous loving. She was relieved when Pitcher ran up the wooden staircase and entered the room, followed by last-minute hoarsely whispered instructions from Emma.

'If you will excuse us, Violet,' her father said. 'I think Edwin wishes to talk in private.'

'Of course.' Still smarting with her lack of guile when Edwin had taken her for the first time into his arms, she went slowly to where Emma stood at the doorway of the small dining room.

'Did he say anything, daughter?' Emma asked.

'I think we'll wait until he has spoken to Dadda,' Violet replied, and she ran down into the cold darkness of the untidy yard to cool her hot cheeks.

When Edwin left the alehouse he was smiling. Pitcher had agreed to the marriage, and from the way Violet had responded in his arms, he had made an excellent choice.

He was still smiling as he stood at the window looking out at the progress of building work on his house. The day was almost gone and the servant had not yet arrived to light the lamps, and he dreamed of what the future held: a wife to grace his table, bring excitement to his bed and give him what he sorely lacked – company and laughter to liven the old house. With his thoughts drifting pleasurably, he barely reacted when a movement caught his eye. But the way the figure moved brought him back to the present hastily.

Someone had passed cautiously across the ground in

front of the window and was heading down towards the almost completed piggeries, crouched, obviously not wanting to be seen. Locking the dogs inside, Edwin slipped silently out and followed.

Kenneth moved with slow caution down the yard, away from the house. Having watched from the shelter of the orchard and seen no sign of life in the unlit house, he considered it unlikely that anyone would see him, but still moved with infinite care – the movement that had roused Edwin's curiosity and suspicion and had prevented him from calling out. Kenneth had no real thought of anyone following and did not look back even when he reached the brick-built pigsties, climbed over the wall and went inside.

He stamped over the floor, peering around in the fading light, touching the walls and even kneeling down and feeling all over the floors. When the shadow fell in front of him, he had no time to gasp before a blow to the head knocked him sick and senseless to the floor.

When Edwin realized who he had beaten about the head, he was alarmed. He had suspected the prowler of snooping to see what had been added to the piggery that was not intended for porcine comfort. But to find it was Kenneth, the letter-carrier of Gower, was a shock.

He did not know what to do as the small man slumped across his feet. He stared out into the black evening, half inclined to return to his fire, pull his curtains and forget what had happened, then deny any knowledge of the affair when it came to light.

That he could not do. He had no idea how seriously he had hurt the letter-carrier, and he could hardly allow him to lie there to die of cold. He examined the prostrate victim and, reassured by his groans, decided that it was safe to move him far from his door.

Taking some rope, he tied Kenneth's hands and feet, placed a kerchief across his mouth, and wrapped him in a thick coat. Gathering blankets from the house, he carried him to the stables and bundled him across the back of a horse. Hidden by the deep velvet night, the horse hardly making a sound on the soft hillside grasses, Edwin reached the quarry behind the alehouse without being seen, and set down his victim against the rocks. He stopped to look down at the alehouse building silhouetted against the lighter sea and imagined Violet asleep and dreaming the dreams of the innocent. An innocence he would have the pleasure of ending.

Through the night he visited Kenneth several times, and found him sleeping contentedly. As dawn began to break, he carefully untied the cloth about the man's face and loosened the ropes. Content that someone would find him before long, he went home to sleep and dream of Violet Palmer.

Men searched for Kenneth at Ceinwen's instigation, when late evening came without his return, all along his route.

Spider went with Dan, and joined others gathered for yet another night-search. The news was spread, children as well as adults arrived, and the searchers quickly swelled into a crowd. Some carried lanterns, all held sticks.

Daniels, the Keeper-of-the-Peace, had been called, and he appeared as neatly turned out as if it had been the middle of a calm day. He began to organize the villagers into groups, giving each an area to search. Spider and Dan came back from following yet another false hope just as Daniels was directing the last groups towards Thistleboon and Newton. The pair set off again, but Dan looked back in time to see the door of Betson's cottage open slowly and the tall figure of the Keeper-of-the-Peace slipping inside.

'Suppose that's as good a place to search for Kenneth as any,' he said, and Spider grinned knowingly. Kenneth would have been surprised at the remark. He believed his visits were known only to himself and Betson-the-Flowers!

No one thought to go as far from Kenneth's route as the quarry. He woke from a drowsy dream once and thought he heard people calling, but, wrapped in the warmth of the blankets, and with a headache making it difficult to open his eyes, he did not fully wake to his predicament. He felt for Ceinwen's form behind him, imagining the softness of her limbs in what was a large piece of limestone padded with folds of Edwin's blankets. His hand, expecting Ceinwen's warm Welsh flannel nightgown, was satisfied, and he dozed peacefully back into a deep contented sleep.

Unaware of the events after Edwin had left her, Violet sat looking out into the night, unable to sleep. Her thoughts went from Edwin and that disconcerting first kiss, to the warm lips of Barrass, whose firm young body was a strong temptation. She knew what she felt for Barrass was lust, the most wicked of the body's weaknesses if the vicar were to be believed. She did not even consider him as a man whose life one day she might share. For her, Edwin was the man to fulfil that role, and she knew that once she and Edwin were married, all thoughts of Barrass and his eager loving would fade.

But knowing Barrass was in the same building, and probably also awake, she was not able to resist slipping on a woollen housecoat and going downstairs.

Her heart was beating high in her throat, and so loud she feared waking the household. But she went on, into the barroom and on beyond it to where the cellar door was slightly raised. She hesitated for a moment, guilt almost overcoming her need, then called his name. It was hardly more than a whisper. Almost immediately his head appeared, a moment longer and he stood before her, his arms enveloping her.

Desire flooded through her and she wondered how she could ever again live without a man's lusty affection. And as he guided her through the muddle of the outside yard to their usual place under the archway, his hands already beginning to caress her, she knew that she could not. An awakening to the sharing of such pleasure meant it was impossible to go back to a life of chastity.

Somehow, even if Edwin abandoned her, she would have to have the companionship of Barrass or someone equally skilled in the art of love. Later she felt shame at the admission, likening herself to those unfortunate men and women who, once they had tasted drink, could not stop taking it to excess. But by the time they had traversed the yard and found their place, such thoughts had drifted away into the cold night, and she had no mind for anything but the next few minutes.

The sacks of seaweed and heather were as they had last left them. Barrass had been repeatedly told to throw them away but even when he had thought her gone from his life for ever, he could not. While they were there, he could nurture the hope of Violet returning to him.

They began to whisper of their love and their need of each other and Barrass's strong hands explored her shivering body. Her hands reached down to touch his hips, to savour his nearness, to slide over his skin, to caress him. Then, as desire reached the point at which neither could resist a moment longer, a light showed in the house and Violet gave a gasp of alarm. Barrass saw it too, and from the position of it, knew that someone was coming down the stairs.

Yet he could not let her go. He forced her down again, soothed her frightened cries and, stroking and murmuring, persuaded her to relax and accept him. It was quicker than any of their many times together. But it was also the most exciting, with the light gradually coming nearer, and both suspecting that Violet's bed had been found empty. They were both heady with more than the typical after-effects of loving, and clung to each other as, astonishingly, Barrass began to feel desire again filling him.

'No, Barrass,' she gasped. 'I must get back to my room.'

The lamp was now near the back door, and they heard Pitcher complaining about the door being left open. Arthur was obviously with him.

'Where's Barrass?' they heard Pitcher say. 'He should come as well.' Then Arthur tripped over something and shouted. His dog barked hysterically.

'Hush, boy! We don't want to wake Emma and the girls!' Pitcher complained.

'Quick, it's all right,' Barrass whispered, and taking

155

Violet's arm he led her around the house to where the new doorway was propped up with large stones.

To his alarm, Arthur's dog had scented them and jumped over the half-hidden obstacles towards them with delight. Barrass hastily kicked it away, but the dog thought it a part of some new game and jumped up to show his pleasure. Barrass opened the door far enough for Violet to slip inside, then, holding her back, with the sound of Pitcher's feet dangerously close, he held her tight, ran his hands around her responsive body and kissed her.

The kiss was no hurried affair, despite the risks. He moved his soft lips over hers in a way that had both of them torn between fear and rising passion. They were both oblivious to the dog, who scratched at Barrass's leg, wanting to be included in whatever was going on. It suffered a further kick and sat with its head on one side in comical offence.

As well as wanting her, love and desire like a flame burning him away, there was the added sensation of a laugh tickling his throat as he finally released her. The occasion was unique in its excitement and daring. He waited as she glided away from him and heard her low husky laugh.

Breathlessly, he called out to her father and announced that he had been down on the beach for a walk as he had been unable to sleep, hoping his breathlessness would not be taken as evidence of a different kind of exercise. Pitcher hastily explained about Kenneth being missing, and Barrass reluctantly set off to assist in the search.

Wearily, when all he wanted was his bed, he helped Arthur and Pitcher to scrabble among the undergrowth and bushes, and along the green lanes. The dog, who seemed to share a secret with Barrass, and attached himself to him instead of his master, kept excitedly dragging him away along unseen trails, but each time it was only the nocturnal wanderings of a small mammal that interested him, and there was no sight nor sound of Kenneth.

Kenneth woke that Friday morning to the sound of bird-song. The ticker-tick-ticking of a robin about to begin searching for his breakfast, the gentle cooing of a wood pigeon from a tree nearby and the kew-kew-kew as a woodpecker dipped across the sky. The sea was a distant murmur.

It was only slowly that he began to wonder why he was in the misty quarry surrounded by damp, moss-dressed stones. He was warm and quite comfortable apart from a drip tickling the end of his nose, and it seemed unimportant to try and work it all out, but gradually he remembered, starting with the blow on his head in the newly built pigsty, and working back.

It was a Thursday, and he had visited Betson-the-Flowers, taking with him a dozen eggs, each one carefully wrapped in the page of an old book, and placed in his leather pouch, a few leeks and a fowl. She had been welcoming and their few short hours together had been pleasant.

It was only as they dressed in front of the large fire on which sweet cherry-wood burned, that his visit was ruined by mention of another of her callers.

'Kenneth, my dear, can I beg a favour?' Betson had smiled.

'Ask of me what you will. If it is possible then I shall willingly do it,' he replied, patting her bottom as it slid into her checked flannel underskirt.

'Will you take this note and leave it for Ieuan-Bricks-and-Mortar?'

'I'll have to take it back to be stamped. But I'll pay the half-penny charge,' he promised.

'No, Kenneth, my dear, it's – private, like. Will you take it now, in the dark? I want you to put it in the new pigsty that Edwin Prince is having built. It's where he's working, see.'

Kenneth looked at her darkly. He knew that he was not Betson's only visitor, but he hated being reminded of the others.

'What's it about, tell me that and I'll take it.' Making an excuse, he pretended a different reason for his hesitation. 'I'm the letter-carrier for the whole of Gower and you

157

know I have to be careful to remain blameless of anything underhand.'

'It's an arrangement. Ieuan-Bricks-and-Mortar has promised to call and – er fix the walls up a bit. I want to tell him when it's best for him to come, that's all.'

'All right then.' He held out his hand for the letter, which was sealed down with sealing wax indented with a pattern edged by black soot where she had heated the seal on the fire. He decided that he *would* deliver it, but he would hide it in some place where the recipient would never see it.

He went to the house of Edwin, and felt his way down the path to the sties. Then, as he was searching for a place to hide the letter where Ieuan-Bricks-and-Mortar would be unlikely ever to find it, the world went black and he remembered no more – except a vague memory of being thrown across a horse – before waking up, warm, cosy and confused, in the quarry.

It was Henry Harris, secretary to William Ddole, who found him. Henry wore a bag across his shoulders in which he had a number of accounts together with the money to pay them. He was on his way from the printers who had supplied the invitations for Dorothy Ddole's party when he decided to take a short cut through the quarry to the alehouse.

He heard Kenneth's cries and, finding him cosy and only slightly harmed, unfastened the ropes that loosely held him, told him to stay where he was, and ran down to fetch Pitcher and Barrass.

Pitcher's first question was, 'What happened?'

'Beaten by robbers after the letters and the money in my bag,' Kenneth lied. 'Beat them off I did, mind, and they called for more of their friends and when there were as many as ten, I succumbed and they tied me and carried me here.'

Barrass's first question was, 'Kenneth, can I go to Swansea for you and carry back the letters?'

On Saturday morning, Olwen rose early. The day was cold,

158

with a wind blustering against the windows and rattling the door, threatening to lift the house and blow it and its contents away. She shivered as she washed in the wooden half-cask of icy water and rubbed herself dry before dressing. She put on new socks, a luxury that heralded the start of winter, and put some paper into the thick boots she had inherited from Dan. Two underdresses, of flannel and cotton, a thick skirt and woollen jumper, covered with an over-large shawl fastened by a simple brooch, and she was ready.

She had no way of knowing the time; like most houses, theirs depended on the chiming of the church clock to tell the passing of the hours, but up here, high above the village, with the sea dashing on the rocks in a roar of powerful ferocity, the clock could not be heard. The wind, as she opened the door and struggled to close it behind her, took the breath from her and she bent and huddled deeper into the shawl. Cold it might be, but she was not going to miss seeing Barrass off on his first journey to collect the post from Swansea.

The tide was almost full, and the smell of seaweed, disturbed and thrown ashore by the wild waves, was fresh and clean. The light was barely sufficient for her to pick out the path to the village, and gusts of wind threatened to knock her from her feet. She pulled the shawl even tighter, convinced that the edges would act like the wings of a bird and float her over the cliff-edge. She was thankful when the path took her slightly inland to drop down behind the houses leading up from the shore called Fisher Cottages, where Ivor and Winifred Baker lived.

Several houses in the row showed lights as men prepared themselves for a day's work. From the sound of the sea, angrily slashing at the shore like a furious parent berating a difficult child, she thought few of the boats would leave the bay that day.

The alehouse was in darkness and her heart sank. Surely she had not missed him? She ran to where chairs and benches were stacked up, pushing her way among them to reach the shelter of the porch over which hung the sign of a pitcher, now creaking in complaint. Shivering, she wondered how long she could wait before giving up hope of seeing Barrass. Then the clock began to rumble preparing to mark the hour, and she crossed her fingers in the sign of the holy cross, offering up a prayer as she counted the chimes. Five. She was not too late, Barrass would set off to the town before six. Then she wondered if Kenneth had refused to hire the horse needed for the twelve-mile journey, forcing Barrass to leave even earlier. Oh dear, why hadn't she asked him?

The cold was biting into her thin body and she was unable to stop shivering. She had no idea how long she had been standing there – if the clock had struck she had not been aware of it. Often she missed its chimes, so much a part of her life, even when she listened for it. She was about to give up and return to her bed, the prospect becoming more and more enticing, when the door opened and Barrass stepped out.

'Olwen!' he said in surprise, 'what are you doing here in such weather?'

'Waiting for you, Barrass. I wanted to wish you luck on the first day of your important new role.' She patted the red waistcoat he wore, which although too small, seemed to make him larger and older and far far beyond her. 'Oh, Barrass,' she sighed, 'there's smart and clever and grown up you are. Will I ever catch up with you?'

'Catch up with me?' he laughed. 'Far ahead of me you are, with a family, a home and a good job waiting for you at Ddole House.'

'I wish I were older, that's all. Then you'd treat me like you treat those others.'

He was embarrassed, so recently come from Violet Palmer, with the sweet scent of her still surrounding him. He was afraid that she might understand most of what happened between him and 'those others'.

'Go home, there's a good girl, you'll be frozen and stuck to the porch if you don't move soon. Thank you for coming

160

to wish me luck,' he added kindly, kissing her lightly on her cold brow. 'You're my most thoughtful and loyal friend.'

'Can't I come with you? Oh please, Barrass, I'll be so quiet you won't know I'm there and I never have a ride on a horse. Please, can I? Go on, say yes.'

'You know you can't. Your dadda wouldn't be best pleased if you went off without telling him, and he thinking you lost again. Besides, I don't know how the horse would take to having a fidget like you on his back!'

'Would you take me if you could?'

'One day you'll come with me, I promise.'

'I could run behind?' She looked at him, wide-eyed and hopeful. 'I can run a-w-ful fast.'

He laughed again. 'Run home, there's a good girl.'

'I bet you don't call those others "good girl",' she retorted as he pushed her gently on her way.

'Go you, and good luck when you start work for Dorothy Ddole.'

'Any messages for Penelope Ddole?' she asked cheekily. The only reply she received was another low, chuckling laugh as he ran away from her towards the stables where a sleepy boy would have the horse saddled ready for his journey.

Her feet felt like balls of ice and refused to move easily as she stepped out into the increasingly strong wind that had wetness in its teeth from the surface of the sea. The shawl seemed as thin as paper and gave no warmth. She tried to run but her legs were stiff and refused to obey her.

Remembering how her father warmed himself after a long cold time in the boat, she stopped near a tree that gave at least the illusion of protection from the fierce gusts and began to bend and stretch, swing this way and that, then tapped lightly on her feet, left, right, left right, stiffly at first, the movements easing as the blood began to flow faster. Then she ran up the steep cliff path to the cottage, where a light now shone, and by the time she had opened the door to her mother's surprised face, she was breathless and glowing.

'I thought you were in bed!' Mary gasped. 'What a one

you are for wandering off without a word! Where have you been to, girl?'

'To see Barrass and wish him luck.'

'Take Dic, will you, and try to feed him some of this thin gruel – and don't show your father. He says it's too like the skilly they were fed in prison, and hates to see me feeding it to his son. Only a little, mind. Just a taste.'

There was no fishing that day and Spider and Dan spent the morning checking their boat and making new nets. At mid-morning Mary wrapped Dic firmly and cosily against her and set out with Olwen to see Dorothy Ddole.

'Will she like me, Mam?' Olwen asked anxiously as they hurried across the fields.

'Be polite and try not to talk too much,' was Mary's instruction. 'She won't want the noise of a chatterbox to add to her other troubles.'

'What troubles, Mam?'

'Never you mind. Just be as helpful as you can to her and you'll be all right.'

Although Olwen had seen Ddole House from a distance many times, the size of it, when she and her mother reached the back door, was impressive. Her own home was tiny – the Ddole kitchen was larger than the two floors put together. Mary left her in the care of Florrie, whose red hair was neatly folded into a bun and half hidden by a lace cap.

'Just go and I'll show her her duties,' Florrie said in her brisk, no-nonsense voice. She closed the door on Mary and Dic before Mary had managed to say her goodbyes.

Olwen felt a knot of fear as she looked around the large room with its shelves and cupboards full of strange instruments. There was a huge fireplace fronted by a contraption of cogs and wheels and long powerful chains which frightened her. If she were to get caught up in its complexities she would never escape. She had a strong impulse to run for the door.

'I want the vegetables prepared,' Florrie announced, and Olwen at once felt relief. Preparing a few potatoes and washing the leaves of cabbages was something she often

162

did. But the potatoes and carrots and turnips that arrived in front of her were in bucketsful and she thought she had never seen so many cabbages except in Dadda's plot of land on the cliff.

When the task was finally finished, her hands were raw and tender, and she looked out at the storm-tossed trees and hoped that she could now go home. She thought of her mother and the smell of a savoury meal cooking in the small overcrowded room and compared it with the huge, impersonal kitchen in which she stood.

'Come on, Olwen,' Florrie called, 'take them peelings out for to be boiled for the pigs, and wash out the bowl under the pump. There's plenty more work for you, slow as you are. You've saved me a bit of time today and you can save me some more by getting to wash these pots.'

Olwen stared in dismay at the pile of dishes and pans that Florrie had been using to prepare the luncheon for the Ddole family.

'There's a lot of dishes for only three people,' she gasped. 'How d'you make so much work? You wouldn't suit my mam at all! We all have to wash up as we go!'

Florrie frowned and with arms on her hips looked ready to scold the girl, but instead her face broke into a smile and her laughter rang out.

'Plenty to say, that's what your mother said about you, and she's right!'

Olwen looked at the red-haired woman and decided that although she scowled a lot and spoke with a bark like Arthur's dog, she was going to be all right. Dozy Bethan was dreamy but kind enough, and thankfully, Carrie Rees had been promoted to the house. She could not have worked with Carrie, hating the girl because Barrass liked her. She had seen them together several times, walking in that slow yet purposeful way towards their private cwtch in the beach. A place where they could hide from passers-by. She climbed onto a stool and reached for the first of the dirty pans.

By the end of that first day, she began to enjoy setting the muddle of food preparation to rights. She sighed her

163

satisfaction when the pans were hung on their hooks, and the dishes neatly stacked on shelves, and did not complain too bitterly when she was set to scrub the huge expanse of slate floor with a hard broom and a bucket of sand to remove the spilt grease.

'Small you are,' Florrie remarked as Olwen put her shawl around her to go home, 'small, not to say skinny, but no one could call you idle. You've done well here, and I'll be telling Mistress Ddole the same. There's no doubt she'll keep you on, you've got a job for life just so long as you keep going as well as you've started. No idling or skimping on the work you're set, mind, or she'll have you out of here faster than straw burns.'

Weary so she doubted if she could walk home, her arms feeling pulled half out of their sockets, hands stinging with soreness, Olwen had the fleeting thought that she would be nothing but relieved if Florrie had told her she would not be wanted any more. Then she looked at the coin in her hand, and up at the firm but kindly face of Florrie, and nodded.

'Thanks, I'll see you bright and early on Monday.'

'No, I'll see you in church tomorrow!' Florrie said firmly. 'All the staff sit with the family. Remember to look your smartest not to let the master and mistress down, mind. Boots shiny and your hair as neat as neat.'

'I don't sit with Mam and Dadda?' Olwen asked in surprise. She had always shared a pew at the back of the church with her family. 'That will seem very strange, watching them from another seat.'

'And don't forget to sing loud!' was Florrie's parting shot. 'They can't abide not being heard above the rest.'

'It's my brother Dan you want, then. I sound like the organ with holes eaten in the bellows by mice!'

The church was full when the Ddole family and their servants arrived. As they entered the old building, heads turned to watch them settle into their usual places. Olwen, nervous as she walked in behind Florrie, Carrie and Dozy Bethan, scuttled to the end of the pew behind the one used by the

164

family, with the stable boys and the rest filing in behind, and she bent her knees unnecessarily to sink out of sight. She was dragged out by Florrie, who insisted that she stood beside her.

'Where I can listen to make sure your voice is acceptable,' she said firmly.

When the vicar began to sing the first hymn, Olwen couldn't find a voice at all. Used to having her brother's strong voice one side and her mother's sweet soprano on the other to swell out and give her confidence, the idea of Florrie actually listening to her and judging whether or not she sang well, was too much for her.

'Sing, child,' Florrie urged.

'I can't, got a cold and my voice has gone to my stomach,' Olwen whispered back. 'Sound like a frog I would, if I tried to join in. Perhaps next week, is it?'

Florrie clenched her mouth in a disapproving and disbelieving grimace. 'Sing, or I'll have you standing on the table practising in front of the other servants when we get back home!'

Wide-eyed and anxious, Olwen sang.

CHAPTER TEN

During the first few days that she worked for Dorothy Ddole in the kitchen, Olwen gradually explored the big house. Her days there were so different from her life in the small fisherman's cottage, she exhausted herself with curiosity.

Her first foray from the big kitchen was through the thick door which led, by long dark corridors, to the dairy at the back of the house. There she met Dozy Bethan idly turning the up and over churn to make butter. After each half dozen turns of the wooden cask, she would press her eye to the peep-hole to make sure she was not turning for a moment more than necessary, although from the sluggish way she worked, Olwen doubted that the butter would ever come.

'Like working here, I do,' Bethan told her dreamily. 'Better than being at home. My mam has had another baby and there's nothing but noise and frantic activity, with all of us falling over everyone else. Fourteen we've got now and all surviving and running about like their feet were on fire. Peaceful here, I love working for Mistress Ddole.'

Olwen nodded politely but wondered how Bethan could call what she was doing, work.

'Cook sent me for the buttermilk. Seems she's expecting Henry Harris to call and he loves it, so she says.'

Bethan ponderously peered in through the eye-hole in the cask, shook her head slowly, and replied, 'Nowhere near ready,' and to Olwen's amusement, added somnolently, 'you can't rush these things, you know.'

Before running back to tell Florrie that the butter was not turned, let alone washed, she could not resist opening the door into the stillroom. She knew it was where Dorothy Ddole made her medicines and ointments, and the soaps and polishes that were used in the household. At home her mother dealt with that part of her housewifely duties where she dealt with everything else – beside their one fire. She wondered how different this household was that it needed a whole room for such things.

The room was painted white and everything looked spotlessly clean. The measurements were far less than the dairy, but the lightness gave the impression of greater space than she had ever seen in a building. Frightening almost, this emptiness. She crept a few steps in from the door, but could go no further, trepidation at being caught there making her unable to let go of the door edge.

There were bowls and containers of every size and shape and she longed to examine them, perhaps to recognize some found in her own home, but she had already learnt a healthy respect for Florrie's hand, and did not want to risk feeling the sting of it on her ear. She was just closing the door when a voice startled her.

'Is that you, Olwen? Do come in.'

Quaking with fear at being caught where she had no right to be, Olwen slinked around the door to see Penelope behind it, holding some candles.

'Come inside and see what we do here,' Penelope said with a friendly smile.

Olwen's face twitched as she tried to smile back, a tic moving her cheek like some terrible ague.

'Sorry, Miss Penelope,' she stuttered, 'I was waiting for the buttermilk and – '

'You'll wait for ever if Bethan is dealing with it,' Penelope whispered conspiratorially. 'Best I come and help her if Cook has need of it.'

'Thank you, Miss.' Olwen bobbed a curtsey as Florrie had taught her.

'Have you seen the rest of the servants' area?' Penelope asked. 'Through there is the pantry which leads back into the kitchen. Come and I'll show you.'

Still nervous, her voice too unreliable for questions, Olwen's eyes nevertheless took in most of what Penelope pointed out. She saw the slate trough where pig meat was salted for winter, and the jars and small buckets for salting fish. Dry-cured bacon hung above them from the beams on

S-shaped hooks, and cheeses were stacked on airy shelves above a marble-topped table in one corner, near the enormous cheese presses that looked fierce enough to hold her a prisoner if she stood too close. Earthenware jars of butter stood on a shelf near the cheeses. Penelope took down one of the jars and asked,

'Can you carry this? Best we don't wait for Bethan to finish, she'll be ages washing the butter before it's ready.'

'It wasn't butter she wanted, Miss, Henry Harris is calling and he loves a drink of buttermilk,' Olwen burst out.

'Oh dear, I think he'll be disappointed today,' she laughed, stretching up to replace the unwanted butter. 'He'll have to make do with ale.'

As Penelope stretched to replace the jar of preserved butter, something fell out of her pocket. Olwen stooped to retrieve it but before she could return it Penelope heard her mother calling, and making hurried excuses, left the room. Olwen stood there holding the piece of paper, and idly opened it. Moments later, while she still stood undecided whether to take it to Florrie or go through the door after Penelope and try to find her, Penelope returned and snatched it from her angrily.

'What are you doing with that!'

'You dropped it, and as I picked it up you went from the room.' The unfairness tacit in the words and the expression on Penelope's face made Olwen forget her position and glare at her, head slightly forward, hands on hips.

'You opened it. Did you read it? You've no business to open letters concerning other people – did you learn no manners?'

'I didn't read it!' Olwen glared back, then lowered her eyes and added, 'I can't read, no one's ever tried to teach me.'

'I'm sorry. I shouldn't have shouted like that.' Penelope was concerned with the contents of the letter being revealed and forgot she was talking not to an equal but to a newly acquired servant. She looked at Olwen and felt a warmth towards the small, fiery girl.

'Sorry I spoke like that. Mam warned me I shouldn't,'

Olwen said. 'Will I have to leave now?' She felt a surge of hope that this girl would send her away from the strangeness of Ddole House where she had to be mindful of what she said and how she said it: back to her comfortable home where she could be her natural, lively self and where no one expected her to act a part.

'Do you think you will like working here?' Penelope asked, crumpling up the letter and pushing it deep into her pocket.

'I feel a bit like someone performing in one of the Interludes, the small plays showing stories from the bible that I sometimes go to see,' Olwen admitted. 'I'm told how to talk and when not to – and that's the hardest part for me, for sure! I have to think about everything I do and not act natural like I do at home. But I think I'll like it well enough, and Mam is glad of the few pence I take home for her.'

'No, you won't have to leave,' Penelope smiled. 'Now, come through this door and you'll be back in the kitchen.'

'To get a clout from Florrie no doubt for wasting time and coming back without the buttermilk!' Olwen groaned. 'You couldn't come with me and explain, could you?' she asked hopefully, then groaned again. 'I'm a-w-ful sorry Miss Penelope, I'm forgetting the part I'm to play again.'

Penelope laughed and said, 'Don't worry too much about me, but you'll have to be very careful not to annoy Mistress Ddole. My mother has a very sharp tongue and she expects servants to behave impeccably.'

'Don't worry,' Olwen said, then added quickly, ' – Miss Penelope!' She smiled as she said it, a reminder that she was beginning to accept her position, even if she still lacked the necessary subservience. 'Mam told me not to worry Mistress Ddole, she having enough problems at present.'

'What problems?' The sharpness was back in Penelope's voice, startling Olwen. 'What do you know about my mother's trouble?'

'Only that she's ill and doesn't want to believe it,' Olwen replied, frowning. 'It's not forbidden for me to feel sympathy for her, is it? Funny old place if I can't be caring about someone.'

169

'She doesn't want people to know. She would be angry if she knew that you had been told.'

'No secrets in this place! There's never a baby coming, or a sick person going, without we all hear about it. Kenneth is better placed to tell the news than those news-sheets they have in the town, for sure. But I won't talk about it, I promise. Now come and explain me to Cook or she'll knock me into the middle of next week!'

Penelope hesitated a moment, then asked, 'You're a friend of Barrass, aren't you? Does he have work now and a place to live?'

'He was helping Pitcher at the alehouse, but now Pitcher is out of prison with the rest, perhaps he'll have to find something else.'

'Why? Is he not a good worker?' Penelope asked.

'Barrass can do anything!' Olwen retorted. 'Good at everything he is, and that strong you'd never believe.'

'Then why is he being made to leave? Pitcher needs someone besides Arthur, surely?'

'Pitcher is feared for his daughters.' Olwen pulled herself up to her full height and spoke the words proudly. 'As if Barrass would want to bother with any of that fussed and pampered trio!'

'There's someone else he follows?' Penelope asked. She knew she should not be talking to the servant girl like this, but curiosity led her on – though caution made her lower her voice for fear that her mother might overhear. 'There's a young woman he is fond of?'

'Yes,' Olwen said proudly. 'Me!' She pushed open the door into the warm kitchen with its bustling activities and, when Florrie glared, Olwen pointed nonchalantly over her shoulder with a thumb, and said,

'Talking with Miss Penelope I've been, and she'll explain that it wasn't my fault.' But Penelope had gone, hiding her laughter from the girl, wondering how Olwen could think that a man like Barrass would show her anything but kindly interest.

'Miss Penelope indeed,' Florrie began, starting towards her with a floury hand raised for a blow to her ear.

'Hit me for being too long and I'll tell Miss Penelope, mind!' Olwen said boldly, bending back from the threatening hand, and Florrie turned away.

'I don't believe you, so make sure you don't use such a poor excuse again,' Florrie grumbled, surprised by the impudence of the little girl. 'Now get on with filling the buckets for washing the dishes. Two buckets at a time, no dawdling with one and that only half filled, mind! Though I think you could manage more than two. Your tongue's tough enough to carry a third, *no* mistake.' Florrie's voice was softer than normal, amused by the small, wiry girl with the oversized idea of her own importance.

Grinning at her, Olwen hurried to do what she was asked.

It was a surprise to both Olwen and Florrie when, just as they were finishing clearing the kitchen after luncheon, Penelope came in and looked around, asking for Olwen.

'Yes, Miss?' Olwen pushed her untidy fair hair from across her face and hid her blackened hands. She had been adding coal to the fire to heat the oven for Florrie's cakemaking, and her face was aglow with the heat.

'I wish to speak to you in the drawing room,' Penelope said, and walked away.

'Oh dear, in trouble I am for sure,' Olwen wailed. 'Why did she come for me and not send one of the servants? Oh, what have I done, Florrie?'

'Cook. You will call me Cook, that is my title,' Florrie said firmly as she hurriedly wiped the worst of the coal dust from Olwen's face and arms. 'Now go. Bethan will show you the way, and remember to be polite, and look down, don't stare up at her with those bold eyes of yours. There's nothing makes them more angry than us looking as if we feel as important as them.'

Holding her breath and trying to still her beating heart, Olwen walked behind Bethan to the wide panelled door of the drawing room.

She tried to remind herself that to leave was what she wanted, to return home to her safe, comfortable life with her parents, but she knew that being told to leave was a disgrace. As well as her mother losing the money she earned, there was the uncomfortable feeling that everyone would know, that she would be discussed and thought unable to behave well enough to work in a big house. No, she wanted to work here and learn from these people, right up to the time she left to marry Barrass and bear his child. The thought of Barrass's approval gave her strength and the threat of tears was gone as Bethan opened the door and announced her with a curtsey.

'Olwen the scullery maid,' Bethan said in her slow, sleepy voice.

'Come in, Olwen,' Penelope said. She was sitting on a richly padded armchair near the fire, a fire screen tilted to protect her face from the glare. She wore a full-skirted, long-sleeved dress of blue plaid, the bodice tight-fitting, a bow of taffeta under her chin. The collar was square across her shoulders and in the same blue plaid frilled with pale blue lace.

'I am willing to teach you to read, if you so wish. I don't like to have a servant, even one as lowly as a scullery maid, who doesn't know her letters.'

'Thank you!' Olwen immediately forgot her place and her concern, and stepped impulsively towards the elegantly dressed girl. 'You mean you will teach me yourself?'

'It will be in your own time of course.'

'Yes, of course!' Olwen's blue eyes glowed, her mind rushing on to the time when she and Barrass could share the thrill of reading some of the books like Pitcher and Mrs Palmer boasted of owning.

'I'll work really hard, I promise,' she gasped, sinking to the floor by Penelope's chair. 'I really will.'

'And you'll remember that you don't sit in my family's presence without being invited to do so?' Penelope smiled to show she was not angry at the impertinence and her smile widened as Olwen stood hurriedly and almost lost her balance by standing on her own long skirt.

While Olwen was gradually accepting the limitations of a working girl, Barrass was learning the long tedious task of thrice-weekly collections and deliveries. On the nights he returned home to the cellar he began to tell Arthur of his adventures, but both were tired – Barrass with the miles of walking and Arthur from the extra work Barrass's absence caused. Before the church clock had struck two quarter hours, the friends had fallen into an exhausted sleep.

Arthur had been fascinated by how through two days, Barrass had journeyed across Gower and called at many of the farms, hamlets and villages where men had built fine houses and depended on the letter-carriers to keep in touch with their businesses.

'At first,' Barrass told him, 'I was constantly afraid. Figures appeared out of the gloom in the early morning as I rode towards Swansea to collect the bag, and I expected each time that I would be killed for the few letters I carried. But it was only people waiting either to add to my bag, or to ask that I gave a message to a relation or friend as I passed. I soon learnt to carry a piece of slate and a chalk so I didn't forget the many messages entrusted to me.'

'What sort of messages?' Arthur asked. 'Weren't you afraid of being given reports dealing with – that which you should not know?'

'I am always very careful, as I am sure Kenneth is. These people involved in smuggling know I am against them even though I did forget my disapproval of it and help Dan, Spider, Pitcher and the others. They wouldn't risk involving me.'

Arthur nodded, and in the darkness of their shelter, his eyes turned to where the door leading to Pitcher's illegal stores was hidden by innocent-looking barrels.

'Everyone knows how straight you are, Barrass, your reputation is such that no one would believe you would ever stand anywhere *near* anything suspect.' The darkness hid his smile as once again his eyes turned to the hidden doorway.

'I have to stay well clear of it, Arthur, I want to work for the King's Mail, remember. People have to trust me.'

Arthur did not point out to Barrass that, because of his blatant disapproval of the boats and their cargoes, no one was likely to trust him. Perhaps one day, when Arthur was able to talk to him with complete honesty, he might point

173

out the reason for the lack of friendship among the villagers. But not while Barrass harboured this fantastic conviction that to become a letter-carrier he needed an impeccable character.

Each day, Barrass reported to Kenneth on the day's activities and each time he approached the bank and climbed up to knock at the door, he held his breath, dreading to be told that Kenneth was ready to recommence his duties. On Tuesday evening, Enyd opened the door to him and invited him inside. He went to where Kenneth sat, a dejected figure, wrapped in several layers of blanket and with a huge bandage around his head. His eyes were moist with anticipated sympathy, and he gestured painfully to a chair beside him.

'Sit down, boy, and tell me how you have managed today.'

'I collected three letters from Peter Downes addressed to a shipping firm in Bristol port,' Barrass began. 'Then there were seven letters to distribute around the route which I did not bother to take into Swansea for marking, as you instructed me. Here are the monies I collected and the notebook with all the transactions noted.'

'Good boy, you're doing a fine job,' Kenneth said in a weak voice. Then, as Enyd went to answer the door to another knock, he poked Barrass urgently and said, 'Boy, will you remember not to finish your route earlier than nine o'clock on Thursday.'

'What d'you mean?' Barrass asked, but he was hushed by another dig from Kenneth's enshrouded elbow, which despite several layers of blanket, was firmly felt.

'Hush, boy, she'll be back in a minute and her with ears sharp enough to hear a penny drop in Pitcher's bar! For reasons you need not ask about for I won't tell you, I come home very late on a Thursday. Now if you should finish early *this* Thursday, my wife will, not unreasonably, wonder why I regularly do *not*. So stay somewhere pleasant, and don't show your face in the village till after half past nine of the clock.'

Barrass was about to ask a question, but the man groaned

174

a warning as Enyd re-entered the room, and Barrass could only nod agreement.

As he stood to leave, having handed to Kenneth all the information about his journey, he managed to whisper, 'This is nothing to do with the trade from the boats, is it, Kenneth?'

'Indeed not.' While still managing to emphasize his weakness, Kenneth looked outraged at the idea.

'No, of course, in your position you would not.'

'Could not!' Kenneth insisted, his self-righteous expression convincing Barrass of the needlessness of the question.

Barrass was curious over the deception, but guessed that the most likely explanation was a woman. Talk about Kenneth and Betson-the-Flowers had reached his ears via Arthur, who seemed to learn the latest gossip while it was in the process of being made.

During the week he acted as Kenneth's deputy, Barrass learnt a great deal about the area in which he lived. The people who waited to see him walk up, with the red waistcoat and the big leather bag, were varied – old women who waited on windy corners wrapped in little more than rags, to earn a halfpenny, cottagers handing him the rent to pay for them with dirt-grained hands, small boys who crumpled the letter they had been asked to deliver into his safekeeping, and smartly dressed and impatient young men with important business letters for London and Bristol.

He learnt about the lime that was delivered and paid for between Gower and Somerset and Devon. About the ships that sailed across from the West Country with rocks for ballast, which they deposited on deserted Gower beaches before sailing empty into Swansea docks to fill up with coal for the return journey. Wool was transported from the small farms and the money for the sale of it brought back to buy supplies for the winter. All this he learnt from asking questions about the letters he carried, and from the requests he had to deliver messages across the length and breadth of the peninsula. He learnt also that fear of the letter-carrier being robbed had led to the practice of bank notes being torn in two and each half sent separately so the thieves would not be able to spend the money they had stolen!

His fear of being attacked had been strong at first, but soon he had forgotten the possibility of thieves setting upon him and taking the precious bag from his shoulders. He strode out, walking tall and with a look of pride on his handsome face that had many young women staring after him with longing.

Olwen, tied to the Ddole House for most of the day, could do nothing to alleviate her fears that he was dallying with a dozen young women at each village. She imagined him standing on the steps of a house, or on the green, his thick curly hair blowing about him, his eyes tempting every older woman to mother him and all their daughters to dream of loving him.

She saw him in her mind's eye, calling and blowing Kenneth's horn to attract the attention of all the house-holders, and knew that every female would rush to offer him hospitality. She hoped that it was only bread, cheese and a mug of ale they offered, but suspected that there would be other things available. She also knew that Barrass was unlikely to refuse.

On the Thursday afternoon she could bear it no longer, and when Florrie told her she could leave for home a little earlier, she ran gratefully out of the house. But she did not take the road home, turning instead along the green lane with hedges of hawthorn so thick that even lacking leaves they offered shelter from the evening breezes blowing across the fields towards the sea.

She was surprised to see Barrass heading not for the village, but towards the cliffs beyond her house. She set off following him, determined to spoil any arrangement he might have made to cuddle with a girl in the deepening dark.

Barrass had made his own arrangement to fill in the time as Kenneth had requested. Now, walking towards the rendezvous with Blodwen, he became aware of someone

176

following him. He touched the bag on his back, suddenly reminded of the responsibility he carried. He should have gone straight back and ignored Kenneth's instructions, pretended he had misunderstood. If he were robbed out here, far from his route, it would be difficult to explain, he might even be accused of complicity and that would finish for ever his dream of becoming official letter-carrier for the king.

Leaving the cliffs and his intended meeting with Blodwen Baker, he slid down the grassy slope to the footpath and hurried along towards the village. There, as he made for the dunes that lay along the shore, he realized who it was. Olwen of course, when was she not following him? He had hoped, now she was busily employed at Ddole House, that she might be less tenacious in her efforts to keep him from enjoying his spare time. She really was insistent, but he was fond enough of her not to feel anger, only amusement.

Smiling now, he slithered up and down the sandy mounds, and at a suitable place he waited, holding his breath while Olwen caught up with him. He quickly slipped off the telltale red waistcoat and tucked it into the bag. His grin widened on hearing her panting up the dune towards him. It was almost dark, the surf a line of white lightness that suggested luminary power but had none.

Unaware, Olwen walked on, her feet sliding so deeply into the soft, golden sand that she thought her progress must be negligible, but she gradually gained height, crawling, her head raised for the first sight of the lights from the road, where the alehouse was busy with customers, concentrating so hard on the effort of moving that she forgot to listen for Barrass somewhere in front of her.

He jumped from his hiding place and she squealed in fright as his hands clamped down on her shoulders, almost pressing her face into the shifting sand. She recognized his laughter immediately and, small as she was, fought to free herself from his powerful arms as he lifted her up, showering sand like petrified rain. Her struggles made him lose balance and they fell and fought like two puppies. When they finally stood and smiled at each other, sand was released from their clothes in thin trickles, a gentle shushing in the almost silent evening.

'You shouldn't follow me about all the time, Olwen,' he scolded. 'One day someone will jump out on you and it won't be in fun. There are many very sensitive to being followed, as you well know.'

'I'm not following you! Why should I? Great lumbering lout that you are.'

'In case you do decide to creep around to see what I'm doing, let me tell you,' Barrass said, holding her arms as she threatened to start fighting again. 'I'm going back to the alehouse, but I don't want Kenneth to know how early I've finished work, so I'm going to creep in without being seen. All right?'

He followed her, which he thought was a change, and made sure she was safely indoors before hurrying to meet Blodwen. When he reached the shallow depression in the hillside where they had planned to meet and talk and perhaps share a few kisses, it was empty. Thanks to Olwen, he had kept her waiting too long. Disconsolately, he walked back to the village, and climbing over the wall and struggling through the litter of building materials, he crept inside the alehouse to wait until the church clock struck nine and he could go and hand over the results of his two-day journey to Kenneth.

He did not go to the cellar, but waited out of sight from those passing to and from the barroom with replenishments, in a corner of the back entrance near the staircase. Emma and her daughters were at home and he knew they rarely came down while Pitcher was busy, preferring to pretend that their father's business was separate from the way they lived, a necessary, unpleasant and rarely mentioned way of providing for their many wants.

When he heard footsteps descending he pushed himself further into the darkness. He recognized Violet, holding a candle in front of her and slipping swiftly towards the door. He wondered if it were he she was looking for.

'Violet,' he whispered. She blew to expel the light and joined him in the dark corner.

178

'What are you doing here?' she asked. 'I saw you from my window. If you've finished your deliveries, why aren't you helping my father?'

'Kenneth made me promise not to arrive before half past nine o'clock,' he whispered back, and amid giggles he explained about the supposedly secret meetings between Kenneth and Betson-the-Flowers.

'Where were you going?' he asked.

'I have an appointment,' she said mysteriously.

'With whom?'

'Granny Hughes,' she told him.

'You don't want love potions, do you?' he laughed. 'That's something you don't need any help with. Perfect you are, Violet Palmer.'

'Barrass, I am getting married to Edwin, next year. I won't see you any more.'

'For a year you'll wait to be married and you won't see me? Why?'

'It wouldn't be right. I want to say goodbye to you here, now.' The urgency in her was unmistakable

'Here, with your father likely to walk past at any moment?' His eyes were accustomed to the darkness and it seemed impossible that people walking past with the bright flame of a candle in front of them could not see as clearly as day into his corner.

'Yes.' She was breathless with excitement, her voice seeming to lack strength as she pressed herself against him. 'For the last time, Barrass, now, please, hurry.'

Granny Hughes was no one's grandmother. She had never married and had never had a child. To everyone young and old, she had been Granny Hughes for as long as memory went back. How old she was no one knew, but the most ancient person in the village, a toothless, wrinkled crone called Meg Morgan, could not remember a time when she was not there.

Granny Hughes was the local gwrach, the wise-woman, to whom everyone went when they were in trouble with a sickness that refused to clear, or when they needed help with a love affair going wrong, or wished to mend a quarrel.

It was not until they had made love and were lying together in that wrapt wonder of spent passion that Barrass thought to ask what Violet, whose parents could afford the treatment of Doctor Percy, could want with the old woman.

'Nothing really, just a little problem I cannot talk to my mother about,' Violet said. 'Some questions about marriage that I want to understand.'

Edwin came to see Pitcher to discuss the marriage date.

'You'd better come and see my wife,' Pitcher said. 'There's nothing I know about such things and even if I had an opinion, I doubt Emma would allow me to pronounce it.' He led Edwin upstairs, leaving Barrass and Arthur sweeping the area in front of the door where men still sat when the wind was not too keen. It was Friday, a day on which there were no deliveries or collections, and instead of resting, Barrass was helping Arthur with the never-ending chores of keeping the place clean and orderly.

Emma was fluttering like a bird caught in a trap, her face rosy and her hair flying about with a mind of its own. She continually patted it in a vain attempt to bring it to order.

'Edwin, my dear. You have come to discuss the wedding plans?' She turned to where Violet sat at a window seat, embroidering a cloth for a small table. 'Daughter, you may greet your betrothed.'

Edwin went over to Violet, and kissed her briefly on the cheek. She did not look at him, but smiled distantly and went on with her sewing. Emma looked at her in surprise – there was none of the usual excitement in her daughter's face that showed when Edwin called unexpectedly.

She sighed. Surely the dear couple had not quarrelled already? She had better get on with the arrangements. With plenty to do, their minds would be too full to indulge in silly arguments. She, Emma Palmer, would take everything in hand. She sighed even deeper and puffed out her plump bosom like one of the pigeons in the trees outside the window.

180

'Violet, put down your sewing this instant and talk to your visitor. I will arrange for tea and cakes. So industrious she is, Edwin, as you see, she hates to waste a single moment.' She snatched the material from Violet's unwilling hands and glared at her silently out of sight of Edwin's admiring gaze. 'Such an industrious child,' she smiled.

When tea had been poured into the fine china cups of which Emma was so proud, Edwin sipped, then told them of the progress on the new house.

'I believe the workmen will be finished sooner than they promised, Mrs Palmer,' he said. 'I am at the stage when I require the assistance of you and your dear daughter to choose the materials and furnishing so it can all be made ready for when we move in as man and wife.' He looked at Violet, wondering why she seemed so distant.

Emma too was anxious, but smiled at Edwin, showing him that she at least was interested in his news.

'Shall we go into town tomorrow, Violet?' she coaxed. 'Or would it be best to go and look at the newly finished rooms so you have a better idea of what to choose?'

'I can't marry you, Edwin,' Violet said softly.

Emma gave a wail, her fingers going to her mouth in a vain attempt to stop it. Edwin stood up and they both stared in disbelief at Violet, who sat quite calm and apparently undistressed.

'You can't marry me? But why? Have I said something to offend you? I beg your pardon if that is the case, although I can assure you such was never my intention.' Edwin walked over and took her hand in his. His mind whirled, trying to fathom out what he had said or done to account for her unexpected change of heart.

'You have done nothing, Edwin.' Her voice was firmer now. 'It is I.'

'You can have done nothing that would make me change my mind about you,' he said gallantly, but he frowned as he waited for her to continue.

'I went to see Granny Hughes yesterday and she assures me I am to have a child.'

'A child? But who -?' Edwin began, then he ran to try

181

and catch Emma as she collapsed in an untidy heap on the floor.

Kenneth felt decidedly weak when he returned to his post deliveries, and he asked Barrass to take over again and do the ride into Swansea and the long walk across Gower. He still had an almost continuous headache and it was too tempting not to ask Barrass, who had proved his honesty and reliability, to help him for a while longer.

It was as Barrass was returning early with the post from the Swansea sorting office that he saw Olwen near the shore. He left the horse in the care of Arthur and ran to join her for a moment.

'Olwen, I've had a message from Ben Gammon, he has news of my father – at least, that's what it sounds like. Look.' He showed her a piece of paper, and pointing to the words, read it for her:

> There's a one what might be your father, in the village of
> Nant Arian. Go and see him. I declare you will find it worth
> your time.

'There, what d'you think of that?' he hugged her in his excitement. 'I'm sure it must be a true indication of my father's whereabouts, else why would he leave a message when he will surely see me before too long?'

'But it doesn't have his name on it,' Olwen said doubtfully. 'Isn't it proper for people to write their names on the end of letters of such importance?'

'It's from Ben Gammon, I'm sure of it, who else would be writing to me about my father?'

He went to the alehouse to collect the horse, in a state of such excitement he wondered how he would manage to spend the whole day travelling and the night sleeping before he came to the part of his route near Nant Arian.

So wrapped in his hopes that he was not looking where he walked, he strolled into the alehouse without a worry, a smile of undiluted pleasure on his face, and when Pitcher came up to him and punched him on the chin – making

182

stars appear hours before their time – he did not feel the pain or the shock of it for several seconds.

Pitcher offered no explanations, he just threw the small collection of clothes belonging to Barrass at his feet and walked off.

It was up to Arthur to explain.

'Seems you are to be a father, Barrass, and Violet is no longer engaged to that Edwin.'

'What?' Dazed and confused by the suddenness of the blow, and the unbelievable news, Barrass stared childlike at Arthur, his liquid eyes showing hurt and dismay.

'And what's more, you're without a home again,' Arthur added.

Barrass, still unable to take in what had happened, rubbed his chin and winced at the tenderness. Like a child, in a voice higher than normal, he looked at Arthur and said,

'Will he change his mind if I ask him?'

'You've still got all your teeth and most of your face, I wouldn't chance it if I were you. Go before he kills you.'

'Why would he want to kill me?'

'Because Violet is going to have a child and you are the father!'

'Oh. Oh I see.' The smile came back to his face, a bit lopsided owing to the already swelling bruise. But it was not until he was halfway to Kenneth's house with the post-bag that realization finally came.

183

CHAPTER ELEVEN

Penelope woke to the sound of voices and slipping on a dressing gown, opened her bedroom door and looked along the landing. There was a light showing from her mother's room and she tiptoed towards it, wondering whether to knock.

Listening at the door she heard the deep voice of Doctor Percy and the weak cries of her mother. She knocked and heard her mother's voice, strong and angry, shout,

'Go away!'

'Mother, it's me.'

'Oh, then please go back to bed, my dear – and – we'll – ' The voice went frighteningly weaker and her father strode to the door and opened it. He carried a candle and in its wavering flame Penelope saw tears on his cheeks.

'It's all right, my dear, your mother ate something that did not suit her tender stomach, that's all. Go back to bed and sleep. She will be fine after Percy has given her something to soothe the pain.'

Reluctantly, Penelope went back to her room, but she did not sleep. For the first time she considered seriously what would happen if her mother died.

She was almost sixteen and at the age to marry, but there was no one in her life that she would consider for a husband, and besides, if Mother went from them her role would be here, running the house for her father. Marriage suddenly became an urgently desirable state!

Her thoughts went first to Barrass, the ragamuffin who had been transformed suddenly into a tall, strongly built, handsome young man. But he would not be considered even for a moment by her parents, so it was no use thinking about him as a husband. But the image of him, standing before her in the clothes she had given him, those amazingly deep brown eyes so full of admiration and appreciation for her small gift, and the memory of how excited she felt at the thought of him undressing so near to where she sat, remained to torment her.

There was Edwin, now betrothed to Violet Palmer. For a while she had dreamed of him being her husband, but, although he was rich, he had lived until recently in such a small, poky house that she could not have been content there. She had not thought of the house being made larger and more suitable.

Her father's friend, John Maddern, who appeared occasionally between visits to London, was a possibility. She tried to think of him holding her hand, and how it would feel to be kissed by him, but it was the image of Barrass which came to her mind and she turned in the bed as if to escape from his attraction. Thinking of Barrass was a waste of time, and if her mother were really ill as she suspected, then time was not on her side. If she did not find a husband soon, then she would remain here running the home for her father and gradually sinking into premature old age. The thought frightened her.

The fire in her room was almost out, but there was still some wood and coal by the hearth. Restless, she rose and revived it to a fine blaze, and sat in its welcome warmth to decide on a list of possibilities.

Sinking her hands into the pockets of her gown for extra warmth she felt the crumpled paper of the letter that Olwen had found. It was from her dressmaker, and asked politely for the enclosed account to be settled. That was another worry. Unbelievably, their finances seemed to be a problem. She sighed and read through the statement again, although she knew it by heart.

Nothing had been paid since Easter, and here it was November passing into December, time to order her dresses for the Christmas festivities. But how could she until this account had been cleared? Surely they weren't so short of money that poor workers like the dressmaker could not be paid? She had tried speaking to Henry Harris but he had been evasive, promising that she had nothing to worry about, that all was well, he was in full control. Her father she dare not tackle. He would be angry with the dressmaker for bothering her, and that would be an embarrassment when there was not another seamstress so clever within a day's ride.

She dozed off eventually, having failed to think of anyone she might seriously consider as a husband. She sat and dreamed of someone like Barrass, with a house and stables and the means to make worries about the dressmaker's bill a forgotten anxiety.

She was still sitting beside the glowing ashes when the servant girl came with hot water. She dressed and went at once to her mother's room. Her father was sleeping beside the bed, his head on his chest and his hand holding onto the thin, white hand of her mother. Fear clutched her as she entered and gently touched her father to rouse him.

'I'm not sleeping, child,' he whispered, 'but your mother is at last. I'll come away so we don't disturb her.' He bent to kiss the now composed, sleeping face and followed Penelope out of the room.

'What is wrong with her?' Penelope asked, although she dreaded to know the answer. She was frightened for her mother, but human enough to realize that the time she had left to choose a husband was less than she had thought. On both counts she was filled with trepidation.

'She has a complaint of the stomach, but Percy assures me she will come right again with a lot of care. Don't show your concern, my dear, you know how she hates it.'

The days that followed were filled with visitors. Besides the doctor, who called three times and finally found his patient sitting in a chair with colour returning to her thin cheeks, Edwin called, a prearranged appointment with her father. Markus arrived soon after with a servant to guide him, and Kenneth called but did not stay. He was still sporting a bandage and came with letters, which Penelope quickly snatched to prevent her mother seeing them in case they were further unpaid bills.

As they were shown into the drawing room, where Dorothy sat ensconced in a deep armchair, Penelope heard her mother call insistently for brandy. The doctor acquiesced, unnerved and worn down by the determination in the eyes so recently ringed with fever and sickness. It was not spirit the woman lacked, he thought sadly as he offered her an extra cushion to sit higher in her seat, but help such as he could no longer give.

'You went riding again yesterday, Mistress Ddole,' the doctor said nervously, waiting for the tirade of anger from his patient, but none came.

'I ride while I can,' she said, narrowing her eyes and daring him to argue.

'But it takes so much of your strength and energy. Save it, I beg you, save it for getting strong again.'

'There will be a time when I cannot. Until then I want to do everything this treacherous body will allow.'

She glared at the doctor, who bent his head and concentrated on his brandy. They made occasions like this so much worse by their braveness, the stubborn ones. If they acquiesced and allowed death to creep up on them like the autumn and winter after a glorious summer, then he accepted it with them and did not grieve for his uselessness.

'I will call tomorrow, Mistress Ddole, but should you need anything before then, please send one of the servants and I will come immediately.' He bent to pat her arm in a fatherly gesture, but the warning glare in her eyes reminded him not to be so condescending and he touched the arm of the chair instead. After accepting another glass of brandy to warm him on his way, he left, railing bitterly against the minimal improvement he could offer after his years of study.

When the doctor had gone, seen on his way by William, Dorothy called to their guests and announced,

'Soon I will be having another party. Perhaps during the Christmas celebrations. This house needs livening up.'

Her voice was stronger, Penelope noticed with relief.

'What kind of party, Mother?' she asked, and sat on a stool near her mother's feet to listen to the plans that, she guessed, were only just forming.

'All the most handsome young men in the district,' her mother said with an attempt at a laugh. 'Got to concentrate on getting you wed, young lady,' she whispered, raising

187

herself with difficulty to talk close to her daughter's ear. 'What about you, Edwin, will you come and bring that fiancée of yours?'

Edwin hesitated, the shock of Violet's announcement still painfully fresh, but he smiled and nodded.

'I will come for a certainty. Thank you.'

'And you, Markus, will you break the habit of solitude and come to celebrate with us?'

'I hardly come under the heading of the most handsome young men in the district,' Markus said gruffly, 'but if you wish me to make up the numbers, I'll come.'

'What about the annual Interludes?' William suggested. 'I've heard that preparations are already under way, and I'm sure they would be willing to perform for your party, here, in our drawing room.'

'I can usually follow the stories as long as they speak up and give me time to form pictures of what's happening,' Markus said.

'That's a good idea!' Penelope began to imagine the scene, with the audience crowded into the room, and the space near the door used by the players. They would serve mulled ale and mince pies and decorate the room with the traditional holly and ivy.

'That's settled, so you can get about your business,' Dorothy said and she settled back into the chair and closed her eyes.

Penelope stared at her long after the men had gone into her father's study, until her mother opened an eye and smiled up at her.

'It's all right, daughter, I'm not going to die just yet!'

'Mother, I wasn't thinking such a thing -!'

'It was in your eyes, but please don't let others see it. I'd hate to see pity in every face. Bad enough with your father.'

'He loves you so much.'

'I know, that's why it's so hard.'

'Can I get you anything?' Penelope asked, her voice catching at the sight of her strong mother now weakened by sickness and succumbing to its inexorable power.

'Be off and make sure your father's guests have everything

they need, then you can fetch me a pen and some paper and we'll begin to make a list of the invitations.'

When Penelope returned with the requested items, her mother was sleeping, and she left them silently on the small side table for when Dorothy woke. At least the task would give her something to think about. She looked at the firm mouth now dragged down in sleep, the fierce eyes closed, and wondered what was in the medicine that arrived at the house with increasing regularity.

Barrass had spent the night in a shallow depression up on the hill not far from the old barn he had once thought to make his home. He was bitterly cold and had hardly slept. The early frost had rimed his clothes, and the sacks that Arthur had thoughtfully provided for his friend to use as blankets were frozen in stiff ridges, offering no warmth. He was hardly able to move. Around him, spiders' webs glistened in the early morning sun, dressing the grass and bushes as for a pageant. His nose felt hard as though it might snap off should he be foolish enough to touch it.

He wondered momentarily why he was here, but then remembering the events of the previous day, hoped that Kenneth did not want him to deliver the letters today. If he were to survive the winter, he had to spend the day putting a roof over him.

He slowly uncurled. The pain of stretching was immense as he had tensed himself against the cold, even as he slept, and allowed his muscles to stiffen. He bent and stretched, turned and pivoted, until most of his muscles allowed movement. His feet felt more like stones, giving no sensation of life as he forced himself forward.

As the day warmed, he gradually felt the strength returning to his body. He was hungry but ignored the discomfort and set to work building himself a shelter. The barn was blackened from the fire and would take an age to clean and to disperse the smell of burning. Using an outside wall of the old place and the garden wall which ran some seven feet away, he thought a reasonable shelter could be made within the space of the short day.

189

First he needed tools and he went to ask Mary for the loan of a spade and axe. She heard his story with tight lips, not pretending to approve but concerned enough to help him find himself a home.

'There's a couple of old woollen blankets when you've finished building,' she promised. 'And a kettle that's more mending than kettle that will do you for a start. And here's a packet of cheese and a small loaf – I expect you'll find hunger makes the work harder.'

He thanked her, then set about his work, laboriously chopping down trees and searching the beach for driftwood. Once he had covered in the space between the barn and the boundary wall, and built a rough wall to one side, he waterproofed the top with turves patiently dug from the field nearby.

At midday, when he had stopped to eat, and drink some water from the spring close by, he heard footsteps approaching.

'Hey,' Dan called. 'Want an extra pair of hands? Finished the fishing and Mam has gone with Dad to sell it. I can spare you an hour or two.'

Companionably the two young men worked to make the small shelter safe from the worst weather, and by the time darkness fell a few hours later, Barrass had a home. They had built up the walls with stones robbed from the old barn, and had even begun to build a hearth and chimney. Soon, unless someone came to throw him off the land, he would be comfortably set up for the winter.

When Dan had gone, Barrass sat contemplating his life and wondering what to do next. It was only then that he remembered Ben Gammon's message, a clue to the whereabouts of his father. It had been the second blow that day to be told that Kenneth no longer needed his assistance, and that, on top of the news of Violet's condition, had put it out of his mind. It was too late, and he was too tired to even think of the long walk into Swansea to meet Ben and learn more. He curled himself up in the blankets, and slept.

Next morning he woke with none of the discomfort of

the day before, and stepping out from the low building, he was pleased to greet his first visitor.

'Dan!'

'Mam insisted I brought you some food,' Dan said. 'She knows we would be in difficulties if you hadn't got the boat for us, and she's grateful.' He handed Barrass a cloth bag from which the appetizing smell of freshly cooked girdle scones came. They were still hot and dripping with honey. Barrass stood and ate them there and then, licking his lips like a child, while Dan went back to the boat.

He had a second visitor that morning – a small boy, shabbily dressed in thick, oversized boots tied with string and a waistcoat over his thin, torn shirt. He told Barrass he was to go and see Markus – and at once.

The meeting at Ddole House, which began with Dorothy's announcement of a Christmas party, was delayed by an hour. William had arranged the meeting to discuss future business plans with Edwin Prince, John Maddern and Markus. John was a late arrival, having just stepped out of the coach from London, and ridden from Swansea on a hired horse.

He was travel-weary and dishevelled, but he at once asked for Penelope and, defying William's request for urgency, stopped for a few moments to talk to her. He extracted a promise of a walk around the garden before luncheon, then went to join the others.

They discussed the arrangements for the cargoes expected the following evening, and the storing of them in the room below Edwin's piggeries.

'It's inconvenient, Kenneth being so ill. Damned unfortunate him being hit by a thief,' William grumbled, as if the attack were the fault of the sufferer.

Edwin nodded agreement, his head down in case the sharp eyes of his host saw the guilt in them.

'It has meant the letter of instruction has not yet been sent,' William explained.

'Is there no one else we can ask to deliver it?' John asked.

'I did think of that Barrass fellow,' William mused. 'He

has made a big fuss about not becoming involved, yet helped to prove that we were all innocent -or – ' he added amid laughter, – 'or at least not so clearly involved! Some nonsense about keeping a good name for when he becomes a King's Messenger. What does he think Kenneth does to earn the fat bank balance he has, pick stones for the local farmers in his spare time? If the letters he handles were counted there would be a serious shortfall, and no mistake! Our self-righteous and pompous Kenneth is not above a little dishonesty to swell his bank balance, whatever stories he fills the boy's head with!'

'With his letter-carrying, our deliveries and Betson-the-Flowers he certainly has a very busy life!' Markus said, looking from one to the other as if his eyes were not sightless.

'We could trick Barrass into helping us. Then, when he complains, we'll promise not to tell Daniels if he helps us again,' William said.

'That usually works,' Markus agreed, stroking his smooth cheek in a worried gesture, 'but Barrass is not greedy, and he has no vices that I've heard about.'

'I know of one to my cost,' Edwin said quietly, and he told his friends about the disappointment in his plans to marry Violet, whose pregnancy was blamed on Barrass. Their reaction was thought-provoking.

Markus laughed again, turning in the direction of the speaker unerringly, and said it was Edwin's own fault for being too hesitant.

John said it at least proved the girl was capable of giving him a child, and that was never certain.

William's response was kinder.

'I have never wanted any other woman but Dorothy,' he said. 'I have no understanding of men who have to prove their irresistibility by finding women who succumb to their attractions and their money. It has always been sufficient for me that I won the love of one woman. I suspect, Edwin, that you are not clear of guilt, and it's only the impossibility of blatant proof of your behaviour – such as a woman cannot

192

hide – that prevented her from feeling the same distaste that you are feeling.'

'Damn it, he's right,' Markus said. 'If she has done no worse than you, why not wed her anyway?' He laughed again. 'A man can never be *sure* the child he gives home and love to is his own. What difference that you know the truth from the start?'

'I confess my first instinct, when I was told of her – condition, was to go and seek comfort with Betson-the-Flowers,' Edwin said. He was looking very thoughtful as the subject was further discussed, but jerked out of his reverie when John spoke.

'I have a strong premonition that Barrass is not to be trusted in any way, not only with a pretty woman,' he said. 'I never feel easy about a man who runs with the hare and the hounds. I cannot understand fully what he and Arthur were doing on the beach the night Markus's tubs were taken by the soldiers.'

'He does say quite openly that he disapproves of the trade, refusing to see how poor the village would be without the money it brings them all. How does he think they feed their families?' William said.

'He is no fool, yet refuses to see how impossible it would be for the cottagers to survive and bring up a houseful of children without the extra money the trade brings them? For a couple of hours' work they can add to their income almost as much as they earn from a long hard day's labour,' Markus agreed thoughtfully.

'He refuses to understand. He has this addiction to honesty that distorts everything in his mind. Yet,' John went on slowly, 'he willingly assisted Olwen in that most dangerous plan of gathering the harvest of tubs in the belief that it would save the men imprisoned. How can he be so adamant on one side, yet turn easily to the other?'

After a long discussion, they decided to spread the word that Barrass was to be considered an enemy and treated accordingly.

'We will help him with food, and make sure he does not

freeze to death this coming winter,' William said. 'I cannot condone his being harmed.'

'Of course, but he must never work in the alehouse again, and if Olwen continues to befriend him, then she too must be watched and treated with caution.'

'I will have a word with Spider,' John promised.

As the meeting ended, John went to find Penelope, and Edwin spoke to William again about Violet's disgrace.

'I will consider what you have said, William,' he said as they walked towards the stable for his mount. 'It would be a mistake to abandon the idea of marrying Violet for I suspect that once she was under my roof I would have little desire to visit the cottage of Betson-the-Flowers again, nor she to even think of the likes of Barrass!'

Barrass went down the cliff path to the isolated and gloomy house where Markus lived. The door was opened to his knock by a small servant girl in muslin apron and cap over a black, full-length dress that swamped her thin body, the sleeves falling over her red hands, the hem threatening to trip her up. When he gave his name, she stepped back to allow him to enter and, holding the offending skirt high above her trim ankles, led him to Markus.

The day was bright, with a weak sun showing in a watery blue sky, but inside the house all was dark. Being blind, it seemed that Markus needed no brightness and begrudged it others. Only the fire burning in the great hearth offered any welcome, and it was towards it that Barrass stepped.

The man he had come to see was sitting in a large armchair half hidden from him. The man's head bobbed forward and faced him without rising.

'I have a letter for you to deliver,' Markus said, appearing to stare into Barrass's eyes, although the boy had not said a word.

'Begging your pardon, but it's Kenneth you want. I only carried the letters for a while after he was hit by thieves.'

'This one is urgent and needs to be carried at once. Will you do it? There is sixpence for you if you do.'

Sixpence would pay his weekly allotment to Mrs Powell

for the boat, he thought at once, and he nodded, then, remembering that the man could not see, said,

'Yes, thank you, sir. I'll see it gets to its destination without delay.'

'Best that you do, or I'll have to remind William Ddole that the old barn needs pulling down to make way for more corn growing,' the man said with apparent politeness.

'It will be seen to at once,' Barrass said.

He stepped forward to take the proffered letter, and felt his hand grabbed. Pulled towards the seated man, bent over trying to retain his balance, Barrass listened while Markus reiterated his warning, staring up with those sightless eyes and a dangerous smile on his face.

Markus looked thoughtful as Barrass left the room. He wondered if the message would reach its destination without its contents being disclosed to the Keeper-of-the-Peace.

Once Barrass was out of the room, even the pretty ankles of the servant girl could not delay him. He ran as fast as he could down the long drive to the narrow track, not even looking to see where he needed to go to deliver the letter until he was too breathless to run any further. Then he saw with dismay that it was addressed to Pitcher – and he had forgotten to ask for his sixpence!

Kenneth was still suffering headaches, and failing to find where Barrass had gone, set out on the two-day journey. He asked Enyd to find out from Olwen where the boy had got to, but warned Enyd not to go to see Barrass herself. He did not want a baby to add to the difficulty of finding his daughter a husband!

Enyd decided that Violet's disgrace might be something she could benefit from. Perhaps Pansy and Daisy were right and she was capable of catching the attention of someone better than Dan. Instead of calling at Ddole House to talk to Olwen, she went to Edwin's house where the new building work was almost complete. On being told that he was not at home, she pushed confidently past the servant and walked in.

She went through the older part of the house and looked at the new extensions. While she sipped an ale brought by the servant girl, she looked around her, imagining how she would furnish the place should she be given the chance. She did not find herself particularly drawn to Edwin, but a marriage to him, one of the wealthiest of the local farmers, was worth considering. He was handsome enough and she would have plenty of time to decide whether she could happily become his wife. With Violet shamed and abandoned by him, now was the time to get under his guard, while he was vulnerable and hurt.

She sat down and spread her skirts becomingly about her, pulling at her hair and retying her ribbons to make as pretty a picture as she was able.

As he rode home, Edwin contemplated what his friends had said with regard to his feelings towards Violet, and decided to go and see her to discuss reviving the plans for them to wed. Being told he had a visitor, and seeing Enyd waiting, he was irritated at the delay.

He did not listen to her first remark, but assumed that due to her father's sickness, and Barrass's absence, she had called for the letters. He thrust them at her, politely thanked her, and ushered her out before she could find her gloves. Humiliated and angry, Enyd walked back home at a rate that had her breathless.

On the cliffs she paused and, seeing Mary washing clothes in a barrel by banging them with the end of a thick stick, she went to talk to her.

'Mary, I was passing and called to see if you've heard the news about Violet. What a shock it must have been for "Lady" Emma to find her dear daughter had succumbed to the advances of a common orphan.'

'I'm afraid that isn't the end of Barrass's troubles,' Mary said, thankfully resting from the steady thump-thump of the washing dolly. 'Shall we have a mug of tea while I tell you about it?'

While they sat near the fire and drank the warming tea, Mary explained to Enyd the distrust felt by the local men regarding any involvement by Barrass in the smuggling scene.

'Will this mean that Barrass can't help my father any more?' Enyd asked. 'He is still far from well and there are days when he is glad of a helping hand.'

'I think for a while people will be afraid to be seen talking to him. Messages have gone around, warning people that he is not to be trusted, and it will be a long time before things will change for him.'

'I think the men are jealous of his good appearance,' Enyd said hesitantly, 'and the women glad of it! I fear there will be more announcements soon, and the population of the village will increase rapidly, unless he finds a wife and remains true to her.'

'There is another girl in trouble?'

'Unless I'm mistaken, Carrie Rees, the servant at Ddole House, will be wearing more layers of loose clothing soon in an effort to delay the inevitable request for her to leave.'

'Surely not Barrass?'

Enyd nodded affirmation.

Dan and Spider walked up the path from the beach as Enyd stood to leave, and Dan offered to walk with her. He was taller than her by a head, and a pleasing companion. She was still smarting at her curt dismissal by Edwin Prince, and because of it she took his arm and smiled her pleasure at his invitation.

'Will you come with me to the Interludes?' he asked as they walked across the wet, prostrate winter grass.

She hesitated for a moment, thinking regretfully of her brief hope of interesting Edwin in her acquaintance, but then she smiled and nodded.

'Yes, Dan. I would like that.'

Dan stopped and turned her towards him, his head lowered in the expectation of a kiss. She again hesitated and he allowed her time to move away without too much embarrassment. The movement she finally made was slight, but Dan read in it her consent, so held her tightly in his arms

197

and kissed her. She responded more strongly than he expected and his heart began to race with the hope that she had at last accepted his love. He kissed her again more firmly, but still half afraid of offending her, with the result that the kiss was without much skill, and unsatisfactory to them both. They walked on in silence.

They had not gone far, each with an arm about the other, when the sound of a galloping horse approaching made them stop again. Dan looked towards the sound, then, with a shout, grabbed Enyd and fell into the bushes with her. They were just in time to escape from the hooves and allow the horse carrying Dorothy Ddole to race over the spot where they had been standing.

Enyd had screamed with fright, and now she groaned with the pain of the thorns sticking into her flesh. Dan was contrite.

'I'm sorry, Enyd,' he said, pulling her free with gentle concern. 'I should have pulled you on top of me and protected you from the thorns, but there was so little time. All I could think about was you being trampled. Come, we'll go back to Mam and she'll make you comfortable.'

'No, I want to go home. There isn't an inch of me that isn't screaming with agony.'

'Then I'll carry you.' He scooped the sobbing girl up in his deceptively strong arms and walked down the path, his face set with anger. How could Mistress Ddole ride like that, with such complete disregard for others? He wanted to run after her and tell her what she had done – injured Enyd, and made *him* feel ashamed for not being able to prevent it. But he knew that talking to such as the Ddoles would be a waste of time. They made the rules to suit themselves and no one would support him if he dared to complain. Walking fast, filled with impotent rage, he carried Enyd back to her home.

'What's happened?' Ceinwen said as she watched the couple approach. 'What have you done?'

'It wasn't Dan, Mam,' Enyd sobbed. 'He saved my life, I think. It was Mistress Ddole and that wild horse of hers.'

'Nearly ran us down, she did,' Dan said, handing Enyd into her mother's care.

'Well, there's not anything we can do about that, then, is there?' Ceinwen said with low anger.

Dan agreed, but reliving the moment later that day, he saw again the face of Dorothy Ddole as she had pelted across their path, and knew the woman's stricken face had been blinded with tears.

Barrass nervously approached the alehouse and handed Pitcher the sealed letter from Markus. The raised arm, palm ready to swipe him, made him explain his business quickly and leave without any delay, and he went slowly through the village street, kicking disconsolately at sticks and stones and the occasional dead rat. It was not apparent at first that those he met did not stop and talk to him. He was still too upset by the loss of Violet and his job at the alehouse to notice. But when three people actually turned away and refused to answer when he called a 'good day', he began to wonder.

He thought it strange, but decided that Violet's disgrace must be public knowledge now, and the mood of anger against him would be a temporary thing. He spoke loudly to everyone he met after that, pretending not to notice the lack of a reply, but he began to feel more alone than when he had been a flea-ridden infant. At least then people spoke to him, even if they had kept their distance.

He spent a little while adding strength to his temporary home, then went down again to the village. Surely the whole population would not ignore him? But he began to feel real alarm when even Blodwen looked at him and looked away as if he were invisible.

On the dunes the next morning, he sat in a sheltered hollow and taking the lines and hooks he usually carried, began to prepare to catch fish from the rocky gulleys further along the coast. He was very hungry and bitterly cold, so his fingers slipped as he tried to tie a knot to hold a hook in place.

'What are you doing, Barrass?' asked a voice, and he gave a cry of relief when Olwen appeared.

'Olwen!'

'I shouldn't be talking to you, mind,' she said, appearing below him where the marram grass was thickest. 'Mam and Dadda would be very angry with me if they knew.'

'But why? Surely it isn't because of Violet?'

'You don't know?'

'Of course I don't know! I haven't done anything except use an old barn to stop myself from freezing to death, and no one has told me I shouldn't.'

'They think you are a spy for the revenue men. Are you?' she asked.

'Of course not. How could you of all people think that! Didn't I help to get the men out of prison?'

'They believe you were on the beach that night to give the revenue men those tubs, and *not* because of Dadda and the rest. They won't believe Arthur and me when we tell them different, because we're your friends.'

She was panting slightly from her walk across the uneven sandy ground and looking up at him from her lower position on a slanting sandhill. Her brilliant blue eyes were slitted against the morning sun that was just clearing the top of the sand in dazzling brightness and giving touches of gold to her shining hair.

'Why do they think that?' He held out a hand and beckoned her to come up beside him. 'I've never approved of the boats, you know that, I've never kept my disapproval a secret. But I *helped* that night. You know I did. I did it because *you asked* me to. Haven't you told them that?'

'They won't believe me, Barrass. I've tried, really I have! Dadda asked me to tell you that he and Dan will pay the money for the boat, they can't accept it as a present, not now.' She looked sad, her head bent, her hair falling like a curtain in front of her so he couldn't see her face. 'I'm to tell you that, then I mustn't talk to you any more. They think it's best you go somewhere else to live. Oh, Barrass, how will I manage if I don't see you?'

He pulled her up beside him and put his arms around

her. Spider's refusal to accept his gift was hurtful. The rest he could half understand – him being an outsider all his life – that for the slightest of reasons things continued the same, but to refuse the boat he was buying for them. That was near to being an insult. He determined that whatever they thought, he would earn the money somehow and pay Mistress Powell the rest of the money he owed. The boat was a gift and he would not allow Spider to refuse it. He realized with an aching heart that he faced loneliness and homelessness again, and hugged Olwen closer to him.

'And how will I manage without my best and most loyal friend?'

'Am I your best friend, Barrass?' She slipped down so her head was on his shoulder. 'Better than Violet and the others?'

'They are different,' he whispered against her golden head. 'You are the one I can be my true self with.'

Olwen sighed with deep contentment. They sat for a while, Olwen delighting in the rare intimacy of the moment, and Barrass wondering how he would survive.

'Have you eaten?' Olwen asked when she felt him begin to stir and knew the magical moment was about to end.

'No, but don't you worry about me. I'll catch some fish later.'

She pointed down the slope to where she had stood. 'I've brought you some,' she told him. 'Five small dabs. And a fine hammering I'd get if Dadda knew I'd taken them from the cart.'

Barrass smiled his thanks. 'Pity you can't come and cook them for me,' he grinned.

'I don't doubt you'll find someone willing to cook your fish, and do whatever else you need,' she snapped, back to her usual bantering manner.

'I'm not so sure,' he said quietly, 'I'm not so sure. Thank you for your thoughtfulness.' And he kissed her lightly on the forehead. He felt utterly lonely when she had disappeared from sight. Searching his pockets, he found one shilling and sevenpence. He collected the fish Olwen had brought and went up to pay Mrs Powell another one shilling and sixpence off the cost of the boat.

At the top of Fisher Cottages he stood a moment and looked at Mistress Powell's bare front garden where the boat had scarred the tangle of weeds to a yellow paleness that still showed. The house was in a dangerous state. The walls had several wide cracks and the end wall bellied out like a giant saucer set on its edge. He knocked, desperate to find her in, needing someone to talk to more than ever before in his life. He took a deep breath as he heard footsteps approaching and smiled as the door opened a crack.

'Good day to you, Mistress Powell,' he said breezily, as if nothing was wrong, hoping that she at least had not been told to ignore him. He held out his hand with the coins. 'I've called to bring you another payment for the boat. I think there is only sixpence left to pay, and you will have it very soon, I promise.'

The wrinkled old hand came out, claw-like, and took the offered money, and he glanced at her face waiting for some acknowledgement. She glared at him, then pulled in her shawl-draped arm and slammed the door.

'Best not to do that too often, Mistress Powell,' he shouted, hurt and dismay making his voice louder in defiance, 'or you'll have the lot about your ears!'

There was no reply, and with this new rejection raging in his heart, he sang loudly all the way down the hill and up through the wooded slope to his shelter, telling himself that he needed no one. But his throat was tight, and eating the fish Olwen had given him was a mite difficult.

CHAPTER TWELVE

It was Olwen and Arthur who fed Barrass after he was shunned by the rest of the village. He woke each morning in his small shelter and there would be a few fish, some ale and, occasionally, some bread and cheese smuggled out of the alehouse by Arthur. He took their gifts gratefully and, when they met, greeted them with joy. He avoided the village and its disapproval, and spent most days wandering around the cliffs and shore, gathering wood to warm him through the winter.

Once or twice he went to church, childishly hoping that someone would heed the lessons monotonously intoned by the vicar about Christian forgiveness. But the frowns aimed his way by the women, who turned and unblinkingly showed their annoyance at his entering the House of God, made him give up. He listened instead to the old and young voices wavering out through the doorway, watching from behind the yew trees as the congregation came out. They all wore their best clothes, with hats beribboned and decorated according to their means and imaginations with feathers and flowers, bows and intricately fashioned corn dollies.

The men all showed their calling with freshly laundered smocks of finest linen, their dogs and shepherds' crooks and even a carrier's whip left in the porch while they entered into worship with their employers and their families.

Barrass watched with sad envy as the throng then separated to their homes. He suffered the pain of increasing loneliness, imagining how each one went back to a fire, company and comfort plus the prospect of a full belly on this special family day. As much of the daily work as possible was abandoned in favour of bible study and contemplation, as instructed by the vicar, but food and fire had been well prepared for on the previous day.

He saw Violet with her family as they came out of the

ancient stone doorway and stopped to talk to the Ddoles. Violet showed no interest. She looked away from the animated conversation between her mother, and Penelope and her father. Is she thinking of me, he wondered, and if so, was it with regret for the loss of our loving? Her face showed nothing. A cloak trimmed with fur, with the hood up around her face, put her expression in shadow, and he was left to wonder if unhappiness showed and, if so, whether it was for the loss of Edwin, or himself.

It was on a Sunday afternoon when Arthur and Olwen arrived with some excitement, to call his name almost before they were in sight of his poor home.

'Barrass,' they chorused. 'Barrass, hurry, we've got news for you!'

He stood up from the back of the shelter, where he had been skinning a seabird he had caught earlier.

'Don't tell me Pitcher has offered me my job back?' He smiled as he greeted them and Olwen felt a rush of love for him. The sun shone on his face, still tanned from the summer, his teeth gleaming white, the hair he still refused to cut in long curls around his head.

'Ivor Baker is coming to find you with a big stick,' she said, sadness for the predicament she had come to report overwhelming her with dismay. 'Blodwen's waist is thickening and she says it's your fault.'

Barrass frowned momentarily, then he started with surprise. 'You mean there's another baby on the way?'

'And that's beside the one Carrie is trying to hide! Thrown out of the Ddoles' house she's been. Barrass, why can't you leave the girls alone?'

'Best we hurry.' Arthur looked back along the path anxiously, his adam's apple jerking with agitation, his thin face a picture of trepidation. 'Seen that Ivor Baker in a temper before, I have. Come on, Barrass, we've got to hide you where he won't find you till he's been soothed.'

Voices came across the quiet fields, where the trees, skeletal now winter was upon them, gave few places to hide. Barrass recognized the bull-like roar of Ivor, and the quieter sound of those trying to calm him.

Olwen held out her hand, and with Arthur and his dog scooting behind, they ran, bent low over the rotting grass, to the furthest side of the field, through the hedge and on, across the bracken-patched hillside and down onto the rocks below the high land. They stopped when they thought they were safe from the searching eyes above them and stood, panting and red-faced, wondering what to do next. It was Olwen who made the decision.

'Could you find the place where I landed when I was caught in that storm?' she asked Barrass. 'If we could get you down there, where the descent looks so impossible from above, no one will find you.'

'But I can't stay hidden in a cave for ever. I think I'll have to do what everyone wants, and leave,' Barrass said. He spoke casually but Olwen could see how afraid and hurt he was at the villagers' rejection.

'Not everyone, Barrass. I don't want you to go,' she said, squeezing his hand.

'Nor me,' Arthur said. He held the terrified dog under his arm, the creature's eyes rolling as he tried not to look down at the foaming sea, or up, where somehow he knew he should be.

The sea was not fierce that day, settling into an almost gentle rhythm as if in respect for Sunday propriety, but its thrashing was sufficient to prevent them from hearing sounds from above.

'I think you should leave me here and let me find my own way to the cave,' Barrass said, looking up to the overhanging turf. If you meet Ivor, you'd best tell him you haven't seen me.'

'We'll come each evening with food,' Olwen said, accepting the sense in his decision. She climbed the easy route to stand once again on the firm grass above Barrass, and helped Arthur with the almost pop-eyed, struggling dog to join her. Without looking back, in case someone was watching them, they set off back to the village.

They saw no sign of Ivor or his followers, but when they reached the old barn they found evidence of their passing. Barrass's crude shelter had been torn down, sections of it spread across the field and the few miserable contents broken. Even the newly skinned bird had been trodden into the earth and spoilt.

Barrass found the cave without much difficulty but there was nothing there, apart from the remnants of a fire, and he knew he would have to find some way of keeping warm. Driftwood was there in plenty, and to give himself some sense of purpose he gathered some, and sorted it into piles to dry above the waterline. From what he had seen before the light failed and what he had learnt from Olwen, he knew there was no permanent beach, that the tide came close to the edge of the cave entrance: the undisturbed ashes of the fire convinced him that at least it did not enter.

In the dark, stumbling awkwardly along the unfamiliar terrain, he went to his shelter intending to gather blankets and a few comforts. When he arrived he could not understand at first what his hands were finding. Then he knew that he had once again lost everything. He sat in the wet grass in the dark field and, with his arms around his knees, considered his dilemma.

Why had he succumbed to the charms of Violet and the others? Why did God give such a gift then insist they deny themselves its joys? Self-pity made him blame the girls momentarily for enticing him, but he was honest enough to admit that he needed no encouragement once he had tasted the delights of a woman's body.

Becoming conscious of how uncomfortable he was, he stretched out on the grass, which felt like a frozen sheet of water but which he vaguely hoped would warm up with the heat from his body. Almost unaware of his discomfort he continued with his thoughts. He would have to leave. It was clear that by staying he risked a beating or worse, and even at best, he would be forced to marry and provide for one of the girls who carried his child. How could he provide for anyone? He had nothing, and at almost nineteen, no prospect of getting even the simplest shelter. With no one willing to give him work, what alternative had he? He must leave.

He was bitterly cold yet he didn't care. The wet grass had seeped its frozen fingers insidiously through his thin clothes, and from head to foot he shivered. Perhaps, he thought with a burst of anger, I should stay here and die. Then they would feel some remorse. The idea of dying to cause uncaring people a momentary guilt was so ludicrous that he laughed aloud, stood up stiffly and began to exercise to warm himself. No matter what he decided, death was not one of the options.

The night was spent walking around the field, searching with hands in the dark and managing to find two of the three blankets Mary had given him. By the time dawn had broken, bringing with it a mist and drizzly rain, he had rescued the third and, feeling rich by comparison with the previous evening, he ran back to sleep in the cave.

Food arrived regularly from Arthur, and on Sunday afternoon, when Olwen was free for a few hours from her duties at Ddole House, she called with her pockets filled with what she had managed to find for him.

What Barrass valued most was the company of his two friends. They would sit in the cave entrance and share their news, Barrass drinking in eagerly the happenings of the village.

'Violet Palmer is getting married next Sunday,' Olwen said on the second week of his banishment. 'Seems that Edwin is willing to accept the baby as his own.'

'Perhaps I'll be able to come back soon, then?' he said, trying to hide his pain at the thought of Violet sharing her body with Edwin.

'Pitcher misses you. He still hasn't finished that drawing room of Emma's and says he never will without a good reliable worker like you,' Arthur told him.

'Tell him I'll risk the anger of Ivor and Winifred if he'll let me come back. I'll work for sixpence and my keep. I owe some money, see, and hate not to pay it,' Barrass said without looking at Olwen. He was thinking of the sixpence he still owed Mistress Powell for the boat, still smarting over the hurt of Spider's refusal to accept the boat as a gift. He would pay the remainder of the money and show contempt for Spider's attitude.

'With Emma still calling you every name that's allowed for a "lady" to use, I think that's naught more than a dream,' Arthur said sadly.

On the day of Violet's wedding, Barrass rose early and set off to walk to the village. He planned to hide in the church-yard and see Violet in her wedding dress given by her father to Edwin Prince, and hoped the sight would drive the urgent need of her from his heart.

By getting to the church early he thought no one would see him and he could settle in one of the yew trees. But as he walked past the stone relics of former villagers, he bumped into Pitcher.

For a moment, neither spoke. Then Pitcher looked at the tall young man and groaned softly.

'Why did you mess everything up, boy? Couldn't you be satisfied with the others? If you had left Violet alone we could have persuaded people to forgive you, but, well you know what Mrs Palmer is like. No chance now of us ever working together.'

'I didn't mean it to happen, it was just a sudden need on both our parts,' Barrass stuttered. He was embarrassed at talking to Pitcher, whom he considered a friend as well as an employer, about his own daughter.

'Never imagines it with your own children,' Pitcher went on. 'Always sees them as babies and lacking the more vulgar feelings of grown people.'

'She's twenty-two,' Barrass said softly. 'I doubt you were feeling childish at twenty-two.'

Pitcher smiled reminiscently. 'No more did Emma,' he confided. 'But,' he added briskly, 'there's no chance of Emma forgiving you. Although I have tried, boy, I have tried.'

'Thank you.'

'Why are you here?' Pitcher asked.

'I came to see the wedding.' Barrass hung his head. 'I shouldn't stay, I know that. No one should stay when every-

208

body wishes them gone, but I've been around the village since I was less than two. Where can I go?'

'I'll have a word at the next meeting of the village elders and see what can be arranged. Seems to me that if I can forgive your trespasses, then others should.' Pitcher touched the boy's arm and said, kindly, 'You come-along-a-me and I'll show you where you can stand and not be seen.'

A small window, devoid of glass, was hidden behind a bushy yew tree growing against the church. Squeezing between the wall and the tree's branches, and stretching up onto his toes, gave Barrass a perfect view of the inside of the church.

Emma and the twins had been there on the previous day to decorate the church with late flowers and the fruits of autumn. It was Pitcher's idea to use berries and the still colourful leaves; he dared not tell her that one of his customers had told him that was how Betson-the-Flowers overcame the shortage of blooms.

Emma was among the first to enter, with the twins in close attendance. The three of them wore heavy plaid cloaks under which glimpses of pale cream dresses showed. The twins looked about them with a superior expression on their rather plain faces, and Emma looked near to tears. Edwin, who arrived next, with Thomas, a neighbouring farmer as his support, wore a strikingly smart suit and cloak in lovat green, with accessories in cream. His trousers were full at the top and tight below the knees, on which buckles gleamed. Polished shoes of fine leather with rather pointed toes made Barrass wonder how many times the man had fallen foul of them. They seemed impossible to wear without tripping up on every piece of litter. Chattering, pointing and even stifled giggling from some of the newly arrived guests did not appear to worry the wearer of the newest fashions. And he even walked to and fro to give them a better view.

William and Dorothy Ddole were there with Penelope, who wore a soft blue woollen dress and jacket, with a shawl of white lace across her shoulders and head. Beside her sat John Maddern who was – to Barrass's mind – as outland-

209

ishly dressed as Edwin, in those strange shoes, a suit of nankeen yellow with a shirt so frilled it made him look pigeon-chested, forcing him to hold his head up at an uncomfortable angle to avoid being buried in the lace.

William and Dorothy seemed dowdy by comparison to John Maddern and Edwin. Barrass guessed the two friends had been to London or Bristol for their wedding clothes. He touched the frayed collar of the shirt given to him by Penelope, and felt the roughness of the serge trousers in appreciation. Clothes did make a difference to how a man felt about himself. He knew that better than most.

He remembered the pride he had experienced when first dressed in the clothes belonging to Penelope's brother, Leon. Perhaps that same feeling was in the two men being stared at, admired and whispered about by the congregation in the slowly filling church. He felt an empathy with the two men, an understanding that transcended his poverty and lowly state. One day, *he* would be dressed in fashions that would make others stare.

When Violet entered on her father's arm, Barrass felt a weakness overwhelm him, and tears threatened. He stepped back from the vision of the woman who rarely wore any other colour than brown, who was dressed in a rich blue taffeta gown that trailed along the ground in a way that made her appear to float down the aisle to stand beside her intended. Her hair was in a thick plait down her back, half covered by the veil that hid her face from him.

The murmured chanting of the marriage service reached him but he hardly heard it. He stood a silent sentinel to her leaving him for ever, watching as her lips moved in the repeated recitations. Then as she lifted the veil from her face, he gave a strangled groan.

He jerked his head back and a branch slipped from behind him and forced its way into the church through the opening. Violet looked up, and for a moment, across the church, their eyes met. It was she who lowered them first, and he saw her shoulders shake with a sensation of horror, before he left his hiding place and ran away.

*

When he reached his part of the cliffs he saw that in his absence Arthur had been with a dish of bread and milk. He sat without any real hunger to eat it, then climbed down to the cave. Thoughts of Violet made him careless of anyone seeing him, and he did not approach the cave with any attempt at caution. Sitting at the entrance was Blodwen's father, Ivor. In his hand he carried a thick, crudely carved stick: bulbous at the top, slimmed to an easily grasped handle at the bottom.

'Ivor!' Barrass gasped. He turned to get back up to the cliff top, but Ivor called him.

'Stop, boy. I want to talk to you. You'd best not try to run, I'm as handy at throwing this as hitting with it,' he warned, tapping his other hand with the weapon.

'What d'you want?' Barrass hedged, knowing full well what the irate father had in mind.

'My daughter has lost her place. Worked in the laundry of the workhouse she did and earned a good wage. With a belly swelling almost as you look at it, she's been told to leave. She had a job for life she did and now you've messed it all up for her!'

'I'm sorry – ' Barrass stuttered.

'So are we. Now we've decided that if you were to marry Blodwen, then come and work for me, then we'll forget about breaking your head, and be friends.'

Barrass looked longingly at the cliffs above him. He should have followed his first instinct and run away. He was fond of Blodwen, but the prospect of being married to the amiable but none too bright girl for the rest of his life terrified him. He didn't know what his life would hold, but he knew he had to aim higher than Ivor's daughter.

'I would not make her a good husband,' he muttered.

'But she would be churched, and might even get her job back, so she won't be much of a burden to you.'

Barrass looked at the sea, frothing and foaming, rising and falling, and the prospect of risking himself to its mercy, to avoid the man standing threateningly before him, looked worth considering. But he thought he might as well risk the heavy stick in Ivor's hand as oblivion in the powerful sea.

'No,' he said firmly.

Penelope rode home with her parents trying to pluck up the courage to ask her father about the debts they were incurring in the village and town. She had managed to prevent her mother from seeing them, by developing the habit, even in these cold winter days, of going for a short walk and meeting Kenneth as he called with the letters. She knew that it was Henry Harris's job to break the seals on them, but she did so herself, while Kenneth sat with Florrie and shared the latest news. She placed the opened letters on Henry's desk, and made a note of each overdue debt with increasing anxiety.

If only Leon would come home, but with his regiment in America it was unlikely he would be home for a very long time. She was tempted to speak to Henry, but each time she prepared herself to tackle the subject about which women were supposed to understand so little, she lost her nerve and asked him instead if he was well, and if Bessie Rees was proving to be a suitable servant.

One morning just a fortnight before the celebration of Christmas was to begin, she counted up the bills she knew had not been paid and learnt to her alarm that they amounted to over eight hundred pounds. Something had to be done, but who could she approach? The decision was made for her when Olwen came in with an embarrassed expression on her young face and asked to speak to her.

'What is it, Olwen? There is nothing wrong, is there?'

'Mistress Penelope, I found this and – I'm sorry but I read it. Your teaching me my letters has brought such a lot of excitement for me I can't stop my eyes translating the scribbles into words now, no matter how I try.' Breathlessly, Olwen handed Penelope a note, torn across but clear to read.

It was a demand for payment of monies overdue, for the purchase of two horses and seven couples of hounds.

White-faced, Penelope stared at Olwen, who backed away as if from a blow.

'Sorry I am, but once I'd read it, I thought you should

see it even if I got a wallop for my trouble,' she said at speed. 'Sorry I am, but I thought maybe you didn't know and your father, he trusts that old Henry Harris who's old and a bit dreamy, to see to it all and I thought, perhaps he'd forgotten.'

'Yes, that's probably what happened. I'll see him as soon as he comes. In fact, he's late. He should be here by now. Go and see if his horse approaches and tell me the moment he arrives, will you?'

'You aren't going to hit me for reading something I had no business to read?' Olwen looked in surprise at the girl, only a little older than herself. Since she had worked at Ddole House, she had received more smacks than in all her previous years.

On her fifteenth birthday in September when she had asked Florrie to allow her to go home a little early to eat the special food her mother had prepared, she had been soundly smacked for impertinence and told that people like fishermen's daughters had no right to remember a birthday, let alone celebrate it. She had celebrated it nevertheless, by a late night visit to Barrass, where they shared a basket of food she had saved over three days, in a midnight picnic.

Now she stared at Penelope in surprise.

'Thought I'd be smacked for sure,' she said. 'I nearly threw it at the back of the fire and pretended I hadn't seen it.'

Penelope smiled grimly. 'I'm glad you didn't.'

She asked the girl to go outside and wait for the secretary and bring him straight to her.

'I'll make sure he explains to me exactly *what* is going on,' she muttered half to herself.

When Olwen had gone to keep watch, Penelope stood at the window and looked out at the gently rising land behind the house. The grass was still a rich green in the fields that had not been ploughed, although the frosts had killed most of the flowers she grew in the beds near the house, and the heather had lost its colour and showed only as patches of black on the distant hills.

The sky was a sombre screen with the threat of rain or

even snow in its lowering cover which had a hint of purple in the grey. She felt very alone. As she watched, sleet began to fall, and the hills swiftly vanished from sight. Remembering the girl outside watching for the secretary, she rang for Bethan and ordered her to go and bring Olwen in.

All morning she waited for the man to make his appearance. So intent was she on what she would say to him, and how she would handle his protestations that he was able to cope with his work efficiently, she did not realize that her mother was also long overdue. Dorothy had ridden daily this past week, and on her return did not seek Penelope out but went at once to her bed.

Darkness came early, with the sleet turning to snow which settled on the paths and trees and made the once sombre day into one of magical beauty. The silence made the house seem isolated and the reflection of the limited light on the white ground gave it a sense of unreality. Only thoughts of the inadequacy of the ageing secretary spoilt her enjoyment of it.

When Bethan came to ask her if she should serve tea or wait for the return of Mistress Ddole, she was startled into realization that her mother had been gone for hours and might be lost in the steadily falling snow.

'Bethan, is my mother in her bed'

'No Miss, she hasn't returned yet from her ride.'

'Not returned?' She stared at the servant in disbelief. 'But she must be! She's been gone for more than four hours!'

'No Miss Penelope, I've just been to see if she would like me to serve tea in her room.'

'I've been so remiss! Send the stable boys out to find her, will you? At once. Get everyone you see to help find her. Oh, how could I be so forgetful?'

The boys from the stables and those who were working in the barns dropped their tools and, pausing only to gather lanterns, hurried off into the storm. Penelope put on her thickest coat and went out through the kitchen door, intent

214

on walking around the immediate area in case her mother should be talking to one of the cottagers.

Florrie called to her and begged her to stay inside.

'Sure to find her soon, Miss, and she'll need you here to comfort her.'

'Cold she'll be, I'll get the fire roaring in her room.' Bethan, moving as speedily as she was able, slowly picked up the coal bucket and walked half dragging the heavy load from the room.

'I'm going to ask at the cottages,' Penelope said firmly, quelling Florrie's pleas for her to stay. 'I'll come back soon in case my mother has been found.'

'Shall I come with you, Miss?' Olwen asked, and Florrie gave a glare that would have silenced anyone else.

'Hush, girl,' she hissed.

Unrepentant, Olwen looked at Penelope and said, 'Best you don't go on your own, Miss Penelope. It wouldn't help anyone if you slipped and we had to search for you as well.'

'She can come,' Penelope said as Florrie raised a hand to slap Olwen. 'Come on, but make sure you are well wrapped. It's warm in here but we won't retain that warmth for long once we go out there.'

Tight-lipped with disapproval, Florrie helped Olwen into a coat too large but thick enough to keep the worst of the cold from her. Then, as the two girls slipped out of the door, she added more kindly, 'Now do as Miss Penelope tells you, mind, and be careful.'

'I'll look after her,' Penelope promised, but as she left, Olwen couldn't resist whispering to Cook,

'Me look after her more like!'

After leaving the courtyard they were horrified to see that the snow had already obliterated everything so it was impossible for them to know where they were after only a few minutes of walking. They set off in what they hoped was the direction of the row of cottages to the north of them, but after finding themselves walking back over their own footsteps, they felt a fear that made them hug each other and wonder where to step next.

'Best we go back,' Olwen said. 'It wouldn't help if we got

ourselves frozen to death. Let's get back while we can still see our footsteps.'

It was not as simple as she hoped. The marks made by their boots were already filling in. It was only Olwen's keen eyesight that brought them to the bulk of a building and led them around its comforting presence to the kitchen door. They fell inside and while Olwen removed the coat Florrie had found for her, the other two servants helped Penelope to remove the wet outdoor clothes, slip on a warm dressing gown and sit near the kitchen fire.

'See you to your room, shall I?' Bethan asked.

'No. I think I'll stay here. There's bound to be news soon.' But the brave words were a sham. Having been out and seen the ferocity of the sudden snowstorm, she already doubted if she would see her mother alive.

'Pity it is that Mr William is away in that London place,' Florrie said. She always spoke disparagingly of any place larger than the village, convinced that the extra inhabitants were all evil.

'He is on his way home,' Penelope said. She was staring into the fire, her voice vague, her thoughts on the sick, defiant woman probably wandering around in the blinding snow, growing weaker and weaker. She sobbed as she thought of having to tell her father of her lack of care, her forgetfulness which must surely end with her mother dying in the cold, white wilderness. She started as Florrie pressed a cup and saucer into her hands, then sipped the tea gratefully, feeling it trickling down inside her and spreading in a warm comforting stream.

She cried in trepidation as there was a knock at the door. Florrie patted her soothingly before she opened it to admit Daniels.

'Carter Phillips called me,' he explained as he stamped the thick snow from his boots and came to stand near Penelope. 'Is there any news yet?'

'Nothing, but so many are searching she will surely be found soon.'

'It's more than likely she is already warm and safe in some cottage and instructing them how to care for her horse

216

and telling them the correct way to prepare her tea.' He smiled to persuade Penelope to believe it, but in his heart he feared that the desperately ill woman who rode to defy her mortal disease had found the sudden storm too much for her failing strength.

Florrie and Daniels sat in a corner talking in low tones, while Bethan went to and from the window, looking out in the impossible hope of seeing someone returning with news. Penelope sat hugging the empty cup with Olwen sitting on a stool close by her silently comforting her.

When the first men returned with no news except that the storm was worsening, Penelope accepted their defeat calmly and asked them to continue as soon as they had eaten and rested.

It was after three thirty and as dark as night when Carter Phillips came with the worrying news that Arthur and Barrass had been helping with the search and had found a body.

'They told me to hurry on ahead of them and warn you,' he told the Keeper-of-the-Peace. Don't tell Miss Penelope yet, mind! It's by no means certain that it's Mistress Ddole. Just starting to dig it out they were, like, after tripping over it on the path above the sea.'

'Is it my mother?' Penelope whispered, her face a mask of pain.

Carter looked shocked, seeing her for the first time.

'Miss Penelope! I didn't recognize you sitting by there or I wouldn't have broken the news so baldly. I didn't wait until they – until they learnt who it was. Told me to hurry so the household is prepared, like,' he said, gulping in his embarrassment. 'Could be a vagrant!' he added brightly. 'Plenty of them about. Yes, that's most likely, for sure.' He took the mulled ale Florrie handed him and sank his face into it before his tongue could add any more to Penelope's distress.

The kitchen was almost as cold as the air outside, as Penelope constantly asked either Bethan or Florrie to open the door and listen for the approach of the searchers. Daniels had left Florrie's side and was standing just outside the door, watching for someone to appear out of the whiteness. His trousers and cloak were sodden, his feet and hands a dull ache, the centre of his back a river of ice, but the discomfort was preferable to seeing Penelope's stricken young face as she watched the door for news of her mother.

The body was that of Henry Harris. Stiff with cold or rigor mortis, Daniels could not know. He would have to leave that for the doctor to decide. Sufficient for now that it was not Mistress Ddole.

Olwen left Penelope briefly and went to hug Barrass and Arthur. Oh how she missed them, stuck away here in a house filled with strangers, with rules of behaviour that were even stranger. The possible death of her mistress and the certain death of the secretary could not dull the joy she felt on seeing her two friends walk through the door out of the storm.

'Best you take him to the barn,' Daniels said, pushing the girl away from her frantic welcome of them.

'Come on, Miss Penelope,' Olwen said, as Barrass and Arthur went out again. 'I think you ought to go to bed.'

'Olwen,' Florrie scolded. 'It isn't your place to tell–'

'It's all right, Florrie,' Penelope said. 'I want to stay here anyway.'

She smiled at the returning Barrass and Arthur who were red-faced with their struggle through the snow, and soaked from bare heads to their poorly shod feet. 'Get these two something to eat and a drink to warm them, fresh clothes to wear while their own are dried. What are you thinking of that you forget our hospitality?'

Florrie glanced at Daniels and whispered, 'Seems she's taking her mother's place already!'

Barrass sat beside Olwen, near to Penelope, and stayed silent while Florrie went to find clothes.

Even though he had helped find and carry home the body of the secretary, he expected any moment to be told to leave to find himself a place to spend the night as well as he could in the now several feet of snow. Olwen sensed his need to be quiet and she held her tongue from the thousand questions she wanted to ask.

Daniels seemed unable to find a way to help. It seemed pointless to go out and wander around in the hope of finding out something. Best he stayed here and kept Florrie company. The company of Florrie with her sharp tongue, kindly heart and delicious food, was something he was enjoying more and more.

The night passed with nothing more heard of the search. No one had returned with any news of where they had looked, and Olwen suspected that most had gone home to sleep with the intention of beginning the hunt for the missing woman again after daybreak. She was content, with Barrass dozing beside her, his warmth touching her with unbelievable joy, and she did not want the night to end. It was as if his isolation were nothing more than a bad dream. Surely no one would want to send him away again, after he had helped through most of the dangerous night to find Mistress Ddole?

As morning dawned, the snow began to retreat. As suddenly as it had fallen, it started to melt. Dripping was heard like an army of tiny feet from every corner of the house, the snow trampled on the paths changed from white to a moist blue, and people began to appear from every side.

The first to arrive was a boy from one of the cottages, who was crying for someone to come and help his brother. Daniels went, with Barrass and Arthur following, and found the body of a boy of about five years, lying near the gate to the drive.

'It was Mistress Ddole who sent him out,' the boy sobbed. 'Sent him to tell Miss Penelope she was safe. No matter about my brother!'

'Mistress Ddole is safe?' Daniels asked, turning the boy away from the sight of Barrass and Arthur forcing the body out of the snow that seemed unwilling to release it.

'Came past on that horse of hers and demanded that we shelter her and stable her horse and then she sent my brother through the storm to tell them she was safe. He was only five.'

Between them, Barrass and Arthur carried the small body

to the barn and placed it beside that of Henry Harris, then went back to Ddole House.

Daniels did not tell Penelope about the death of the small boy, only that her mother was safe, being cared for by one of the cottagers. Bethan took her up to bed to rest, and Olwen asked Florrie,

'Can I go home for a while, Cook? My mam would be glad to know that I am safe too.'

Olwen walked joyfully between Barrass and Arthur, pushing through the snow that was a wonderland of brilliant whiteness in the shamefaced sun. Every colour of the rainbow shone in the melting snow and its softness was an excuse for them to slide and slither and throw sloppy snowballs at each other, so, when they arrived at the house on the cliffs where an anxious Mary and Spider were watching for them, they looked like drowned rats.

Even Barrass's tight curls had become a straggling mat of moisture-beaded strands around his face, and Olwen's golden hair was a dark fringe of rat tails. Arthur's sparse hair was flattened to his head so he looked as if someone had scalped him. His face seemed even thinner than usual, the adam's apple a huge knot in the sinews of his scrawny neck.

Forgetting their intention of treating Barrass like an outcast, Mary and Spider welcomed them all and began drying them off as they shared news of what was so far known of the deaths in the snow.

CHAPTER THIRTEEN

The snow did not completely melt that day. The deceptive sun faded before the afternoon, and as darkness fell the ground froze, leaving the snow hard and treacherously slippery. The air was still, there was not the slightest wind, but the chill seemed to rise up, spreading through his body and reminding him of the dangers of sleeping outside. The cave was not a cheerful prospect and he turned his back on it and went to the brightly lit house of William Ddole.

As he approached the door, he glanced in through the slightly steamy window, hearing the busy sounds of Florrie and her assistants as they prepared an evening meal for Penelope and her mother. So many people to look after so few family. He sighed. All he wanted was a barn and some bread to fill the ache in his stomach.

He moved closer to the window. Vague shapes passed to and fro, dark colours and some, even with the misted windows, clearly seen to be a bright and startling white. Voices came to him and he moved closer to listen, the vicarious companionship a comfort.

He was lost in wistful imaginings of belonging to a household such as this, so that the hands suddenly gripping roughly on his arms, pinning them close to his body, made him shout in alarm. As he struggled to be free, he turned his head to see one of the stable boys holding him, glaring at him.

'What are you doing here? Spying on us, maybe?'

David was ten years older than Barrass and powerfully built. With ease, Barrass was pushed in through the back door, where Olwen ran to him and begged Florrie to let him at least sit a while before the fire.

'Frozen he'll be if he stays out there with so few clothes on,' she said. 'You don't want another death laid at the door

221

of Ddole House, do you?' she added as doubt showed in Florrie's face.

'What is happening here?' Penelope came into the busy kitchen, where food and the preparation of it was spread across the large table and dishes and pots were stacked against the small table and the sink. 'Barrass?' she looked questioningly at the shivering boy, and at the hands still holding him. 'What *is* going on?' She looked at Florrie for an explanation.

'Snooping he was, Miss Penelope,' Florrie said.

'Were you?' Penelope asked Barrass.

'I'm cold and I have nowhere to sleep. I was drawn to the window for the sight of people and the food and warmth I lack,' he told her.

'Nowhere to sleep, on a night such as this?'

'No, Miss Penelope.'

Penelope gestured irritably for the stable boy to release him and said firmly, 'No one should be turned away on such a night. See that he finds a warm place with the horses, David.'

The stable boy nodded. With a jerk of his head, signalling for Barrass to follow him, he went towards the door.

'Can we find him some food as well, Miss Penelope?' Olwen asked, although from the look Florrie gave her she knew she was chancing another slap for impertinence.

'When you have all eaten, you may send something out to him,' Penelope said, and with a half apologetic glance towards the boy who had spent most of the previous night searching for her mother, she left the room.

Penelope pressed both hands to her burning face. She refused to admit that the cause of her excitement was seeing the orphan, as her mother called Barrass. What was it about him that made her forget who she was? She had only to hear his name to find herself longing to catch a sight of him. On the rare moments when she was in his company she warmed to him as if he were an equal. In moments of wild fancy, she imagined that his father would be discovered to have been a wealthy man, that he had rich blood in his veins. She impatiently pushed away the threads of where that idea might take her. Really she was no better than a servant who harboured impossible longings of a marriage to her master!

She hurried along the passageway and up the stairs to her mother's room. She must forget silly fancies and concentrate on someone who might make her his wife, like John Maddern. But the thought of John, who was at that moment on his way from London with her father, did not even make her aware of her beating heart. The sight of Barrass, in his once-smart clothes now wrinkled with damp, and his dark soulful eyes, made her heart threaten to jump from her body.

Olwen stayed at Ddole House that night. Florrie had insisted that the weather was too bad for the girl to run home at a late hour. She shared a bed with Bethan who, even in the bitter cold, seemed to take for ever to undress and slip between the icy linen sheets.

She tried to talk to the girl, find out more of the way the Ddole family lived. All she knew after her weeks there were the times and contents of their meals. But before her first question was formed and uttered, Bethan was asleep.

Olwen lay awake for a long time, the coldness of her bed, without a fire below adding warmth to the room as it did at home, the strangeness of the attic and her uncommunicative companion all held back sleep, as did the thought of Barrass sleeping in a nearby barn.

A tear slipped from her eye as she wondered if he would ever have a home and the luxury of friends again. If only Mam would let him stay with them. She would willingly give up her bed – or share it with him. Then he would do to her all the things he did with others, like Violet, Carrie and the fat Blodwen, and, she suspected, what he wanted to do with Penelope. She had seen the expression in both their eyes when they had looked at each other down in the kitchen.

She growled like a puppy. Why couldn't he forget about girls just for a little longer? There was no sense in him, she decided. None at all! A deep frown settled on her face as she finally slept.

Barrass woke from a dreamless sleep, warm and comfortable and with crease marks on his face and arms from the hay as evidence of his luxurious accommodation. He was undecided whether to stay or leave. He might be accused of scrounging if he stayed but the thought of some of the bread he could smell baking in the kitchen decided him. He would go when he was told to go, and not before.

It was David who came with food. Bread still hot from the oven and a hunk of cheese, still on the knife. There was an apple, wrinkled from storage, and a mug of ale with which to wash it down. Barrass had never felt so comfortable in his life. If only he could stay. He boldly decided to ask for Miss Penelope and see if she would find him work to pay for his keep.

He knocked on the door, and it was Olwen who opened it, her face lighting up in delight. He handed her his metal breakfast plate and said,

'Will you ask if I can see Miss Penelope, Olwen? I have a hope that she will let me stay, for a while at least.'

Olwen's smile was wiped away by a look of irritation.

'So you want to get around her with your big eyes and your look of a whipped dog, do you?' she whispered, bending forwards in her favoured position for scolding him, small hands on her sacking-covered hips. 'Well I'll warn you, she isn't the sort to be taken in by the likes of you!'

'Who is it, Olwen?' Florrie demanded and, when told that Barrass wanted to see Penelope, she told him to come back later, as it was 'far too early to bother decent people hardly risen from their beds!'

It was too cold to stand and wait, and he didn't want to risk criticism by re-entering the barn without permission, so he went to the small steep woodland leading down to the beach, and spent the morning gathering fallen branches which he intended to sell. Mary allowed him to use Spider's tools

224

again, and he soon had six sacks filled with logs and kindling.

He sold them all within a few hours of starting out, one at a time on his back, and when he had earned sixpence, went with it to the house at the top of the hill and knocked on Mrs Powell's door.

'I've come to pay the last sixpence, and to thank you for waiting,' he said, handing her the coins.

'Selling wood, are you?' she asked.

He thought of the remnants of his day's activities and shook his head. 'Not to you. I have enough small pieces to fill a sack and I'll bring it to you without cost,' he smiled.

When he returned with the sack of wood, he was about to leave it at her door, but knocked and waited. He looked up at the end wall of the house and was alarmed to see how much more weakened it had become. The recent frosts had widened the cracks and made the structure more unstable.

'Best you get Ivor-the-Builder to look at this house,' he said, pointing out the huge cracks. 'Or ask William Ddole to get it fixed, he takes your rent and should make sure it's safe to live in. Dangerous it is, with water in the cracks and the winter frosts hardening and thawing to make the cracks wider.'

'He won't do anything,' the old lady sighed. 'Asked I have, time and again.'

He accepted her thanks for the wood and looking back at the precarious house wall, went up through the fields and on to Ddole House. He felt that he was safer in a barn than some people were in houses, and he determined to mention the woman's plight should he manage to talk to Penelope.

'She won't see you! Too busy for a ragamuffin like you she is!' was Olwen's gloating greeting.

'Oh, then I have nowhere to stay tonight,' he sighed, glancing at Florrie, who was in the act of handing a cup of tea to the Keeper-of-the-Peace.

'She says you can stay, but only for a few nights while you find yourself somewhere else,' Florrie said.

'Thank her for me, will you?' Barrass said, his eyes shining in relief. The barn had been so cosy, he would have hated to return to the cave.

He spent the next three days carting wood and stones to the cliffs above the cave and, throwing them down, used them to make a shelter within the cave. At least here, he thought, no one will destroy it, unless Ivor decides to pay me another visit! He shuddered at the thought that Ivor's temper might be less easily controlled when they next met.

He found a few items of clothing amid the strewn rubble of his last home, stiff with new frost, and he put them to dry around a small fire. Content with what he had achieved, he set out to find himself some work. A safe shelter was the first consideration, but money for food was a close second. He could not go on depending on Olwen and Arthur. He went into the village to beg.

Pitcher threw a volley of bottles at him. Ivor threw an axe. Spider told him it was more than he dare do, to defy the rest of the village on his account, and at Ddole House he was not even seen by Dorothy or her daughter, but told to go away and stay away, by Florrie on their instructions.

On his way back to the cave, he gathered more wood for his store, but on passing the house of old Mrs Powell, went to her door to leave it as an extra gift. If things were difficult for him, then they must be worse for an old lady like her.

As he raised his hand to knock on the door, dust was spreading through the air, and he closed his eyes at the discomfort of it. He became aware of a sound, a slow trickling sound and he waited, listening curiously. Then a few stones fell, some landing near him, and as the sound increased to a roar, he ran away just in time to avoid being covered. The house collapsed with an unbelievably loud noise that went on and on, becoming a part of his existence, filling his head with painful reverberations that he thought would burst his ears.

When he opened his eyes the dwelling place was a pile of screaming rocks and rending wood. All he could see was dust rising like smoke from a giant fire, the house vanished within it. The noise lessened but still echoed within his

226

head for an age. He stared, momentarily dazed by his narrow escape, then realization hit him and he ran towards the moving pile and called with increasing alarm for Mrs Powell.

Pitcher saw him running towards him and raised a bottle ready to throw. But when Barrass called out in obvious alarm and ignored the threatening missile, he lowered it and listened.

'The house has fallen abroad like paper in the rain! Quick, she's inside. Mrs Powell's buried under her house!'

Without waiting to see if Pitcher was following, Barrass ran back up the hill. People were already standing looking at the devastated building, none apparently aware of it being occupied.

Arthur was close behind him as he reached the road where the spread of fallen rocks began, some rolling towards them down the steep hill like a game of skittles. With the dog barking in excitement, they began to climb over the shifting rubble. Once they started to remove the stones and broken timber, others joined in until there was a tunnel of sorts through which Barrass crawled. Ivor Baker called for him to stop.

'No sense you killing yourself,' he said gruffly as Barrass's heels disappeared and more stones fell to hide his passing. 'Take the end of this rope at least,' he shouted, 'then we'll be able to find you if – ' More stones fell and he stopped, convinced the boy would never be seen alive again.

'Old she is,' he said to the crowd who stood around, spuriously anxious looks barely hiding their excitement. 'Old and ready to meet her maker! Barrass, fool that he is, is but a boy.'

Arthur had taken the rope Ivor offered, and attempted to follow his friend under the rubble, but he had no luck, the passageway that had opened to allow Barrass through had been blocked.

'Shout to me, Barrass,' the boy called, tears running through the dust on his face. He listened and then his gaunt face brightened, the eyes widening as he heard sounds below him. With Ivor and Pitcher assisting, and others forming a chain to take the stones he moved, Arthur cleared an area until they could see below the collapsed roof timbers to where a tent-like space was formed.

Mrs Powell was crouched with Barrass leaning over her protecting her from the occasionally falling debris.

'Move everything slowly,' he called to the dirt-streaked, upside-down face that stared, wide-eyed, at them. 'As soon as you've made a space, we'll get her out.'

'Someone's gone to fetch Doctor Percy,' the face reported, coughing and spluttering in the dust before withdrawing into the outside air.

It took all day for the old woman to be brought safely out of the house. As darkness became complete, the house breathed a last sigh and with a groan of distorting wood, the roof timbers surrendered and fell, filling in the space where she and Barrass had been sheltering.

Doctor Percy examined Mrs Powell and after casually assuring her that there was not even a broken bone, he went off leaving others to decide how she was to be cared for.

'You could share my shelter,' Barrass said, 'but I doubt you'd be able to get there.' He stopped as he was about to explain where it was, afraid that once again it would be found and destroyed by those who wanted him gone.

Spider and Mary had arrived and they promised to give a home to the old lady until a better one could be found.

Gradually the crowd dispersed until there was only Pitcher, Arthur, the dog – who had changed from white to dirty grey in a matter of hours – and Barrass. Barrass looked at Pitcher uneasily, wondering how the man would react now the danger was safely passed.

'Best you come home-along-a-me and get yourself cleaned up,' he said gruffly.

'Thank you.' Barrass sighed with relief – perhaps he would be saved yet another night in that cave.

'Best you stay out of sight of Mistress Palmer, mind,' Pitcher warned.

He slept in the cellar with Arthur and the dog, who smelt of soot and old mortar. He was stiff and tired from his efforts in the ruins of Mrs Powell's house, but content, with a roof over his head, some company and a stomach filled with a thick lamb stew left from the family's meal. In the morning, long before it was light, he was hauled out of his warm bed by Pitcher and told to go.

It was a Wednesday and he was sitting on a wall outside the alehouse in the darkness, pretending indifference to the harsh coldness that rimmed everything with white, when Kenneth passed on his way to collect the letters from Swansea.

'Can I come with you, Kenneth?' he asked.

'Can't trust you, boy,' Kenneth said sadly, his breath forming a cloud around his face.

'But why? What am I supposed to have done?' Barrass shouted. Above him a window opened, and Emma threw a bowl of water out.

'Making more noise than the cats, you are!' The window slammed shut and curtains swung across obliterating Emma from his sight. The figure of Kenneth disappeared more slowly, steam from the horse's nostrils blending with the mist of the winter morning. Barrass stood up and stamped his frozen feet. So, he was on his own, what was odd about that? He made his way slowly up the cliff path to see if Mary would give him some breakfast.

Dorothy Ddole was tormented by dreams of children. She had lost three children of her own to infant mortality, but it was not their tiny faces she saw in the darkness of the night. Knowing she was approaching death made her remember with regret all the things she had done that had caused distress to others. There were so many, although the unkind acts towards adults were not responsible for keeping her awake. Only the children.

There was the boy or girl, she knew not which, whom she had chased on horseback only recently as it climbed down from a tree and ran across her path. She had not pulled the horse back but encouraged it onward, used the child as sport, and even laughed as the terrified face

229

screamed out before falling backwards through the hedge and into the stream away from her fearsome, snorting steed.

Another occasion was the night of the snowstorm. She had settled herself comfortably before the fire of one of the cottagers, who dare not deny her. She had eaten their food, made sure they had stabled her horse, and then pointed to the small child who was about to settle into his truckle bed beside the one used by his parents, and insisted they sent him to let her daughter know she was safe.

The snow had looked like a lace curtain of unbelievable beauty when he had opened the door, the surface silently rising and already higher than his hips. She had ignored the pleading eyes of his mother, and told the child to hurry, pulling the blanket the woman had given her closer about her and glaring with disapproval at the open door.

When she had been told that he had died, buried in the snow before walking more than twenty yards, she had felt no remorse, not until the nightmares had begun.

She knew it was knowledge of her own approaching death that made her feel guilt. It was only a labourer's child and they had plenty more. Everyone knew they did not feel things the way people like she felt them, didn't they? But she could not forget the haunted look in the eyes of the child who fell away from her into that stream, wide-eyed in terror, or the sight of that small figure pushing his way out into the snow.

The nights were long, and weakening muscles prevented her from spending too many hours sitting up and reading to pass the lonely hours. Bethan sat in a chair near her for a part of each evening now, but, dozy as her name, the girl slept as soon as she settled in the big, comfortable chair and would not be roused without being hit with a stick and even then she would quickly return to slumber.

Tomorrow William would be home, and perhaps John Maddern with him. She momentarily forgot the way she had caused the death of the cottager's child and piously asked God to allow her to live long enough to see her own daughter betrothed.

Arthur was finding work at the alehouse very hard. He hinted to Pitcher that they needed an extra pair of hands, but Pitcher refused.

'I'll work-along-a-you for the whole morning, boy, and we'll get the work done, somehow.'

Pitcher wanted Barrass back, finding in the boy the fulfillment of his long-felt desire for a son. But although he had pleaded with both Emma, who burst into tears every time the boy's name was mentioned, and with the village council, neither would change their mind about him.

'We couldn't rest easy knowing he was about the place gathering information,' Ivor had insisted. 'Until we can be sure that he is one of us, then he stays an outcast.'

'Best that he goes right away, then we won't have him driving the girls and their mothers to tears of pity and much else besides,' another added.

'I think we should ask the vicar to repeat his warnings about the weakness of the flesh,' came the voice of Carter Phillips' old grandfather whose age no one knew. 'The boy's a danger to young and old.'

So Pitcher deliberately made work difficult and refused to continue with the untidy mess that was to have been Emma's new drawing room, in the hope that eventually Barrass would be allowed to return.

Olwen couldn't find Barrass. She searched frantically during the few spare hours she had, but no one had seen him. Arthur had told her that Pitcher had allowed him to stay for one night, but since then there had been no sign. Florrie told her not to worry about him.

'Found himself a safe place for sure. He's been looking after himself since a baby, that one,' she said in her sharp voice.

The days were short and very cold as Christmas approached, and Olwen was kept busy with preparations. Dragging herself home after hours scrubbing floors, washing shelves or standing at the many tasks Florrie found for her, she would force herself to go to the cave, or to some of the cottagers, asking if there was news of Barrass, but for three days there was none.

On Sunday afternoon, when she was allowed a few precious free hours she went to see Enyd. She was invited inside the house on the earthen bank by Enyd, and was surprised to see her brother in the living room.

'Anything wrong at home?' He stood up immediately.

'Come from work I have, not to fetch you,' Olwen explained. 'I wondered if Kenneth has seen anything of Barrass.'

'Dadda won't talk to him, not now,' Enyd said firmly, glancing at her mother. 'What with one thing and another, no one will spare him a thought.'

'Well I will!' Olwen said aggressively. 'Disappeared he has, and *I'm* thinking about him for sure! It's never been so cold as this week, and him with nowhere to sleep. Searched for Mistress Ddole all through the night of the snowstorm, and saved old Mrs Powell from her house, then sent off as if he were a scabby old dog!' She took the seat her brother offered, but continued to glare at both him and Enyd.

Ceinwen offered the girl a cup of tea and a Welsh-cake, still hot from the girdle. She was red-faced from the heat, and her eyes reflected red from the flames.

'Don't fuss yourself, girl,' she said. 'He'll have found a place, that one. Never been without a bed and a feed yet. Someone'll take pity on him.'

'He doesn't want anyone to "take pity".' Olwen sighed as she sank her teeth into the hot, flat, spicy fruit-cake. 'He's a part of this village and should have a place, not be depending on handouts from anyone who feels pity!'

She left after a while, with Dan promising to wait until Kenneth returned from his rounds.

'I'll ask for news, there's no one more able to tell you where he is, even if he doesn't talk to the boy,' Dan said. 'Hears everything, Kenneth does.'

Olwen went next to the alehouse. It was closed and dark apart from a flickering light from a back room. She banged loudly on the door and window until Pitcher came complaining that the glass would be smashed and him with enough to pay for already.

'No, I haven't seen him since Wednesday,' he said. 'And thank you for *not* banging on the glass when it's nothing more urgent you have to say.' He closed the door on her as from upstairs he could hear Emma shouting, demanding to know who was calling.

He stood behind the closed door for a moment, ashamed of the way he had turned the girl away, ashamed too that the village was ignoring a homeless person in this weather. Repaying his kindness by fathering a child on his daughter was inexcusable, but the boy did not deserve to die out in the frosts like a sick old fox.

Emma's voice was becoming a wail, and he reached for a cloak hanging behind the door. With an irritable shout to explain his intention, he ran after Olwen, to see her safely home. Spite couldn't include little Olwen no matter how loyal she was to the boy.

Olwen heard Mistress Powell's gentle snores coming from below her, and imagined the old woman sitting in the chair near the fire, so much a part of their home now, she was hardly noticed. There was an occasional crack as a stick was fed to the flames, and the shuffling of falling coals. Small sounds, familiar and soothing. Then she heard Dan returning from Enyd's and, hoping for news of Barrass, she hurried down the ladder in her nightgown and a woollen hat – and screamed with delight to see Barrass standing beside Dan, both glowing from their walk up the cliff path.

Her eyes were huge with sleep, her smiling face small yet perfectly formed, framed by the hat which covered her ears yet allowed her hair to cascade down her back in disarray. She was startled by a look of surprise and admiration on Barrass's face, and blushed in the wonder of it. Unrecognizable sensations suffused her body, starting deep within her and spreading until even the tips of her toes were warmed by them.

'I've been looking for you,' she whispered, her voice sounding as strange as the feelings his eyes had stimulated.

233

'I've been sleeping in a barn so near you I could have called and you would have heard me,' he smiled. 'At Ddole House, with the connivance of Florrie and David.'

She thought she would hear if he called from a hundred miles away.

'If Mistress Ddole found out – ' she said, wishing that the look had not already faded from his dark eyes.

'I'm gone long before the family is up.'

'I thought you might be off on some trip to find your father,' she said, as Mary prepared a drink and food for them.

'William Ddole is back now, delayed he was with the ice and snow. I can't sleep there any longer,' Barrass told them. 'I'm off to the cave, but don't tell anyone where I am, will you?'

'In more trouble? Been fathering more babies?' Olwen whispered to him, and he laughed.

In the corner, Mistress Powell opened rheumy eyes and winked at the tall, dark young man as if with a shared secret.

'You shouldn't know about such things, Olwen, you're only a child,' Barrass whispered back, deliciously close to her ear so his breath filtered through the woollen hat.

'Mamma, Dadda, we can't let him go to the cave at this time of night, now can we?' she said firmly, willing her words to be heeded by her stony-faced father and her gentle, concerned mother.

'Spider?' Mary said, looking at her husband.

'All right, but not a word to anyone or I'll have some explaining to do,' Spider said gruffly. He did not like leaving Barrass to fend for himself, but was afraid of disobeying the council. 'Cwtch up on the seat near the fire and out you go before anyone is about in the morning. Right?'

Olwen went to bed to dream of that look returning to Barrass's face, warmed by the memory of it, and the knowledge that he was sleeping near her.

Barrass stayed awake for a long time thinking of Olwen, and to his surprise his first thought in the morning was of her, wearing that childish hat with the fastenings tied under her chin, that had made her look so unbelievably beautiful.

234

Mary and Olwen watched as Barrass set off to re-inhabit his cave. Mary had given him some extra clothes and some old, rather worn blankets made years before from the sheep's wool she had collected from the hedgerows. Spider walked with him to carry the gifts which included food.

As they reached the place where the path lay dangerously near the edge and gave them their first view of the sea, Barrass stopped and pointed. Below them, washed this way and that by the waves were planks of wood and other debris. Spider looked at the boy and, deciding to trust him, said slowly,

'It's the boats that were lost on the night of the snow-storm, boy. They didn't read the signs of the approaching storm – took many of us by surprise, it did. They should have turned back, or at least stayed well clear of land with visibility practically nil.'

'It was a cargo from France, was it?' Barrass asked. When Spider nodded, they climbed down to search the beach for bodies.

There were none to be found. Of the cargo they saw only a spoilt bale of silk, a solitary barrel, which they dragged above the tide line and hid among pebbles and rocks, and a few empty and broken boxes. Sadly, thinking of the lives probably lost, Barrass and Spider went on their way to the cave.

'I'll go later and tell them at Ddole House,' Spider said.

'I'll go if you wish,' Barrass said, hoping that if he was trusted with such a message by Spider, others might recon-sider their treatment of him. Spider shook his head again.

'Best for you and me if you don't mention this,' he said and Barrass sadly agreed.

Spider waited until Barrass had lit a fire and made the place as comfortable as possible. 'Sorry I am, boy,' he said, 'but until the council change their mind about you, I can't do more.'

'It's work I need,' Barrass said, 'I'm not asking for charity, just a chance to earn my bread. But I don't want to leave the village to find it. No one wants me but I still feel this is where I belong.'

'You won't get work near people with young daughters,' Spider warned him grimly. 'Made a big mistake getting tangled up with half a dozen girls, and not wanting to marry any one of them.'

'I'd have married Violet. I'd have worked alongside Pitcher and been a good husband. But Emma wouldn't even consider me for *her* daughter.'

'Can't blame her for that,' Spider laughed. 'Nothing but a cave, and that filled with stuff others have no need of. Compared with that Edwin, you aren't a very good catch, now are you?'

'But I'm going to be somebody one day,' Barrass said firmly. 'Just you wait. You'll have Emma regretting she didn't get me for a son-in-law.' He swallowed to fight back the tears threatening and they were silent for a while, watching the flames.

'What do you remember of my mother?' he asked when Spider stood to leave. 'There's so little I can truly recall and I need to hang onto what little there is.'

'She lived around the village, finding work here and there for most of the year. Much like you're doing now,' Spider told him. 'She was pretty, but always very thin and undernourished in spite of the help people gave her. One day when she had been away up in the north shepherding through the summer months, she told Mary – Mary was her friend – that she was carrying a child. You were born two months later. About this time of the year it was.'

'And my father?'

'You've asked me before,' he said solemnly.

'I keep asking in the hope that someone will remember some little thing my mother said, something to guide me to him.'

'Best you forget and clear your mind of what's past and gone. Who's to say it would help if you did find him, eh? Might be nothing but a problem, and it seems to me you've plenty of those already.'

When Spider had gone, Barrass worked for a while tidying the place that seemed likely to be his home for the foreseeable future, his thoughts still on his father. Tall he

236

was, he told himself, and with dark, soulful eyes. His plentiful hair was a rich brown touched with red like the polish on a fine wooden table. He chanted the few facts like a litany, forcing himself to remember them, afraid that even the pathetically few remembered words would fade like the rest, into false, wishful imaginings.

The memory of the message came to him so suddenly he cried out his stupidity at having forgotten it. He tried to bring to mind the day when Ben Gammon's message had arrived with its promise of news about his father and, searching in the pockets of his jacket that had suffered so many soakings, found the piece of paper, almost pulped. The message was blurred and impossible to read. Why had he forgotten something as important as this? He closed his eyes, screwing them up tight in the effort to remember what it said.

'Nant Arian – Silver Stream – that was the name of the place,' he muttered. 'Someone there who might be my father. How could I let that slip my mind?' Now he had remembered, he wanted to go there without delay. Perhaps it was already too late? The day was hardly started, he would go at once.

He knew where the small hamlet was to be found, a small crossroads near a fast-flowing stream that gave the place its name. He had passed there once or twice when delivering letters for Kenneth. The day was sharply cold but a weak sun showed and, once he had started the blood flowing, he enjoyed the walk. There was some purpose to his day for the first time in weeks.

He stopped once to eat some of the bread Mary had given him, but it tasted of mildew from his pocket. He threw it down for the jackdaws that hovered hopefully near him, calling their name. He was glad to move on again. Hunger was not an urgent problem, he would be back at the cave before dark.

Swinging his arms to shake off the cold that the brief stop had allowed to seep through the damp cloth he continued on his way. He would spend the rest of the day drying his clothes before they were too mouldy to use. Once he had realized how badly his jacket smelt of mildew, the stink seemed to hover around him like a cloud.

As he approached the small community, following the stream, he met a couple of boys about ten years old. They were poking at something at the edge of the water, and pulling faces as if enjoying some huge joke.

'What have you found?' he called, and they beckoned him closer.

'It's the bachgen man,' one of them shouted. 'Come and see.'

The body of a small person, his back curved and distorted, lay huddled in the mud. Remnants of clothing clung to the body which, Barrass guessed, must have been no more than three and a half feet tall.

'A child?' he asked, sympathy clouding his face.

'No, a bachgen man, a little boy-man, drowned he did long before the snow came.'

'Why isn't he buried then?' Barrass frowned.

'A joke,' the first boy laughed. 'It's left for a joke, see.'

'There's someone coming who's been told that his father is here,' the second boy went on. 'When he comes, we're to show him this!' Both boys went into paroxysms of laughter, hugging each other in glee, and did not see Barrass stride angrily away.

CHAPTER FOURTEEN

The death of Henry Harris affected several lives. Bessie Rees lost the regular payment for looking after him in the small house near the village. She was elderly and the money he gave her for washing his clothes, cleaning his house and cooking his simple meals would be sorely missed. Especially now, with a baby soon to feed and Carrie having lost her position at Ddole House.

Florrie grieved the loss of a friend, who had called regularly and taken food and drink in her kitchen and shared with her the daily happenings of their employer's family. He had known about forthcoming events as soon as the family had decided on them and the advance knowledge, which he had willingly passed on in her kitchen, had given her an important place in the village as well as the household. Her life would be poorer for his passing.

For the Ddole family, there was relief mixed with their sadness.

'He has been a faithful servant,' William said when he was told the news, 'but the time has come when we need a fresh young brain to cope with our business affairs.'

Penelope agreed, wondering if perhaps with a new secretary the accounts would be settled more promptly and no more unpleasant letters would arrive to worry her.

She handed three of them to her father after dinner on the day he and John Maddern returned from London.

The first thing William did was talk to his bank, and explain that there would be new signatures on future correspondence. The bank replied that unless funds were added to his account swiftly, there would be no need for further correspondence. He tried to bluff it out, pretending he knew nothing of the unpaid bills, but the owner of the bank was adamant. He would cash no more bills of hand, until the money was back where it should be. An imperious finger pointed to the large withdrawals that had been transacted during the past weeks. William left Swansea with the anxiety that, with Henry Harris dead, he had no way of finding out why the removal of funds had taken place. What could have happened to make Henry Harris deplete his funds in such a way? There was no sudden and unexpected debt to explain it.

He took John Maddern, a close business associate, into his confidence. The man had expressed his hope to marry Penelope so it was only just that he was made aware of the difficulties facing her family.

John was a serious man who rarely smiled. Listening to William explain the mysterious situation to him, in a quiet corner of the alehouse, he promised to both look at William's accounts and find him an honest secretary to take hold of the reins once the crisis was past.

'Be sure it is only a temporary crisis, William,' he said. 'There has obviously been something amiss with Henry and we will find out what it is and put things right.'

'You sound very sure,' William said. 'What a homecoming: my wife looking sick to death, and so unlike her normal brave self I am afraid to go into her room for fear she has already left us. Penelope anxious and afraid, having carried the burden of this alone, while I have been away. A valuable cargo lost and fine men drowned in the snowstorm. Everything is at a variance with normality, it seems, yet you think this is a temporary state of affairs?'

'Your wife is indeed very sick and I fear there will be no happy outcome there. She has suffered a great deal of pain and her eyes show that she is giving up the struggle. Something depresses her mightily besides her sickness, I think.'

'And the rest?'

'I can make Penelope forget her worries and persuade her to enjoy the forthcoming festivities. Perhaps if we announce our betrothal, that will have a good effect on your wife's spirits, as well as on Penelope?' He looked thoughtfully at the stained wooden table, lost in his thoughts – as was usual for him once a problem presented itself for his solving. He said little as they finished their drink and headed towards Ddole House.

'Do you have land you can sell?' he asked finally.

'Will I need to?' William frowned.

'It depends on just how Henry Harris behaved. If he was an honest man then the solution will be there for us to find. If he were dishonest, then you will have to find a way of making money fast.' John spoke with such slowness that William found his thoughts racing ahead, hardly hearing the man's words. There was the land on the clifftop, where Spider and his family lived. Spider was a fisherman and could surely manage without the piece of land, so long as he had enough somewhere else for a cow and a few pigs?

He was aware of the danger of allowing someone they could not trust to buy the land just there with a clear view of the sea, but there was surely someone who would be both suitable and interested?

When he slid from his horse and called for David to attend to it, he walked in having almost forgotten the man with him.

John had a fine business brain, and the ability to see and consider a problem from many sides, playing with each before abandoning it, until he found the right way of dealing with a situation. But his slowness made him hard work to converse with at times.

William went first to his wife's room, where he found her in a chair near the fire.

'My dear, you are feeling better?'

'Much,' she smiled. 'I have spent the afternoon ordering a few new things. Spending always cheers me. I sent for the seamstress and have instructed her to make three dresses for Penelope and a housecoat for myself. I feel the draughts more, this winter. A horse to replace the one grown too irritable for Penelope to ride safely and a new Aubusson carpet for the drawing room, my dear. And I feel so much better too for getting out of that dreaded bed.'

'Don't stay out too long, my dear, or you will be stiff like the last time.' He tried to speak calmly but was horrified at her casual spending. But how was she to know of his problems? For the first time ever, he had not shared his worries with her.

'To escape from the prison of the bed for a while is worth the discomfort of an aching back and a raw agony in my other parts. I feel then I deserve to take an extra dose of the medicine that fool Percy gives me.'

He kissed her, aghast at the porcelain frailness of her body as he touched her but hiding his broken-hearted grief until he had closed the door. Leaving her with a cheerfulness that had him choking back the desire to howl, in a bravery that had to match hers, he stood for a long time with his hand still on the door latch, wondering how long before he opened it to find her gone.

'John,' he said, when they had finished their meal, 'I want you to stay here for the festivities. You know how well my wife loves a party, and we'll give her the best yet.'

'Can you afford it?' John asked, wearing his most serious expression.

'Oh, could we? Mother has arranged for the performers to act the new Interludes for us,' Penelope told him.

'Then we will make sure they come and bring as many of their followers as we can squeeze into the house,' William said. 'Will you make all the arrangements tomorrow? Make sure we have plenty of victuals, my dear, and that everyone knows they are invited?'

'I will go with you,' John offered, thinking that with William temporarily out of credit, his own pocket might be needed.

All next day, Florrie and her staff were frantically busy counting out the stores they had and what they would need for the party. Olwen was sitting on the floor, sorting the contents of the many jars and tins and boxes containing everything from oatmeal and flour to the jars of expensive spices and herbs that Cook used. The amount of each item was written down, and the shortfall noted, ready for the shopping trip to Swansea on the following day.

When Penelope stepped into the kitchen with the list of

guests, Florrie wailed that the kitchen would need to be double the size for the meat alone to be cooked.

'Send some out,' Penelope said. 'Most cottagers will be able to cook at least one joint for you. It's a party for the villagers so it isn't unreasonable that they are asked to help.' She added another name to the list before handing it to the irate cook, who was trying to stay calm amid the flurry of Christmas preparations as well as the unexpectedly large house-party.

'There'll be need for more help on the day, too, Miss Penelope,' she said with a warning shake of her head, 'and to add to the fun, Bethan saw a rat in the laundry today, seems they're back for the winter.'

'Did she catch it?'

Florrie looked lugubriously at her mistress and asked, 'Bethan, Miss Penelope?'

'Send for Collins the rat-catcher at once.'

'Yes, Miss Penelope,' Florrie sighed. 'At once.' She looked around at the chaotic state of her usually neat kitchen. 'I'll do everything "at once".'

As soon as Penelope had gone, Florrie slapped Olwen's ears and said, 'Take this list and put it in the drawer, then go and tell Collins that we need his services, "at once". Then clear all this stuff back into the cupboards, "at once". Then, when you've done all that, see that this afternoon's meal is ready to serve, "at once".' Still repeating 'at once' in a low mutter, Florrie went to the corner and, flapping her apron to cool her face, sat and closed her eyes, dreaming the mess would be gone when she reopened them.

Olwen held her ears where Florrie's hand had landed, and opened the drawer to slip the list of guests inside, but she could not resist glancing to see whose was the name added as an afterthought. Her lips tightened with disapproval when she pointed to each letter and laboriously spelt out: Barrass. What does she want with him, she wondered, then aloud she asked,

'Cook, shall I leave early and go and tell Barrass he's invited?'

The apron over Florrie's face rose and fell and snores

came from behind it. Florrie, overcome for once by all she had to do, had fallen asleep.

The short plays using stories from the bible, or on occasion the theme of an enjoyable sermon, were written by Dan and Arthur. Between them they discussed an idea, then began planning the rhymes. Eventually Dan wrote it all down for the players to learn. Several of the performers could not read, but during the rehearsals soon became familiar with the words and the tone in which the composers wanted them said.

Dan wrote the music but this they did not write down, neither knowing how, so he would sing the simple melodies over and over, until the group knew all the songs.

'Important,' Dan insisted, 'because should some or one of us be taken ill, someone else must be ready to take our place.'

Rehearsals took place either in Kenneth's small house or, when Pitcher was in an amiable mood, at the alehouse. For this favour, Pitcher insisted that the first performance should be his. Shortly before Christmas, the newest Interludes had their first showing.

Arthur, because of his high-pitched voice, played a woman. He wore an old dress once belonging to Emma, and told of the sadness that befell those who did not love their neighbours as themselves. The story showed how a woman ignored the plight of her penniless neighbour and refused to help feed her children, then, several scenes later, how the neighbour became rich and, when the opportunity came, forgot the previous unkindness and gave generously to the one who had refused her. The scene ended with Arthur, the generous woman, raised up on ropes on a complicated pulley system devised by the blacksmith, apparently on her way to heaven.

The first time this was tried the rope broke, catapulting Arthur into the audience who were staring up at the rafters in awe of the magnificent effects. Emma, who with Pansy and Daisy, had been seated closest to the stage, thought it was an avenging angel, part of the performance, and hearing the applause from her fat little hands, others joined in. After a hurried consultation, a bruised and aggrieved Arthur agreed to go along with the idea, but fervently hoped he would not be expected to do the death-defying fall at every performance.

It was at a barn near Thistleboon that they performed for the second time, and the rope was in the powerful hands of Carter Phillips. Used to handling a pair of heavy horses, he assured Arthur that he could not be in better or safer hands.

He wound the rope carefully around the pulley with the aid of a handle made by the blacksmith, but in his excitement, caught up in the dramatic ending to the story, he forgot which way to wind it and changed direction several times as he became more and more embarrassed at his mistakes. For several terrifying moments, Arthur was winched up and down, struggling to free himself, while the audience blocked the door trying to escape his flailing feet.

For the benefit of those unable to pay to see the Interludes, the generous group did a special outdoor production. Arthur was eagerly looking forward to it.

'At least you can't half kill me in a field,' he said, his adam's apple wobbling in a frenzy of relived fear. He dressed up, rehearsed his words and went to the field, with his dog trotting beside him, at peace with the world. Then he saw the oak tree.

He began removing the dress. The weather was still very cold but he ignored it as Dan, Phillips and the others ran towards him.

'What are you doing?' Dan demanded. 'It's nearly time to start!'

'I'm taking *everything* off if necessary,' Arthur said, showing his skinny legs as his woollen trousers, worn under the dress, began to slide downwards. 'I won't stop undressing until that there rope is taken from that there oak tree.'

His shirt was thrown to the ground, where the dog began to shake it as if it were a rat, then the vest which had seen better days and was an embarrassment both to him and to the audience now gathering.

'All right, all right,' Dan groaned. 'You can walk off backwards, and that will have to do.'

Arthur smiled and began dressing again – all except the shirt, which the dog and taken and which was never again found.

It was the eve of Christmas day when their visit to Ddole House took place. The large living room had been emptied of furniture apart from seats for Penelope and her mother. William and John stood behind them, leaning against the wall near the fireplace.

Those who could not get inside stood in the hall or up the curving staircase, and even outside in the dark garden, climbing on one another to share the view through the windows. To accommodate all the guests, they were to perform twice. Arthur reluctantly agreed to rise on the rope for the second and final performance only.

Those who had seen the first showing moved with difficulty to allow others to take their places, and Violet, who had stepped into the dining room with Edwin, found herself face to face with Barrass, who was standing at the door into the garden.

'Miss Violet,' he said, backing away.

'Get out of here,' Edwin snarled, his arm raised threateningly. 'You have no right to be anywhere near here. Leave the village, you aren't welcome.'

Barrass was cold and hungry, and the invitation which he had received via Arthur gave him courage.

'Told to come, I was,' he said firmly. 'Told to come and see the Interludes and have a bite of supper.'

'I'll see to this!' Edwin moved off, calling for William, and Violet was left staring into Barrass's glowing eyes.

She held her mouth a little agape, drinking in the sight of him: large, strong, confident beyond belief for someone in his unenviable situation, his bedraggled clothes seemingly unimportant. A longing for him made a sob escape her parted lips. Edwin, suddenly remembering that he had left them alone, came back, pushed angrily against Barrass, who did not move, and went out again, dragging Violet in his wake.

Edwin came back shortly, this time without his wife, and said threateningly, 'Go, you. If I ever find you near my wife I'll kill you.'

Barrass was trembling, not because of the threats, but the sudden sight of Violet and the knowledge that she still wanted him, as he longed for her. Memories flooded back and he felt the urge to run, to go somewhere to sit alone and dream of her and their brief and wonderful moments together. There had been plenty of others, but Violet was very special, their time together unforgettable.

He went into an empty room and closed the door, unable to decide what to do. He wanted to go away but the thought of food held him, and the chance of another glimpse of Violet to help him through the lonely night. He looked up with hope as the door opened, but it was Penelope who came in.

'Barrass,' she whispered, 'I am so sorry to put you through this embarrassment, but I think you must leave. My father and John tell me you should not have been invited.'

'I was going anyway,' he said.

'Wait a moment,' she said, 'I cannot let you go without food. There is a fine supper laid in the barn with plenty for everyone. Please come with me now and I will see that you are fed.'

Barrass could not refuse either the thought of a few moments of her company or the supper.

They ran across the yard to the brightly lit barn. Apart from three specially hired servants known to neither of them, the place was empty. Already the long trestle tables were groaning under the weight of the supper. Candles had been lit and placed around the walls on metal sconces, each one decorated with twigs of holly and garlands of ivy. On the table between the dishes of meats, cheeses and bread and the dishes of preserves, more lights glowed, giving the place a magical air.

In two corners of the room were barrels of ale supplied by Pitcher. Rows of pewter mugs stood waiting to be filled, most brought by their owners for fear of losing a drink for lack of a pot. Many others had their mugs safe in their pockets for when the performance ended and supper was called.

The three servants were setting the last of the plates and arranging the benches for a few more important people to sit. Twenty at a time would be allowed into the feast, the rest would wait, anxiously watching the depleting piles of food, and the gradually emptying barrels. The settings done, the servants quietly left.

'Give me your scarf,' Penelope said and Barrass tried to unfasten it from his neck. Troubled with the knot in the wet material, he bent his knees for Penelope to undo it for him.

The touch of her fingers on his neck did strange things to him and he glanced at her to see two frightened eyes, luminous and large, staring into his own. He held both his breath and her gaze, his expression softening into that of love, moisture filling his brown eyes as she continued to stare at him. His hands covered hers and together they unfastened the knot. His hands lay lightly over hers and the scarf dropped onto the straw-covered floor.

'I'll fill it with food to last tomorrow as well,' she whispered, her hand limp and submissive in his.

From the house came the sound of Dan singing a slow, sentimental song, the words only a blur, the music an accompaniment to the sensations shared by the ill-matched couple. She wore a dress of dark red taffeta and a shawl of creamy wool, he was in a crumpled jacket that had been soaked and dried repeatedly, and trousers that had once been the latest fashion but now bore evidence of his having slept in them for many nights. Penelope's hair was smoothly held back and up from her slender neck, the lamps picking out the golden glints, his was a wild bush of deepest black, framing his features and shadowing his intensely powerful eyes.

The words of the song were in fact pious, telling of a flower of eternal life planted in every heart, being fed by kindness to others or dying of neglect, but the distantly heard melody and the sweet voice made a love song for the two people in the barn.

Florrie was shouting orders, making the servants, including an exhausted Olwen, run to and fro and bump into each other in the large kitchen. She supervised as meats were piled on platters and carried to the table, where she would add the finishing touches before nodding satisfaction that they were fit to be served. Olwen tore loaves apart and piled them into deep baskets and all these were put ready for replenishing the tables in the barn. Florrie was finally satisfied that nothing had been forgotten.

Everyone was tired, but the need to get the work done forced them to forget their aching legs, and get on with the seemingly endless tasks. Between sorting out the enormous supplies of food for the barn, the red-faced cook was trying to look into the room where the performance was taking place, to see if Daniels and his children were there. She had never seen his five children and was curious to see how well he cared for them. Daniels was always neatly clothed and she wondered if his finery was at the expense of his children.

She settled the troupe of seventeen servants, who were falling over each other in their haste to please her, to wash and tidy away those pans, pots and tins she had finished with. All that remained was to carry in the hot dishes. Giving Olwen a large dish of hot pease-pudding and boiled, sliced ham with capers to take to the barn, she slipped once again into the passageway to look into the crowded audience for the face of the Keeper-of-the-Peace.

She saw him between bobbing heads as the audience stood and sat, cheering and booing the characters in turn. He was standing against the far wall, his children dropping in size like steps to one side of him. The oldest and youngest were girls of about fifteen and six. Between them were three boys and all were dressed as neatly and expensively as she could imagine.

The girls wore identical dresses of a beautiful red plaid, full-skirted, and white lace-frilled aprons tied at each side with a full and lacy bow. Their coats were over their arms as they stood hardly able to move for the crush, yet uncomplaining and obedient. Framing delightfully pretty faces were poke bonnets over long, shining hair.

The boys were neatly dressed in red plaid trousers, white linen shirts and leather shoes shining with polish. Florrie's heart sank – there must be a woman somewhere in Daniel's life for his family to be so well turned out. She returned to the kitchen and shouted impatiently for Olwen.

Dan's song had finished to wild applause and was swiftly followed by the high straining voice of Arthur in his role as righteous woman. The contrast, to Barrass and Penelope listening in the barn, caused them to smile. A smile which, fed by uneasy forbidden excitement, turned to giggling laughter. Barrass leaned forward to take Penelope's weight against him, and for a moment she froze, then he felt her body relax and soften against his. Her head lifted and he stared once again into those serious, wide hazel eyes. His head bent towards her almost without his intention and their lips touched, trembled and blended into a kiss.

Olwen pushed against the door with her back as her arms were holding the warm dish and taking all her strength to keep it from slipping. She rolled around the door and stared in disbelief at the couple almost beside her.

'Barrass!' she said, and the couple sprang apart as if on a cart-spring.

'Please put down your dish and go back to the kitchen,' Penelope stuttered. 'I am finding some food for Barrass before he leaves.'

Cheekily, Olwen said, 'Food? Yes, I suppose kisses *are* food for such as him!' She placed the dish on the table and, fishing out a slice of ham, threw it at Barrass – to see it land on his cheek, held there by the pease-pudding. With a glare of unrepentant defiance for Penelope, she ran from the barn and burst in through the kitchen.

'Best we set out the rest of the hot food, or we'll be

250

crushed in the rush,' she shouted at Florrie, and the cook was so surprised at her impertinence that she obeyed.

When Florrie went into the barn Penelope was placing bread and cheeses and some cold pork into Barrass's scarf. Florrie curtsied politely to Penelope then, seeing the smear of pease-pudding across Barrass's face, scolded him for starting before the rest. She did not understand why both of them laughed.

In the packed living room, the final Interlude was coming to an end. Emma, standing beside her daughters and Edwin Prince, was unable to decide whether or not she should, as a lady of some importance, be amused by the antics of those on the stage. She looked for a lead from others, and seeing the Ddoles obviously enjoying themselves, thought a cautious nod of approval might not be misunderstood. She did not feel at ease. Evenings like these were a real bother, some performances were acceptable to everyone – and others, and she was not sure which, were definitely not. She wished she had pretended one of her headaches and stayed away. Best to be absent than to be considered less than ladylike in the way she chose her entertainments. Musical evenings were best. She knew where she was with a musical evening.

Arthur was still adamant that he would not be hauled up by ropes over the beams by the blacksmith and Carter Phillips. Then Pitcher asked him.

'I want you to pretend to hurt yourself,' he whispered, a weather eye on his wife. 'If Emma thinks you can't work then she'll support me in my efforts to get Barrass back. She knows I can't manage the place on my own, and even with you it's nigh impossible.'

Reluctantly, Arthur agreed. 'For Barrass, mind,' he muttered, 'and I want a promise that you'll pay me when I can't work if the pretence goes on for more than a day.'

Under the dress the ropes were attached and partly hidden. Behind the scenery they stretched up to the thick rafters under the roof. It looked a long way up to Arthur as he prepared for the final scene.

In an effort to hide the surprise of Arthur rising to

251

'heaven' – in his long and well-padded dress, eyes raised to greet his maker – from those who had not seen a previous performance, the thick rope was coiled on the stage where actors and banks of greenery hid it from view. Unfortunately, Spider, who was assisting with announcements and by dragging holly and evergeens to and fro as scenes changed, tripped and knocked the rope under Arthur's feet.

The result was that as he was raised to heaven in a chorus of aahs and oohs from an impressed audience, the rope around his feet altered his position to hanging upside down, with Spider being hauled up beside him. Spider's long legs flailed wildly, knocking over the banks of greenery and disclosing the rest of the cast partially undressed as they changed costumes for the final applause.

Emma's doubts returned and she shouted for the twins to close their eyes, but found herself unable to look away from the sight of the men in the attitude of prayer, as they knelt down and tried to hide their most private possessions. Spider managed to swing across and reach the beams and, with the blacksmith's assistance, lowered Arthur to the stage where he fell into a heap. Spider swung himself down, completing a feat of acrobatic ability that raised a cheer and would be a talking point for many weeks. John and Edwin picked up the fallen greenery, and eventually order returned.

William hugged his wife, laughing helplessly, and could not make the speech of thanks he had planned. It was Penelope who stood amid the ruins of the stage and announced that supper was ready in the barn.

The valiant actors sat, hidden by the banks of restored greenery, and gathered their senses.

'Do you think it was a success?' Arthur asked in his high voice.

'Put it this-a-way. Best we go and find ourselves some supper before they throw us out,' Pitcher laughed. He offered a hand to Arthur. 'I think Mrs Palmer would believe a disturbed and sprained ankle bone, don't you?'

Ivor and Winifred Baker led their pale-faced daughter

252

Blodwen in for supper. Scuttling in their wake, hoping to avoid too many comments, came Carrie Rees. She stood beside Blodwen, both girls wearing very full skirts to hide their increasing fullness. Blodwen, always a fat child, was already showing her pregnancy in spite of her efforts to hide it. Her face had extra roundness, an added fleshiness about the chin, and her sad eyes showed undisguised dismay at her condition.

'I don't know why she insisted on coming,' Ivor grumbled to Winifred. 'Makes me feel uncomfortable it does, escorting *two* girls whose condition is rising into prominence by the hour! People will think it's me that's the cause if Carrie hangs around us like this! Bad enough with my own daughter growing a child and the father unwilling to lay claim to it!'

'I wanted to come and make the Ddoles ashamed for what they did for me,' Carrie told him, having overheard his complaint.

'What the *Ddoles* did?' Ivor turned on her and several people stopped eating and talking to listen. 'I thought you said it was Barrass?' he hissed out of the side of his mouth.

'The Ddoles threw me out, not caring that I had no man to keep me, and me not likely to find another place,' Carrie pouted. 'Mam hasn't spoken to me since.'

'You don't think it's *Barrass* and not the Ddoles to blame for your difficulties?' Winifred exploded.

'Never. He didn't do it alone,' Carrie said with a smile shared by Blodwen. Her smile widened a little when Winifred turned and slapped Blodwen, as the reminder brought fresh anger against her wayward daughter.

Bessie Rees pushed her way towards them, a linen bag tied around her waist, hidden inside her voluminous skirts. As she helped herself to food, she dropped pieces of meat, bread and cheese down to fill it. She ignored her daughter.

When one of the servants came and asked Bessie to go and see William Ddole, she unfastened the bag with a wail of dismay, shaking her hips to free herself of it. They'd seen her helping herself! And her only grabbing a bit of food to see them through the next few days! Stepping over

253

the incriminating false pocket, she followed the boy through the festive crowd to William Ddole's study. Quaking with fear, her head filled with half-prepared excuses, she went inside.

William had John Maddern with him.

'Mistress Rees. My friend and associate Mr Maddern has a mind to stay in the area for a while and plans to take the cottage recently used by Henry Harris. He would like you to look after him as you cared for Mr Harris, if you will.'

The relief was so great that Bessie could only mumble her thanks, and make an unsuccessful attempt to promise her best endeavours at all times.

'I will call on you when the festivities are over and we will discuss what I need from you,' John said.

With more disjointed thanks and promises, Bessie backed out and hurried back to the barn.

She was delighted. If John Maddern paid her as generously as Henry Harris had, then she would manage well enough, even without her daughter making a contribution. She did not go to share her good news with Carrie, but went under the table to retrieve her false pocket.

Olwen searched for Barrass. She guessed that he would not go while the party continued, but would stay and watch, enjoying vicariously the social gathering, the merriment of friends. She found him in the porch outside the back door, staring in through the tiny window. He was hugging his scarf, swollen with gifts of food, nursing it like a baby in the crook of his arm.

'Barrass,' she whispered, 'if you come round to the kitchen door, I'll find you some ale.'

'Olwen,' he sighed, pulling her close to him. 'Why am I always on the outside of everything? What have I done that no one will befriend me?'

'I've just seen Blodwen and Carrie! And there's Gaynor too! And that Violet Palmer is hereabouts! You can't say no one will befriend you! And what did I see when I went into the barn? You and Miss Penelope kissing. Really Barrass, you are a problem to me, indeed you are!'

Her scolding brought the laughter back into his eyes, barely seen in the poor light escaping from the house.

'Teasing you I was,' he admitted. 'I thought I'd make you forget what you saw in feeling sorry for me.'

'How can I forget, when there's evidence of your "loneliness" all around me. Try to forget I do, every day I give it a real try. But the way you carry on with every girl in the village except me – ' she gave a huge sigh – 'Barrass, it's a-w-ful hard.'

She took his hand and led him around the house, stumbling in the dark that was made more difficult by the occasional light spilling out from the house. He put the bundle of food inside his jacket and protected her with his arm as they manoeuvred the woodpile very close to the house, and skirted the edge of the barn from where the sounds of happy laughter came. Olwen wanted to walk slowly, she was warmed by his arm and the feel of him so close to her. On impulse she hugged him.

'Always be my friend, Barrass,' she sighed. 'Whatever happens to us, stay my friend.'

He touched her forehead with his lips and said, 'My special, my most loyal friend. No matter what I do or what happens to me, you're always loyal. Even when I was ridden with fleas you didn't shun me. Worth more than anything that is, and I'll never be less than a friend, I promise.'

As they reached the kitchen door, something ran across their path.

'A rat!' Barrass said, and picking up a piece of wood he threw it after the scuttling animal. They chased it in the dark, its shadow sometimes looming large as it neared a lighted window, then thinning and disappearing again. His hand held hers tightly and she felt a part of him, knowing that he was enjoying the foolish game because she was sharing it with him. The rat was joined by two more and Olwen screamed with disappointment as they disappeared down a grating leading to the cellar. In the sudden excitement he dropped his bundle of food and Olwen kicked it aside, happily spilling the contents over the cobbled path.

'Don't worry, Barrass,' she smiled, 'I'll do better than Penelope, I'll see that you have plenty of good food. Don't I look after you always?' Leading him into the kitchen where the servants were wearily sorting out the chaos of the evening, she refilled his scarf with fresh food, smiling her satisfaction as she thought of the ruined food given to him by Penelope.

She glowed as she thought over the words he had spoken, long after the party was over and she had dragged her weary body up the stairs to the bed she was to share with Bethan. What did he mean, never be less than a friend, did he mean that one day, when her body finally decided to grow up, they would be *more* than friends? That he would kiss her like he kissed the others? She smiled as she slept, pursing her mouth occasionally as she imagined his lips softly pressing against hers.

CHAPTER FIFTEEN

Penelope did not enjoy Christmas. She found John's company boring and spent a lot of time sitting with her mother, imagining Barrass alone and uncomfortable in his cave near the sea. Her father and John pored over books and lines of figures in the study most mornings, and at some convenient time during the day John would invite her to walk a while with him in the chill of the garden to 'Refresh themselves in the clean salty air'. These walks, which took place mostly in silence, interspersed with occasional empty flattery, became a burden.

The bitter cold of November and early December had softened somewhat, and the ice had given way to rain. To walk in the garden meant having heavy boots on her feet, and the regulation half-hour walk that John insisted on meant coming back wet, cold and in need of a complete change of clothes and a warming drink.

'You have to spend so much of your day in the sickroom,' he explained, 'that I fear for you getting ill yourself.'

'Please don't talk of my mother's room as a sickroom, John,' she asked. 'She is much improved since the night of the party. I think the merry crowd did her more good than all Doctor Percy's medicines.'

'She had been downstairs more, I agree, and has even – against your father's wishes – wandered over to the stables to look at her horses.'

'You know she has bought two more?' Penelope asked. 'David has gone now to fetch them from the south of Gower. Two Welsh mountain ponies which she insists will be a joy to ride, so sturdy and patient.'

'She will never ride again, you must know it?' John said.

'Perhaps believing that she will, gives her the strength to fight her illness.'

'But she is sorely ill and indeed will not last the winter,'

John insisted, determined that Penelope should not deceive herself with false hopes. He did not understand her determination to cling to the belief that her mother's sickness was temporary, that her death would be faced when it happened and not rehearsed over and again beforehand.

Penelope walked a little ahead of him to hide her anger. How could he not see that for as long as her mother lived she would support her in her dreams? She refused to say out loud that her mother was dying. It would seem to be letting her down. She had tried to explain this to John, but his black and white approach to everything convinced him she was living in a dream, to which there was only one end, disappointment and sadness. He could only see the end and not understand the here and now.

They walked in silence for a time, Penelope wishing that she could leave John and visit Barrass, knowing instinctively that he would understand the game of pretence that her mother was playing and recognize her need to share it. She glanced at John, seeing that once again she had annoyed him. He thought her a foolish female in need of the common-sense protection of a man. She saw him as an insensitive wife-seeker, who thought of a woman as an extension of his business requirements. She shivered, wondering how insistent her father would be that she married him.

That John was considered a good prospect she knew from previous conversations with her father. She also knew that her father, in his present difficulties, leaned on him and valued his advice. It was like a trap closing in on her.

Since her father's recent return from London with John, she had not been included in discussions on their financial situation. She had explained her fears, and had been told to leave it to them, order some new dresses and forget her anxieties. It irked her that she had been left to deal with the running of the house and her sick mother and all the day-to-day problems that occurred while they had been away, yet was now forbidden to ask the simplest question. After all, her future as well as her father's was affected by their financial position. Unless she married John.

Another glance at his stern expression dispirited her further and she turned back to the house.

'I have had enough health-giving fresh air for today,' she said firmly.

He looked about to argue. It had been his intention that they should walk to where they could look down on the sea. There was a bay he wished to study, and having Penelope with him was an excellent excuse to stand and stare. But seeing the rare light of battle in her eyes, he smiled and took her arm, gently guiding her back.

The sound of shrieking women and the lower rumble of men's laughter greeted them as they reached the grounds of the house. Penelope looked at John, whose face was a mask of concentration. He was obviously unaware of the strange sounds.

'John, can't you hear?' she said, picking up her skirts to run towards the house. 'Something strange is happening.'

Brought back to the present, he followed, catching her up and then insisting she waited until he had investigated.

She stood at the wide gate to the drive and, on tiptoe, tried to see beyond his running figure to the source of the excitement. She saw him stop and talk briefly to Florrie, who was standing on top of an upturned barrel supported by the-Keeper-of-the-Peace. He did not come back to explain what was happening, and she began to step closer, hoping to overhear what was being said by the shrieking voices surrounding Florrie.

The group near the kitchen door and at the side of the house all held sticks with which they occasionally beat the ground to added shouts and screams. Then, when Penelope thought she would have to defy John and run to see for herself, a small figure detached itself from the rest and ran towards her, skirts held high above knees and bare feet.

'Olwen! What *is* happening?' she demanded as the flying figure reached her, blue eyes sparkling with fun, hair streaming back in the wind of her speed.

'It's Collins-the-Rats, Miss,' Olwen said breathlessly. 'It's been such fun you'd never believe!'

'Fun?' Penelope laughed.

'Oh yes, Miss. He's chased them into his sack and so many have run past him that the house seems to be moving away from them instead of the other way about. Cook has sent all the furniture out into the garden, and the carpets, including the new one just arrived from the town, are all out having a beating as if the creatures are hiding in the weave.

'Terrified they are, all of them. Daniels was sitting drinking an ale all peaceful like and suddenly there was one of the beady-eyed little brutes at the toe of his fine leather boot. Cook threw a saucepan at it and Daniels thought she had gone mad, like Gregory Pugh did, and suddenly there was nothing but uproar.'

'Yes – ' Penelope failed to hide her smile – 'It does sound like fun. What a pity I missed most of it.'

'Come and stand up by me. There's no danger of being bitten,' Olwen promised. 'Oh, I wish Barrass could see this! I've never seen Cook in such a tizzy!'

Forgetting her place as she frequently did, Olwen took Penelope's hand and, laughing, dragged her towards the house. Penelope saw that the doors leading to the cellars were open and beside them stood her father in angry discussion with Collins-the-Rats. She did not listen to what was said, but went past them to stand on a box where she could see all that went on. Olwen stood beside her, pointing out the rats that still darted for freedom through the screaming servants.

John saw her and ran to help her down.

'My dear, I'm so sorry you are frightened like this,' he said, holding out his hands for her. Penelope brushed them away.

'John, it's the best fun we've had all through the festivities! Do go away, you are blocking our view. Oh look!' She nudged the girl beside her. 'There goes a pair of them.'

'Look out, David, they looks mean!' Olwen joined in, glancing at Penelope for her to share the mirth.

Penelope ignored John's impatient shrug and watched the stable boy aim his stick at the pair of rats scuttling towards him. He missed and disappeared into the barn in pursuit.

'Please, Miss,' Olwen dared to say when order had finally been restored, 'can you ask for me to have a hour or two off so I can go and tell Barrass? He'd love to hear about it and it's an a-w-ful long time since I saw him.'

Penelope nodded. 'I will tell my father I have fish to buy and we will go together.'

Olwen thanked her, hiding her disappointment at not visiting Barrass alone in a final laugh as Florrie set about ordering the return of the furniture.

'Best I go and help now.' She jumped off the box and offered her thin arm to help Penelope down before running back to the kitchen and the much-delayed preparations for luncheon.

John did not attempt to conceal his annoyance at Penelope's unruly behaviour. Penelope had described the disastrous rat-catching episode to her mother who had livened up and regretted that she had not been called to witness it herself. Dorothy had felt well enough to join them in the dining room, but the obvious annoyance felt by John had both women subdued before the meal had begun.

'I have annoyed you, John?' Penelope said when Bethan brought the last of the courses. 'I should not have shown such enjoyment?'

'Not in front of the servants.'

'But John, this isn't London with your formal ways,' Penelope protested. 'Here we take every opportunity for laughter. If I had been fast enough, I would have let loose some of the hounds! Then we would have had some sport!'

'I intend to live in London for most of the year,' John said stiffly. 'I would wish for a wife who knew how to behave in the social setting I enjoy there.'

'Then London is the place to look for a wife, surely?' Penelope ignored her father's surprised look and went on daringly, 'I wonder why you spend so much time here with the likes of us if we are not to your taste, sir.'

'You are very much to my taste,' John replied. He glanced at William, who nodded, then he went on, 'It is my dearest

261

wish that you become my wife, dear Penelope. I feel sure that you and I can have a happy life together, once we have sorted out a few small difficulties.'

The fork dropped from Penelope's hand. What manner of man was he that he asked her like this, with her parents listening, and the servants likely to wander in to gather more gossip for the kitchens? She stood up, colour suffusing her face, and walked to her mother's chair.

'Mother, I think it is time that you went back upstairs. Shall I call for someone to help us?'

'I will take your mother to her room,' William said firmly. 'You stay and – entertain John.'

As soon as the door closed behind her parents, Penelope stormed out and went to her room. Summoning a servant, she asked for her coat and boots, then went to the kitchen and told Florrie that the kitchen would have to do without Olwen that afternoon as she needed the girl to accompany her on an errand.

Seeing how ill prepared Olwen was for a walk in the chill misty afternoon of early January, Penelope sent Bethan to her room for an extra cloak.

They walked across the wet fields talking easily, forgetting the pretence that they were not friends, until they reached the edge of the cliffs. There, stepping as close to the edge as they dare, Olwen called for Barrass. He came almost immediately and his eyes lit up as he saw his visitors.

'You are well come,' he said, picking up Olwen and swinging her about him as if she were a child. He saw that Penelope had a basket filled, he guessed, with food, and he thanked her more solemnly, looking deeply into her eyes and seeing what he had come to recognize as the desire for more than friendship.

'Will you visit?' he asked, pointing down the ill-defined path to the sea.

'Barrass!' Olwen said disparagingly. 'Miss Penelope doesn't want to see your old cave, and besides she can't manage the pathway.'

'I'll help her,' Barrass promised, knowing Penelope would not refuse.

'We cannot stay long,' Penelope said, but allowed him to take her hand and lead her to the dangerous descent. 'You go first, Olwen, and show me how it's done.'

Olwen scrambled down and, looking up, wondered at the unnecessary slowness of Penelope's steps, and the way that Barrass held on to her waist for an interminably long time.

'Hopeless she is, it isn't *that* difficult,' she muttered, pretending not to understand.

Barrass had made the cave quite comfortable, with blankets both to sleep on and to act as a screen against the wind that came off the sea with almost every tide. A fire burned sluggishly, sending smoke out across the rocks in a blue haze. There were cooking pans, a supply of tapers and a few good thick candles with a flint beside them, a jar of water in a corner away from the fire, and a shelf on which lay a few crusts. He had most of what he needed, but Penelope grieved for the way he had to live. From what she had learnt from Olwen, Barrass had never lived in a true home for more than a few weeks at a time, and none of those occasions lately.

They stayed a little while but Olwen was unhappy. She felt the air sparking as in a thunderstorm, something passing between Barrass and Penelope that isolated her and made her feel she was not needed. She slumped against the rocky wall, damp with the approach of evening, and looked down at the sullen sea, rising and falling against the rocks so close to her.

'It will soon be dark,' she said, urging Penelope to rise by standing up and taking hold of the empty basket.

Barrass again helped Penelope to negotiate the steep and dangerous climb, dismissing Olwen's puffing and panting with a casual request for her to 'stop showing off'. She glared at him, daring him to touch Penelope's hand as they said goodbye, her blue eyes buried in a frown.

He stood at the top of the cliff for as long as they were in sight, waving whenever one of the heads turned to look back.

'Why won't people help him?' Olwen asked. 'They tried to make him go away.'

'I learnt from my father, when I mistakenly invited him to the Christmas party, that he is not to be trusted,' Penelope said.

'Not with girls for sure.' Olwen glanced at her companion, who seemed not to have heard.

'The boats have been reported on several occasions, and until they find out who *is* spying they will continue to believe Barrass is responsible.'

'But he wouldn't!'

'He complains loudly and adamantly that he does not approve of people cheating on the king's taxes. How are they to believe this does not include helping catch the guilty ones?'

'But my *father* is one of the "guilty ones". Barrass wouldn't risk harming him, *or* Dan. He wouldn't!'

'I believe that, but how do we convince the others?'

They walked on silently as the mist of the closing day folded in around them. When they reached their first sight of Olwen's home, they stopped. John Maddern and two other men were pacing the land on which Spider kept his pigs and grew his crops.

'What are they doing?' Olwen asked. 'Why are they measuring out Dadda's land?'

'I – I can't imagine,' Penelope said, swiftly turning away. 'Best we go around by the stream. I don't want to explain to John Maddern where we've been.'

It was much later when Olwen discovered the reason for the activity around her home. Spider called at Ddole House while she was washing the huge cauldron in which Florrie had recently made a leek and chicken cawl. The thick soup had burned onto the cauldron and she was so busy trying to remove it she did not hear him arrive.

'Can I speak to William Ddole?' she heard him say and jumping up, gave him a hug.

'Dadda. What do you want with Mr Ddole? He hasn't complained about me, has he?'

'No, love. It's a business matter, nothing for you to worry about.'

Olwen disappeared again inside her pot, determined to be there when he returned from his interview. He was twisting his hat in his long, thin hands and there was a look of concern on his kind face.

That he did not stop to see her as he left, worried her greatly and as soon as she could, she ran home to find out the cause of his anxiety.

'It seems that William Ddole, for reasons he won't tell us, is wanting to sell this house and the land,' Mary told her. Olwen stared at her parents, who, in the few hours since they had known, had aged frighteningly. Mary's hair, usually so neat and orderly, was hanging out of her scarf giving her a bewildered look, Spider was slumped on the bench seat as if his long, sinewy back had failed him. Baby Dic was wailing his complaint at being ignored, in his basket near the fire. That her mother took no notice of his distress was alarming. Olwen picked up the little boy and cuddled him.

'I'll talk to Penelope,' Olwen said when the matter had been discussed fully, every prospect considered. 'She will help. I'm sure her father can be persuaded that, as this house is a tai unnos, a night house, built by my grandfather, and ours by right, they can't throw us out of it.'

'Tai unnos rights are not strong against a determined landowner,' Spider said sadly. 'A group of paid bullies could demolish it in no time and who's to argue for it then? And the land that was originally ours was minimal and I've gradually extended it as my family grew so what I use for the animals and the crops is not legally mine. No one has ever argued the rights and wrongs of it – until now.'

The house was a simple dwelling of compacted mud, built with walls two feet thick on a stone base. The bedroom floor was a wattle of woven hazel branches and the roof was straw thatch over gorse. The walls and roof, window and doorway had been built in one night by Olwen's grandfather with a group of willing friends. As they had traditionally succeeded in completing it and having the hearth made and filled with a fire with smoke going up the chimney before dawn broke, it had been accepted to be his by right for

265

ever. But as Spider had explained, many a tai unnos had been demolished when its position became inconvenient.

'But what can he want with this strip of cliff top?' Spider asked. 'There's no one would want to build a big house here, and besides, the land is too small for anyone of substance to want.'

'Together with the rest of the land stretching back to the stream, it might be worth more than the same land without our little piece,' Mary said, taking Dic to sleep against her warmth.

'There's a spring close by and the land is good,' Spider added. 'It would fetch a good price, but surely the Ddoles aren't hungry for the pounds it would fetch?'

'There's talk that they aren't paying their debts,' Mary said. She rocked the baby in her arms, holding him close in a protective way, bent over him, warding off all dangers. Olwen moved to sit near her, an arm across the baby, and Spider sat up as he watched them, straightening his back preparing for battle.

Olwen walked back to Ddole House in a sober state of mind. She dare not question Florrie, who in any case had little to do with the affairs of the house purse, simply ordering what she needed and taking delivery of it. Bethan would know little more except what she might glean from listening at doors. Dare she impose on Penelope's friendship and ask her?

The opportunity arose that same day, as Penelope came into the kitchen to confer with Florrie. Dorothy Ddole had invited seven people to supper and their likes and dislikes were the source of a long discussion. When the decisions had been made, Olwen managed to be outside the door as Penelope passed through it.

'Can I talk to you about something private, Miss Penelope?' she whispered.

Penelope nodded and led her into the small study used by her father. She smiled at the girl, hoping for news about Barrass. When Olwen told her that the house on the cliff top was to be knocked down and the family evicted, she put both hands to her cheeks in horror.

'But my father would not do such a thing!'

'With that John Maddern telling him how to make money he would!' Olwen said rudely. 'The rumours are that your father can't pay his debts and the houses will go until he has made enough to put himself right with his debtors.'

'Olwen. You must not talk to me like that.'

'And why not?' Olwen scolded, her hands on her hips. 'How can you expect me to say nothing while your family is threatening to put mine out in the cold winter weather, with nothing between them and the loss of their home but you saying it won't happen?'

'I'll talk to my father, I promise,' Penelope said, but there was fear in her heart that her pleading would not be enough to alter his mind. She knew only too well how impossible it would be to continue without finding some money from somewhere.

Turning the knife, Olwen added, 'Want us to end up like Barrass, do you? Homeless and driven out of the place where my father has lived and his father before him. On the road we'll be, Barrass with us, and your family to blame.'

Olwen realized she had gone too far, had spoken rudely to the girl who she was employed to serve and who was in no way to blame.

'Miss Penelope, I'm sorry. I forgot who I was talking to. I should never have spoken like that. Please, will you forget it? I won't be that rude again, I promise.'

'Go now, and I'll talk to you when I have seen my father.'

Olwen went back to her work but for once, her speed was less than Dozy Bethan's.

Penelope did not talk to her father. Taking Bethan with her, she went to call on John Maddern. John had settled into the house previously rented by Henry Harris, and, as it was her first visit to him in his new home, she carried salt and holly to ward off evil from the house, plus a gift of small cakes made by Florrie and a bottle of wine. When they arrived, the door was open and Bessie Rees was scrubbing the yard with a long-handled broom.

'Mistress Ddole! Come inside do.' Bessie rubbed her

267

dirty hands on her sacking apron, then untied it and threw it to one side as she showed the visitor into the small but neat living room. 'My oh my, Mr Maddern will be disappointed. Gone to talk to that Kenneth-the-Post, he has, with some letter for delivery to the Swansea office. There's a man for writing letters! Never a week goes by without he has letters to give to Kenneth.' She prattled on as she tilted the huge black kettle to pour boiling water onto a pot of tea leaves. When the tea was poured into a delicate and tiny cup, she handed it to Penelope proudly.

'Ever seen anything so pretty before? Came from London by the stagecoach they did, along with all manner of fine things. Whoever marries him will be the envy of everyone, with a husband able to provide such stuff.'

Penelope let her chatter, hardly needing to add more than the occasional word, while she looked around the room. It was well furnished indeed, with a fine long-case clock in one corner rumbling before it chimed the midday hour. China and pewter ornaments filled the mantelshelf and cluttered the window sills. There were pictures of dreamlike scenes of beautiful countryside. The staircase was wooden, and under it was oak panelling which Penelope suspected was a door.

'What is in there?' she asked when Bessie finally paused for breath. 'Surely not a room?'

'Oh no. That is where poor dear Henry Harris kept his things, papers and the like.'

'Now used by Mr Maddern, of course.'

'Well, no. I didn't tell him, like.' The woman looked guilty. 'I told him there was nothing but a stone wall, made to support the stairs for fear they would give under the weight of a man.'

'And that isn't true?'

'Kept things there, he did, and I think that they should remain his secret. Supposing he *is* dead, the man has still lived, he doesn't suddenly vanish together with all memory of him and I wouldn't like people to laugh and think – '

'The key, Bessie.'

Knowing she was bested by looking into Penelope's cool

268

and determined eyes, she gave up her efforts to keep the man's secret and said, 'There ain't one, you just pull by here – ' Bessie bent down and pulled at the edge of the panel and the understairs was revealed. To Penelope's disappointment there was nothing inside but a small wooden box. Bessie and Bethan carried it into the room. It had no key and Penelope slowly opened it, with Bethan peering over her shoulder, and Bessie standing, wiping her hands nervously and unnecessarily on her skirt.

It was filled with pages of pressed flowers. Each bundle showed the progress of a season, starting with the first snowdrops, daffodils and celandines, and including silk-like welsh poppies and lacy fumitories, going right through the year with all the grasses and flowers of summer, to the bronzed leaves of autumn.

Penelope knelt down and sifted carefully through them, too involved in the beautiful collection to wonder why Henry thought it necessary to keep his work a secret.

'He was afraid people would laugh at the idea of a man doing something so feminine,' Bessie explained. 'You won't tell, will you? He wouldn't like people to laugh at him.'

'I can't imagine anyone laughing,' Penelope said, getting more comfortable on the carpeted floor. 'I wonder if John will let me have them?'

'Have what, Miss Penelope?' John Maddern appeared in the doorway. 'And what, may I ask, are you doing sprawled on my floor?' He stepped towards her and as Bessie and Bethan scuttled out of the room, offered her a hand to rise, but she pointed to the pages of dried flowers and said,

'John, aren't they beautiful? Please forgive my impertinence in finding them. May I take them home and study them?'

'I would have given them to you before if I had thought you might be intrigued by them.'

'You knew about them?'

'I searched the house thoroughly when I first came, hoping for some information that would help your father,' he said. 'Now, shall we put them back in the box and I will send them over to you before the day is out.'

He went to close the panelling, but Penelope stopped him.

'Isn't it smaller inside than out, by a little?' she asked. She bent down and all but disappeared under the wooden stairs. She backed out and pointed. 'I do believe there is something else to find.' She stood and allowed John to look.

He called for Bessie to bring a taper and went in and stared around the small cupboard space thoughtfully, then disappeared as he knelt down, throwing strange shadows. Penelope stood waiting for him, her eyes constantly drawn back to the pressed flowers still spread over the rich carpet. Eventually he came back out and he was smiling.

'There is indeed something else. The supports to the first stairs are hollow and in them are some papers. Will you please excuse my manners if I ask you to go at once and tell your father to come here? I don't want to involve the servants. Thanks to your sharp eyes, my dear, I think we have discovered Henry's other secret.'

Penelope walked home in excitement, thinking more of the wonderful collection of wild flowers than the possibility that John and her father might be able to find the missing money. She planned to ask her father to buy her some books in which she could store the flowers, and began to consider how she would arrange them. Bethan rarely chattered so they were both silent until they reached the house.

Florrie and the other servants were outside, all perched on barrels, boxes and window sills. Some had even climbed drainpipes and were balancing on the low roofs of outbuildings. David was sitting on the eaves of the stables with an armful of stones which he was throwing down.

'What is happening? Penelope asked.

'Rats, I suppose,' Bethan said in her slow voice. 'Collins-the-Rats is back.'

Then she saw them. The ground was moving in a sea of brown backs, undulating waves of fur changing direction as if under the orders of a drill sergeant, as they tried to escape the stones and sticks of the servants. Ignoring the calls to keep away, and leaving Dozy Bethan sitting on a window sill with the others, her feet raised inelegantly to avoid the pests, Penelope ran to find her father. He was marching up and down his study in a rage.

'Father, I have just seen a plague of rats and – Father, what is it?' Immediately she was filled with fears for her mother. 'Is my mother – well?'

'She has had a terrible shock, my dear, and I am in the mood to kill Collins-the-Rats for causing it.'

'What happened?'

'He didn't get his money – I – er – forgot to pay him last time he came, I understand. This time, he was impatient and when I did not pay him he was very rude so I told him he would not ever be paid nor would he work for me again. He came this morning shouting impertinently for his money. When I refused, he opened the sack he carried on his back and emptied several dozen rats out in Florrie's kitchen.'

The request for her father to visit John was forgotten and she ran up to her mother's room.

'Mother, are you all right? Don't worry about the rats, David and some of the others will soon rid us of them.'

'It isn't the episode of the rats that upset me, daughter.' Dorothy's voice was strong, and she stood upright and unsupported at the window, looking down over the stables, pigsties and storehouses to the distant hills. 'It's how I have been so stupid. I have lived for more than forty years and spent it being stupid.'

'How can you say that, Mother?' Penelope went to hug her, but Dorothy pushed her away.

'Why didn't you tell me of our precarious situation? Why wasn't I told that money was short and creditors were lining up for their money?'

'I – did not know for certain, Father was away and – and I thought it pointless to worry you until he came home, believing it to be but a temporary situation due to the sudden death of Henry.'

'It went back further than your father's recent visit to London.' Dorothy's eyes, deep-set in the skull-like thinness of her face, glared accusingly at her daughter. 'You allowed me to arrange expensive parties, to order three new horses, dresses I can hardly be expected to use, so bad is my health, and a new carpet for the drawing room and curtains costing more than most cottagers have to live on for many a year. You said nothing as I restocked the pantry and ordered grain-seed and the like, sent the blacksmith's account sky high with repairs and new lights and a dozen unnecessary things. All the time knowing we hadn't the money to pay for any of it.'

Penelope bowed her head, then she looked her mother firmly in the eyes and asked, 'You think because of this that you have led a useless life? It is the husband's responsibility to deal with finances. Yours to give him the kind of home he desires. That you have done and he would have no complaints.'

She helped her mother back to bed, finding her rigid with barely suppressed anger. Giving her a spoonful of the medicine which Doctor Percy had delivered to her almost daily, she tucked her under the covers, and seeing the fire was burning low, went with the promise to send Bethan up to attend to it. She went down, thinking only of the sad state of her once lively and strong mother, sad that her father had been made to admit the difficulties they were undergoing. She still forgot the message for her father.

Dorothy lay on the bed but her eyes were wide open and sleep no longer a possibility. She had watched as Bethan built up the fire, stared as the flames flickered and grew and eventually wrapped themselves around the new coals and reddened them to a heat-giving glow. She was useless. Even in such disaster as poverty facing them, she had not been considered able to help. They were treating her as if she were already dead. She forced herself to look around the room, taking in everything she had not looked at properly for years, wanting to see the room in which she had spent so many hours during the past months, to soak in its beauties and its ugliness. She turned her head and studied the small chest between the two windows on the opposite wall. It was in need of a polish. The picture above it was a little off centre. She raised herself as if to go and straighten it but sank down again. It was really too much trouble.

She tried to relax. Doctor Percy had warned her that she must conserve her strength. But for what, she asked herself? For more days spent like this one, uselessly existing? Costing money they no longer had. She closed her eyes at last, to squeeze out the very first tear of self-pity.

As her lids dropped, blocking her view of the room, she saw at once pictures of the small boy walking off into the snow, and the child backing away in terror from her horse's legs. What a selfish life she had led, best there was no more of it.

The decision to rise from her bed forced remaining reserves of strength into use, the mind refusing to accept the body's weakness. Taking a coat from the cupboard, she as soon allowed it to fall. It was too heavy for her to lift, let alone wear, its weight would drag her to the floor before she left the room. Taking instead a lighter, thinner jacket, she pulled on boots, shuddering at the thinness of her legs in them, and went to look out of the window.

The excitement of the rats was over, the house was back to its normal quiet. With an ironical smile she paused to straighten the picture before going down the stairs and out through the back door into the cold air. She walked slowly until she reached the corner of the stable yard, then mustering all her strength she walked to where David was laying out a row of rats, counting them with the pointed stick which he had used to dispatch them.

'David, my horse. And hurry if you please.'

He looked startled but jumped to obey her, saddling her favourite bay. She could not lift herself on to its back, even with the use of the mounting block, and he hesitantly asked if she should wait until she was stronger.

She slapped her whip towards him.

'Get me on. I don't care if you have to use the block and tackle. Get me on. Tie me if necessary, but *get me on*!'

She took it slowly at first, the horse patient in spite of the friskiness of the newly released. Then she pressed her stick-like knees against its flanks and urged it on. She nearly

273

fell as they turned a bend in the lane, but by crouching over the horse's neck felt more secure. She shouted for it to go faster and faster until, as strength failed her, she aimed it at a hedge. She flew through the air with a curling, rolling motion, as light as a dandelion head, and as the horse landed gracefully on the other side, her body rested among the branches of the hawthorn and was completely still, her head at an impossible angle.

CHAPTER SIXTEEN

Although they had been expecting it, hour by hour, minute by minute, Dorothy's death was a shock to William and Penelope. William went with the bier and a party of servants to bring home her body, then he closed himself in his room and refused to see even the maid who wanted to rebuild the fire. Penelope went to find Kenneth, to send a letter to her brother who was serving somewhere in the Americas on the service of His Majesty King George III.

Penelope did not hurry back. Dressed in clothes of black and grey, she could not face the further greyness of the house in mourning. She wandered up the cliff path towards Olwen's home. The girl was busy in the Ddole kitchen, but her mother, Mary, was someone to whom Penelope felt drawn at this lonely time.

'Miss Penelope, come in for goodness' sake and warm yourself, frozen you are, without a good coat across your shoulders.' Mary ushered her inside the small, cosy room and seated her near the roaring fire. She busied herself near the hearth, preparing a cup of tea, in the only china cup she possessed, which she kept for special occasions. 'Drink this, you need warming inside and out.' She took the thin shawl from Penelope's shoulders, giving her instead a thick woven blanket.

'My mother is dead,' Penelope said softly.

'Yes, the news reached us before middle day,' Mary replied softly. 'Pity for her, but she was so ill and in pain, best she's safe in the arms of Jesus, her suffering done.'

'But what will I do?' Penelope looked at her, eyes filled with the need for tears, her mouth sagging a little as she pleaded for some guidance.

'You'll do what your father needs you to do of course.' Mary spoke more briskly, sensing the need for matter-of-fact advice rather than maudlin sympathy. 'You will carry the burden of the household until arrangements can be made. You're young, my dear, but very capable I'm sure.'

'I could be swamped by it all.' Penelope's eyes were wide with distress.

'But you won't be. When things have settled, your father will make arrangements for someone to run the house and you'll be free to marry your John Maddern – if that is what you want,' she added curiously as a pained expression crossed the girl's face. '*Is* that what you want?'

'It's what my mother wanted.'

Mary said no more. She refilled the girl's cup and offered food, but sensed that she wanted to talk more than eat, so Mary sat, rocking Dic, who was restless with the discomfort of cutting his second pair of teeth. After a while Penelope put down the cup and asked,

'You are happy, you and Spider?'

'I don't think about it, so I suppose I must be! When we decided to spend our lives together, he was not a rich man, living day to day with what he earned from the unpredictable and cranky fish shoals. He promised me all I needed and much of what I wanted. I think he has kept that promise. In return, I promised to care for and love his children and give him a home of comfort, love and good food. I think he is not dissatisfied with my half of the bargain.'

'You *are* happy.' Penelope looked around the simply furnished and overcrowded room. 'I would have so much more, but perhaps, with John I would not be so content.'

'Settling for comfort and enough money to keep the worries at bay is what many would gladly accept.'

'Perhaps.'

Penelope stood to leave, handing the precious cup back into Mary's hands. Mary watched her go, a sadness for the girl making her hug her baby and be glad she had no such decisions to make. A simple life brought few surprises but many compensations in its lack of the need for brave decisions. The next meal, the day's tasks and she was done, sleep coming easily, contentment so normal she rarely thought of it. She waved as the girl disappeared from sight. I think she has helped me more than I helped her, she thought, as she began to prepare a nourishing and filling meal for when Spider and Dan returned from the tide.

Penelope wandered back to Ddole House where teeming servants were preparing once again for hordes of visitors, this time to say goodbye to the mistress of the house. She went to her room and only then realized she still wore the blanket lent to her by Mary. She would give it to Olwen, or perhaps walk over again to return it. The poor house on the cliffs offered something she seemed to lack. Then she thought of the threat to take the house from the family, and decided that as her father was in no mood to discuss the situation, she might as well go and talk to John. He was not what she desired for a life partner, but he would willingly help her in this.

She called Olwen away from her work and they walked through the fields to where John was living in Henry's cottage.

'No matter who lives here from now on, it will always be Henry's cottage, won't it?' Olwen chattered as they approached the neat, whitewashed building.

John was in the small living room, in his neatness already a part of the surroundings. He called for Bessie to take their coats and ordered tea, and then left them while he took the papers on which he was working to another room.

Penelope shared her enjoyment of the pictures on the walls with Olwen.

'I think they must have been brought by Mr Maddern together with the fine carpet and hangings,' she explained, but Bessie, overhearing her, disagreed.

'Oh, no, Mistress, they belonged to Henry Harris. Very fine aren't they?'

'Indeed. I did not imagine him as a collector of beautiful paintings,' Penelope said.

'Not a collector, Mistress, Mr Henry did each and every one of them himself.'

Penelope was surprised.

'But why did he not tell anyone?' she asked as she re-

277

examined one of a woodland glade filled with bluebells that particularly appealed to her.

'Afraid of being laughed at. What a waste of a talent. Like the vicar is telling us, a talent, like the money in the parable, is there to be used and developed.'

'It's very sad that we found out too late to do anything about this.'

'But not too late to enjoy them,' John said as he returned. 'You can choose which you would like for your new home, my dear.'

Hurriedly changing the subject, Penelope asked John for his advice on the 'vexing problem of Mary and Spider's cottage'.

He looked at Olwen, head down in what was, for her, a very subdued and anxious attitude.

'I think, my dear, that is something we should discuss when your father is recovered somewhat.'

'Take them from their home and they would be destitute. Without a hearth and proper warming food, Spider would soon be too ill to work and then they would all weaken. We see it happen so often, and despite the best endeavours of the council, people, even whole families, die.' Penelope saw Olwen flinch but was determined to persuade John to intervene. 'I think if we continue with the plan to take their home, I will have to offer them a share of my own.'

John smiled, the rare relaxation warming his eyes and softening his firm mouth. But he shook his head.

'That will not be necessary, my dear, and that is all I will say until we have discussed it with your father.'

The funeral waggon was followed by almost all the villagers, the line of people fanning inwards across the fields as people left their scattered homes to join the mourning procession. William stood with his daughter in the small church and beside the grave, stony-faced and gaunt.

'It's as if his spirit left with hers,' Mary whispered to Spider as, with clothes still smelling of recently caught fish, they joined the throng.

Dan was with them, his eyes constantly searching for and

finding those of Enyd. Olwen stood with the rest of the servants from Ddole House, wondering where Barrass had got to, and if he had been turned away. John Maddern stood beside Penelope and her father, his sober expression hiding his excitement. Today, when all the crowds had gone, he had some cheering news for his friend.

John found William later that evening sitting in his wife's bedroom, staring sightlessly at the empty bed. When John broke into his reverie he stood and punched a dent in the pillow, unable to bear its neatness.

'William, I have news that will brighten the shadows just a little.'

'Not now, John, this isn't the day for business.'

'Not even to be told that I have found your missing money?'

William raised his eyes from the bed and looked at his friend, raising a quizzing eyebrow.

'Is this a joke to break me out of my melancholy, John? I warn you, today it cannot be done.'

'I found your money and the explanation of its disappearance in Henry Harris's house – at least, your daughter did. Penelope noticed that the under-stair cupboard was of smaller measurements inside than out. I searched and found papers and boxes of money and promissory notes.'

For the first time since a shepherd had found Dorothy's body, William's expression became animated.

'But why?' he asked.

'I do not know for certain, but I suspect that as he was getting old, and had fears of losing his strongest supporter in Dorothy, he made everything about the accounts as difficult as he was able, hoping that you would not dismiss him.'

'But I had no intention of dismissing him – although, yes, I admit he was becoming forgetful and I considered taking on a younger person. But to help him, not to replace him. I should have told him.'

'He feared poverty, abandonment, the few years left to him lonely and useless ones. So, he refused cash and took promissory notes, gradually removed all monies from your

279

banks, paid in cash when accounts became due, and generally muddled things up, like eggs after a housewife's whisk, so no one but he could unscramble them.'

They talked long into the night, with John showing William the lists of monies due and offering to travel around on the morrow to claim the payment of the bills of hand, and settle all the overdue accounts.

'Thank you, John for your honesty and friendship. I am ever grateful.'

'Then may I beg a favour?' John asked, that rare smile suffusing his features. 'It is not really honest, but a small enough thing in itself.'

'Anything, my dear friend, anything.'

'May I tell Penelope that we no longer plan to demolish Spider and Mary's house, and that it was due in some part to my persuasions?'

On the following morning John set out carrying a large leather bag. Borrowing one of William's horses, he went around the village and the town settling accounts and receiving overdue payments. It was dark when he reached home, and a frost was sparkling on the cobbled yard in the thin light of a D-shaped waxing moon. He had been tempted to go at once to tell Penelope of the change of plan, wanting her to be able to give the family the good news, but he had held his patience, the work for William must be attended to first. Tomorrow he would tell her and perhaps they would go together and share the pleasant task. He called for water to wash himself, and fell into bed exhausted but content.

On the following morning he rose early and set off for Ddole House. Today he would persuade Penelope to name the day on which they would marry. He felt stirrings of excitement at the prospect. She was comely and capable, what more could he ask? That she was a mite unwilling he did not see as a problem; he was certain that his persuasion would be as enjoyable as it would be successful.

She was as delighted with his news as he had foreseen, and happily agreed to go with him to tell Mary and Spider.

280

They rode together, their horses having to press against each other in narrow places as he was unwilling to move from her side. He glanced admiringly at her as she chattered brightly about how she would word the announcement, smiling gaily as she imagined the couple's pleasure and relief.

Her hair began to escape from its habitual plait, so that an early and over-bright sun picked out red tints that fascinated him. She wore riding clothes of black, bought for mourning her mother, but the glow in her cheeks and the bright lights in her hazel eyes made the sombre clothes less than stark, seeming to add to her contrasting vividness.

Penelope felt warm towards him. Since the death of her mother and the discovering of Henry Harris's secret, he was more relaxed, and his expression, usually so dour, had become that of a man who found her pleasing. She began to see him with less than previous doubts. Perhaps after all he might not be an over-serious husband too wrapped up in his business affairs to care for her properly, they might even be companions in the way her parents had been. She smiled at him, a dazzling, shared smile tinged with a hint of a closer relationship to come.

When they called on Mary, he stood back and allowed Penelope to tell the good news, then he added,

'It is due entirely to Miss Penelope. Her sharp eyes and great intelligence saw something I and many others had missed. I cannot explain how the reprieve came about and you must not ask. Sufficient to say that William, who regretfully thought to move you to a new home, has now no need to make any such change.'

Mary curtsied to Penelope who laughingly asked that instead of thanks, she and John would like to be served with some of her excellent tea and bake-scones, which she could smell cooking on the griddle near the fire.

'Oh! And burning most like!' Mary gasped, running to save them. Penelope followed her in, and stopped with surprise as the large frame of Barrass stood from a corner seat to greet her.

'Miss Penelope, I – I regret hearing of the death of your

281

mother,' he said, and John stood, with a hand on the top of the door lintel, wondering why the boy was so familiar.

'Go if you please,' he said sternly, 'we wish to talk.'

With another moist-eyed look of sorrow for Penelope, Barrass thanked Mary for her hospitality and pushed past John to stand in the winter sun.

Penelope, from the semi-dark of the room, looked at him standing there, uncowed by John's dismissal, the low sun a glowing nimbus about his eclipsing silhouette. Inexplicably the morning was darker for his leaving, the joy of the ride with John scarcely remembered. A coldness filled her as she looked again at the stern face of John, disapproval showing in every inch of him. She had been foolish to imagine that she and John could ever have a loving relationship. Not while there was Barrass.

Penelope had further news of Barrass a few days later, when she met Olwen at the pantry.

Have you seen Barrass of late?' Penelope asked.

'Yes, Miss Penelope, he visits with my mother often, since no one else will either speak to him or feed him,' Olwen said in her forthright manner.

'It is not my doing, Olwen.'

'Sorry, I'm forgetting my place again. I never will remember how I'm supposed to talk different to you than to others.'

Penelope smiled. 'As long as my father doesn't hear us I don't think it matters.'

'Will you marry John Maddern?' Olwen asked. 'Rich he is but I hope you don't because I hear that he is moving to London so if you do marry him I won't see you and I'll miss talking with you.' She drew in a long breath after the non-stop speech and leaned against the wall to relieve the strain of holding a heavy cheese.

Penelope called for one of the boys to carry it for her.

'When you go home tonight, I will send a cheese for your mother. We have plenty and she will be glad of extra.'

'Thank you.' Olwen frowned. 'You are kind to us, but that is not why I will miss you,' she said, her blue eyes staring, willing Penelope to believe her.

'If our roles were reversed –' and they almost were, Penelope thought to herself – 'I am sure you would be as kind to me.'

'Would you mind if instead of giving all the extra cheese to Mam we took some to Barrass? He would love a cheese, and only has what scraps Arthur can occasionally find for him. I fear he will have webbed feet soon, for all he seems to eat is fish and an occasional loaf of bread.'

'Not a word then,' Penelope whispered. 'We will go tomorrow.'

They went across the fields loaded with a cheese and several cakes and loaves. They had waited until William and John were out about their business and stole through the yard like thieves, giggling like children at the furtiveness.

When they reached the cliff above the cave, they called softly, but there was no reply.

'I'll go down and wake him,' Olwen said. 'Lazy he's getting to be sleeping this late.' But the cave was empty. She made several trips down the precarious path with the food, then they departed, disappointment making them silent.

It was Arthur who told them where to find him.

'Swansea he is. Gone to talk to them at the sorting office. Ben Gammon is sick, see, and Barrass is after his job.'

'But he isn't old enough?' Penelope said.

'That won't stop him. Old enough to father children, he can convince them he is past twenty for sure. Anyway, he isn't sure how old he is, what with his mother being dead and no one bothering to remember.'

The girls walked back to Ddole House, Olwen pleased that he was at least close to achieving his dream, but afraid that it would take him away from her. Penelope was wondering if she could find an excuse to go into Swansea and 'accidentally' meet him.

Barrass had been up and about early that morning and, seeing Kenneth, had called a 'good morning'. Kenneth, still complaining of a headache from the attack that had left him

283

in the quarry, told him to come along into Swansea if he wanted a chance to take over Ben Gammon's job whilst Ben was sick. Barrass needed no second telling.

Barrass mounted behind him and the horse took them steadily towards the town. They stopped occasionally to collect letters at some of the larger houses along their route, and Kenneth stayed mounted, glad for the young man to do the running about.

When they reached the town, it was quiet. Most of the litter from Saturday's market had been either swept away or scavenged by people or animals and there was nothing on this dark morning to entice folk from their beds. Apart from an occasional man walking to his work at the boats or the collieries, the streets were silent.

'I hate a Monday, always have,' Kenneth said, bending forward and sliding his leg over the horse's rump to dismount. They were early, so they left the horse to graze and went to sit on the wall outside the inn. Kenneth lit up his long clay pipe with the pattern of a pitcher on the bowl – the design made specially for Pitcher to sell in his alehouse – and puffed gently on the aromatic tobacco.

'Any more trouble with young women, then?' he asked, with a hint of a smile behind the pipe. 'Or are you trying to behave yourself?'

'I wanted to marry Violet, and I think she would have had me,' Barrass said, colouring slightly.

'Fat chance. Not with that Emma Palmer pretending to be someone she's not,' Kenneth said. 'Spoilt them girls and lost them the chance of good marriages, if you ask me. That Edwin is all right, mind, but it's a better life if you marry the one who makes your heart leap at the sight of him. Better than having your mother choose for you, specially a mother like Emma with her rings and plush curtains and her talking like she had a mouthful of quails' eggs.'

Barrass chuckled. 'You chose, did you? Ceinwen made your heart leap, did she?'

'Never you mind about that, boy, but I tell you this, when Enyd wants to marry, I won't try to persuade her different. That Dan, he's a fine fisherman and an upright solid citizen.

284

I can't see what she sees that makes her want him, but if she chooses Dan, I won't raise no fuss and bother. Trouble is, boy, Emma and them twins of hers tried to tell Enyd that she could do better than Dan, could have someone smarter and richer, and I fear that Enyd will listen to them and lose her best chance of happiness.'

'I doubt that Enyd will be persuaded, if she wants something really bad,' Barrass said thoughtfully.

If only Violet had had as much determination he might not be sitting here, glad of the slight offer of friendship Kenneth offered. He would have taken his place at Pitcher's alehouse, and been on the road to being someone of importance.

People had gathered outside the inn and were looking hopefully along the road for the arrival of the relay carrier bringing the bag from Monmouth. He soon learnt that the post had not arrived on the previous evening, and began to think hopefully of his chances of filling in for Ben Gammon. Best he forgot Violet and brought his thoughts back to what could be achieved.

The door of the sorting office opened, and the postmaster came out and shouted across to the inn. A boy ran out with a tray containing three pewter mugs of ale which he took into the office. Kenneth looked along the road, then shrugged as if giving in to the inevitable.

'I suppose I'd better buy us some nourishment, boy.' He felt in his pocket for some coins which he gave to Barrass. 'Go and find us some food and an ale. I think we'll drink it inside, though, there's an air of lateness about the morning. I fear we'll still be here when the sun is up and trying to shine.'

A few carriers were already settled at tables near a sluggishly burning fire. Barrass sat and listened to the talk around him, of difficult journeys and even more difficult customers; of loves found and lost. Tales shared, and enjoyed, and which he soaked up like a thirsty pup soaks up a puddle.

Melancholy flowed over him as he saw the number of hopefuls waiting for a chance to start work in place of Ben.

He wanted to be one of them, but what possibility was there of himself being chosen? Even the people he had thought of as friends no longer gave him a greeting – only Kenneth, when he had need of company to pass the boring journey, and Spider, and Pitcher, he thought disconsolately, unconsciously counting on his fingers. Plus the women of course. They refused to ignore him, and for that he was grateful, even if it meant the possibility of more trouble.

He had spent several pleasant hours of late in the company of Carter Phillips' sister Harriet, who seemed well pleased to give him some of her time, but who was without the enthusiasm for his loving that Violet had shown. Nor did she have the fullness of body that had so delighted him with Blodwen. Carrie had given him pleasure with her shyness and hesitation, Gaynor with her boldness, but Harriet seemed coldly calculating and he suspected she had a strong determination to marry him. Lucky she didn't know where he lived. He smiled when he thought of young Olwen, always his champion and protector. He went out to look along the road for the first sight of the much-delayed post.

There was a large crowd by the time a horse came into view and many were surprised to see that the rider was a stranger.

'Ben is still sick,' the stranger told them as the postmaster impatiently snatched the overdue bag. 'Came to tell you I did, but I can't make the trip again mind. I'm on my way to Llanelli for to stay. He says to tell you this:'

Sliding down from his horse, he said in a voice so like that of Ben that people applauded his performance,

' "Ho," Ben Gammon says to me, "I fear that this illness will make me hug my bed for a few days yet. But worry not, for I say there is a man who makes me think, Why I do declare he will do the job as well as myself! Name of Barrass from Mumbles. Ask him," he says to me, so, Postmaster, them's Ben Gammon's words for you to ponder. Knows the route as he's ridden it with Ben, he has, so go and find this Barrass and let him take over till Ben is recovered.'

286

Heads turned to look at Barrass and there were mumbled complaints at the boy being chosen.

'I'm here,' Barrass said, excitement rising like fire inside him. 'I'm here and ready to take responsibility for Ben Gammon's route as soon as you say.'

The postmaster decided to follow Ben's recommendation. For today, a replacement rider had already been hired if – as it turned out – Ben Gammon could not ride the route. But from tomorrow morning, Barrass was to be the official replacement until Ben was fit to work again.

Barrass could not stop the smile from spreading across his face. That one day when he had accompanied Ben had resulted in him having his chance. He forgot the teasing that Ben had tried to arrange with the corpse at Nant Arian, and thought of the man only with kindness and appreciation.

'Coming back with me, boy?' Kenneth asked. 'Or are you going to stand there with that stupid grin on your face all day?'

'Come back I suppose,' he said, his eyes shining, his head thrown back in a laugh.

They returned to the village, dropping off two letters on the way. Children occasionally came out to meet them, following them for a while before returning to their homes. When they reached the first houses with gardens almost touching the edge of the tide, a fishing boat was being dragged up onto the shingle and Barrass recognized the gangling figures of Spider and Dan.

He called to them, shouting his news across the silent morning, and voices echoed back congratulating him, cheering him. People appeared out of the houses and waved without knowing the reason, so the solitary horse with its two riders seemed like a procession.

He did not light a fire when he reached the cave. He rarely did, considering it best to run across the fields and get thoroughly warm before wrapping himself in the thick blankets to sleep through the worst of the icebound nights. That way he stood less chance of someone finding his home and destroying it. Smoke was an insidious giver away of secrets.

He stood looking out over the sea, the excitement in him allowing no thought of anything but his wonderful experience. His only regret was that he had no one with whom to share his news. He stood tall and with added confidence, having been chosen by the Swansea postmaster for the responsibility of being Ben's replacement.

His face glowed with remembered pleasure and his eyes shone bright and full of optimism. His height matched that of Spider but his frame was larger and already he was broadening with the maturity of a man, his neck thickening and sloping wide to his powerful shoulders. Standing at the mouth of the cave, even in his shabby clothes he was an impressive figure – strong, with an inner strength that showed in his fine eyes and the way he stood, upright and proud, as well as the muscles already so well developed.

He almost stumbled as he went deeper into the cave to bring his blankets out for a shake and some fresh air, and looking down, he saw the food which he was sure could only have come from Olwen and Penelope. The sight filled him with joy. There were at least two people who would share his excitement. He would go and thank them for the gift and tell them of his appointment. He savoured the word – appointment – the one used by the postmaster. It had a ring to it, the sound of importance. He had been appointed to assist in the transportation of the King's Mail. He hungrily tore at the bread and cut himself a chunk of cheese, and with it in his pockets to eat as he ran, he climbed up the cliff and hurried towards Ddole House.

Penelope was in her mother's bedroom with Mistress Gronow, sorting through Dorothy's clothes and deciding what she could, with a few alterations, keep for herself and which she would take into town to dispose of.

'If you marry, Miss Penelope, your future husband will have ideas of his own about what you wear,' Mistress Gronow said tentatively. 'He might not like you using cut-about clothes. Men are often fussy that way. Proud of the way they dress their wives.' She could not ask, but was dying to discover if and when her client was to marry John Maddern.

'It will be some time before I have to ask permission to wear what I like, if ever,' Penelope said firmly. 'Now, if you please, will you help me off with this cotton dress? It will be many months before it is warm enough to wear it, even indoors.'

She took off the patterned dress of yellow and white which her mother had bought for a garden party some years before, and threw it on the floor. She was already bored with the task which she had set for the seamstress. She wished someone would interrupt them so she could forget clothes for a time. Even John would be better than this quick-fingered and gossipy woman who sometimes amused but often irritated.

The servant's door in the corner, through which buckets of coal were brought and the night-soil bowl taken to be emptied, opened quietly and with relief she saw the small, hesitant face of Olwen.

'Please, Miss Penelope,' Olwen asked in her most polite voice, 'Please for a word?'

Penelope dismissed the seamstress, promising she would see her on the following afternoon.

'What is it?' she asked when the woman had gathered her measuring stick and her pins and was gone.

'It's Barrass, come with great news. What Arthur told us is correct. He's been made a letter-carrier for the king! And will be at least until Ben Gammon has recovered from the fever that torments him and stops him travelling the route.'

'He is here?'

'Out in the old coach house. Can you talk to him, or shall I send him away?' She closed the small door behind her and stepped towards Penelope. 'Come to thank you for the food he has,' she whispered.

'I will go and see him. You get back to the kitchen and I will try and slip past the window without being seen.'

Olwen helped her to put on a cloak and hood, then returned down the narrow wooden staircase to the kitchen.

She did not like the idea of Penelope and Barrass being alone, but there was nothing she could do about it, and besides, would not disappoint Barrass in his need to tell of his good fortune.

As she worked, cleaning the spoons and two-pronged forks with a polishing cloth and sharpening the knives on a stone, she kept stretching up to look out at the distant coach house, wondering if they were kissing, wondering why it was that she loved Barrass while she was too young for him, and he was too impatient to wait until she was not.

Penelope approached the old, overgrown building, which sprouted bushes from cracks in the neglected stonework and with a roof undulating with the weakening rafters. With a furtive glance to make sure she was not seen, she quickly entered. The place had the feel and smell of disuse and she shivered with the still coldness of it.

Since her father had given up most of his business affairs and the wealth that went with them, they no longer had need of a coach or the specially trained horses to pull it. She walked past the abandoned stalls where there was room for four horses. The hay mangers were empty, the slatted wood already falling away from the walls. They only had horses for riding now, with a small waggon which they occasionally used when they went visiting.

She pushed against the door separating the stables from the half where the coach was kept, and it stubbornly tightened against the hard-packed earthen floor. Then she felt the handle move without her turning it and it was pulled open and Barrass stood in front of her.

'Miss Penelope. You shouldn't have come, it is so cold here,' he said in a low, caring voice.

Behind him the shape of the old coach loomed out of the darkness.

'I cannot stay.' She backed away from him, for he seemed to overpower her with his presence. 'You wished to see me?' She tried to keep her voice calm, using the tone saved for the servants.

'To thank you for the food. And to tell you my news. I

had to share it with someone and apart from Olwen and her family, there is no one who would care enough to listen.'

'Tell me your news. As for the food, you are more than welcome.' She shivered as she stared at him, and his eyes filled with such longing that her heartbeat increased in an alarming way.

'Shall we sit?' He gestured to the shabby coach behind him. 'I think there might be a few complaints from the inhabitants, the mice must be disturbed only rarely.'

He opened the creaking door and helped her up into the once beautiful seats where generations of mice had burst through the plush, padded upholstery, the stuffing showing through in untidy flower-like extrusions. It smelt musty and damp, reminiscent of ancient cupboards, old clothes, dead flowers and funerals – of which there must have been hundreds in the dynasty of the mouse kingdom that surrounded them.

Penelope knew she should go, indeed that she should not have come. What was she doing here, in the eerie old coach house with someone whom decent people would not even talk to? She shivered again and realized she was wearing only soft house slippers.

'You are cold, let me warm you.' Barrass moved closer to her and placed an arm around her shoulders, pulling her against him.

'I have only slippers on my feet,' she said, a tightness in her chest making it hard for her to breathe. He smelt so clean, redolent of the fields and the hills and the seashore, as if the winds had swept over him and taken away everything but the cleanliness of the open air and the special maleness that was Barrass and no one else.

She stiffened as he stretched down and touched her ankles but relaxed as his hands began to stroke her feet, warming them in a way that she had never before experienced. When his hands rose higher, encompassing her shins and knees in their hypnotic movements, she lay back against him and became aware of nothing except the effect of his touch.

The hand on her shoulder began to move, creeping down

towards her breast, which seemed to stretch achingly to reach it. When he kissed her the world seemed to explode into a galaxy of stars, the brightest one containing herself and the other half of her that was Barrass.

She eased herself out of her cloak, making soft cries as his lips touched her slender neck and went lower until he had pushed aside the neck of her gown and found the place she longed for him to find. Then she lay across the old, smelly seat which, in the emotional upheaval of her first loving, became transformed into a beautiful thing. His weight was on her, seeming so right, his warmth pervading her until, when she thought she would scream with the joy of it, his possession of her rose to encompass her whole body in emotion and joy. Then they were both still.

A shyness overcame her as her body calmed and she turned away from his kisses and pulled her clothes hastily around her.

'Penelope, you are perfection,' he said, and forcing her to face him, waited until she moved once again towards him, her eyes already beginning to close.

CHAPTER SEVENTEEN

Barrass walked into Swansea, frequently bursting into song. That he had been unable to afford the hire of a horse for the journey did not seem a problem – he ran for parts of the way in sudden bursts of joy. When he arrived at the sorting office he was tense with excitement, his dark eyes glowing with an inner fire, his expression that of a child at seeing some longed-for treat. He walked in to greet the postmaster, unable to contain his happiness, collected the bag, and listened with care to last-minute advice and warnings before going out to mount the horse that awaited him.

He had forgotten in his excitement that the only times he had been on a horse were when Kenneth or Spider had allowed him to sit behind. Climbing up onto the back of the fresh young horse from the post stables was something very different from either experience.

At first he jogged painfully, falling first one way then to the other, teetering on the brink of crashing to the ground but always at the last moment righting himself again. The horse complained as the reins were pulled in an effort to keep him upright, and it jigged across the path as if considering throwing its inconsiderate rider into a convenient holly bush.

He finally remembered that if he rose to each alternate step things would become easier; then after a while the horse made it clear that walking was preferable once it had got rid of the high spirits resulting from a long stay in the stables. So eventually, he remembered more of what he had been told and gripped with his thighs instead of hanging on to the reins, and they got along well enough, but with unresolved dislike, each for the other.

Stiffness wore into him as muscles held too tight began to complain, but with the stiffness came a sense of achievement and he realized, as he approached the point where the bag would be handed over, that he was enjoying himself.

When he reached the end of his uneventful journey, he saw Ben's son waiting for him. Barrass had forgiven Ben (and his son, probably its originator) for the trick played on him at Nant Arian, so now he greeted the son with a smile as he handed over his precious leather bag.

'So, they gave the job to you. Well, are you pleased? I said, "My goodness me what a treat it would be for the boy who searches for his father to follow in his footsteps", I said. So Father, he said, "Goodness what an idea, I do believe they would do it if I suggested it," so, here you are!'

'Thank you,' Barrass said, as usual a little confused by the way Ben's involvement was told. 'I suppose there is no news of anyone who could be my father?'

'Dear me, no. Now, if you've a mind, there's a mulled ale to cheer you before you set off home.'

'I thought your father stayed overnight and went back – ' He faltered as the young man shook his head.

'No need, my fine friend. Your work is done and done well, and so I will say to any who asks. No, all is well again and Father'll be up and running afore you can touch a pillow with your head. Fit as a flea and twice as lively he is. "Why I do believe," he says to me, "I do believe that me ague is gone like a sea fret in the summer sun." Now over there is a fresh horse so when you are rested, you can be off back to all the girls that cried to see you go.'

Darkness had returned when Barrass reached the Swansea sorting office. He handed his horse to a stable boy who was not pleased at being woken to attend to him, then set off wearily on the walk back to his lonely home. His legs ached dreadfully, the muscles on his thighs, overstrained by lack of experience, were painful and filled each step with dread. He thought he would do better to find somewhere to sleep and walk home on the following day, but a million stars showed in the heavens, the trees and hedges sparkled with frost, the ground was hard underfoot, and he knew that he would not find anywhere safe from the bitter winter night.

He was disappointed that his new position had lasted but a day, but the prospect of seeing Penelope sooner than he had expected cheered him and he walked along more easily, anticipation giving a sprightliness to his steps.

He slept long into the next day, rousing occasionally but retreating back into sleep in face of his aching muscles and the icy cold. The only sounds were of waves thrashing impatiently at the rocks close to where he lay, and an occasional scream of a seabird. Then he slowly realized that the call was too regular and he opened an eye reluctantly to see Olwen standing at the mouth of the cave, her face shadowed.

'Olwen!' He was awake in an instant, rising from the layers of blankets to greet her, groaning as the sudden movement reminded him of his strained muscles and sore flesh. 'Come in, warm yourself or you will be frozen into a statue.'

She moved slightly and her face was revealed. She was glaring at him, and the sight of her smallness, showing such an adult scowl, made him laugh.

'Come and warm yourself in my bed,' he said, pulling the covers back and inviting her to sit among them. 'Come on, you will freeze and what would I do without you?'

'What you always do, find yourself a woman to give a baby to.'

For a moment his heart seemed to stop. Had there been another claim of fatherhood to lay at his door?

'What d'you mean?' he asked warily.

'Penelope Ddole – and what her father will say I daren't think! Oh, Barrass.' She left the entrance and ran to him. He put his arms around her, his cheek resting on her fair head.

'You don't understand such things,' he said.

'I do! I know that you can't look at a girl without wanting to crawl into her bed, burrowing under her clothes like the fleas you carried for so long!'

He led her to the still warm covers and persuaded her to sit. She surprised him by clinging to him. Her amateur

295

lips screwed up like a fir cone, her eyes tightly closed, she planted a kiss on his lips that made him laugh all the more.

'There,' she said, glaring angrily. 'I can kiss too.'

'Oh Olwen, it was lovely,' he laughed.

'Was it? What was it like?' Her heart was beating fast and there was a reciprocal tic in her cheek but the feeling was swamped by anger as he laughed even louder and said,

'It was like being kissed by a dried walnut!'

She hit him and they fought like they often had in the past, but this time the anger in Olwen was real, the disappointment of his rejection cruelly felt. After a moment, Barrass realized it and he held her arms tightly, crooning to her like a baby until her struggles and tears subsided.

'Olwen, you are my best and truest friend, what I feel for you is something completely different from what I feel for people like Violet and Penelope. The loving is almost a game, one I cannot resist playing when it is offered so readily. But I would never treat you like them. Or,' he added in a firmer voice, '*or* allow anyone else to treat you in that way. Kill them I would, and don't you forget it.'

'I think I will kiss Arthur,' she mumbled, 'he has shown that he would like to. If you won't kiss me I must try others.' If she expected him to argue and insist she did not, she was again disappointed.

'Arthur is a good friend and if you put your trust in him I don't think he would treat you any way but properly.'

She began hitting him again.

Sitting amid the blankets, arms around each other, they talked for a long time – something they had not done for many weeks. They shared their experiences of both Olwen's work at Ddole House, and Barrass's journey on horseback to replace Ben Gammon, albeit only for a day. The companionship they had always enjoyed but which had been lacking of late seemed easily repaired and both were happier for it. Then Arthur appeared at the cave entrance, the dog under his jacket, puffing.

'Barrass, you'll have to move and be quick about it.' He began pulling at the blankets they were wrapped in, saying nothing to Olwen, but urging Barrass on.

'But why? What has happened?'

Arthur began throwing out the rocks that formed a wind barrier at the cave mouth. 'Help me hide all evidence of your staying here, I'll explain later,' he said, his voice almost a squeak. 'Move if you value your life and ours.' He recognized Olwen's presence for the first time.

The dog sat against the dead ashes of the fire while the three people jettisoned the wood and stones that had made the place habitable, then he was once again deposited in Arthur's jacket.

'The customs men are coming here, they've been told the cave will be used for contraband on the next tide. Hurry! There's a crowd of them already in the church collecting guns and weapons from the town chest! Hurry!' His thin face white with fear, his adam's apple dancing madly, he handed the blankets to Barrass and the cooking pot to Olwen, and dragged her out. Barrass was kicking the fire ashes over the edge when Arthur ran back, Olwen still in tow.

'Too late, they are already at the top of the cliff. We'd better hide in the cave.'

They waited in the darkness, Barrass hugging Olwen and Arthur soothing the dog, when a shadow crossed the mouth of the cave, and silhouetted against the sky they saw, not an excise man, but Penelope.

'Barrass?' she called softly, 'are you there?'

She looked doubtfully around her, surprised to see the emptiness, her heart falling at the thought that he had moved away.

'Over here, quickly,' Barrass called and he darted out and took her arm. He shushed her involuntary scream, then Olwen spoke and their secrecy was hurriedly explained.

'Did anyone see you?' Arthur asked.

'I am sure not,' Penelope replied. She was excited by the turn of events, disappointment changing in an instant to thrill at the prospect of an adventure.

They had just settled quietly when they heard footsteps and the figure of Daniels appeared, closely followed by a tall, uniformed man, a gun held at his side. The soldier was

297

followed by others until in front of them, like the opening of an Interlude, the stage was set for the arrest of the boat crew expected on the next tide.

The soldiers and customs men made no effort to be silent, but chatted and laughed, with one standing outside and listening for the warnings to be shouted down from others dotted about the cliffs. The guns and the makings of shot were casually placed beside them as they lolled comfortably against the rock walls. Some settled at once to sleep, wrapped in their cloaks. Others ate or drank and even lit pipes, although orders promptly came to put them out, as the smoke would be smelt by the wary boat men.

Barrass thought it worth trying to move further inside the cave while there was a chance of their not being heard. He had explored a short distance, and now, with tapers and a flint filling his pockets, he whispered his plan to the others, placing a kiss on Penelope's soft cheek in the darkness as he did so.

Using his hands to feel the way, Barrass guided the rest in line-astern convoy through the dry black passageway deep under the hill. When he was certain they had turned enough corners for the light not to be seen, he struck the flint and lit a taper. Soon they all carried one of the cheering yellow lights and they sat to explore with their eyes the place where they found themselves.

Penelope was worried. As soon as the excitement had eased, she thought of her father, and John, both undoubtedly involved in the deliveries to come, and both likely to walk into the trap.

'My father will come,' she whispered. 'They will capture him and this time he won't escape prison, or worse. We have to do something. *Please*, Barrass, help them. I couldn't bear to lose my father so soon after my mother's death.'

'There is nothing we can do, except go on along this passage. The air is not stale, there's hope of another entrance, but where it will be I cannot imagine.' He had little belief in a second entrance – he could feel no draught and surely if there was an opening, they would feel some movement of air?

He and Arthur led the way along the uneven path which sometimes narrowed and occasionally appeared to end, but always widened out again, allowing access. He urged them to be silent, afraid that sounds would echo and alert the men. Then to Barrass's amazement, they turned a corner and a gust of wind blew out his taper.

He warned the rest to stay well back, afraid that their route had led them in a circle and they were back facing the sea. His pupils widened and seeking light, he realized with a flood of excitement that in the distance, the blackness was less dense. Slowly, feeling his way, he moved towards it. The opening in the rocks was so sudden that the daylight all but blinded him. He did not recognize the place, but that he was among fields and not close to the sea was apparent. Birds sang and the trees were tall and straight, not bent and distorted by the relentless sea-driven winds.

He was tempted to explore before calling the others, and stepped out into the weak sunshine. To his utter disbelief, he came face to face with Violet.

'Barrass!' she gasped. 'What are you doing here? Why did you come?'

'Yes, that is a question I would like answered too!' Edwin appeared beside her. 'Well? Have you come to disgrace my wife further?' Edwin stood, fists raised in a threatening posture, and Violet, ungainly with the expected child, stepped back with a shout. Servants came running and in moments Barrass was surrounded.

'I've come to warn you,' he said quickly, 'the cave at the far end of this tunnel is full of soldiers waiting for the boats coming in on the tide!'

'What's this? The tale is a fancy one – you do not lack imagination!' Edwin stepped closer, his arm bent ready to strike a blow. And he would have, but out behind Barrass came Arthur, the dog a bulge under his coat.

'It's true and you haven't much time to warn the others!'

Disbelief brought a foolish expression to cover the rage on Edwin's face, and then it became even more comical as out behind Arthur and the dog stepped Olwen, with, last of all, Penelope Ddole.

He believed them then, and sent his servants scurrying with messages for the local people who had intended to help unload the boats that evening.

'Come with me,' he told Barrass, 'we'll have to light a fire on the cliffs.' He turned to Arthur. 'Take these ladies home and tell Pitcher what has happened. *Run!*'

Running beside Edwin made Barrass's stiff muscles protest and he was afraid that he would be accused of delaying the warnings. He forced his legs to keep up with Edwin as they sped across the fields to the cliffs.

A tangled pile of cut gorse had been set ready, needing only to be lit to be seen far out to sea. But when Edwin reached the spot it was gone, kicked over the edge by the sharp-eyed Keeper-of-the-Peace.

'No time to gather more,' Barrass panted, 'we're likely to be spotted at any moment. He snatched the flint box from Edwin's hand just as voices called and they saw men coming in their direction – though they hadn't yet been spotted.

'Go you,' Barrass said, 'show yourself and make them follow you. I'll see that the fire is lit.'

He hid out of sight while Edwin ran down the slope away from him, then struck impatiently at the flint. It lit at last, and he blessed the weather that had dried the grasses and heather. Once the flame grew in strength, the hillside began to rip and roar with it. The fire began to surround him and he was hard put to escape from its furious progress. Though not a concentrated beacon, the flames would be enough to make the boats abandon the landing.

Dirty, stiff with running and half choking on the smoke, Barrass managed a laugh. He had saved the men from capture mostly by good luck, but once again, unbelievably, he was without a home!

'Tonight,' he muttered, 'surely tonight no one will refuse me a bed!' He skirted the cliffs, moving cautiously until he felt he was safe from the soldiers, and made his way to Olwen's cottage.

Dan and Spider were sitting by a low fire, Mary was

300

hugging Olwen whilst rocking baby Dic's cradle with a foot, and Mrs Powell, now a confirmed resident, was dozing in a corner. They smiled a welcome when Barrass walked in, Mary easing Olwen away from her and rising to make him food.

'Tomorrow,' Spider said, 'I will call a meeting of the council. You will surely be believed after this day's work.'

Penelope was escorted home by Arthur and his dog. She went through the kitchen, an almost unrecognizable figure with her cloak filthy and her hair falling from its plait. Bethan followed her to her room and arranging for bath water and fresh clothes, settled her in a chair to wait for them.

'Your father is out,' Bethan said lazily. 'Best you get to bed before he sees the state you came home in.'

'I think he will not be angry,' Penelope said, allowing Bethan to remove her soiled shoes and stockings.

Curiosity was never strong in Bethan, it seemed to be too much trouble to try and work out puzzles like this. She went to fetch the hot water, and by the time the second pair of buckets had been carried into Penelope's bedroom, she had forgotten any questions she might have harboured in her slow brain.

William heard the story before he reached home – the story quickly concocted about Arthur, Penelope and Olwen being on the cliffs to ask Barrass about his journey with the letters, seeing the soldiers and customs men and, being afraid of involvement in some violence, hiding in the cave. He was doubtful when Penelope suggested that the adventure cleared Barrass of suspicion so far as informing the customs was concerned.

'The men arriving while you were there might have put him in a difficult situation,' William said. 'He had to invent a story to hide his involvement. And how did he know about the cave leading to Edwin's garden?'

'He didn't, Father, I'm sure he didn't,' Penelope said hotly.

William smiled at her. 'There must be something special

about that boy. He has survived unharmed through the winter without home or food –' he raised a quizzical eyebrow, but she did not respond to the tacit question – 'and has fathered babes on some of the village's prettiest women. And, my dear, I suspect that even you, my level-headed daughter, are more than a mite smitten.'

'I was with Olwen, and the rest happened around me. He led us to safety and could have escaped unseen. But he chose to face Edwin and warn the men. I can't think how you can still suspect him of being the spy.'

'Oh yes. He risked his life on the cliffs too, setting the heather ablaze.' He smiled again, patting her head as she sat against her pillow, the candle light showing the red amid her brown hair. 'Very well, I will ask the council to consider carefully the case for believing him innocent of befriending the law-enforcement men. But if there is any further reason to doubt him, I fear he will disappear over the cliffs where he spends so many hours of his time. Tell him, will you? If you should see him? That for a while it's best he stays away from the cliffs?'

Barrass was on the cliff path as William spoke. Spider had given him the message that Markus wanted to see him. With some trepidation, he had left the cosy bed Mary had prepared for him on the opposite side of the fire to Mistress Powell, and set off in the darkness. He whistled as he went, making sure that should anyone still be about, his appearance did not in any way seem furtive. He was deathly tired, but kept up the cheerful whistle, even when someone appeared out of the bushes and walked by his side.

'Sent to escort you,' a voice said. 'You and the little maid.'

'What?' Barrass turned and stared back along the path. 'Olwen!' he accused. 'Is it you?'

She stepped forward and took his hand. 'I thought you might be lonely,' she said, 'and if you were, I wanted it to be me you had for company.'

The unknown man chuckled. 'I've heard about you, boy,' he said. 'Age no barrier, young and old treated alike.'

302

Barrass raised a threatening arm but the man laughed again and led on. Barrass followed with Olwen close behind him, still clinging to his hand.

At night Markus's house looked unwelcoming, the late hour adding to the threatening, crouched appearance of the place. The windows showed not a chink of light. Dogs, barking and scratching at some unseen door, sounded like a threat, the heavy trees overhanging the drive an added repellant. Barrass felt his hand grasped tighter as the man called and knocked at the dark door that seemed thicker than the one on Swansea prison. He wondered if he would ever be allowed out again. He pulled free of Olwen's hand and put an arm around her instead, holding her close so she shared the beating of his heart.

The door, opened by an unseen hand, revealed nothing but blackness. Their escort struck a light and a candle blazed briefly before settling into a small useless glow. They followed it, stumbling, across the hall.

'Light the sconces,' a voice commanded, and the room in which they found themselves was revealed as a library, with books on three walls, the fourth wall having four large windows, uncovered by curtains. Arthur was in a huge arm-chair with his dog, small, thin and curled up, and creased almost to nothing by anxiety. He managed to offer them both a sickly grin.

'Lights matter not at all to me,' Markus said, 'but I want to put you at your ease.' He smiled in their direction and gestured to a chair. 'Please sit. Miss Olwen, how pleased I am that you could come.'

They sat, Olwen as close to Barrass as was possible. Ale, port and brandy were offered, which they refused.

'I wish to hear your version of what happened this after-noon,' Markus said. 'All of it, the full, truthful story, and I warn you, I know enough to be able to judge the honesty of it.'

'I will tell you all I know,' Barrass began, but Olwen interrupted,

'The first part of the story is Arthur's, I think.'

'Then please begin.' The man's head went unerringly to where Arthur sat nursing his dog.

Between them they explained every moment of the time from Arthur overhearing soldiers' conversation at the ale-house, and of Olwen's calling at the cave to wake Barrass. Then they waited for the man to comment. He frowned, the sightless eyes open but showing no emotion. Olwen was stiff with sitting tensely for so long in one position, but she dare not move. Barrass wondered how he could save her if their story was not believed.

'I see,' Markus said finally.

Two of the candles had gone out, their wicks, weakened by lack of trimming, collapsing in the hot wax. Knowing that Markus could not know, they said nothing. But Olwen shivered as the uneven light distorted the man's face, making it threatening and as unwelcoming as the house.

'I believe you.' Markus stood up and smiled, the smile oddly pleasant in spite of not reaching his blind eyes. 'My men will see you safe home. Sleep well.'

Olwen did not go to her bed that night but sat close to Barrass beside the fire, holding his hands, sleeping against his strong shoulder. Spider woke them early the next morning as the cockerel crowed.

'Best you come fishing with Dan and me until we know what's to be done with you, boy,' he said. 'As for you, my girl, you'd best be off if you don't want a hiding for being late for work.'

Olwen foolishly believed that Barrass belonged to her after that night spent in his arms. But when she next went home he was gone. She wandered disconsolately down to the village to see Arthur.

'He's back here,' Arthur told her excitedly. 'Pitcher, he persuaded that Emma of his that it's the only way she'll get her room done and finished.'

'Where is he now?' Olwen asked, a shyness preventing her from relaxing and cheering the news with the jubilant Arthur. 'I want to talk to him.'

'Well, as for that, I think you'll have to wait a while.' He shook his head with a smile of amused disapproval on his pale face and, not knowing how hurtful his words would be, whispered, 'Gone to see his latest lady-love, I suspect. That Miss Ddole, would you believe!' He shouted in offended surprise as Olwen hit him and ran off.

It was soon widely known that Barrass was acceptable again, but the mothers still feared him, especially Emma.

'I don't want him near us, Mr Palmer,' she shouted when she had finally been worn down into agreeing that he should sleep in the cellar with Arthur and the dog. 'He isn't safe with decent girls – he's ruined one of your daughters and I fear for the other two!'

'Heavens above, Mrs Palmer, is it your daughters you can't trust? What sort of schooling did I pay good money for if you tell me you can't trust them round a fellow with a strong body and a weak resistance? Takes two, Mrs Palmer! It takes two!'

'Mr Palmer!'

The inevitable tears ended the argument, with Barrass allowed back but strictly forbidden to climb the stairs to the rooms used by Pitcher's family.

Barrass looked wistfully at the arch behind the house, and went to see Penelope.

The disused, musty old coach became for Penelope what the archway had been for Violet. Whenever Barrass was free of his work for Pitcher, he made his way to the coach house and let himself in. Penelope would be waiting for him, breathless with love and longing.

No one seemed aware of their meetings, but Olwen, who knew Penelope well enough to guess when she was doing something she should not, knew each time they met and felt the growing pain of it. She did not tell, but suffered each meeting as if the time was taken from her own life, making her older and yet further away from Barrass than ever.

One day she could bear it no longer. As Barrass slipped out, she confronted him at the side of the coach house.

'Olwen! You did give me a fright!'

'Nothing to the fright you'll have when her father finds out!'

'You wouldn't tell, you're my friend,' he coaxed.

'Wouldn't I? Just come here once more and you'll find *him* waiting for you instead of her, with her fluttering eye-lashes and her pouting mouth!'

'Come and walk with me, Olwen. I'll explain what it's like.'

'No need. I'm not a child.'

'Of course you aren't, although you are a child in some respects. The ways of a man and woman are something you aren't ready to learn.'

'Teach me,' she said, facing him, hands on hips and blue eyes blazing with anger. 'Kiss me like you kiss her and see if you think I'm too young.'

'One day you'll find someone worthy of you. I'm not. I couldn't stay true to one woman, even one as deserving of loyalty as you.'

'Dadda is loyal, Dan will be when he gets Enyd to agree to be his wife. Why do you have to be different?'

'I'm greedy.' He smiled, then went on, 'I suppose I was lacking in everything relating to love when I was a child, and having grown up and discovered the pleasures of women, well, perhaps I am recouping what I'd missed. You are constantly hugged and shown affection by your family. I had never been touched except in anger or disgust until I was fifteen. Discovering the liking young women had for me was balm to my loneliness. Do you understand?'

'You don't really love them, not like Dadda loves Mam?'

'That's right.'

'Not like I love you?'

'I'm afraid not.'

She seemed satisfied with his attempt at an explanation and left him, to return to the kitchen and bear the cuff of Florrie's hand with a stoicism that surprised that lady, who was used to a fiery retort. All she had to do was keep Barrass from marrying one of his brief loves, until she could make him see her as the one true love in his life. Somehow

306

the task did not seem so difficult now it had form and could be put into words. But she could not pretend not to mind when Barrass and Penelope met so close to where she washed pots and scrubbed floors.

Dismay, jealousy and anger built up in her as the day progressed. Why should he treat her, his real true love, with such disregard? Suddenly it all boiled over.

'I think someone is using the coach house as a home, some tramp probably,' she said to Florrie later that day. 'Shouldn't it be firmly locked for fear of a fire?'

While Penelope walked across to seen John Maddern to tell him she would not be his wife, Florrie set David to work fitting a new lock and an extra bolt on the coach house, hanging the key in the kitchen where it could be easily seen.

'But why?' John asked when Penelope broke the news. 'I will give you everything you want. A London house and the social life that goes with it, a home here as well so when I need to see your father we can make a summer visit and you can invite all your friends.'

She waited, hoping even then for a declaration of his love for her.

'You wouldn't be broken-hearted,' she said sadly, 'by losing me.'

'I don't understand such words,' he said with a smile. 'I do know that with you as my wife my life would be complete, without it there would be a great lack. Will that do for you? Will you now put me out of countenance completely and deny me the happiness you represent?'

'A lot of words, but no emotion,' she replied.

'Emotion comes later, when we are married and begin to know each other in the way men and their wives enjoy.'

He took her blushes for innocence, but she was looking at him and wondering how he would compare with Barrass.

'I'm sorry, John,' she said, giving him a slight touch of her lips as a goodbye.

She walked home light-hearted. Now she would begin to persuade her father that Barrass was worth considering as a son-in-law. If only she could find him a responsible job. There was nothing more telling on a man than the way he earned his living.

Olwen heard the news with dismay.

'Barrass is a fool, with less sense than he was born with,' she told Arthur over and over. 'Why I bother with him I really don't know.' But as she lay in her small bed each night, she knew why and realized that even if her body was still and small and child like, she was growing up.

In the bed behind the partition, she heard Dan tossing and turning in his straw-filled bed and guessed that for him too, life had problems. She lit a candle, pulled a coat over her night-gown and went to sit on the end of his bed; a small face in the woollen night-cap looking at him with sympathy for them both in her clear blue eyes.

'Growing up isn't very nice, is it, Dan,' she whispered. 'Not nice at all.'

CHAPTER EIGHTEEN

William looked thoughtfully at the new key hanging in the kitchen. He had a wild suspicion about who was using the coach house, one that he was trying not to believe. He lifted the key from its hook and told the cook that he would keep it in his study.

'I must think about getting the place repaired one day,' he said as excuse.

'There's a lot of work to be done before it's usable,' Florrie warned. 'And where will you put the coach? That won't last either unless something is done a bit quick.'

'I will talk to Ivor when the spring comes. It's been neglected for so long another month or two won't matter.' He tapped the shining new key on the palm of his hand, and frowned as he went out of the kitchen.

A few days later, Penelope put on her warm cloak, slipped out of the door and made her way to the coach house. She saw no one, the path she took rarely used by the servants. Her face glowed with excitement at the prospect of an hour or two with Barrass. They had made the tryst at church, passing in the crowded doorway as people paused to adjust their hats and hoods against the heavy rain. Careful not to be noticed, she had whispered a time and a day, and walked on, taking her father's arm and nodding to her acquaintances with polite smiles.

Time had passed slowly, until the day she saw her father off to a meeting in Swansea with hardly contained excitement. She did not notice the scar on the coach-house door where her father had removed the recently fixed lock, only curling her fingers around the worn wood and pulling it open. Barrass was standing there, not running to greet her as normal, but still and silent. Beside him, a restraining hand on his arm, was her father.

'Father? Barrass?' She tried to bluff her way out of the dangerous situation. 'I thought I heard a noise and came to investigate.'

William let go of Barrass's arm and stepped towards her. He raised his hand just once, almost knocking her off her feet with the slap to her face. Barrass stepped forward with a shout and the men began to wrestle.

'Stop it!' Penelope shouted. 'You will have the servants here in a moment. Stop it, I say!'

William dismissed Barrass and guided his sobbing daughter towards the house.

'If you harm her – ' Barrass threatened.

'I will not touch her again,' William muttered. 'But I cannot say the same about you!'

Penelope sat trying to look chaste and offended but succeeding only in looking guilty and dejected. She had known it would be difficult to persuade her father that Barrass was the man she wished to marry, but now, having been caught so embarrassingly, like a servant girl, she knew it was impossible.

'What are you going to do?' she asked.

'You are going away from here. Right away. We have friends in London. I will write to them at once and ask if they will have you there for a year or so, until you have grown up!'

'A year or so? I don't want to go to London, Father. I like it here.'

'You go to London, and the only way you can escape living with Gerald and Marion Thomas is by agreeing to marry John – if he will still have you after this. Be sure I will tell him.'

She was silent for a while, sitting on a stool with her father standing before her, a threatening figure, alien in his fury. The silence stretched uneasily.

'I will go to London if you promise not to punish Barrass. I have already told John I will not marry him. Father, the fault was mine. Barrass would never have approached me without encouragement,' she whispered.

'You are not in a position to argue,' William said, then he relented and nodded wearily. 'All right, I will say nothing of this to anyone.'

Barrass strode to the kitchens angrily and, ignoring Florrie, dragged Olwen outside.

Growling ferociously, like Arthur's dog protecting a bone, he said, 'So, you call yourself my friend, do you? Loyal friendship doesn't include telling William Ddole about my meeting his daughter! He slapped her. Do you know that? He slapped his daughter and almost had her off her feet.'

'Barrass, I didn't – '

'Of course you told him! No one else knew.'

'Someone must have. I didn't tell, I promise you.' She was frightened for a moment, then the anger faded from his dark eyes, restoring her composure, and she said cheekily,

'I knew, so why shouldn't others? Not very clever at keeping your assignations to yourself, are you, Barrass? Especially when your partners in love have a bulging belly to show for your attentions. Can't keep anything quiet then, can you, Barrass Bull!'

She thought she had gone too far and backed away. Barrass was glaring at her, breathing hard, and she was relieved to hear footsteps and see the tall, well-dressed Keeper-of-the-Peace arrive. She backed away from Barrass and, opening the door, called,

'Daniels is coming, Florrie.' She turned back to Barrass. 'Got to go, I've work to do.' She met his glare with a frown that knitted her fine brows together, and slipped in through the door.

Barrass moved away after greeting Daniels, but did not go far. Daniels had left the door slightly ajar, and Barrass stood blatantly listening.

'I've called to see if you have caught anyone at the coach house,' he surprised Barrass by saying. 'Did you leave some-one watching as I suggested?'

'Didn't get a chance,' Florrie explained. 'As soon as I told Mr Ddole he took the key and said he would see to it. Said he's going to get it rebuilt, he did.'

311

'There was something else,' Barrass heard the man say, coughing nervously. 'Will you take a walk with me and my children after church next Sunday?'

Barrass stepped away, not wanting to hear any more. So Olwen had not spoilt things. He felt a momentary guilt at his treatment of her, then his thoughts returned to Penelope, wondering how her father would choose to deal with her.

He was still undecided about what to do, not wanting to leave in case, somehow, he could help Penelope. He moved back from the kitchen door and stood trying to think of a way to see her and find out if she was all right. William Ddole came around from the stables and, seeing him, strode across to berate him for ignoring his demand to leave.

'Is she all right?' Barrass asked before the man could speak.

'No thanks to you if she isn't!'

Any further words were silenced as Florrie came out of the kitchen door followed by Daniels. The couple walked in a friendly way a short distance from the house and they saw Daniels' hand gently squeeze Florrie's as they talked and laughed, their heads close together.

Barrass and William forgot their quarrel and exchanged glances. They were both thinking the same: Was Florrie the means by which the law knew of the movements of the supply boats?

When Penelope set off for London on the coach from Swansea, there were few to see her go. She stepped up into the vehicle with John, and found a seat next to the window. Huddled miserably as closely to the padded interior as she could, she remembered that other coach, with its families of mice and unsavoury smells, where she had been so happy with Barrass. She hardly lifted her eyes from the floor, where straw was spread to offer some warmth for the long hours ahead. It was only when she heard a slight gasp of anger from John, who sat opposite her, that she looked up, and saw two figures standing waiting to wave her off.

'Olwen,' she called, and waved a perfumed handkerchief furiously. The other figure, taller, broader and so much in

312

her thoughts that she at first believed him to be a figment of her imagination, was Barrass.

The handkerchief faltered in its movement, and before she could call out anything further, John leaned across and pulled down the blind. Grimly, he glared at her, daring her to raise it again before the coach had lumbered out of the inn yard. She stared, white-faced, at the floor, determined that she would not speak one word to him in all the five-day journey.

Winter had begun early with a sudden snowstorm and it ended late with another unexpected fall.

'Daffy snow,' Pitcher told Arthur and Barrass as he set them to clear a space outside the alehouse door. 'Gone as soon as it's arrived, with the daffs growing through it without any harm done.'

'Then why are we wasting our time shovelling it in piles if it'll be gone before evening?' Arthur grumbled.

It lingered for an extra twenty-four hours, but when it had melted into the warming ground that early April day, it left the countryside shining and newly washed. As Barrass and Arthur walked up the hill to visit Spider and Mary, they saw as if for the first time the purple haze of the new shoots on distant birch trees, and the bright new green of the hawthorn leaves.

Flowers were appearing everywhere, spring squill patching the cliffs with blue, snowdrops with their dancing skirts of white and green, and daffodils pushing their leaves through the soft, warm earth in quill-ends of green, as they prepared to display their blooms. Star of Bethlehem, whose roots were sometimes roasted to provide food, and even a few early pansies were seen raising their faces to the sun.

Arthur bent to pick a bunch of the small pansies, tying their slender stems with hair from his head, and putting the posy in his pocket.

'For Pansy,' he blushingly explained. 'I always gather a few of the first ones for her.'

With Penelope gone to London, Barrass had felt that his

life would never again be happy, but the snow had livened his spirits in some indefinable way and the morning had enriched his feelings of wellbeing. When they reached the small white house on the cliffs they were both smiling with the exhilaration of the climb and the joy of the new season's beginning.

Their happy mood was lost as soon as they came in sight of the open door and heard voices raised in anger: Dan and Enyd. Abandoning their intention of visiting, they turned and went back down to the village. They did not want the glorious day spoilt by quarrels.

Ceinwen and Mary sat on the bench at an angle to the fire, where a pot of cawl was simmering. Dan and Enyd sat on the floor facing each other, quarrelling.

'But Dan, it's a chance you'll never have again!' Enyd said. 'Markus is offering you work! Staying on dry land, and never facing the dangers of the small boats. You're a fool not to take it.'

'Enyd, love, you know I can't stay away from the sea, it's my life. I've followed my father since I was barely five, and would have gone even before that if Mam hadn't tied me to the door each morning until the boat had left the shore!'

'You say you love me,' she pouted prettily. 'Aren't I worth getting a proper job for, then?'

'If you love me, can't you see that I would be a different man if I left the work I know?'

Enyd rocked the cradle in which Dic was sleeping, her agitation showing with the speed of the movement. Mary gently bent down and moved the baby towards her.

Since Ceinwen had arrived with her daughter to give Dan the news of Markus's offer, the two older women had said nothing, determined not to interfere.

Both mothers were surprised when Dan agreed to go to Markus and inquire what the new job entailed. Mary's face showed shock, Ceinwen's a small satisfaction, but neither spoke.

'But I'm going alone,' Dan said firmly.

Later that day, when Enyd sat at home waiting for his decision, Dan walked to Markus's house and sat down against the gatepost. He picked a stalk of newly sprouted grass and chewed the sweetness for a while, staring across the fresh green bracken that was uncurling itself towards the sun. He dozed for a while undisturbed, enjoying the warmth on his weather-browned face, then rose, stretched, and walked back.

'No,' he told Enyd firmly. 'I could not work for Markus. Now, will you settle for what I am and marry me?'

'No,' Enyd said equally firmly.

Barrass had hardly seen Olwen since he had apologized rather coolly for believing she had told William about his meetings with Penelope. He had felt foolish for his unreasonable anger and she knew in her heart that by mentioning the coach house to Florrie, she had in fact been as guilty as he thought her.

Each day he hoped that she would appear and begin chatting to him in her usual enthusiastic way, their disagreement forgotten, and each day Olwen went about her work at Ddole House hoping he would find some way of meeting her. But days went by and they did not meet. In such a small community it seemed that fate was separating them.

Barrass was surprised at how he missed her. Olwen had been his shadow for so long it seemed odd to walk along the cliffs and meet a girl without having her dogging his steps and spoiling his plans. It was so empty without her cheerful chatter that he stopped meeting Harriet and took to spending what spare time he had either with Spider and Dan on their fishing expeditions, or walking with Arthur and the dog.

When they eventually met it was, surprisingly, at Pitcher's alehouse.

Pitcher, with Barrass's help, had finished the new room and Emma happily began preparations for a party to celebrate. For months Pitcher had seen her arriving back from Swansea with materials and pieces of furniture and the enormous bills to go with them, and wished he had been strong enough to say no when she first asked him to build the new room. But he smiled as she came in with the twins in tow, her plump, red face glowing with delight at the final purchases. If she wanted something, he knew he would always get it for her.

The days before her intended supper party were days he hated. She had no time to do anything but prepare his food, and pass the occasional peremptory word, lost in a world in which there was no place for him. She bustled about the house, sorting out even the most rarely used cupboards and drawers to make sure that everything was spotless for her guests.

'What makes you think they will look in small corners, Mrs Palmer?' he said irritably one morning when he found her half disappeared under a chest of drawers.

'I would,' she said with a glare, '*I* would!'

The food was cooked in their own kitchen but with the help of extra servants. Finding it difficult to hire girls locally and unwilling to have them living in, even for a brief period, she spoke to William Ddole when he and Pitcher were sharing a quiet few minutes in the barroom.

'I will speak to Cook,' he offered, 'I am sure she will lend you a girl.'

So Olwen, to her surprise and delight, found herself working in the same building as Barrass a few days before Emma's party. Admittedly they were separated by a staircase which was guarded by Emma with the ferocity of a soldier protecting his fort against a horde. But they managed to speak, and to send messages by Arthur, who, being almost a part of the building he had been there so long, was allowed to come and go as he needed.

Olwen was coming down the stairs with a pail to empty outside when she saw Barrass emerging from the cellar, his dark head appearing over the trap door, then coming into view in the shadowy area behind the barroom.

'Barrass,' she whispered, 'I'm helping "her upstairs" to get the house prepared and supper cooked, and on the day I'm staying to serve at table. What d'you think of that then?'

'Olwen! It's so long since I've seen you, where have you been hiding?'

'Thought I'd been sent to London with Penelope, did you?'

'Don't talk about that, I'm sorry I blamed you,' he said in a low voice.

He had come to stand close to her so they could whisper in the dark passageway undisturbed. Olwen soaked in his presence like a balm, a comfort so needed and sadly absent over the recent days that she wanted to hug him and bury her face in him, revive the memory of his smell and the sensations of him holding her close. Parting without properly healing the breach in their friendship had made her suffer rejection for which she had to accept the blame. She wanted to throw herself at him and thump him with her small fists as she had always done in the past, but there was some emotion preventing her from the childish act.

It seemed that as she waited to grow up and become the woman he would turn to for love, they had instead grown apart; her maturing had developed into an obstacle, so she was unable to be natural and hug him as she would once have found it so easy to do. She forced herself to reach out and put a small hand on his arm, shyness making her arm heavy to raise, an inexplicable reluctance holding it back.

The warmth of him through the sleeve of the Welsh flannel shirt produced a response from her body that shocked her, engulfed her in new knowledge, so she backed away, although her need of his touch was an urgent clamour in her heart and her heavy arms ached to enfold him. She knew that her days of being a child were fading away and she would be filled with new sensations and needs that he might not recognize. She slumped against the wall, swamped in ineffable sadness. Without putting it into words she knew that days of fancy-free happiness were over and that new joys were still a long way off.

Emma's voice as she came clattering down the wooden stairs made Barrass push her on her way.

'Best she doesn't see you talking to me,' he whispered. His lips briefly touched her hair and he was gone.

Stunned with the bewilderment of emotions so rare they were like pains, she stumbled towards the back of the house to retrieve the pail she had abandoned seemingly hours before. For the rest of the day she worked like the hands of Pitcher's clock; the movements automatic and unmanaged by her dulled brain.

On the day of the long-awaited supper party Olwen arrived at the alehouse as dawn slipped silver fingers across the horizon and speared the dark sea with gradually spreading light. She let herself in and settled herself into the kitchen to begin the vegetables. It was still early in the season and there were only a few rather dried-out carrots, wild parsnips and some leeks already thickened with seed-head stalks. She concentrated on making large quantities of cawl with some small chickens for flavour, and tried not to think of Barrass only a few paces away.

While the cook and Emma argued about the correct way to deal with a saddle of lamb and the fish that Dan had brought, Olwen kept herself busy. Between shouted instruction from either Emma, who could not keep away from the centre of activity, or the more and more irate cook, she found cleaning to do – polishing the cutlery and wiping the plates, cleaning up the drips of fat from the meat the moment they appeared, until Cook shouted for her to 'Keep from under my feet!'

She went outside to tidy the abandoned trimmings of the meat and vegetables and the hastily sorted oddments that Emma had discarded to make her home neater and less cluttered. Among the items thrown out were several books, and with her rapidly growing skills in literacy, Olwen examined them with interest. She began reading first pages, and finding them to her liking and well within her ability, she decided to keep them.

She went through the house and into the barroom, where men were already sitting in groups around the fire and at the window, long pipes issuing blue smoke, heads bent in earnest discussions. It had been her intention to look for

Arthur, or so she told herself, and it was with mendacious dismay she greeted Barrass.

'Looking for Arthur I was,' she said, wailing silently at the prickly unease she felt at seeing him, convinced he sensed her discomfort and wondered at it. She avoided his eyes and looked around the room vaguely as if Arthur would materialize from under a table.

'Gone on a message for Pitcher,' Barrass smiled. 'What have you got there?'

'Books,' she said inanely.

'That much I had guessed.' His smile widened as she glanced at him.

'Thrown out by her upstairs and I thought I would use them to practise my reading,' she explained, holding them behind her so he could not see that they were romances. She was not able to take teasing, not now, and from Barrass.

'That is an excellent idea, the more varied your reading the greater your ability will be.' He held out his hand. 'Shall I mind them for you? I will take them home for you, or keep them here, whichever you wish.'

'I thought Mam would like me to read them to her.' She blushed as he took them from her.

'That would be kind,' he said softly. He frowned then, his face darkening as his brows knitted. 'Olwen, is something amiss? Are you still angry with me for doubting you?'

'How could I stay angry with you, Barrass?' she forced herself to answer lightly. 'I have to go now, or her upstairs will be shouting my name for all the village to know I'm avoiding my duties.'

In the late afternoon Olwen was allowed a few hours off, to change her clothes before serving the guests with their meal. She ran home, clutching the books that Barrass had hidden for her, and showed them to her mother. There was no time to start reading them though, Mary had several tasks for her daughter to complete during the luxury of a free afternoon.

'Go and help Dan bring up some seaweed from the beach, will you?' Mary greeted her as she ran breathlessly into the small room. 'It isn't too early to start replenishing

319

the pile to dry for burning. And if there's any driftwood, put it aside for when your father goes down later.'

Disappointed, imagining a brief moment of her mother's time to share the stories, she wandered back down to the beach. Dan was piling up some planks brought in by the midday tide, ready for breaking into firewood, and sitting watching him was Enyd.

'If you two are going to quarrel all afternoon, I'm going back to the alehouse!' she said as she approached them. 'There's enough row going on there with that Emma scratching the eyes out of everyone she sees and accusing them all of time-wasting, but I'd rather that than seeing you two tearing each other to bits with your barbed tongues! It's a-w-ful wearying, truly it is,' she added with a sigh. Then she opened her blue eyes wide, the whites seeming to reflect the sky as she stared at them. They were both smiling. 'Friends are you?' she asked in amazement. 'Never!'

'If only Enyd would accept that I can't ever be anything other than a fisherman,' Dan said with a sigh. 'Getting married then, we'd be.'

Enyd opened her mouth for a sharp reply but Olwen hurriedly told them she didn't want to hear their nonsense. The couple smiled and set off back to tell Mary once again about their difference of opinion, begging her to help them resolve it.

Olwen watched them go and felt no pleasure at their happiness, only a deflating sadness. Was she becoming an old misery already and her not more than fifteen? There was no point in going back to the house so, ignoring her mother's request for once, she spent the rest of her free time sitting on the chilly beach, hugging her knees and looking out across the huge expanse of the water, daydreaming of a wedding in which she was the bride and Barrass, tall and handsome beside her, the proud groom. The disconsolation now a constant partner to thoughts of Barrass engulfed her again and she walked back to the alehouse, her head bent as if searching among the pebbles for favourite seashells to add to her collection, but seeing nothing.

Part of her depression was the sensation that she was

overlooked and unimportant. She was pushed this way and that in the kitchen as last-minute preparations were completed around her. She eventually stood against the wall watching the others. It was as if she were invisible yet still managing to be in the way! An unwanted stranger there, she wished she could run away back to her mother and never leave home again. Her thoughts were muddled between a determination to accept this new adulthood that she teetered on the brink of, and wanting to sink back into being a dependent child at her mother's knee, doing as she was told and with no rebellious thoughts of her own.

When the guests began to arrive, on a collection of carts and waggons and a few carriages, she still kept out of the way, watching with interest as the beautifully dressed people were ushered past the barroom full of craning necks and curious eyes, and up the staircase, where they were relieved of their cloaks and hats by the constantly bobbing maids.

Olwen forgot her mood of melancholy in listening as the visitors passed, their voices artificially loud, apart from some confidentially whispered remarks of regret for foolishly having accepted an invitation to visit a family who lived in a common drinking house.

William Ddole's sharp eyes saw her and he nodded kindly to her, managing to whisper a few words of encouragement. She was surprised to see Dan there as a guest, accompanying Enyd and following Kenneth and Ceinwen with their son Tom, resplendent in the uniform of private soldier in a foot regiment. She wondered how she would manage not to laugh as she offered her brother food, in her temporary role of serving maid.

Excitement began to bubble deep in her throat and the evening was viewed with less and less apprehension as guest after guest arrived. Violet came with a stern-faced Edwin, a far larger Violet than she remembered, and she spared a thought for Barrass, wondering how he felt at seeing her married to another man while carrying his child.

The tables were barely sufficient to hold the twenty guests, each chair scraping against the one adjoining and knee pressed intimately against knee, a situation that some enjoyed thoroughly and unselfconsciously. It was difficult for Olwen to reach between the closely packed diners to pass food through.

Long before the meal was ended she was exhausted. Her legs felt encased in lead as she ran up and down the stairs bringing fresh courses and removing the remnants of others. She saw Barrass several times as he served the men in the barroom, and once he defied Emma's orders and carried a laden tray up the stairs for her.

'You'll drop the lot if I don't. A titmouse given the load of an eagle, that's what you are.'

He paused to peer through the edge of the door for a glimpse of Violet, and in her suddenly acquired maturity, Olwen allowed herself a moment's sympathy for his lost love. Then she pushed him out of the way.

'Want to get us both in trouble, do you?' she hissed, then calmly went into the noisy overfilled room with the heavy tray.

There were several people she did not know, and guessed they were school friends of Pansy and Daisy. She looked at them curiously, and thought that apart from the strangely artificial voices, they were much the same as herself.

'For you'd think from the way that Emma's been carrying on these past days they were so special they wouldn't look like the rest of us at all!' she grumbled to Arthur as he pushed past to bring more wine.

'It's Emma who's different from the rest!' he whispered. 'Cracked and heading for the Dark House, if you ask me,' he said, referring to the place where those whose minds had become disordered were kept.

When the meal was finally over, the moment Emma had been dreaming of arrived. The ladies moved into the new and splendidly furnished drawing room. Emma's face was redder than ever and her fat, beringed hands waved in apparent dismissal of the compliments she received. With a sigh of relief, Olwen carried down the last of the food, leaving the men to sit at their port and illegally imported cigars. She had already noted that Daniels had not been included in the gathering.

When the door closed behind her she sank onto a stool, hoping that she might go home without being expected to assist with the piles of dishes and pots. She had felt invisible during the hubbub of preparations, now she wished she were.

To her surprise, the men did not settle to enjoy their port as she had been led to expect. William, Kenneth and Pitcher crept downstairs to where several of the evening's previous customers sat waiting for them. With Barrass and Arthur, who had been dismissed with a wave of William's hand, Olwen watched them gather near the roaring fire and discuss something in low tones. The three watchers guessed they were planning the next landing of the boats.

Their business did not take long, and they went back up the stairs, trying to avoid the creaking of the wood and the squeaking of their leather boots. Their descent and ascent were hidden by the sound of music coming from the new parlour, where Dan and others were entertaining the ladies. As clapping announced the end of an item, the footsteps doubled their speed and they were back in the dining room before it had subsided.

In both rooms there were chamber pots hidden by a screen, so it was with surprise that Olwen saw Kenneth slip back down the stairs and out into the yard. She thought the pots must be over full, but did not mention it for fear that she would be given the unpleasant job of emptying them.

Exchanging glances of curiosity with Barrass and Arthur, she was even more surprised when the two young men followed him. She thought it politic to stay where she was, then curiosity overwhelmed the possible embarrassment of catching them urinating against a wall, and she set off after them. Anything was better than starting to sort out those endless dishes.

She had to run fast. Kenneth was already halfway up the steep wall of the quarry and Barrass and Arthur, carrying his dog to keep him quiet, were ready to climb the moment he disappeared at the top. She made an inspired guess at where Kenneth was going, skirted the quarry, ran up the road and crossed the fields to where the Keeper-of-the Peace lived.

She forced herself to run even after her legs began to tire and threaten to collapse under her, and she was in time to see the letter-carrier disappear inside Daniels' house. As Barrass and Arthur arrived, she showed herself.

'Go you,' Barrass said, 'back to the alehouse before you're missed. Serve in the bar if needed, and tell anyone who asks we've gone for more ale.'

'What will you do?' she panted.

'Arthur will go and tell William, I will go and warn Markus. Late as it is, he will want to know.'

'I'll come with you so he'll believe you,' Olwen insisted, and Barrass, seeing the sense of it, agreed.

'Best you keep with me, mind, or I'll leave you to find your own way.'

'I've been watching Kenneth,' he explained as they ran along. 'I didn't believe that Daniels would have risked implicating Florrie by asking her to spy for him. He cares for her, you can see that for sure.'

'You don't care for me, then! You don't mind *me* coming on this errand with you!' Olwen said.

There was silence between them for a while, apart from puffing breath. Olwen was glad of the darkness, afraid to see his face and the irritation it might show. Then to her relief he laughed.

'When could I ever stop you doing what you have a mind to do, Olwen-the-Fish?'

'So, Barrass, you are with us after all,' Markus said when they had made their explanations.

'I was never against you,' Barrass replied, 'I just refused to be a part of even this dishonesty.' Wryly he added, 'I thought that if I wanted to be a carrier of the King's Mail, I needed to be above suspicion.'

'You can work for me if you've a mind.'

'Thank you, but no. I have my mind set on what I want to do and achieve,' Barrass said firmly, 'but if you would kindly make sure I don't have my head pushed into any more rabbit holes it would be a kindness.'

Markus's rare laughter followed them as they walked back home.

Walking with Barrass holding her hand to guide her, Olwen felt a resurgence of depression. He thought her still a child with no part in his future. He had dreams of being a fine wealthy man with a houseful of servants to wait upon him. He would marry someone like Violet who would fit into such dreams, while she would remain a little girl even when she was old and bent up and as bald as he had been for his first fifteen years!

He is a fool with as much common sense as a fly that buzzes until someone swats it, she thought irritably. She quickened her pace, pushing against him in the darkness, showing her impatience to be home.

He talked about the implications of the night's events, and she only nodded invisibly in the darkness or replied with a grunt that could mean either yes or no, whatever he preferred. She wanted to hit him, hurt him so he at least noticed her.

As they approached the cottage, he pulled her to face him.

'What *is* the matter with you, Olwen-the-Fish?' he demanded.

Suddenly the scales tilted, the depression and anger slid away like water along the side of a speeding boat, and she was a child again. She pulled furiously on his long hair, then ran giggling at his shout of rage, as he chased her. Choking with the effort of trying to be quiet, she burst through the door, and stood behind it while he whispered insults through the crack. With a whispered 'Goodnight' she climbed the ladder to her bed.

CHAPTER NINETEEN

Kenneth disappeared from the village and no one, not even his wife, knew where he had gone. For several days, Ceinwen wandered the streets and houses wailing her misfortune at losing her husband and provider, leaving Enyd to deal with the post as best she could. Enyd at once sent for Barrass and asked if he would take over the collections and deliveries until she could decide on the best way of coping. Barrass accepted with unbounded excitement.

'Olwen,' he called as he ran up to the white cottage, 'I am to be the temporary letter carrier!'

'So? It will be just another excuse for you to chase girls. What is so wonderful about that? It's not the position of letter-carrier you want, Barrass. It's the position that gives girls your babies to carry!'

'Olwen. Aren't you pleased for me? It's a step towards my dream,' he said as he held her arm and walked with her towards the cliffs.

Olwen's lovely face softened then, her blue eyes crinkling with generous delight. 'Of course I'm pleased,' she smiled. 'Glad for you I am. But don't spoil your chances by making it more a round for loving than for delivering the King's Mail.'

'You talk like an old woman, little Olwen.' He showed strong white teeth in a laugh, his attractiveness hitting her like a sudden wild gust of wind.

'Young I might be, but I am an old wise-woman compared to you when it comes to common sense!' she snapped.

She stepped apart from him, pressing her shawl against her as the edges fluttered in the breeze. His hands, helping to fasten it around her slim body, disturbed her greatly and she turned away, afraid that her growing love for him would show. They stood together looking down over the still water in the fresh early morning.

'Come with me tomorrow morning to collect the letters from Swansea,' he suggested impulsively. 'Ceinwen will have to pay for the hire of a horse or I'll never finish. You can sit behind me and we can talk, and you can meet all the people at the inn I've told you about.'

Olwen was tempted, but she shook her head. How she would love to go with him, to enter this new life of his and meet his friends as if she were his partner. She ached for him, but afraid of spoiling their very precious friendship, she pretended to be the child that she looked, and said in a horrified voice,

'No, I *can't*! Florrie would kill me for sure if I was late for work. There's a lot of cooking they do in that old Ddole House! You'd think there was an army to feed instead of only William Ddole and his friends.'

'Do you hear news of Penelope?' Barrass dared to ask. He was relieved when Olwen did not lose her temper at the reminder that he had been responsible for her going away.

'No word reaches the kitchen of how she is coping with being so far from home, but I know there was a letter from her for her father, Kenneth told me that.' She moved a little away from him, the memories of the coach house rendezvous painful for her. 'I miss her, you know. She was kind and didn't treat me like I was little better than the pigs and cattle, like some of the others do.'

'I cared for her too,' Barrass said. 'Everyone I care for goes away,' he added softly. Then he smiled. 'Except you, Olwen.'

For a long time after he had left Olwen, Barrass's thoughts were on her. She was so much a part of his life and he could not imagine ever living where she was not. He set off back to the alehouse and his day's work with Pitcher, the wind blowing gently through his long, black hair and ruffling his shirt into ripples of bubbling warm air. Tomorrow he would go in the early morning to collect the letters, and for a while at least he could pretend he was stepping out following the footsteps of his unknown father. But even this gratifying turn of his fortunes was somehow subdued and without the intoxicating thrill he had so often imagined. Inexplicably, the fact that Olwen was not free to enjoy it with him had spoilt the excitement almost completely.

Emma Palmer was in a happy frame of mind. She had found a small jar of wild pansies in her daughter's bedroom and guessed that Pansy had a secret admirer. She at once began to imagine the romance that surrounded the gift of flowers. Her plump face was rapt as she sighed and touched the small petals, each flowerhead so perfect, just like the girl she had named after them.

For several hours of each afternoon, when she had no visiting or shopping to attend to, Emma read romances. She was convinced that on one occasion they had saved her sanity, giving a false explanation for her daughter Violet's inexplicable behaviour with Barrass. But today she could not settle to read, she was far too excited and needed to talk to someone. She stood up and rang the small hand-bell for the servant and asked for her outdoor clothes. There was, of course, only Ceinwen-the-Post, but she was better than no one and at least she listened without too many interruptions!

Ceinwen was sitting beside her fire, having walked around to every house she could think of where Kenneth could be hiding. She had even asked Betson-the-Flowers, going to the woman's door with trepidation and asking if she had seen Kenneth. The woman had laughed and retorted that she saw *every*one. A few more questions from Ceinwen elicited no further information and she walked down the green lane from the tumbledown house red with embarrassment and unreasonably angry with Kenneth for putting her in the position of having to go to that notorious place.

'Not that I expected her to have seen him, mind,' Ceinwen told Emma when they were settled near the fire with a cup of tea to hand. 'Never one for the ladies, was Kenneth. Too fond of his home.'

'For sure,' Emma soothed, eyes glazed with determination not to tell. She sipped her tea and began to think it had been a mistake to come. She had expected that as usual Ceinwen would want to hear all her far more interesting news, but here she was, after almost half an hour, still listening to Ceinwen's tale of woe. She shuffled purposefully in her chair, making preparations to rise. Ceinwen took the hint and said at once,

'But here's me going on and I'm much more interested to hear what has been happening to you, Emma. The girls, are they well?'

Emma launched into her news.

'My dear, I do believe my Pansy has an admirer. I found a small posy half hidden behind a curtain in her bedroom and I am certain if they had been from someone – well ordinary, she would have shown them to me. Don't you think it romantic that she keeps the gift a secret even from her own, loving mother?'

'Very romantic,' Ceinwen said obediently. 'Have you a clue to who gave them to her?'

'One or two, my dear Ceinwen, one or two.' Emma shook her head mysteriously and placed a fat finger over her reddened lips. 'But for the moment I will say nothing.'

'I hope that the romance will go well, and that Pansy will have a better beginning to her marriage than Violet,' Ceinwen could not resist remarking. She looked at Emma to see if there was any dismay, but Emma smiled at her and said,

'That too was *so* romantic, wasn't it? Just like in the book I read last week. The innocent and utterly beautiful girl falls for an undeserving man, and at the very last moment, she realizes that the other, wealthy and much more admirable gentleman is the one she truly loves. His love for her transcends all their problems and they live happily afterwards.' She sighed her satisfaction at this slightly distorted summary of events, and held out her cup for more tea.

When she had discussed with Ceinwen all she had to say, Emma apologized for the briefness of her visit, explained how busy she was, and asked for her cloak. As she was being helped into it by her hostess, she heard raised voices and at once stopped her preparations to leave, curious to know the cause. The door leading to the room used as the sorting office burst open and Kenneth stumbled in, followed by Enyd, who hastily pushed the door shut and leaned against it in her determination to keep others out.

'What's ado?' Emma demanded, moving into a safe corner.

'It's Dadda,' Enyd said, panting with the effort of holding the door. 'Help me, will you, or they'll kill him before our eyes!'

Ceinwen and a reluctant Emma both leaned against the door and a frightened Kenneth joined them. After what seemed an age, those on the other side of the door stopped pushing and Enyd cautiously opened it to see that the room was empty.

'They've gone,' she sighed. 'But you can't stay here,' she added to her father. 'Kill you for sure they will.'

'I didn't do it, I didn't do it,' wailed a white-faced Kenneth.

'Oh, I'm so glad to hear you say that,' Ceinwen sighed, but her relief was short-lived.

'- I didn't get them imprisoned. Did that to themselves they did, caught stealing,' Kenneth went on. 'Doing my duty I was, for King and Country.'

Ceinwen reached for the girdle sitting on the hearth and hit him with it.

'Fool that you are!' she shouted. 'We live here, don't we? They're our friends, aren't they? You can't hand over your friends like that.' On the second smack, Kenneth sighed, smiled sweetly and sank to the floor.

'Come with me, Enyd,' Emma shrieked. 'I can't leave you here with these two maniacs!' Grabbing the girl's arm, persuading her to come for Emma's own protection more than the girl's, she pushed her way past the recumbent letter-carrier and his irate wife and out of the door.

They ran past the men and women who had been chasing Kenneth, now herded into a shouting, complaining group by Daniels, and into the alehouse. Puffing and gasping,

Emma dragged Enyd up the stairs and into the sitting room where Pansy and Daisy were just being relieved of their outdoor clothes.

'Kenneth is back from hiding and Ceinwen is on the edge of derangement!' Emma announced. 'Look after Enyd, my dears, it isn't safe for her to return until everything has calmed down!'

Once the servant had been dismissed, Pansy and Daisy demanded to know what had been happening.

'I don't really know,' Enyd said with regret. 'Your mother bustled me off before I could learn a thing! All I know is that my father has turned up again. He's been missing since it was found he was telling the soldiers and excise men a few little things here and there. Not spying, mind!' she emphasized and the girls shook their heads in disbelieving unison. 'Just a bit of chat that he picks up on his travels, like.

'Well, where he's been hiding I don't know, but he suddenly appeared at the corner of the bank and ran up shaking as if he was on his last legs. He must have been chased for miles, poor dab! He pushed his way into the house and the mob following him tried to push in as well. But we held the door until they gave up.

'They're still there, mind, and there's threatening they look, too! Not all of them our people, but a few from the next village I believe.' Enyd stopped her recital and gradually regained her breath. 'There's exciting, isn't it? But what will happen to us now we can't work the letters I daren't think. Because for sure, they won't allow Dadda to remain as the letter-carrier now this has come out. Killed he'd be if he set foot outside without protection.'

'Why, you must marry,' Daisy said, as if finding a husband was the simplest thing to do. 'If you don't you will spend your whole life caring for your mother and father, and what life is that for a girl like you?'

'Marry Dan, you mean?'

'No, no, not Dan the fisherman. You have to be told time

and again, don't you, my dear friend? You are worth far more than Dan!'

'I think Dan is a fine man,' Pansy said. 'He is as good a catch as the fish he brings in.'

'Really, sister,' Daisy sighed. 'A fisherman, for someone like Enyd?'

'I would prefer to marry someone who is honourable and who truly loves me, than a man who has a fine position but no love in him,' Pansy said firmly. 'Take heed of our sister Violet. Would you take her place?'

'Hush, dear. Violet was foolish, and if you ask me she got off remarkably well – and for that we have to thank our dear mother.'

Pansy did not reply. She and Daisy were the firmest of friends, and as close as twin sisters should be, but on this they disagreed.

Her gaze drifted to the ceiling, thinking of the flowers that were hidden behind a curtain and which had been given to her by one with no pretensions to being a gentleman, but to whom, if he were older, she would gladly hand over responsibility for her future happiness.

Kenneth continued to smile unconsciously as Daniels walked into the house and began to understand what had happened.

'I fear that your husband, for his bravery in helping to stop the smuggling, will suffer at the hands of his friends,' Daniels told Ceinwen. 'I will do what I can, and I have taken the names of all those presently outside, warning them that if a hair of his head be harmed, I will come to them for explanations. There is little more I can do. Will you go away from here and start again?'

'No,' Ceinwen replied quietly.

Ceinwen was a woman whom few noticed. She seemed to slide into the background of whatever company she found herself in. Quietly spoken, unassuming in dress and manner, she was ignored because there was nothing memorable or interesting about her. She did her work calmly and efficiently and bothered no one. The fact that no one

332

bothered her seemed to matter not at all. Now, with her softly spoken refusal to leave the village, Daniels looked at her as if for the first time.

'You will stay and risk the anger of everyone?'

'You call Kenneth a brave man, I call him a fool,' she surprised him further by saying. 'I will not let him drag me from my home. I will stay here and hope that eventually people will forgive him – I know I am talking against the law-abiding uniform you wear, but I still say it. I hope they will forgive him for his greed and stupidity. There, now you know for sure where I stand. I am not against you, Daniels, but neither am I for you.' Then her gentle voice added, 'I am on the side of peace, but not in the way your title represents it.'

It was the longest speech he had ever heard Ceinwen make and he stared at the dark eyes, the unkempt hair, the wrinkled and rather dull face, and wondered what the person behind the colourless facade was really like.

Kenneth began to move and Daniels helped the small man up into a chair. He gestured to the pot of tea left from Emma's visit and Ceinwen poured a cup. Daniels held it while the man drank thirstily and then handed it back to Ceinwen to be refilled.

'I think it might be wise to send for Doctor Percy,' he said. 'There's no knowing how badly they have hurt him.'

'They didn't hurt him at all,' Ceinwen told him.

'Then why was he unconscious?'

'I gave him a smack with the girdle,' Ceinwen said in her calm, quiet voice. 'I hope I haven't buckled it, makes for burnt cakes it does, if the girdle is not straight and true.'

Daniels did not trust himself to reply.

Ceinwen continued to gather in the letters for the post, and worked with Barrass as easily as she had with Kenneth, the only difference being that Barrass reached his destination earlier, and finished on a Thursday at a remarkably early hour.

Kenneth stayed inside, only venturing out to use the earthen privy after dark. No one came to threaten him, but he was certain, as he bent low and peered nervously over the window sill, dark eyes darting in an attempt to look in all directions at once, that men were out there just waiting for him to show his bandaged head.

Enyd had not gone straight home when she left the ale-house. The persuasions of Daisy, that she should look for someone grander than Dan, unsettled her. And Pansy's opinion that Dan was a fine man, instead of helping, only added to the confusion.

It was not as if there were that many choices. There were a number of young men who worked on the farms and laboured long hours on their own small patches of land, but who else would look at her, the daughter of the dis-graced letter-carrier, for a wife? She thought of Thomas, and Edwin Prince, and John Maddern from London. They had soon put her in her place on the few occasions she had met them. Her face warmed as she remembered her foolish visit to Edwin Prince.

It was all very fine to listen to people like Daisy, who had the advantage of an education as well as contacts with other business and monied people, but for herself she would be better served to remember how lowly she really was.

The late afternoon was getting cold, the wind, so benign earlier in the day, was seeping into her clothes and touching her skin with icy fingers. Her hair blew out behind her and she smilingly imagined herself at the prow of some ancient ship, seeing her craft and its crew into safe harbour. Then the thought of ships brought Dan back into her mind and she frowned.

She stood silently enjoying the growing strength of the sea-cleansed air, smelling the seaweed and tasting salt on her lips. The singing entered her consciousness gradually, so sweet that it might have been a part of the sea's sound, or one of the ghostly voices that the sailors say comes from the newly dead as they search for their loved ones. But the voice was familiar and, she realized with a smile, not far away. Dan was coming into the shore with his catch.

She moved closer to the cliff edge and saw the small boat

easing its way around the headland. Dan was standing with a hand on the mast, waving to her.

'Enyd, come and meet me,' his strong voice called, and seabirds screamed a chorus. 'How did you know it was me?' she shouted back, but she knew the answer. In a crowd of hundreds, she would pick out Dan, as he would know her. In that moment, she admitted that whatever fancy imaginings had filled her mind, Dan-the-Fisher was the only one she could love.

Laughing like a child, she ran down the steep path, losing her balance and shouting with mock fright, slithering on the loose stones and sliding on the grass, until she was in his arms.

That Dan was delighted with the uncharacteristic welcome was in no doubt. He lifted her up and swung her around him before kissing her lightly and demanding of his father that he be let off sorting the fish.

'Dadda,' he pleaded. 'I need to talk to Enyd. And the moment is one not to be lost,' he added in a whisper. 'Go now, can I?'

'All right, boy,' Spider grinned. 'Glad I'll be when you and Enyd are settled in your courting! Best work we'll get from you then.'

Dan guided Enyd to where they could sit sheltered by the sand dunes and took her hand. With the wind for accompaniment, he sang:

My love is like the morn,
Sweet as each new dawn,
Fresh and sweet as each new dawn
My love is like the morn.

My love is like the day,
Sweet as new-mown hay,
Fresh and sweet as new-mown hay
My love is like the day.

My love is like the night,
She gives my heart its light,
My secret love my own heart's light

335

Sets cupid's arrow on its flight,
Fills me with such sweet delight,
My heart is like the night.

They sat for a long time, talking only occasionally, and of nothing personal or important: admiring the colours in the sea, the gentle lapping of the waves and the musical sounds of the wind in the trees and the tapping of ropes on the masts of the now idle fishing boats. Each one conscious of the feelings they held for the other, and content to savour them in amicable silence.

Kenneth, at Ceinwen's insistence, went back to his work, after a week during which Barrass coped efficiently and with great enjoyment with the collections and deliveries.

'So good he is that soon there will be talk about how much sooner he delivers than you, and how willing he is to go extra distances to serve the people in the most isolated houses and farms,' Ceinwen warned her pale-faced husband. 'Yesterday it was raining so hard that he went early and took several letters right to people's doors so they wouldn't get themselves wet and cold waiting for him!'

'Fool that he is,' grumbled Kenneth, heaving on his coat over thick padding to keep out the cold wind. 'Making a rod for a fool's back!' He put on an ancient top hat which he had stuffed with seaweed in case he should be beaten about the head, and lifted a stout stick in his hand. There was nothing more he could do to protect himself. He had suggested to Ceinwen that he should invite Barrass to travel with him for the first few days, but she had refused. Still angry with him for his treacherous behaviour to their friends, she would allow no extra expense.

'You pay for what you do, your payment is constant fear. Go now and hope that others will not be as cold and uncaring as you are!'

He looked at her in surprise. She was always surprising him lately. His quiet, mild, inconspicuous wife had become a scold.

Almost pushed out of his door, he stumbled down the

336

bank and scurried, bent almost double to avoid being noticed, to the stables where the horse was harnessed in readiness for him. Barrass stood in the shadows – hoping, Kenneth guessed, that he would lose his nerve and ask the boy to work one more day.

'It's all right, boy,' he said with an attempt at casual confidence. 'I am fully recovered from my wife's beating.' The horse skittered as he climbed nervously and awkwardly onto its back and, still seeking the second stirrup, hurried out of the village on the road to Swansea.

The ride was a nightmare. Although he had told no one apart from Barrass that he was recommencing his route, he feared every shadow of every bush. The sun, low on the horizon and as yet without much strength, cast distorted shadows and had his heart leaping in panic every few moments. When he reached the inn, where there was already a crowd waiting for the sorting office to open its doors, he felt sick.

He dismounted and offered the reins to the stable boy but the boy impertinently refused, turning his back and pretending to be busy with something else.

'Hey boy, take my horse,' Kenneth blustered, looking around for support from lookers-on. In every face was disapproval. Many turned away from him. Some spat on the dusty ground and even the small boys who were always about seeking to earn a penny would not take his horse. He felt fear rising and half imagined the crowd closing in behind ready to attack as he walked the horse over to the corner and tied the rein himself.

No one objected when he carried water for his mount, and there was hay available which no one begrudged. But for himself, there was no ale to be supped, and not even a spare seat to rest while he waited for his letters. Outwardly everything was the same as on other mornings – laughter and woeful confidences, loud talk and secret whispers – but Kenneth stood amid the tumult as if invisible.

Conversations ceased each time he approached a lively group, and even Ben Gammon, who was always ready for a pleasant sharing of news, ignored his greeting as he set off with the Swanzey Bag towards Monmouth, waving and shouting to his friends. With dread, Kenneth took the few letters that were silently handed to him by a disapproving postmaster, and remounted to return to the village.

'Damn the expense,' he grumbled to the stable boy at the village. 'I'm a sick man. Get me a horse for the two days of my route.'

It will be safer risen above the crowds and it makes for a faster getaway if there's any trouble, he thought, and I won't dismount at all if I can help it, or not until I'm sure no one wishes me ill.

By three o'clock he was barely able to stay on his horse. Craning his neck in an attempt to see around corners and staring at every bush and tree for fear they hid an assailant, he had exhausted himself. He had reached Penrice Castle and delivered the three letters from Bristol and the one from London, then, unable to stand the strain, slid from the horse's back and sat with his back against a tree to rest. Frightened as he was, he slept.

He finished the first half of his journey and with some trepidation went to the house at Middleton, near Rhosili, where he normally stayed. What if they too refused to acknowledge him? He forced himself to shed his anxieties and knocked loudly on the door as he usually did, calling for Mistress Griffiths to let him in. As the door opened, he walked in and demanded an ale and some bread and cheese to revive him and hold his hunger until it was time for her excellent evening meal.

She appeared not to treat him any differently from normal, but when her husband came to carry his bag and show him to his room, he was taken out through the kitchen and into a small, draughty lean-to that had been built to house chickens. The walls had been whitewashed and there was a bed with a low frame to keep it out of the cold air seeping under the ill-fitting door.

'Room's occupied for tonight,' Mr Griffiths informed him. 'This is all we can offer, and glad you should be that

338

we don't send you to find a place in a sheepfold up on Rhosili Downs.'

They gave him food with little politeness, and he went to his poor bedroom and barricaded himself inside before huddling miserably under the shabby blankets that smelt of horses, and tried to sleep.

He reminded himself that it was Wednesday, that the following day was Thursday, the day on which he visited Betson-the-Flowers. Having that to look forward to – should he survive the night and the journey back – he closed his eyes and pretended he was beside her warm fire with her soft body wrapped around him.

The following morning he hurried on his way after a mean breakfast served by a scowling Mistress Griffiths. One of the few letters left to deliver was for far-away Penclawdd where the women went out on the sands to gather cockles at each low tide, but he decided to forget it and go on the almost direct route for home. It was rarely that he did not deliver the full collection, and he knew that he would be severely reprimanded if anyone should think to complain, but he decided that today, of all days, was the one when he could break the rules. He had never felt so weary.

With only the one letter in his bag for delivery and twelve to take into the Swansea sorting office, he came in sight of Betson-the-Flowers' house. He dismounted and found he could barely drag his feet the last few yards. He did not look up to check whether the window was draped as a warning that she was occupied with another visitor. It rarely happened, as his own calls were regular and she always made sure she was free.

He had almost reached the door when a movement caught his eye. The frilly, warning curtain twitched and spread across the shining glass of the front window. He gave a groan. Of course. She would not have known that he was back on his route. He eased the bag from his shoulders, threw down the stick he had carried unnecessarily for the two days, and went to sit beside a tree out of sight of the door to wait. He did not want to see who was leaving, best he pretended that he was her only visitor.

It was earlier than his usual time to call too, he had forgotten that in his haste to be finished, and riding instead of walking, he had cut hours from his journey. She would be cross with him for changing the habit they had enjoyed for years. He smiled when he thought of her anger, put on, short-lived and utterly exciting. His tiredness fading, he sat and listened for the sound of her door.

He could not have said how long he sat there, but the sun was lowering down the sky and a cold dampness seeped from the earth and chilled his body, making the wait more and more uncomfortable. Impatient at last, he thought perhaps he had missed the departure of Betson's guest and wandered casually back to her door. He listened and there was no sound from within. He began to call, pushing against the door as he did so.

'Get away, pig!' she called and the door was pressed firmly shut against his hands.

'Betson?' he whispered. 'It's me, Kenneth.'

'Pig. That's what you are! I hid you, didn't I? Saved you when there was a chance you might have been murdered? I believed you when you insisted you were innocent I did. Lied to me you did. Pig! Pig! Pig!'

Cold, tired and hungry, longing for her loving, her fire and her food, he stared foolishly at the door for a while, then gave up, convinced that she would forget in time, that those happy moments were not gone for ever. Replacing the bag on his back as regulations insisted, but ignoring the stick, he dragged his feet towards his mount and crawled up onto its back. Deciding to take a shorter route home, he later dismounted and guided the horse down the stony path towards the quarry.

He had the Penclawdd letter as proof for Ceinwen that he was sooner than usual because he was too ill to finish his rounds. There was no reason why he couldn't go home early and be comforted. A sharp stab of concern flashed through his brain as he thought that those days *were* possibly over. That Ceinwen, like all the rest, no longer considered him deserving of even the slightest kindness.

As he approached the top of the quarry, five men

appeared from the trees. Each one carried a stick which they tapped against a palm in a threatening manner. Kenneth gasped with disbelief. Not now, when he had reached sight of the smoke from his own fire! He tried to remount, but his foot could not find the stirrup, his legs lacked the strength to lift him and he abandoned the animal to its fate.

He turned from them and, revived by fear ran like a hare for the quarry. He practically threw himself over the edge, not giving a thought to how he might place his feet, and ran uncontrollably down the steep slope. He tripped over a bramble that had crept across his path and rolled like a ball, dashing himself against numerous jagged edges, and settled in a painful heap almost at Pitcher's gate. He risked a glance upwards to see the five men standing on the horizon, one already beginning to find a more orderly route to join him.

'Pitcher!' he screamed. 'Barrass! Arthur! Pitcher!' A window opened and Emma's screams joined his. As the five men worked their way down the face of the quarry, Barrass ran through the arch, scooped up the terrified man and carried him into the yard.

'Never no more!' Kenneth shouted as he was half carried and half dragged inside the house. 'I'm never going to deliver a letter again. Ceinwen won't persuade me after this. Hounded I've been for two whole days, wondering if I will ever see my home again. Hounded, mind! Never no more. Never!'

It took a glass of Pitcher's best brandy to calm him.

'Good isn't it?' Pitcher said as the terrified man slurped shakily. 'Best French that is. Illegal, mind! Should refuse it by rights, shouldn't you?'

Kenneth chose not to hear him until the glass was drained.

Barrass, Pitcher, Arthur and the dog gathered the unexcited horse, then they all escorted Kenneth home, and once through his door, he shouted to Ceinwen that whatever she said to persuade him, he was no longer the letter-carrier for Gower.

'I have already decided that,' Ceinwen said quietly, 'best we offer it to Dan, then he and our Enyd can marry.'

Barrass heard the announcement with an aching heart. His only chance of carrying letters around Gower was gone. He hardly noticed Enyd push past the drooping figure of her father to run up and tell Dan the exciting news.

'No, Enyd, a hundred times, a thousand times, *no!*'

'But Dan! I thought you loved me?'

'That I could never deny,' he said, leading her to the privacy of a huddle of wind-curved trees. 'But neither can I deny that I am a fisherman,' he insisted firmly. 'My father and I work together and never have any of our family or friends gone hungry.'

'But you might die,' she whispered with a sob. 'I am so afraid for you, Dan, that it would be a life filled with misery for me.'

'Only think, your father has several times been attacked and you say that today he has been chased by a horde of ten men armed with knives and sticks – or so he says. I have never even been in danger! My father knows the sea as well as any man in these parts, and respects it. He will never take a chance with his life or mine, knowing that without him, Olwen and baby Dic and my mother would be in difficulties. For them he would always err on the side of safety. For you, my dearest love, so will I. There, you have my promise on it.'

'Olwen nearly lost her life,' she said in a vain hope of winning the argument.

'Olwen didn't take time to read the signs. When she knew she was being stupid she was too prideful to admit it. That is a mistake she will never make again. Pride can kill far easier than the respectful use of the sea.'

'But we would be able to have an easier, more comfortable life, Dan. Why don't you just *try* being the post-carrier? You may even prefer it. How can you know if you do not try it?'

'Fishing is a proud calling,' Dan said softly, taking her in his arms and willing her to understand. 'Didn't they feed the village and many from outside when there was a great famine? And when there were visitations of the plague and the smallpox, and no one dared to leave the village or allow anyone to enter with food? Didn't the fishermen save us then, bringing in good food from the sea, and feeding everyone until the danger was past?'

'I am afraid of it, Dan.'

'Then I will have to teach you not to be.' He kissed her and smiled. 'When you have lost your fear of it, you will no longer be feared for me, and all will be well.'

'That will never be.'

'I *will* marry you, Enyd. Of that you can be certain. And, I will not have to leave the sea to persuade you, of that too you can be sure. Listen to *me*, the one who loves you, and forget the grand and impossible ideas fixed in your mind by Emma Palmer and her silly, fanciful daughters.'

He walked her back to his mother's house away from sight of the sea she so hated, and softly, his powerful voice controlled in a low, sweet whisper, he sang again,

> My love is like the morn,
> Sweet as each new dawn,
> Fresh and sweet as each new dawn
> My love is like the morn . . .

CHAPTER TWENTY

Tom came home again towards the middle of April and Olwen met him three times in as many days on her way to begin her work at Ddole House. Each time he was waiting for her at the end of the green lane and each time he escorted her to the gates of the driveway and watched as she walked down between the trees and out of his sight.

It was simply a coincidence so far as she was concerned, and it was not until Florrie and Dozy Bethan began to make teasing remarks that she thought otherwise.

'Out for walks early he is and what's wrong with that then?' Olwen said in response to yet another pointed comment. 'Ceinwen gets up before the cockerels to get the day started before Barrass comes back with the letters, I expect she pushes him out from under her feet. Like most men he's probably less use than the space he takes up!'

Florrie chuckled as she handed Olwen the empty coal buckets to fill.

'You're probably right at that, girl. With Kenneth hanging around too scared to leave her shadow, and Tom wanting something to do to pass the idleness of his leave, it probably drives the poor woman frantic.'

'Never a chance to be idle in Mam's house,' Olwen grumbled, pulling at the door and pushing her way through with the ungainly buckets. 'What with the animals and the fields, and the fish and the wool – always the wool! Finding it, washing it, dyeing it and then there's the carding and spinning and weaving. There's never a day in the year when there isn't something to see to with the wool!'

'Brings in a good bit of extra with the blankets she makes, your Mam,' Dozy Bethan said. 'Some of the best to be had, Mary-the-Fish's blankets, that's what people do say, for sure.'

'Are you going to stand there all day with those empty

buckets, letting all the heat out, Olwen-the-Fish?' Florrie asked. She chuckled again when Olwen slipped through the door and closed it with careful firmness behind her.

'Still plenty of cheek in that one,' she said to Bethan. 'But she'll do, she'll do.'

'Not for long, then, if that Tom is looking out for her. He comes home so rarely and for such a short time that he'll work fast and make his courting last a few days instead of months. Have to watch them soldiers,' Bethan drawled in her slow voice. 'They works very fast they do, them not having the time to dawdle, like.'

Bent from the waist filling the coal buckets, Olwen was wondering if Barrass would care if she *did* keep company with Tom for the few weeks he was at home. Probably not, she sighed, heaving up a large piece of coal and dropping it on another to break it into usable sizes. She idly thought that would be a nice thing to do to Barrass's head. 'Oh, that Barrass,' she said aloud, 'he's an a-w-ful fool.'

'And why is he a fool?' a voice said and she turned in alarm to see Tom standing at the door of the barn, laughing at her. He was not in uniform, but wore dark brown trousers over which were pulled shiny, polished boots. His shirt was white linen, neatly pleated down the front and with a large, stand-up collar. The collar was turned fashionably up, cradling a cravat of brown only slightly darker than his trousers. He carried a jacket across his arm and a hat shaded his eyes from her, although, from the shape of his mouth, she guessed they would be laughing.

'You shouldn't be here,' she gasped. 'Set the dogs on strangers they do. And that David in the stables, he hits first and sorts out the questions later!'

'I have a letter for William Ddole, it came by the morning post and I offered to deliver it for Barrass,' he said. 'I thought it might be an excuse to walk you home later. So, if no one asks why I'm here now, forcing me to hand it over, I'll see you later. Six of the clock, is it?'

'How do I know!' she said impatiently. 'Cook is quite likely to find me something to do at five minutes off the hour and make me stay until I finish it!'

His sudden appearance had rattled her. It was as if thinking had made him materialize. Pity it hadn't worked with Barrass, she thought angrily. He's probably off looking for that Harriet, or some other pretty pair of ankles he's taken a fancy to.

'I said I will be waiting at the gate,' Tom said.

She brought her mind swiftly back and said, 'I heard you,' although she had not. 'I'm not deaf, and no more am I decided about whether or not I want you to walk me home, Tom-Soldier-Boy!'

'Soldier, but no boy, as I'll demonstrate should you have a desire to learn,' he said.

'Oh go, before I throw this coal over your neat clothes!'

He raised his hands in mock alarm and backed away.

'By the gate then, at six of the clock,' he called back.

She rattled the coal against the buckets and did not answer.

Later that day she was sent on a message to the house of Violet and Edwin. She carried the folded and sealed note in her hand, curious as to its contents but not daring to do more than lift a corner to see what it said. All she could make out was William Ddole's signature, and she sighed in disappointment. Learning to read had been fun, and although she no longer had Penelope to ask if she was stuck on a strange word, she was making excellent progress.

The house that Edwin had dramatically enlarged for the arrival of his bride was, Olwen thought, an ungainly building. Low and long at the front, with the newer, taller building joined on at the back for the full length, with chimneys adorning the ridge like ill-formed teeth, it looked what it was, an attempt to make something grand out of a farmer's dwelling.

The entrance was at the wide opening that had once been the division between the living rooms and the place set aside for the cattle, goats and chickens. The new doors were ornately carved and boasted a huge knocker that seemed likely to defeat Olwen's attempts to bang it. On tiptoe she stretched until she could touch the lowest tip of it and knew that, reluctantly, she would have to do as she was supposed to, and go around to the servants' and tradesmen's door at the back.

She walked around the building where the evidence of recent working was apparent in the neglected bricks and stones and the debris of cutting them that lay all about. She was looking along the building to decide which was the correct door when she heard a scream.

Her legs almost gave out under her, but recovered enough to step closer to the back door. It burst open and a distraught-looking woman shouted.

'Olwen, go at once for Doctor Percy. It's Mistress Violet. Run, girl!'

Forgetting to hand over the letter, Olwen darted around the house and along the paths and small tracks, cutting through fields and disturbing a small flock of sheep. The scream seemed to echo around in her head for the whole time she was running, it chased her, urged her on so she did not pause for breath.

Doctor Percy was at home and, on hearing that it was Violet who needed him, set off at once on his small horse. Olwen sank to the ground, her limbs trembling, her breath painfully tight. Even her teeth felt the agony of it as she drew each breath.

'Olwen! Whatever is the matter?'

She looked up and saw Tom staring at her from the corner of the doctor's house.

'Nothing's the matter, I'm out of puff, that's all.'

'Has someone chased you? Tell me who it is and I'll see they regret it.'

'Nothing like that,' Olwen said as she began to rise. 'I had to run for the doctor for Violet Prince. The baby on its way, I suppose.'

He offered her a hand. She ignored it, but he took her arm anyway, holding her close against him, and walked with her away from the house. She still held the letter.

'I was to deliver this, but the scream emptied my mind,' she said, and he took it from her.

'I will take it. My days are not very full. It will be an

347

excuse to go and see if the reason for the urgency was the arrival of Barrass's baby.'

'Don't say that!' she snapped. 'The baby is Violet's, and as she is married to that Edwin, *his* it will be!'

'Talking to you is like pouring water onto a fire,' Tom laughed. 'Spitting and crackling with every innocent remark!'

They walked together to the place where their paths led in opposite directions. He released her arm and, to her surprise, bent suddenly and kissed her – first on her cheek and then, when she moved to avoid it, his lips held hers. The surprise faded and the sensation was one of sweetness. His arms were around her, pressing her slightly against him, his lips moving gently, moulding hers into an opening flower. He did not look at her again, but gave her the briefest of hugs and was gone.

'Six of the clock, remember,' he called back.

She stared after his retreating figure, stunned by what had happened. She had never been kissed in that way before. Arthur kissed her in fun and Barrass with brotherly affection, but Tom's kiss was different and had caused strange things to happen to her insides. She walked slowly back to Ddole House.

News of the arrival of Violet's baby girl reached them in late afternoon. Olwen closed her ears to the remarks about Barrass's part in it, and pretended not to understand the jokes that passed between the kitchen, the stables and everyone who called at the house. She knew that the baby was the result of Barrass's loving, but there was no advantage in tormenting herself about it. And besides, since Tom's kiss she was no longer so surprised at it happening. The stirrings of the need for loving were already in her, and how difficult it must be to deny them with the one you love. But it was Barrass her body cried out for, Barrass's kisses, and Barrass's hands pressing her close to him. She scrubbed even harder at the pots to take her mind from the sensations that were disturbing her.

That evening she pleaded with Florrie to allow her to

leave early. She did not want to talk to Tom. There was something insistent about him, forcing her to accept her own emerging adulthood. She ran home, and offered to help Mary with the new blanket that was set up on the loom in the living room. Mary was surprised, but wisely did not ask the reason for such industriousness.

Dan needed to show Enyd that the sea was not a fearful enemy, only a friend with capricious moods and an unreliable temper. He talked it over with Spider, who advised him to coax her into a change of mind.

'Get her out on the sea, boy, make sure she enjoys the experience. Be sure to take her out while the sea is in gentle and unplayful mood, then she will gradually realize that she gives pleasure and bountiful gifts as well as danger and death. Just now Enyd is set on remembering only the worst, ignoring the best.'

Dan wandered around, attending to his various tasks whilst trying to think of a way to entice Enyd into his boat. He agreed with his father. Once Enyd had felt the joy of skimming the surface of the sea, being driven along with the wind giving what you asked of it, the craft dancing at great speed and taking on a life of its own, there would be a complete change of heart. But how to persuade her?

It was Arthur who gave him the idea. One day when the tides were quite low, Dan watched from the top of the cliffs while Olwen on a blessed few hours of freedom, and Arthur with his dog, rowed out to the headland of Limeslade Bay and stepped overboard to stand, with water up to their knees only, on the Mixen Sands, the sandbank that was such a danger to unwary shipping.

He waved to them, and as they laughingly climbed back on board the boat, he ran around the headland to meet them as they reached shore near the village.

'Will you do that again?' he asked and, helping to lift the excited dog out of the boat, while Arthur tied it to its moorings, he explained his idea.

Enyd was disconsolately dealing with the accounts. The columns of figures had occupied her for several hours and

349

as the pages became blurred with tiredness, she decided to finish and take a rest. She was filled with melancholy. Having spent an hour earlier taking tea with Emma and the twins, she was again thrown into uncertainty about the decision to marry Dan.

If Emma were to be believed, she would regret becoming the wife of such a lowly man and would spend her days in semi-poverty and drudgery. But she had felt no stirrings of love for anyone but Dan, and that he loved her was in no doubt.

She closed the ledger with relief as she completed the final total on the page, and stretched. If her mother could listen for callers for an hour she would go and walk on the cliffs to ease her stiffness. The tide was at its lowest and she loved the strong smell of the weed part-dried in the warmth of the day. Dan had invited her to walk with him at this hour, and she wanted to feel his hand on hers, and put aside the wavering doubts that he was the one she loved.

Dan was with his mother, repairing a small loom that had become a victim of baby Dic's attentions. When the darkness of the room showed that someone stood at the door, her looked up and smiled with delight.

'Enyd, my love, you've come.'

'I have listened to Emma's boasting and the twins' chatter, and worked over Dadda's books, so I need to feel the fresh air about my ears to wake me up from my dullness,' she said.

She heard a sound outside, and turned to see Olwen running for the cliff path.

'That girl,' Dan said. 'She'll never grow up! Runs around like a demented puppy and never feels fatigue. Off she is to row out around the headland with Arthur.'

He sat finishing the repair while Enyd watched, not speaking very much, but each very aware of the other. When the loom was once again sound, he put it aside and gathered her in his arms.

The kiss was ended regretfully when the sound of Mary coming back with the eggs she had gathered, singing to

350

Dic, met their ears, and they went out to greet them both before setting off towards the cliffs.

Dan appeared to have nothing on his mind apart from Enyd, but he was carefully timing their arrival at the cliff edge to coincide with Arthur and Olwen reaching the sand-bank. He looked down at the beach and saw the small boat being rowed out from the small, narrow stretch of sand, appearing from the distance to almost graze against the rocks jutting out at either side of it. He felt a moment's anxiety, not wanting there to be a real emergency instead of the rehearsed imitation.

He carefully turned Enyd so she would not see Olwen deposit Arthur and his dog in the unlikely shallows so far from the shore and waited impatiently to allow time for Olwen to row to where she could not be seen from the shore. Then he pointed to Arthur, stranded dangerously, the dog in his arms, out beyond the rocks, and called Enyd urgently to follow him.

As they ran, he shouted to her that they must hurry, that Arthur must have gone to rescue his dog, and that she must come with him to effect a rescue or see the boy drown before her eyes.

She did not argue, carried along by his authority. They reached the beach, running down the uneven slope without attempting to find the easiest path, and onto the shore. There, a small boat was waiting for them. Enyd hesitated then, and Dan dealt firmly with her fears.

'I need you to come with me, Enyd my love, or that boy is in danger. Not from the sea, but from his own stupidity,' he said, and pulled her over the gunnels and into the small boat. He released her then, feeling a bit guilty as she clung fearfully to the small bench seat. Pushing the boat out until it bobbed on the waves, he climbed in and began rowing towards the small figure apparently alone and helpless in the sea.

As they reached him, Arthur laughed, and throwing the dog into the water to follow, he swam to Olwen who was anchored just out of sight behind the headland, holding the rope fastened about his waist. She helped the dog and

Arthur over the side and then they pulled up the anchor and set sail, jeering at the victims of their joke.

'If we sail around the headland now and come into the village, we can catch them and give them the hiding they deserve,' Dan laughed, continuing with the pretence. But he was smiling, and pretending not to notice how white Enyd's hands were as she silently clung to the sides. He began to sing, his strong voice riding the waves as easily as the boat, and he confidently hauled up the sheets and allowed the slight wind to flap them. Then as they came out past the headland, the wind filled them and the boat soared away across the surface of the sea, the sound a gentle one, the movement as natural to Dan as breathing.

He glanced at Enyd frequently, but said nothing to suggest he was aware of her being afraid. He saw her hands slowly relax their grasp and he risked meeting her eyes, smiling, and she answered with a wavering one of her own.

They stayed out for more than an hour, and by the time they reached the beach, she had managed to stand beside him, handle the rudder, help pull in the sail, and even – to his surprise and delight – take the oars, though she succeeded in sending them in circles, her right pull stronger than her left.

When she stood on the gravelly shore she was trembling and he carried her up to her parents' home, both laughing with the exhilaration of the experience.

'You cheated me, Dan-Fisher, don't think I don't know,' she said breathlessly, her cheeks and eyes aglow. 'You and that sister of yours, and Arthur, even the dog! You all cheated me.'

'Are you pleased?'

'I'm glad now, but when I first stood in the boat I thought I would never, ever forgive you. Even now I think you're the most – '

Her recriminations were stopped by his kiss.

The only people who were not pleased were Mary and Spider. They threatened Dan that if he ever involved his sister in anything so foolish again, he would regret it for ever.

'We could have lost her,' Mary sobbed. 'The sea is so wild at that point and she's only a child!'

In her bed above the living room, Olwen smiled, shook her head and whispered,

'No I'm not, Mam, no I'm not. I'm growing up and it's a-w-ful hard.'

Ceinwen and Enyd tried once again to persuade Dan to take the position of letter-carrier but he refused firmly, and this time Enyd did not prolong the argument. She went out several times with Dan and Spider, short pleasure trips only, but as her confidence in Dan's ability to look after her grew, so did the conviction that if she loved him, she could not ask him to give up the life he so enjoyed.

They eventually planned to marry in the month of September, and as soon as this was decided, Emma ran across to the white house on the bank and offered her services as advisor.

'There's nothing you can tell me about weddings and the proper way to have things done, Ceinwen,' she said firmly. 'Be guided by me and you'll have no complaints or criticisms.' She lowered her bewigged head that was topped with a large-brimmed hat she had bought second hand from a door-to-door clothes seller.

'I think, my dear, that I might be celebrating the nuptials of my daughter Pansy before the year is out. Besides the romantic flowers, there have been several surprise gifts appearing in her room and although she has not uttered a word by way of explanation, I think I suspect who it might be.'

'Oh?' Ceinwen said with a curious light in her brown eyes. 'Who do you think is her secret admirer then?'

'Why, no one less than John Maddern, the man who comes often to spend time with William Ddole. I've noticed, you see, that the flowers only arrive rarely, and each time it has been when John Maddern is staying. Now, what d'you think of that? A friend of the Ddoles and a London man of business!'

'It isn't him,' Ceinwen said casually. 'It's that Arthur, your pot-boy.'

'Oh really, Ceinwen, you will have your little joke.'

'No joke,' Ceinwen said, maliciously enjoying the shock on Emma's chubby face. 'It's that Arthur who brings her flowers.'

It only took a few moments for Emma to recover.

'I know about *that*, dear,' she lied. 'That poor lovestruck boy, admiring Pansy. That *is* a joke! No, there is someone else and I feel almost certain that it is John Maddern. Now,' she said, rising and reaching for her cloak, 'Pitcher will be wondering where I have got to.'

'Mr Palmer! Come upstairs with me at once!' Emma shouted as she ran in through the alehouse door. 'He will have to go. The boy will have to go!'

'Oh no. What has Barrass been up to this time? He's hardly here!' Pitcher sighed and wearily followed his irate wife up to their living room, preparing arguments for persuading Barrass to stay at the alehouse once he was freed from carrying the post. When Emma explained that Arthur was 'paying court' to their daughter, he roared with laughter and told her to behave before he collapsed with her larking him.

'Arthur!' he said disparagingly. 'Nothing but a boy.'

'That, Mr Palmer, is what you said about Barrass, and we have a dark-eyed granddaughter to prove how wrong you were!'

Olwen would probably have refused Tom's invitation to walk her home by the longest route if she had not just heard the news of Barrass's second daughter being born. Although it was expected, somehow the prospect of the girls giving birth to his children had not seemed real. Knowing that there was a Gabriella Prince and a Maude Rees made her face up to the fact that Barrass loved every woman he met – with the exception of herself.

Tom was standing just inside the driveway when she finished work for the day and although it was late he invited her to walk across to the next bay to see the sunset. He was an attractive young man, she supposed, with his hazel eyes that flashed with amusement and cooled to adoration in moments, as she had seen when he talked with Dozy Bethan at the kitchen door while delivering yet another letter, and the news of Carrie's child.

The sea was green and, to Olwen as she stood at the edge of the tide, the waves seemed like pale green glass. There were a few people walking on the beach and several poorly dressed children played with a couple of dogs in and out of the cold water.

'Catch their deaths they will, bathing before the sea has warmed,' Olwen said disapprovingly.

'Oh? And what about you and Arthur daring to go out to the Mixens then?'

'That was different.'

'For love,' he said softly. 'Do anything for love, would you, Olwen-the-Fish?'

His arm slipped around her waist and he led her away from the water, darkening suddenly as the sun disappeared. She shivered and his arm tightened.

'Best we go up from the sea where it's warmer.'

'Best I make for Mam's fire,' she said.

But she did not dissuade him when he led her away from her home to a small half-hidden place in the rocks, out of sight of those passing. He took off his coat and placed it across her shoulders, kissing her lightly as he tightened it around her. She began to feel excitement as he sat close beside her and held her tightly against him. Then he began to pull her closer to his length, forcing her to straighten against him, persuading her to feel the sudden urgency of his kisses as he did. His breathing became harsh, his demands more fierce, and she became frightened. She cried out and tried to pull away.

'Tom, stop it, you're hurting me.'

'No I'm not, you like it.'

His hands were all over her, pulling and kneading, stroking and exploring, sliding under her clothes until she screamed loudly and long, startling him into relaxing his hold on her. She pushed him away and kicked out at him as she rose to flee, and she ran without looking back, the scream continuing long after she had left the sight of the small hidden place in the rocks.

When she reached home, Barrass was there, and the sight of him made her cry. She had imagined running in and telling her mother she was tired and being allowed to hurry up the ladder to her bed, there to recover from the humiliation of Tom's treatment.

'Olwen?' he said. 'What has happened?'

'Nothing. I'm tired, that's all,' she said, then to justify the tears beginning to slide down her cheeks she added fiercely, 'And so would you be if you'd been running around after others all day since first light!'

Mary turned from the fire where she had been stirring a large pot of broth.

'Tired are you, love? Why not go for a walk on the cliffs, that always calms you down. Barrass will go with you, won't he?' She looked at Barrass, tall now and greatly filled out since he was taking so much exercise and eating so well, and smiled at him. 'Then stay to eat with us, if you don't mind some old broth made with a couple of bones from the bacon.'

'What happened?' Barrass demanded when they were away from the house.

'It's nothing to do with you,' Olwen snapped. 'What makes you think you have the right to ask me what I've been doing, while you go and do exactly what you like with every girl in the village and some beyond?'

'You've heard about Carrie's daughter?' he asked. 'But that wasn't a surprise, was it? You knew, everybody knew she was due to be confined. She says it was mine and so it might be, but why has it upset you so?' He frowned then as the words she had spoken reached his understanding. What was she saying? Had she – but no, not Olwen.

'Olwen, you haven't been – well, trying to imitate my

behaviour, have you?' He felt foolish even suggesting it, but once the thought was there it had to be said. Anger flared in him as he thought of her with some boy from the village, and as she did not answer, he tried to think who it could be. Not Arthur, but he did not know the boys who worked for William Ddole, was it one of them?

'Who was it?' He reached out and stopped her, pulling her to face him. 'Olwen. Tell me what has happened.'

'Stop pulling me about! Go away if you can't be polite!' she said, hands on hips, her shawl fluttering about her: a bird nervously preparing to fly.

Then she ran home and cried some more.

In church a few days later, Olwen slipped as usual into the pew behind the one used by William and occasionally by his guests. He was without family now and his solitary figure saddened her. She looked up at the plaque on the wall in memory of Dorothy Emelia Ddole and thought that with her gone, the man was completely lost. Sending his daughter away must have been difficult. She turned her head, saw Barrass's face in the furthest shadows of the old building, and glared at him. He is so stupid, she thought with an impatient stamp of her small foot.

Ceinwen was there with Tom in his red and white uniform, but without Kenneth, who was still too scared to leave his house. Enyd stood with Dan, beside Mary, Spider, baby Dic and Mrs Powell. Olwen wished her position with the Ddole family did not prevent her from standing with them.

Pitcher was sitting with Emma and the twins, and a little away from them, with the two servants they kept, was Arthur, still employed, but watched by Emma like a dog with a specially juicy bone.

She watched as Violet came in, with Edwin, and carrying her baby. Her eyes drifted to where Barrass stood, just back from his deliveries on Gower, wondering if his face would show any disquiet, but he was looking away, staring up at the wooden carving on the roof timbers. Uninterested, she wondered? Or was he still in love with the daughter of the alehouse keeper? She shivered as the thought took hold.

357

The young couple walked down the aisle and sat beside William Ddole, and were soon joined by John Maddern on one of his frequent visits. William had obviously invited them to sit with him as they were invited to sup that evening at Ddole House after the service.

When the service was done, Olwen hurried outside for a quiet word with her parents before Florrie ushered her back to prepare the meal. To her surprise, Florrie did not seem to be in her usual panic to get back, in spite of having guests to feed. She was talking to the Keeper-of-the-Peace. His five children were there, all in a neat row, with the woman who looked after them silently waiting for Daniels to finish his conversation.

Dozy Bethan was standing nearby, waiting without any sign of impatience, and Olwen joined her.

'But what shall I call you?' Florrie was saying. 'I can't call you Daniels, now can I?'

Daniels lowered his head stiffly and said after a slight cough, 'My name is Ponsonby, but I would prefer if you would continue calling me Daniels.'

Florrie soberly nodded agreement and both girls stifled giggles in their hands.

'Go you,' Florrie scolded them, 'get back and start on cutting the loaves!'

Barrass watched the Ddole party leave, then turned to see Violet coming out on her husband's arm, the baby wrapped in soft woollen blankets against the evening coolness. People were stopping to admire the baby – *his* baby, yet he could never be even the smallest part of the little girl's life. Gabriella. He savoured the name and liked it. Protected by her mother and even more so by the man she would call 'Father', she would probably not come into his sight again until she could walk into church on her own. A few tormentors came and congratulated him on the birth of his two daughters, and he acknowledged their jeering with cold, stony-eyed nods.

As he turned away to go to the alehouse for his meal, a hand touched his shoulder and he turned to see Markus with his manservant, standing behind him. There was no one else near, and the blind man looked up at him as if he could see him clearly, the touch of the shoulder all he needed to give him a guide. He said softly,

'Barrass, we have a cargo coming in this night, will you help us with it?'

Barrass thought quickly, his first impulse being to refuse with slightly outraged disapproval, but he held back the retort and considered. The man was obviously offering an olive branch. He would be a fool to reject it. Then it became clear to him that this was a chance to prove what he had always insisted he felt, that he was a part of the village, a member of the community prepared to stand up and take his chances with the rest.

'Thank you, Markus, I will be happy to help you.'

'Eleven of the clock, boy. You will know where – the cave where you hid for a while and thought no one knew.' The man chuckled and patted his arm before being guided back to his horse.

It was an enormous surprise, not the least of it his own response to the whispered invitation. All these years he had shown outrage at the doings of the illegal importers, and now he was willing to help them cheat the law and the king. He stretched to his full height and smiled widely. A great weight had been lifted from his broad shoulders. He was being accepted at last. He was no longer an outsider, an incomer with no place here, he belonged! He wanted to tell Olwen but she was gone to finish her work at Ddole House, her Sunday freedom refused for this week. He went out with the last straggling churchgoers and walked up the bank to talk to Kenneth.

Ceinwen, Kenneth and Tom were already sitting at their meal, cold meat and a few chopped vegetables in deference to the vicar's demands that no one worked on the sabbath. He thought with a wry smile that at Ddole House, where the vicar was one of the supper guests, they would have found a way round that inconvenience.

He refused their invitation to eat, just wanting a bit of company for a few moments, while he savoured the sudden decision. He knew it was one he dare not discuss with Kenneth, and for a moment worried in case someone saw him come straight to the letter-carrier and think the worst. He stayed only long enough receive his second surprise and to hear the words he had longed to hear above all others.

'Kenneth is still unwell and he thinks it would be best if you accepted the position of letter-carrier officially,' Ceinwen said. 'Best we still use this place as the sorting office, mind, and I will deal with the books until you can find yourself someone to help you.'

She went on explaining how they would arrange the changeover, and how her recommendation would for a certainty persuade the postmaster to allow him to take the post, but he hardly heard. His large eyes seemed moist enough for tears. He thanked them and started across the road to the alehouse to celebrate with Arthur and the dog, but changed his mind and ran all the way to Ddole House. This was something he had to share with Olwen.

It was after ten o'clock when Olwen finished the last of the pans and pots and walked out of the door into the dark night. She had seen Barrass waiting outside and was in an agony of impatience to know what he had to tell her that caused his face to have set in a constant smile. As soon as she stepped outside he blurted out the news of Kenneth's retirement and his willingness for him to carry the letters officially.

'At last, Olwen, I have what I have always wanted. I am the Letter-Carrier for Gower!' He picked her up and spun her around, laughing when the dogs began to bark and the gruff voice of David in his room above the stable warned them to hush.

'I work for the King's Mail!' he shouted, and taking Olwen's hand, ran down the drive, with her dancing alongside him.

Tom went back to join his regiment and for the first time since he had treated her so roughly, Olwen felt free of him. She had not spoken of the incident to anyone, but Barrass guessed that something unpleasant had happened and one day it slipped out and he knew.

'Tom has gone back then,' he said as they walked one late evening on the cliffs. 'Funny life, that of a soldier. No chance to make friends, coming and going and never knowing where you'll be at any time. I don't think I would like that.'

'Best he's gone if you ask me,' Olwen said, then she stopped, wishing she had not spoken.

'Why?' Barrass asked. 'He didn't bother you, did he? A bit of a show-off I gather, and keen for everyone to listen to his adventures. Bored you with his talk, did he?' Then he looked at her face and asked, 'But it wasn't talk, was it, Olwen? Was it Tom who bothered you and made you cry that night you came in near to tears?'

She told him then, of how she had foolishly gone with Tom to sit in the small secret place in the rocks and how he had pulled at her clothes and frightened her. The expression on Barrass's face frightened her even more.

'But how could he bother you like that. You're only a child!'

'No, Barrass, I am not.' She stared at him for a while, then walked away.

That night Barrass worked beside Spider in the cold sea, hauling in the boats and handing up the tubs and packages they contained, helping to push out the empty boats and waiting while they were refilled and returned. No guilt over breaking the law worried him. He was one of the villagers and this was one way of filling empty bellies during the harsh winter months as well as giving the locals a taste of a few luxuries.

Kenneth braved the open air and walked across to the alehouse. Ceinwen had made it clear that he had to begin to meet people, allow them to have their say, then hopefully forget his disloyalty. The first time, he had only stood a few paces from his door, which Ceinwen shut firmly behind him. Then he had run after Pitcher with a letter he had left behind, the open air seeming fraught with unseen dangers. But today he had determined to take the worst the locals could give. He would sit outside the alehouse and face everyone. The sooner he took their abuse the sooner it would all be ended, Ceinwen was right about that.

It was very unpleasant. As news spread through the houses that he was sitting there, the scene quickly developed into something similar to the village stocks, as a wide assortment of rubbish was thrown at him, covering Pitcher's windows and porch with an indescribable mess. It was difficult to take until drink began to soften the edges of the cruel abuse. He forced himself to sit there and take the insults and the physical indignities. Better this than having to move away and start again amid strangers.

He ordered drinks in rapid succession to give himself the courage to stay. Arthur darted in and out of the alehouse door, weaving to and fro to avoid the missiles. His dog managed to find a variety of tasty morsels amid the garbage and seemed not to mind the occasional hit.

It was a Thursday, and when Barrass returned from his route and went to hand the letters and money to Ceinwen, he glanced across to discover the cause of the noise coming from the alehouse, and saw Kenneth sitting there almost covered from head to foot in disgusting filth. Everything from rotten eggs and fish to hard lumps of coal and even a few rocks had reached their target so that, besides the food, Kenneth's face was multi-coloured with bruises.

'What has happened?' he asked Ceinwen.

She glanced casually across, and as if the unfortunate man who sat there was a stranger to her and of no importance, explained,

'I told him he had to face them some time or start wandering to where no one knew him and where no one would give him work or food or even a place to stay.' She smiled amiably and added, 'Locked the money away I have, and refused to cook for him, so he had to face them or starve. Best for you, I told him, and finally he agreed.' She went back inside while Barrass ran across to talk to her husband.

The man was very drunk and, Barrass suspected, past feeling any of the missiles that were still being pelted at him with untiring enthusiasm.

He called for Arthur and together they dragged the almost unconscious man from his seat and into the alehouse porch where he was at least partially protected from the crowd.

'She knows about Betson-the-Flowers, see,' Kenneth slowly explained. He seemed to be having trouble with his tongue, which had become too large to fit properly into his mouth. 'Starve me she will, made me come out and take this, she did. "Best for you," she said, although I don't think she meant it, like.'

Barrass, after seeking Pitcher's permission, carried the small man out into the yard behind the alehouse and settled him in a corner.

'Good to me you are, Barrass, my boy.

'My boy,' he repeated slowly and with great emphasis. 'You are, you know. You are my boy – my son. I'm the father you've been seeking all these years.' He giggled idiotically and went on, 'Fancy you searching everywhere and me being here all the time.'

Barrass, reeling with the shock of it, ran out through the building and up onto the cliffs, trying to shut out the words that were going round and around in his head. Kenneth his father? No, that could not be.

Olwen found him there when darkness had fallen and Arthur had sent her a message to tell her what had happened. She walked slowly up to where he sat, sprawled on the early summer grass, and sat down beside him.

'It cannot be true,' he whispered. 'He is *nothing* like me! How can he have fathered me? Just look at us and compare. He must have been larking me.'

'In their drinking mugs men often speak the truth they no longer have the wits to hide.'

'You believe him?'

'I think it probably is so, yes.'

'But all those things my mother told me – '

363

'Truth in your remembering too?' she said softly. She decided then to cheer him out of it if she could.

'Tall?' she teased, saying the word slowly and in a voice that was low, 'and him no bigger than a pint measure?

'Red-haired?' she added in the same low voice, willing him to smile, 'and him with less hair than one of Ivor's discarded paintbrushes?

'Honest?' Her voice went down to its lowest and she was at last rewarded with a laugh. 'So fade the dreams of childhood.'

He moved closer, his face a half-seen, half-remembered image in the dark, with only the white of his teeth showing her that he was smiling.

'Oh, Olwen, what would I do without you?'

'You will never know,' she said quietly. 'Whether you want me or not, I am yours and will always be there for you.' She stretched up and kissed him, firmly and confidently, on the lips.

She felt him stiffen with shock, and a crease showed in the faintly seen image of his brow.

'Olwen, you are – '

'Just a child?' she finished for him. 'No, Barrass, as I keep telling you and as you will see if only you will look, I am not.'

He remained perfectly still, looking down at her until she began to believe they would still be there when dawn broke, Then they both moved and were soon wrapped in each other's arms.

'Oh, Barrass,' she sighed softly, 'sometimes you are a-w-ful slow.'

71